PENGUIN BOOKS

THE SWEET-SMELLING JASMINE

Jenny Hobbs is a freelance journalist, author and occasional TV arts programme presenter who lives in Johannesburg. She is well known for her many contributions to South African magazines, which include the long-running *Blossom Broadbean* column and for her efforts to promote books and reading.

Her first novel, *Thoughts in a Makeshift Mortuary*, was a finalist for the prestigious CNA literary award for 1989.

D0610965

JENNY HOBBS

———

THE SWEET-SMELLING JASMINE

PENGUIN BOOKS

PENGUIN BOOKS

Published by the Penguin Group
Penguin Books Ltd, 27 Wrights Lane, London W8 5TZ, England
Penguin Books USA Inc., 375 Hudson Street, New York, New York 10014, USA
Penguin Books Australia Ltd, Ringwood, Victoria, Australia
Penguin Books Canada Ltd, 10 Alcorn Avenue, Toronto, Ontario, Canada M4V 3B2
Penguin Books (NZ) Ltd, 182–190 Wairau Road, Auckland 10, New Zealand

Penguin Books Ltd, Registered Offices: Harmondsworth, Middlesex, England

First published in Great Britain by Michael Joseph 1993
Published in Penguin Books 1994
1 3 5 7 9 10 8 6 4 2

Copyright © Jenny Hobbs, 1993
All rights reserved

The moral right of the author has been asserted

Printed in England by Clays Ltd, St Ives plc

For RNH, the original Bear,
With love and thanks

Isabel

She is a middle-aged housewife, past fifty, last child in college, husband floundering in the grey final reaches of the civil service, hanging on by his clean pale fingernails for his pension, only five years to go. They have a paid-for house with a large garden in a nice suburb, two cars and a holiday cottage on the South Coast to which they seldom go now that the children have grown up and moved away.

Seldom go together, that is. Isabel goes there secretly to be alone with her lover. Her husband thinks she is with her sister in Durban, and is pleased that they have become closer to each other. He likes it when Isabel goes away because he has the house to himself and can eat greasy takeaways with chips and play his music as loud as he pleases, drinking brandy and soda until he falls into bed with red stains on his cheeks and nobody to nag him about his blood pressure. He finds life without a woman so simple and restful that he wonders why he ever married in the first place, why he ever bothered with all those girls. He never did enjoy sex much; his prudish virago of a mother saw to that.

Isabel enjoys sex hugely now that she can shout and laugh as much as she pleases, without any children around to hear her. Her lover is a journalist who spent years as a foreign correspondent, and has achieved critical acclaim as the author of several political biographies and three quixotic travel books. Under another name, he has also published a novel whose frank revelations of middle-aged sex have recently thrilled and shocked the nation. It is based, of course, on his stolen months spent with Isabel and their joyful discovery of each other.

They are lying naked on their bed in the cottage, two

singles roped together with a double mattress on top, looking out at the sea through the sliding glass doors. The white cotton sheets are rumpled, pillows everywhere. He is lying with his head between her breasts, fondling one of them in the tender aftermath of their lovemaking.

'Izzy, I wish this were every day.'

'Don't call me that. You know I don't like it.' But she says it lazily, without heat.

'Can't it be?' He raises his head to look at her.

'Can't it be what?'

'Every day. Living here, getting up late, loving and working and sybaritic eating – it would be paradise.'

She sighs. 'If only.'

He props himself up on one elbow. 'Why not? I'm free now. You're emotionally free from that etiolated appendage who calls himself your husband. All it would take is one swift merciful cut and the bonds would be severed.'

Her breasts jiggle as she laughs. 'Etiolated appendage! I've always loved the way you use words. I wish I had the knack.'

'It comes with practice.'

'Easy for you to say.'

'Easy, hell. I've worked damn hard at my trade all these years.'

'While I was merely caught up in the trivial pursuits of keeping house and raising children.' The defensive words spill out before she can stop them.

His hand moves to cover hers. 'Are you telling me it wasn't enough?'

'Oh, you know how it is.' She thinks, Of course it wasn't enough, not by today's standards. But I was so bloody feeble when I was young. So lacking in courage. Maybe I deserve my rotten bird's nest of a marriage.

'I don't know how it is. I don't understand. How could you allow yourself to be submerged like you did?' His mouth is a sea anemone in the grizzled seaweed thickets of his beard; it goes red when he gets angry.

She turns away from his irritatingly righteous question. He mustn't think he owns her. It would spoil everything.

'You'd know if you had married. Children are demanding. Husbands are demanding. I had to cut myself into little pieces

2

all the time and spread them around. You've no idea how exhausting it is bringing up a family and trying to live decently on a civil service salary. I never had the energy to think of doing anything else but be a mother. And a wife, of course.' She is silent, thinking back over the many skirmishes fought on the sexual battleground of their bedroom until they decided by mutual agreement to end hostilities by sleeping in different rooms. 'But the conjugal complications are over with now, thank God. George likes his brandy too much and me too little. I used to wonder whether he wasn't homosexual by inclination; he doesn't like seeing me naked like you do. I've always undressed in the bathroom.'

'He doesn't know what he's missing.' The red lips part in a brief smile. 'But seriously, if he's gay you'd have good grounds for divorce.'

'He's not gay. He just doesn't like women much.'

'How do you know?'

She feels tears pricking under her eyelids. His infidelities still hurt, even now with her miraculous new love lying next to her, their skins sticky with the cooling sweat of their lovemaking. 'He used to have flings with the new secretaries, one after the other. Kiss them behind the filing cabinets, take them to lunch, give them wine, lure them into hotel rooms with bunches of roses and promises. It was quite cynical, an assertion of his power over them rather than a desire for sex. As soon as he'd conquered one, he'd dump her and move on to the next.'

'How did he get away with it?' The writer's curiosity is roused. 'I mean, offices being what they are, you'd think there'd have been complaints. Philanderers don't make for a happy atmosphere.'

'He was the manager then. And he had powerful protectors higher up. That's one of the reasons he's still there, though he doesn't do much more now than keep track of the stationery requirements. Paper clips and rubber bands. He's pathetic really.'

The long-suffering look on her face enrages him, and he pushes himself up and shouts, 'For God's sake, Isabel, why do you stay with the stupid fart? What's keeping you there?'

'The children –'

3

'But they've all gone!'

'Not Ralphie. He hates the residence where he's staying, and comes home every weekend. I feel I have to be there for him.'

'What about me?'

She puts out her hand and strokes his muscular brown arm. 'I'm here for you.'

'But I want you every day.'

She says quietly, 'That's the trouble. Everyone wants me at their beck and call. I've lost track of what I want for myself.'

He jumps out of bed, naked in the sunshine pouring through the sliding glass doors, and stands with his hands flung out and his bare feet planted on the floor, hair curling down his stomach to his still-tumescent curve, face grinning like a gargoyle's. 'You want ME!' he crows. 'Admit it.'

She has to laugh. It comes frothing out like just-uncorked champagne, irrepressible when she is with him. 'I admit it. But there are other things too.'

'Such as?'

'I need work like you have. Something to encourage my mind to send out new roots and start to grow again. Brain compost.' She sits up, wanting him to understand her urgency. 'If I'm to break free of my wife-and-mother restraints, I have to have something worthwhile to replace them.'

'Am I not worthwhile enough?'

'Worthwhile, that goes without saying. But not enough. I need –' She breaks off, unsure of what she needs.

He drops his arms then and kneels next to her, saying in his most cozening voice, 'You need to channel your energy and your thoughts in a new direction. Try writing, Izzy. You use words as well as anyone, and like I said, the knack comes with practice. Didn't you win an essay competition once?'

She nods. 'All those years ago.'

'The ability can't have totally evaporated in the meantime.' He is teasing her. 'Try again.'

'But what?' She has an intricate network of lines round her eyes and mouth, fine as drawn-thread work. Her hair is as grey as it is blonde now.

'Write about Two Rivers. That was a special place at a special time in your life – our lives – and it's all there inside you.'

4

'I try never to think about Two Rivers. Never.'

'Why not? I do, often.'

'You haven't used it in any of your writing.'

'I couldn't. It would have hurt –' He pauses and goes on, 'I would have been trespassing on ground forbidden to me. But not to you. It's your story too.'

'My story. I never thought of it that way.' She gets up now, her body heavy round the hips and thighs but fine-boned; her arms and wrists and ankles are slender. As she raises her arms to twist her long hair into a knot and secure it with hairpins her breasts tilt upwards, tipped with rosy brown nipples.

He says, wondering, 'You are so beautiful.'

She smiles at him under one arm. 'So are you.'

He rises and goes towards her, demurring with the false modesty of a man who knows he has kept his body in trim. 'This battered old cabin trunk? The frame's going in places and the veneer needs a lot of touching up.'

'But it has so many surprises inside.' She twines possessive arms round his neck. 'I love it.'

'I love you.' His hands fall to the full sweet curves of her bare bum and they stand rocking together in the sunshine. 'And I hear what you say. You need to find your self-respect again before you can come to me. Go home and write, Izzy. You have so much to tell.'

Wrapped in the comfort of his arms, smelling the sleep-warm tawny skin of him and the sea in his hair, she thinks, Yes. Yes, I have a lot to tell. It's time I looked back at Two Rivers and tried to understand what really happened there.

Extract from the official report of the Sandham Commission of Enquiry into the Easter 1952 Riot:

'. . . Two Rivers is a small town on the Natal coast a few miles south of Durban, situated at the confluence of the Umlilwane and Umsindo rivers, which then run into a lagoon that becomes landlocked during the dry winter months.

The urban population is approximately 13,000: 3,000 Whites, 4,000 Asiatics and 6,000 Bantu (about half of whom are Zulus and the rest Pondo labourers on six-month contracts); inland to the west are two large Zulu reserves. The town is surrounded by canefields owned by the Herald Sugar Company, which is the dominant employer. Supporting occupations include the civil service, commerce, small family businesses and vegetable farming.

For the purposes of this commission, the outstanding feature of Two Rivers is its single tarred main road, part of the national coastal road between Durban and the Transkei. It runs through three distinct areas. Approaching from Durban and to the north of the Umsindo river is the mill complex with its factory buildings, staff cottages for Indian employees and compounds for the contract millworkers. To the south of the Umlilwane river is the company estate with its offices, sugar research laboratory, White employees' homes, club house and golf course. The town lies in the triangle between the two rivers, separated from the mill complex by a broad belt of Indian-owned market gardens along the north bank of the Umsindo river.

From the point of view of crowd control, this single main road bisected by two rivers would seem ideal, as theoretically it would be necessary only to barricade the bridges to stop major movements from one part of the town to another. However . . .'

1

The official report on the Easter riot lies on the desk where I've just put it down after copying out that piece, written in the bureaucratic jargon of officials the world over. It makes Two Rivers sound like some hick town in a geography book, but I remember it by the smell of jasmine on warm stone.

Jasmine grew everywhere, often tangled with golden shower. It rampaged over the old brick and corrugated-iron houses and up the ugly iron footbridge at the railway station, and hung from garden walls and the gutters of the Cosy Hotel, and crawled over the temple steps. Even where the houses ended and the canefields began, it could be found twisting up the wire stays of the telephone poles that marched away south to Umkomaas and Port Shepstone. In August when I arrived to stay with Stella and Finn, the jasmine was a mass of pointed buds shading from plum to pink to spiralled white that soon burst into starry sprays of flowers, transforming Two Rivers into a glorious perfumed garden. It bloomed again in memory during the Deepavali festival of lights in November, when the scent of jasmine incense overlaid the smell of hot oil from the rows of tiny clay lamps flickering along the windowsills and verandas of all the Hindu homes, lighting them up like birthday cakes.

The one place jasmine didn't grow was on the company estate where my friend Titch McFadyen lived. It was too common a creeper to be admitted there. The gracious company homes (built for a subtropical colony blessed with an inexhaustible supply of servants) had roses and bougainvilleas trained up their stately veranda posts, augmented in spring by explosions of purple petraea. But then everything was different on the company estate: the trees were shadier, the paved roads broader, the lawns greener, and even the river seemed to slip past with bated breath, channelled between prim rectangular beds of red and yellow cannas and the mown fairways of the golf course.

Jasmine also reminds me of the Indian buses that used to roar along the gravel roads through the canefields in copper clouds of dust. They were painted pale blue, with NAIDOO'S FAVOURITE TRANSPORT in big gold letters along the sides. Each had its name written in an ornamental scroll at the back: *Mexicali Rose* and *Divine Wind* and *Baby Come Closer*, *Spy Smasher* and *Aerial Blues*, *Paradise Express* and *Invincible Clipper* and *Tugela Fairy*. But my favourite was the *Sweet-Smelling Jasmine*, the oldest and rattliest bus on the line. Its driver, Ramsamy Pillay, a skinny old man with a white walrus moustache whose head barely cleared the top of the steering wheel, sang all day in a quavering nasal whine as he hurtled along his route, scattering goodwill and pedestrians. Ram Pillay was deaf and couldn't hear bells or shouts; he would only stop if given a sharp tap on the shoulder. Ram Pillay gave free lifts to widows and cripples and to stray dogs if they looked lost enough, though his wife swore every week to make a curry of the next flea-bitten mongrel he brought home.

He gave Titch and his friends and me free lifts up and down the main road too, though he wasn't supposed to because we were white. He made us scrunch down between the seats so Sergeant Koekemoer wouldn't see us if he chugged past on the 500cc Triumph, pride of the Two Rivers police force. Ram Pillay would never take a penny from us by way of a fare, so we tried to repay him by waving whenever the *Jasmine* rattled past and shouting, 'Hullo, Ram!' We knew he'd see our lips moving even if he couldn't hear us. Sister Kathleen Killeally got furious when I did it from the middle of a convent school crocodile and made me say hundreds of Hail Marys for unseemly behaviour in public, even though I wasn't a Catholic. 'I'll save yer wicked little soul yet!' she'd hiss so none of the other nuns could hear.

Twice a day the *Jasmine*'s worn tyres would squeal to a halt at the bus stop next to the pharmacy and stand shuddering and backfiring, with Ram Pillay revving the engine vigorously so it wouldn't give up the struggle and expire before he reached the station terminus. It was often so full that its windows bristled with the heads of passengers gasping for air. Roped to the roof rack there'd be shabby suitcases and rolled mattresses and sacks of mealie meal and rice, surmounted by produce on its way to and from the market: crates of windblown fowls crouching in terror, lettuces and pumpkins and pineapples, bunches of litchis and heavy trusses of green bananas. Boys would be clinging like a cluster of monkeys to the brass rail in the doorway. At each stop they would scamper off to make room for the descending passengers: old people feeling for the steps, fat women landing with a double slap of sandals, sticky-faced children tumbling down. After them came a waft of stale air that had been used and re-used since the last stop, smelling of bodies and hot metal and hair oil. Everyone hurried because Ram Pillay's foot sometimes slipped off the clutch, making the *Jasmine* lurch forward taking unwary limbs with it. When he had relocated the clutch and finished apologising and begun revving again, the bus would let out a foul belch of exhaust fumes before bounding forward in convulsive jerks as the boys grabbed for the brass pole, competing to see whose feet would be snatched up last from the dust.

Two Rivers was a small town then, hardly more than a village grown too big for its boots. Except for the sugar mill which was the reason for its existence, it had no factories, no warehouses, no poisonous chemical effluents or noise pollution – none of the industrial fungi that have invaded our towns in the name of progress.

It was set like a navel in rolling swells of green canefields, bounded by rivers and a lagoon. Flat-spreading flamboyant trees with bubbles of hot scarlet flowers laid pools of shade over its pavements, not only outside the company offices and in the square, but also in the Indian part of town with its bargain shops and sardine-tin houses. Old Man Herald had insisted when the town was laid out that each household should plant a jasmine creeper and all the streets be lined with flamboyant trees for shade, one to each stand; residents who allowed theirs to die of neglect were fined and made to replace them. No one would have dared to vandalise one of his plants; until he died, Old Man Herald with his fierce fly-away eyebrows was God in Two Rivers. Finn told me that some people still believed he was watching them from beyond the grave: glowering through a peephole in the granite obelisk to his memory in the square, making sure that the town he had founded was still shipshape.

Two Rivers. Two Rivers was my home for eight crucial months of growing up. Driving past it on my way back to family responsibilities after my stolen days at the beach cottage, with the need to write about it growing in my mind, I turned off the highway and tried to go back in time.

But the green and dusty Two Rivers I remember has been swallowed by a city hungry for industrial land. Smog and soot and cinder ash hang in the air. The flamboyant trees have withered and died. The market gardens have given way to a blight of factories, and the ambling rivers have been strait-jacketed in stained concrete channels. Only the resolute jasmine has survived to pit its tendrils against the new ugliness, as it has over the temple ruins, covering the jagged fangs of plaster and concrete with its soft living green, an oasis of peaceful growth in the midst of a holocaust.

I sat there for an hour trying to ignore the traffic swishing past on the new six-lane highway as I prised up the memories that lay buried under the jasmine. I thought of the night when the rioting exploded along the main road towards the temple, and the horror of its white wedding-cake tower cracking from top to bottom and disintegrating like a sand-castle. The reek of camphor and incense and rotten fruit and sweat. The bone-chilling sound of hundreds of people scream-ing in the moonlight. I remembered the blood-smeared fea-thers of a rooster that had been brought to sacrifice but not in this way, crushed by a falling statue, and its diminishing struggles as dust gradually filmed its bright black eye. And the death hush that fell over the crowd when the last piece of plaster slipped and lay still. Before the real horror began.

But I remembered happier things too. Sunny days at the beach and Stella's rare laugh. Mr Reddy's grave smile, hands clasped across the middle of his immaculate jacket. The khaki pith helmet Titch often wore, grubby round the edge of the brim with finger marks.

10

And Finn, of course. His way of speaking with his voice going up at the end of a sentence instead of down, and his self-possessed manner with people that said, I am what I am; take me or leave me. His hands that were furry on the back like a bear's paws. The drained blue of his eyes before they finally closed. The faces of the people who stood round his grave: relieved, curious, stern, embarrassed, nervously smiling, not one of them mourning. Except Titch and me. And maybe Stella, I don't know. No Indians came. He had been their friend and confidant, the one white person most of them felt they could talk to about intimate things, yet they did not come to his funeral. He had broken their taboos as he had broken ours.

But they sent flowers. When the Lutheran pastor had finished, Stella snatched up one of the gaudy marigold garlands that lay on the heap of red earth dug out of the grave and tore it to pieces. There were murmurs of approval. Then the wind began to blow and everyone went away, grateful to leave the mangled orange flowers and the raw new cemetery like a bleeding wound hacked into the green canefield.

Getting up, I left the new Two Rivers behind me – but the one I remember lives again as I write.

Isabel

She looks at the pages she has now rewritten on clean lined paper and stapled together in the upper left-hand corner, thinking, When does a piece of writing become a manuscript? This looks like one of my school essays.

'Write your essay out in neat before you hand it in,' she remembered every English teacher saying. 'I won't mark messy essays.' Yet a lot of the vibrancy of a first draft is lost when it is written out 'in neat': all the words you tried that didn't work and had to be rejected, the crossings out and scribblings in and sudden inspirations added afterwards, the omission marks and arrows and dog-eared corners and multiple coffee rings that are the evidence of long and careful deliberation.

I won't throw my first attempt away, she thinks. It's a beginning, at least. But I'm going to have to concentrate much harder on what I'm trying to do. Remember with more clarity what I saw and felt, and try to find better words.

On a blank page she prints THE SWEET-SMELLING JASMINE across the middle, starts to write 'by' under it, then crosses the 'by' out. It would be tempting fate to write her name.

She gets up from the desk and goes into the kitchen to make yet another cup of coffee to ruminate over as she plans the next bit, the real beginning of the story. It should start with the train coming into Durban station, she thinks. That first day with Stella and Finn, when they realised that I was no longer the little girl they had left behind and they were taking on more than they'd bargained for.

2

I didn't know what to expect when I first went to Two Rivers, packed off to my older sister Stella after Pa died and Ma had a nervous breakdown. I hadn't seen Stella for six years, ever since the day she came home with Finn and said they had just been married by a magistrate, and Pa told her to get out of the house and never come back again. It was like one of those Victorian melodramas, only real in a way that was horrible: Pa raging at her for throwing away her education and his money, Ma moaning into her hankie, Stella shouting out of a white face that made her red lipstick look as though it had been scribbled on with a crayon by a child.

She was supposed to be meeting me at Durban station and I wasn't sure if I would still recognise her. I knew she wouldn't recognise me. There were eleven years between us, a big gap for sisters, and I wasn't the little kid she remembered.

It was a morning at the end of August – early spring on the Reef where I had come from, but you couldn't call it spring in Durban where there are only two real seasons: sauna and windy. The train had been crawling for hours through the Valley of a Thousand Hills and suddenly there was Durban – a jumble of houses, mostly white with red tiled roofs, on tree-covered hills next to a hazy blue line of sea. The train went under a lot of bridges then stopped near some signal boxes. The two old women sitting across from me, who had been talking nonstop ever since the steward brought the morning coffee, dropped their voices. It's funny how a train stopping makes you do that, as though some living thing has died. One of them whispered, 'Durban station.'

I unstuck the backs of my legs one by one from the green

13

leather seat and knelt on the green bolster under my window to look out. The station lay beyond a spaghetti of railway tracks spangled with unwinking red eyes. The sun beat down on my arms. My face was sweating. Stella would be waiting on the main platform, probably tapping her foot.

The train gave a jerk and started to move again. I could feel the massive wheels that had carried us for five hundred miles rumbling deep inside my body. We passed the signal box and a man in a black peaked cap waved at me. Although I waved back, I felt rather insulted. I was practically grown up; well, fourteen-and-a-half anyway. Too old to be waved at like a child.

The train clacked across a series of points and began to slide past the whitewashed edges of a platform. In the hot shade of its corrugated iron roof a straggle of people stood with raised questing faces, their eyes flicking indifferently past me. Where was Stella? The train began to slow down, then stopped with a final carriage-bumping jerk, hissing steam.

I craned to look up and down the platform. The waiting people were beginning to move now. They waved, called, broke into little runs as they spotted those they had come to meet, reaching up with smiling faces to greet them, ignoring the children anxiously tugging for attention in the sudden confusion. Children always get ignored when grown-ups meet each other, as though they are non-persons, not worthy of formal introductions. It used to make me mad when my parents had people to the house and introduced them to each other while I stood there like a spare part, the nameless daughter waiting to have her head patted.

It wouldn't happen any more now that Pa was dead. I blinked hard and concentrated on looking for Stella. Porters in black waistcoats and peaked caps were swooping towards the train with a fleet of luggage trolleys curved up like bananas at both ends. A tinny voice blared from the loudspeaker, 'The train just arrived on platform two is the morning express from Johannesburg, Heidelberg, Standerton, Volksrust, Newcastle, Ladysmith, Estcourt and Pietermaritzburg,' and went on to repeat it in Afrikaans. Behind a glass-panelled wagon, an Indian food vendor was shouting, 'Hoddogs! Cigarettes! Cooldrinks!'

Where was Stella? I turned my head back to the beginning again and made my eyes move more slowly over the crowd, looking for the red hair that she so hated because it wasn't a romantic auburn but the bleached copper of a ginger cat. She'd worn it swept up into a French pleat when I last saw her, to make her look more sophisticated. She was only nineteen when she left art college and married Finn.

But I couldn't see her anywhere, and felt the beginnings of the crampy pain I always got in the pit of my stomach before big events, like the time I went into hospital to have my tonsils out. What if she wasn't there at all? What if she'd had an accident on the way to the station and been badly hurt, maybe taken to hospital and was on the operating table at this very moment hovering between life and death? Apart from Ma who couldn't help me now and Aunty Mavis in faraway Johannesburg, Stella was my only living relative. If nobody came to fetch me, who could I ask for help? There weren't any policemen in sight, and Ma had warned me since I was little not to talk to strangers because they might be agents of the white slave trade. Maybe the two old women in the compartment with me would help? But when I turned round, they had gone.

In panic I swung back to the window – and saw Stella behind the frieze of people moving along the platform, leaning against one of the pillars that held up the station roof as she took a last pull at her cigarette, in no hurry. Her hair had been cut very short and clung to her head like a bathing cap with wispy edges, and there was a big floppy basket at her feet. She was still wearing the arty clothes that Ma used to call a dog's breakfast: a faded purplish blouse and a long black pencil skirt with a broad elastic belt that pulled her waist in, purple bobby-socks and tennis shoes. This was long before people began to wear them all the time and call them tackies. Then it was definitely eccentric to wear tennis shoes off the court, and unheard-of to wear them with purple socks. Marriage didn't seem to have changed her one bit.

I shouted, 'Stella! I'm here!' but she didn't hear me. She dropped the cigarette, ground it out with her foot, sighed and put her head back against the pillar looking as though she'd rather stay there than come and find me. I told myself I was just imagining it (Stella never enthused over people) and

15

shouted again, leaning as far out of the compartment window as I could, 'Stella! I'm here!'

She turned her head and saw me, and her face looked surprised. 'Isabel?'

It was such a relief to have found her that I couldn't help grinning like a kid. As she picked up her basket and came towards me, I babbled, 'For a moment I thought you hadn't come.'

'Of course I've come! Did you think I'd abandon you to the tender mercies of the SAR and H?'

Looking down at her sharp upturned face and brown eyes that always reminded me of the fox in my book of *Aesop's Fables*, I said, trying to make it sound really adult and serious, 'Please don't start teasing me like you used to, Stella. I'm not a kid any more, even if I sometimes sound like one. I want us to be proper sisters.'

'Proper sisters.' She said it as though she were tasting it for different flavours. People were pushing past in groups behind her, gesticulating and talking, followed by porters with their trolleys piled high with suitcases, but around us there was the little globe of silence that seems to envelop people when something important is happening between them. 'Proper sisters. Yes, I'd like that,' Stella said, and smiled up at me for the first time. 'I'll try not to talk down to you or treat you like a kid, OK? I hated people who did that to me when I was your age. It's as though they negate you as a person, isn't it?'

She was saying just what I'd been thinking. I felt the crampy pain in my stomach begin to dissolve and thought, I can begin to have a family again with her and Finn.

'For starters, you can heave your suitcase out,' Stella said. 'I can manage it with my free hand if it's not too heavy. The taxi rank's not far away.'

'It's the old Samsonite one Pa always used to use.'

'Oh, that.' Her voice went flat again. 'I hope you haven't filled it up too full.'

'There wasn't very much to put in.' I turned to get it down off the luggage rack. My blouse pulled free of my pleated skirt as it always did when I reached up for something, and one of the hated long white socks that Aunty Mavis had insisted I wear fell to my ankle.

16

Stella took the suitcase and lowered it on to the platform. 'I'll walk along to the door at the end of the carriage and meet you there. Tuck your blouse in and pull that sock –'

I glared at her. It was as bad as the man waving from the signal box.

She shrugged. 'Sorry. It's going to take a while to unlearn being your little mother. You'll just have to be patient with me,' and was gone. I tucked in the blouse, dragged up the sock, picked up my school satchel and stomped down the long linoleum corridor to the end of the carriage, where a half-full glass jar of drinking water was still heaving from side to side as though unwilling to lie still after its long journey.

As soon as I was down on the platform, Stella started shouldering her way with the suitcase into the stream of people and trolleys moving towards the exit. 'Come on. We've got to be quick or we won't get a taxi.'

'I thought you said Finn had bought a car?'

'Couldn't have it today,' she said over her shoulder, and plunged behind a trolley.

I tried to plunge after her but the gap closed and I stood hesitating, not wanting to push rudely in front of people laden with parcels and raincoats and babies and bulging travel bags. I had been brought up to mind my manners, when of course my mother ought to have been teaching me survival skills instead. They would have been much more useful in the long run. I found myself being carried along like an anxious cork on the edge of the crowd, with Stella nowhere to be seen.

Overhead the heat from the sun was beating down through the corrugated iron roof, and little freckles of sunlight from empty nail holes ran over people's faces and clothes. The dust rising from the platform started to tickle my nose. I stopped and sneezed and then stood on tiptoe but still couldn't see Stella, not even in front where people's heads were bobbing up the exit stairs. I began to run, sidling past the bodies that got in my way, trying not to push, not to touch, looking round all the time for Stella so that I didn't notice the red fire bucket full of sand and cigarette butts until I stumbled against it, and fell.

17

Out of the crush a hand grabbed my arm: dirty fingernails cracked to the quick and an unshaven face above them. 'Why in such a hurry, girlie? Hey?'

I tried to tug my arm away, feeling sweat pricking out under my arms. The hand grabbed higher, brushing my blouse. 'You lost or something?'

'Let me go!'

I squirmed in his trembling grip and turned my face away from the hot winey breath, but he leaned closer and putting his mouth to my ear wheezed, 'I'll look after you, girlie, yes I will. Come along then, this way, come with me –'

'Isabel!' Stella's voice was furious. She shouted at the drunk, 'Will you leave this child alone?'

People were stopping and turning to look. 'Shame!' someone said and clucked her tongue. It was so humiliating that I wanted to die. I felt a tear slip out and slide down my cheek.

'Just trying to help the girlie, no offence,' the man mumbled, but he let go and veered off before Stella could open her mouth again.

She turned her fury on me instead. 'Why didn't you keep up with me, for pete's sake? That was really stupid, allowing an old tramp to –'

'I couldn't help it! I lost you and I was looking for you and I fell and he just grabbed me.' It came out in a blurt. I pretended to scratch my nose and wiped the betraying wetness off my cheek with a forefinger so Stella wouldn't notice. She hated tears.

'You should have kept up with me. God, I seem to have spent a lot of time bailing you out of trouble. If we're going to be proper sisters, you'll have to do much better than that.' She swung the suitcase round and went charging off again. 'Come on. The taxi rank is this way.'

The taxi we got into was an old black Chev with running boards and dented hubcaps and a smell of hot soiled leatherette. I sat by the window looking out. Durban was a blur of traffic crawling between high buildings, palm trees, rickshaws, trams, people crowding the pavements; the sea was nowhere to be seen.

'Tell me what happened,' Stella said after a while from the other side of the taxi, saying the words fast so they wouldn't get stuck in her throat. I could see she didn't want to talk about it, but she had to know.

I kept looking out my window and said, 'Pa died one morning at breakfast. He fell forward with his face in the cornflakes and when we turned him over, he was dead. Just in a few seconds. There were cornflakes stuck to his forehead and milk running out of his mouth. His skin was all purple. Ma was screaming.' I stopped.

'Go on.'

'Why didn't you come to the funeral?'

'For him? Never. He treated me like dirt. I think the real problem was that Pa thought all women should be as subservient as Ma was. It was a trial to him to have a daughter with different ideas and a mind of her own.'

I had never thought of Ma as subservient. She'd listened to Pa's opinions and done the things he expected of her, but she'd had her own opinions too. Often she'd agree in front of him, then say or do the opposite when he wasn't there. She said to me once when I asked her how she could be so two-faced, 'It's just more peaceful this way, dear. If men have the comfortable feeling that they're in charge, they leave a lot more to you than they would otherwise.'

Nobody was in charge now. I shivered, even though I was sweating in the taxi's heat, and thought, Do I have a mind of my own? How can you tell?

Stella was saying, 'I don't believe in burial anyway. Ma should have had him cremated.'

'She expected you!' I turned, accusing. 'She kept saying that you'd come home now there was no reason to stay away.'

Stella looked surprised. 'But I told her I wouldn't be coming. Over the phone.'

'Still, she hoped.' I reached out and turned the handle to make the window go down a few inches, hoping the air outside the taxi was cooler. It wasn't. 'She kept hoping until the morning after the funeral, then she started crying and couldn't stop. The doctor came and gave her an injection that made her dopey and told her to stay in bed, but she wouldn't. She just sat in that big armchair by the window looking down the drive to the gate, waiting for him or you to

19

come home, I wasn't sure which. In the evening when Aunty Mavis and I tried to make her get up, we smelt pee. She had peed into the cushion. She was still crying. Her face was like melted plasticine.'

I thought about the pee that kept running down Ma's legs into her shoes when the doctor came again, talking in a loud voice. The shoes squelched as he led her out to the ambulance, helped by a man in a white coat.

Stella leaned forward and put her hand on my arm. 'Don't worry too much, Izzy, it's just a nervous breakdown. Nothing permanent. The doctor told me over the phone that it's not uncommon after a bereavement. He thinks she'll be fine with rest and treatment.'

She still hadn't got the message. I said, hard and loud, 'Don't call me that any more.'

I hated my name: Isabel Jane Poynton. How could any normal parent stick a label like 'Isabel' on a child, followed by something as plain and unvarnished as 'Jane'? I was teased all the time in school, usually with the knock-knock joke that ended, 'Is a bell necessary on a bicycle?' and everyone falling around laughing. When you're a kid, being laughed at cuts like knives.

Stella made it worse by calling me Izzy at home, which I hated even more. It was one of the ways she got back at me for being what she called the worst drag in the whole world. Stella was a teenager then and wanted to be with her friends, but because Ma worked and there wasn't enough money for a full-time servant, she had to look after me in the afternoons. It must have been awful for her, but it was no reason for her to go on calling me Izzy after she had made her escape. Izzy, rhymes with dizzy and frizzy.

She said huffily, 'What does your ladyship want me to call you?'

I'd been thinking about that all the way down in the train. Since nobody but Stella and Finn would know me in Two Rivers, it would be a good place to try out a new name. I'd considered Isolde at first (I fell in love with Tristan the first time I read about him) but thought it was probably too different for comfort. I liked unusual, romantic names like Star and Amber and Sapphire, but knew they were too teaseworthy to use. And plain Jane was too close to the bone. 'Belle?' I ventured.

Stella gave a snorting laugh and scrabbled around in her basket for a packet of Gold Flake cigarettes and a chrome lighter. 'I don't quite see you wrapped in the aura of the deep south, kiddo.'

'Kiddo's even worse than Izzy.'

'Sis, then?' She laughed.

'No!' 'Sis' in Afrikaans is what you say for a bad smell or something disgusting. I felt the treacherous tears coming again. You're a nobody without a name.

She must have noticed that my eyes were shiny because she stopped laughing and said, 'Don't worry, we'll hit on something. Meantime it'll be Isabel, OK?'

I nodded.

'Don't fret about Ma. You'll be back home with her before you know it.' She lit a cigarette with a practised flick of the lighter; I hadn't known that she'd started smoking until I first saw her at the station. 'The doctor seems to think it won't be more than six months.'

She'd been checking on how long she was likely to have me hanging around. I said quickly, 'I promise I won't be a nuisance to you and Finn.'

Her voice came through a cloud of smoke. 'Don't be silly. You know we're glad to have you.'

But I didn't know anything for sure any more. My life had dissolved overnight into someone else's. I turned back to the window. 'You don't really mean that.'

The streets had become a road running through vegetable patches fenced off with rusty wire. Behind them were low hills covered as far as you could see with green squadrons of plumed sugar cane alternating with cut sections where the ginger stubble looked like Pa's chin used to in the morning. Stella once told me that the worst thing about her hair was that she got it from him.

'Nearly there,' the taxi driver grunted, wiping the sweat off his forehead with the back of his hand. He was fat and white and flabby, and his backside spread all over the seat. I wondered if he spread all over his wife too when he got on top of her in bed. I wondered things like that quite often the year I was fourteen, and would find my eyes drawn to the bulges in men's pants with a prurient fascination that was frightening. Perhaps I was a teenage pervert?

Stella was saying, 'Of course I mean it.'

I looked sideways and saw her fiddling with the handle of her basket and thought, I've embarrassed her by speaking the truth. I'm going to be a nuisance to her like I was when I was little.

I said, 'Aunty Mavis took me to see Ma in the loonybin before I left. It was weird. All those old women staring and creeping around and whispering in corners. One of them tried to pick me up – she had a red face and buck teeth and she was dribbling – only the nurse made her let go. Ma was dribbling too. She was in a cot with high sides like they put babies in, and guess what? Underneath there was a tube coming out that ran into a little bag, and the bag was full of –'

'You haven't changed, have you?' The words came rattling out like hailstones and I was relieved. We were back to normal hostilities, everything out in the open, no sugary sentiments for the semi-orphaned child. You had to clear the decks first if you wanted to be proper sisters.

We went on in silence after that. Soon there were houses on both sides of the road, wood-and-iron shacks with small windows and sticking-out stoeps hung with ferns in painted tyres, each with its own yard of trampled red earth shaded by mango trees and arching bamboo. Pawpaws leaned like drunk giraffes against the tin roofs, which had stones and pumpkins on them to hold them down. Most of the houses had a cluster of three bamboo poles by the front steps flying small tattered red or white flags; I thought they must be Hindu prayer flags, and wondered what the prayers would be for – the usual stuff like health and wealth, or constantly fluttering praises to the gods? I remembered Ma reading *Kim* to me, and the Lama clicking his rosary and saying '*Om mani padme hum*' over and over again. But it was Catholics who clicked rosaries, and wasn't he supposed to be a Buddhist? The differences between religions were very confusing.

Ahead were the squatting oblong shapes of a sugar mill billowing smoke from tall grey chimneys. After a while in

Two Rivers, you stopped noticing the caramel smell of boiling syrup and the tiny black bits of burnt sugar cane trash that fluttered all day in the air. The mill just squatted at the edge of your life swallowing ton after ton of cane and regurgitating streams of sticky brown sugar into sealed trucks that went to the refinery in Durban, to be transformed into the lustrous ice-white crystals that customers prefer in their sugar bowls. Stella, of course, kept only the cheap brown 'government sugar' in her home. She usually did the exact opposite to what other people did.

I looked sideways at her again as the road went under the conveyor-belt bridge that joined the mill buildings on either side. She didn't look any more married than when she'd been at art school. Wearing tennis shoes and purple socks and carrying a basket were acts of defiance against the hats and gloves and handbags that women wore when they went out then. She sat with her neck at the tense angle I remembered, her face turned away from me, her thin legs coiled round each other.

I was a laat lammetjie, a late little lamb, born when Ma was over forty. From the day she brought me home I must have been a blight on Stella's life. She wiped my nose and my bum and heard my reading and sewed name-tags on my school clothes, probably gritting her teeth against the thought of her friends enjoying themselves unencumbered by small sisters. By the time she escaped to art school and Finn, she must already have hated me with a passion. It was ironic that she should be stuck with me again after six years of marriage, when she had probably just begun to feel safe.

On the terrible day of her confrontation with Pa, I had heard her whisper to Finn after Pa had gone away, slamming the door behind him, 'I don't want this bloody baby. I hate kids!' She had lost the unborn child that had led to the hasty marriage and not fallen pregnant again. I wondered, more savvy about such things now that I was fourteen, whether she had lost it deliberately, and felt like a murderer because I must have been the cause.

'We're here.' The taxi had gone over a bridge and stopped on a street with shops crammed together down both sides. I followed Stella out and stood looking around while she paid the taxi driver.

23

It's hard to remember now what I thought that first morning. Did I notice the smells first, or the irascible honking of one of Naidoo's buses, or a rickshaw puller padding by?

Or was it the mixture of people? Finn's pharmacy had been sited by its original owner at the point where the white shops in Two Rivers petered out and the place called 'Coolietown' began. The white shops had verandas and awnings to protect their display windows from the sun, and they made welcome patches of solid shade on the pavements between the more feathery shade of the flamboyant trees. There were a few remaining trees but no awnings or pavements down at the Coolietown end, only wide sandy paths that also served as bicycle tracks, spittoons, sports arenas and extra display space for the goods that spilled out of the shops. The sand was so thick in places that the paths were ever-changing bas reliefs of footprints superimposed on more footprints made by all shapes and sizes and shades of people.

In the mining town where I came from, people kept themselves to themselves, neatly boxed and labelled. The black migrant mine labourers lived in cramped hostels, the black residents in locations and townships, the few Indian families behind their shops, and the white people like us in houses with servants' quarters in the back yards. Except for occasional forays to the Indian shops for cheap fabrics and clothes and fresh curry powder, we mostly bought things from our own shops. (The fact that you call a person a 'coolie' or a 'charra' or a 'curry-muncher' doesn't, naturally, stop you looking for bargains in his shop.) Until I stepped out of the taxi in Two Rivers, I had never thought of the difference between races as anything other than the unbridgeable chasm between black and white, a simple matter of opposites. Pa would have added in the tired grumpy voice he had begun to use all the time, 'And never the twain shall meet.'

Yet here on this street was extravagant variety: skin of every shade from ebony to walnut to chocolate to coffee to apricot to cream to pinkly sunburnt; hair in all textures from fuzzy steel wool to silk, sometimes minutely plaited all over, sometimes hanging down in one long oiled plait; noses that ran the gamut from straight and high-bridged to broad and flaring. I had been transported from a quiet house with two

24

aging, ailing parents into a noisy subtropical marketplace where people walked and talked and argued with each other, brushing shoulders and mixing together as though the laws we lived under, and I had thought immutable, didn't exist. It was like shaking a kaleidoscope, then finding when you put it to your eye again that the chips of glass had changed colour and fallen into a startling new pattern.

On that first day in Two Rivers I told myself, This is Real Life at last. Capital R, capital L. I didn't have the foggiest idea what Real Life meant then, but I soon learnt. I wonder now if it was the years of running away from what happened in Two Rivers that made me opt for the dull security of marriage to a self-centred civil servant. If only I had kept faith in what Finn taught me instead of burying it with him. If only.

Isabel

Her desk is in a corner of her bedroom by the window, so she can swivel sideways in the old wooden office chair bought at a junk shop and look out at her garden. After a number of unpleasant skirmishes she has managed to convince George that her bedroom is her private domain, even though the house is in his name because he is the breadwinner and he feels he should therefore have access to all of it. Now he doesn't even try to come in while she is there, but she has the nasty feeling that he sometimes lets himself in with a duplicate key while she is out. Though he is careful about disturbing her things, there are signs: the books on her bedside table fractionally closer to the telephone, the hangers in her wardrobe differently spaced from the way she left them, her underclothes in the chest of drawers refolded too neatly. He is probably looking for this mysterious piece of work she is busy on, which he won't find because she hides it elsewhere before he gets home.

It has taken her three weeks to finish the second chapter. The completed, neatly written pages squared away on one corner of her desk are beginning to look like a manuscript. Nearly seven-and-a-half thousand words – she has counted each one – and gallons of coffee and sweat, with occasional tears.

She is thinking about the closing paragraph she has been copying out. What is Real Life? she wonders. I thought I knew then, aged all of fourteen-and-a-half. It was everything that happened outside my narrow child's world of mother, father, friends and school; it was grown-up, serious and seething with endless promise. Now Real Life seems a tarnished parody of the shining dreams I had. Now it's a husband I despise and an absent lover I can only see for brief hours and lack the courage to embrace openly, a home I am beginning to feel trapped in, a son who struggles to connect with the world around him, and two daughters who have grown into people I don't always like. Worst of all, I've grown into someone I don't always like. What happened to the Isabel who thought the world out there was a big juicy magic apple waiting to be bitten into and savoured?

It turned out to be sour, she tells herself, sourly. I made the wrong bloody choices.

She catches herself in the middle of a self-pitying sigh, and with a click of disgust gets up and goes out into the garden to water the seedlings she planted the day before. She has spent years creating this green oasis of lawns and trees and flowering borders out of a suburban wasteland of building rubble and veld grass. Her only helper was an elderly Zimbabwean gardener whose understanding and love of plants was concentrated in fingers cracked like parched soil, and whose reading matter was a cheap album of family photographs which he looked through every afternoon sitting on a kitchen chair outside his room in the back yard. But Joseph has had to be invalided home, brain-damaged and crippled by unknown thugs in a savage street attack one night, and she has not wanted to replace him with a lesser gardener. Now a team from a gardening service comes once a fortnight to do necessary maintenance, and she plants only occasional seedlings. Going out to water them is the best therapy when she gets stuck with her writing.

She stands holding the hose, watching the arc of sprayed water glitter in the midday sun as she plans what to say in her next chapter. It should be first impressions of the house and the pharmacy, and seeing Finn again. The meeting with Titch and Kesaval belongs in the following chapter. The thought comes to her when she thinks about Titch: Of course, I picked up my love of gardening from his mother.

Isabel has a vivid memory of Lilah McFadyen in a gnome-like straw hat advancing on some overgrown roses with her secateurs flashing. Titch always used to say that plants screamed when they saw her coming at them; he maintained that you could hear them squeaking in thin botanical voices. The only way they could get back at her was by pricking her with their thorns.

Titch. When she thinks about him now, about their meandering expeditions round the little sugar town and along the banks of the two rivers that gave it its name, she finds herself smiling. We were so naive compared with today's teenagers, she thinks. So green and gauche and trusting. We believed that life could only get better and better for us. We reached out confidently for the future, expecting so much.

The hose water darkens the dug-over soil round the drooping seedlings, giving off the rich semen smell of hot dry earth slaked with the first drops of rain. It is the smell that people gradually forget when they have left Africa, and the one that most powerfully welcomes them home.

A surge of longing sends Isabel inside to telephone her lover, just so she can hear his voice again.

3

The taxi vroomed and crawled away. Stella picked up the suitcase and walked towards a door set in a high stone wall saying, 'Come on.' But I was too busy looking around to follow her.

To the right of the wall was a prim whitewashed building that rose well above street level, with ORIENT PHARMACY written in a large black signwriter's script across the facade and 'Prop: F Rosholt' in smaller letters below. In front of the central glass door flanked by display windows was a landing finished in mottled grey granolithic tiles with two symmetrical flights of steps leading up to it, as though the pharmacy were a fastidious Victorian aunt drawing its skirts up out of the dusty pathway. In one window an array of cosmetics lay nestled on blue satin, backed by a row of apothecary bottles filled with different coloured liquids. The other window held an assortment of footcare products, bedpans, enema bulbs, crutches, trusses and various orthopaedic contraptions made of leather, chrome and the bright orangey-pink elastic that used to be called skin colour. Looking at them made me burst into one of those mad adolescent giggles. I don't know why trusses and prostheses and enema bulbs viewed naked in shop windows should be so incongruously funny, but they are. Perhaps you're trying to laugh away the dread thought that you may one day need some of them.

Smothering the silly explosion with my hand, hoping she hadn't noticed, I called after Stella, 'Is that where Finn works?'

She stopped by the door in the wall and stuck her chin out. 'That's it. Our temple of patent medicine. You've no idea how much faith people invest in pills and potions.'

I had never thought of her as a snob, but I saw then that she hated living behind a shop – it must have been such a comedown from being an art student. The phantom baby and I had a lot to answer for. The urge to laugh died away. 'It looks very smart.'

'We've done it up, of course. It was in a hell of a mess when we bought it.'

She jerked open the door and I followed her through. Behind the wall it was suddenly quiet, the street babble of voices and traffic noises muffled by greenness and dappled shade. In the angle between the pharmacy and the L-shaped house joined on to it at the back was a shady paved courtyard overgrown with maidenhair and sword ferns and elephant's ear. Goldfish swirled under the lilypads of a stone fishpond; over it stood a frangipani tree starred with creamy yellow-centred blooms, each wax-perfect. Next to the street wall was a bank of deep blue hydrangeas out of which rose the mango tree that was to become my observation post on a new world.

I said, 'What a lovely garden,' thinking that Stella had made it and trying to please her.

'It's Finn's.' She shrugged and went on ahead of me, carrying the suitcase away from her side as though it were contaminated. Maybe it was, for her.

The house was a surprise too: you could hardly see it for the flowering jasmine that swarmed up the walls as far as the roof, dangling from the gutters and falling back in thick scented swags where it became too heavy to cling on. Windows peeped through like inquisitive eyes under shaggy brows, and there was a long low veranda with more ferns growing in pots. It looked like the kind of place you needed a cane knife to hack your way out of in the morning. Jungly. Nice.

Stella pulled open the screen door that led off the veranda and held it so the spring wouldn't slam it shut, saying, 'Come on, Isabel.' I was still dawdling next to the fishpond, but I hurried up then. I really did want to please her, to show how grateful I was to her for offering to have me, but as usual I only seemed to succeed in irritating her. When I got to the door she said, 'I'll show you your room first, then we'll go and say hullo to Finn. It's through here.'

She led the way down a high dark passage to a door which she pushed open with her free hand, motioning with her head for me to go in first.

My bedroom at home had been a nondescript place: dreary furniture, a carpet with carnivorous-looking flowers writhing all over it (a refugee from the dining room) and a worn green candlewick bedspread whose stains chronicled my childhood. The only object of any personal value was the set of bookshelves that Pa had bought for me on an office sale, in which I kept my books and treasures.

The bedroom I walked into could have been lifted straight out of a film set in colonial Malaya or the West Indies. You could imagine retiring there for an afternoon rest under linen sheets with the shutters closed to keep out the heat, and just the faintest scent of orchids and twirled cigars. It was – still is, I think – the most beautiful bedroom I have ever seen.

The first thing you noticed was a curly cast iron double bed with stork legs, covered in a white textured cotton counterpane with a knotted mosquito net hanging above it. Against one wall was a stately wardrobe of dark polished wood with bevelled mirrors on the doors; next to it was a matching wash-stand with a white marble top holding a porcelain basin and pitcher, both strewn with pink cabbage roses. By the window was the sort of wicker chair that stood on verandas then, painted white and given a buttoned cushion lining, and on the floor were woven grass mats smelling of fresh hay. The green leaf-filtered light coming in through the windows made the room seem like the bottom of a pool, cool and still.

I turned to Stella who was standing by the door and said, awed, 'Can I really sleep here?'

'Really and truly.' She was smiling again. 'Do you like it?'

Overcome by the thought of having such a romantic, extravagant room to myself, I blurted like a kid, 'It's the best, most beautifullest bedroom I've ever seen!' But it wasn't enough. She looked as though she was waiting to take a bow. I said, 'Did you fix it up like this?'

'Yes. And I've done some of the other rooms too.' Her foxy eyes had gone warm and shiny. 'It's fun. I scratch around in

31

junk shops for old furniture, and at sales for discontinued lines and other odds and ends like material remnants. It's amazing what you can do without –' She stopped. I could see that she was going to say 'much money' but couldn't bring herself to. Stella hated admitting defeat in anything. The last sentence she had flung at Pa had been, 'I'll come home rich one day and show you!'

I didn't want her to get cross again and looked round for a diversion. 'Are those for washing?' I pointed at the rose-bedecked basin and pitcher.

She shook her head. 'You'll have to wash in the bathroom across the passage. I bought them from Abjee's sale rooms because they look just right for the wash-stand, not really to be used. They're genuine Victorian, you know? The bed's Victorian too; it came from the rubbish dump, and I cleaned it up and painted it myself.'

I said, 'Honestly, this is the sort of bedroom I've always dreamed about. How did you know?'

She lifted one eyebrow (it was brown, not pale ginger any more; she must have had her eyebrows dyed) and said, 'We're proper sisters, remember?'

I try to remember Stella like that, when she was being jokey and understanding, but her sharp edges keep getting in the way. Moments later she was saying in a tone hovering between command and suggestion, 'I'll put your suitcase here in the corner. You can unpack and put away after you've had a wash and a look around.'

She went out, closing the door with a bossy click. I prowled the room feeling pleased and proprietorial. Had a drink of warmish water from the glass flask on the wash-stand. Poked my head into the cupboard (was this what coffins smelled like?). Investigated the commode by the bed and was disappointed not to find a chamber pot covered with cabbage roses too, though it probably wasn't for lack of trying; Stella was always meticulous about details. Then I sat down in the wicker chair to test it and didn't want to get up again. From the first moment I sat there it felt like a thinking chair, the sort you can retreat to while you puzzle things out. Sometimes during the months I lived with Stella and Finn, I even imagined that it creaked answers to my thoughts. Which were, that day, that it was going to be difficult for both Stella and me to distinguish between Izzy the kid and the new Isabel with bosoms and black curly hairs that got left behind in the bath when I forgot to wash it out. It seems to be the hardest thing in the world to convince people to take you seriously when you're fourteen.

Then I washed my hands in the bathroom, brushed my hair for Finn and went to find Stella.

She was in the kitchen, which was one of those huge dark culinary caves that people built at the turn of the century with a coal stove and massive wooden dressers and a scrubbed table in the middle. But Stella had been at work in there too, stencilling a frieze of blue forget-me-nots tied with ribbon above the white tiles and painting the woodwork blue to match. On the dresser shelves were rows of blue and white plates and cups and jugs, each one different, some cracked or chipped, some with flowers in them; on the table was a willow-pattern jug full of white arum lilies. It felt like a farm kitchen where a plump wife made apple pies and crusty bread all day and any minute the farmer would come stomping in with a bucket of creamy milk, calling for his supper. Which was clever of Stella because she had always loathed cooking and wasn't good at it.

She was standing near the back door talking to an old Indian man in a round white cap and a high-collared long grey jacket that buttoned all the way down the front. When she heard me come in, she turned and said, 'Oh, Isabel, this is Mr K K Reddy, the laundry mogul. Mr Reddy, my sister Isabel.'

I was being introduced. Progress. I smiled at him.

The old man screwed up his face into such a mass of smiling wrinkles that his eyes were twinkling at me from deep slits. He joined his hands palm to palm under his chin, reminding me of the two halves of a pecan nut, and said with a little bow, 'Missy Isabel, I am glad to welcome you.'

I said, 'Hullo,' and sort of bowed back, not knowing what else to do. I had never met an Indian – socially, I mean. Only selling things.

Stella was going on, 'I should have called Mr Reddy the ex-mogul. He has just handed one of the biggest laundry

33

businesses in Natal to his brother-in-law to run until his grandson is ready to take over. Heaven knows why.'

The old man made a deprecating gesture. 'In his later years, Mrs Stella, a man must terminate his quest for money and security and bend his thoughts to his spiritual development. It is the Hindu way.'

'Setting your soul to rights?'

'You could call it that.' His wrinkles dropped back into place and his face became serious, even mournful, with the smile gone. 'After a lifetime of double, double, toil and trouble, as your Bard put it, I am able at last to spend the proper time on my devotions.'

He stood earnestly leaning towards her. I shifted on to my other foot, hoping that Stella wouldn't choose that precise moment to start a theological argument. The kitchen was hot. A fly buzzed against one of the windows. Then the old fridge that had once stood in the pantry at home clicked on and began its familiar one/two rhythm, the motor tapping against its mounting as if a dance-band leader were about to start up a foxtrot. I felt the stupid tears seeping into my eyes again. Somebody else would be living in our home soon.

The fridge may have reminded Stella of home too, because she said in an absent voice, 'You're sure you wouldn't like a cup of tea, Mr Reddy?'

He smiled his refusal, inclined his head and went away through the back yard.

I was surprised how neighbourly they were, but even more by a last shrewd glance he gave her as she turned away. White children like Stella and me were brought up to understand that we might know and even love our black cooks and nannies better than our mothers, but after a certain age this was expected to fade to a relationship of mutual respect in which both parties knew their places. I was just past that age. The fact that the old Indian man's eyes could measure Stella in such a personal manner was disturbing.

I had never thought of Indian people as anything other than shopkeepers and vegetable vendors. At home the vegetable sammy had come twice a week, one padded shoulder burdened with a pole carrying laden kidney-shaped wicker baskets at each end, to squat down outside the kitchen door while Ma picked through his carrots and chillies and lettuces and brinjals. His bony brown legs had jutted up on both sides of his white dhoti as he looked away, feigning indifference, but I knew from the sharp glitter of his eyes watching her and the way he folded her coins carefully into his turban before wrapping it again that there were a lot of people depending on his vegetables.

Maybe I would learn more about Indians now that I would be living so close to them. It was quite an interesting prospect – social research of a kind that would never have been possible in the mining town where we had all been sealed into separate compartments. Black and brown people were complete mysteries to me, I realised, and then sighed. Fourteen is a time when there seem to be a lot of mysteries to unravel.

The one that puzzled me most then was the exact difference between sex and love, and whether I would be able to tell one from the other when my time came to have a boyfriend. Because they embarrassed Ma, I had to find out for myself about the facts of life. The first revelation happened when Evelyn Simpson had told us in breathless detail at primary school what she had seen when she watched her parents one night through their partly open bedroom door. It was not reassuring. Among other snippets, she had sworn that her father's thing was as long as her arm, and when we measured it against our flat little prepubescent bellies, the whole procedure began to seem almost certainly painful if not dangerous. No little Simpson appeared to have been conceived afterwards, so it wasn't foolproof either. Subsequent revelations by friends and teachers in biology classes had clarified the physical details of sex, but not how to tell lust from love. In those pre-Pill days it was an important distinction.

'Shall we go and see Finn?' Stella was saying. I followed her down another passage and she opened a connecting door to the pharmacy which led into a small neon-lit room smelling of chemicals, with a gas burner and a stone sink and shelves and shelves of bottles. The bigger bottles, labelled with staccato chunks of Latin and holding various liquids and powders and ointments, were on the lower shelves; above them were rows of small brown ribbed bottles in different sizes waiting to be filled. There were flasks and lidded jars ranging from big to small like a family; a string bag full of new corks; a bundle of wooden spatulas next to a white marble mortar and pestle; a delicate brass scale.

'The dispensary,' Stella said, using a loud explanatory tone where I'd expected hushed reverence. Despite the harsh brightness of the light, didn't she feel the spirits of the old alchemists in there? Or the dangerous power of the poisons and drugs in those bottles, the guardians of Life and Death: the sleeping pills that could soothe or kill, the morphine that could bring both ease and addiction? (I had been reading a lot of gothic novels that year.) Trying to ignore her, I felt a delicious chill down my spine and closed my eyes to enjoy the feeling. But when I opened them again, I saw that it was just the room where Finn worked. The bottles were higgledy-piggledy on the shelves, some teetering on the edge. There was an untidy bunch of prescriptions spiked on a nail. The brass scale with its tiny coin-like weights was tarnished. A scatter of powder trailed across the floor. Against one wall some wooden drawers hung open, one with a red rubber tube coiling out of it.

Stella said, 'He's so damn untidy,' and went to the sink for a wet cloth to wipe up the powder. She jabbed the tube back and elbowed the drawers shut and began to straighten the bottles, saying as she crashed them against each other, 'Hang on while I get them into some sort of order again.'

So I stood there while she had an orgy of tidying up, feeling like the sorcerer's apprentice. But I was released from the spell by Finn, who threw the door open and came in wearing an unfamiliar starched white jacket that buttoned up the side to his shoulder, and a huge smile that took up most of his face. 'So, you've come.'

I thought, Maybe living in Stella's house won't be so bad, and blurted, 'It's jolly nice of you to have me.'

Stella didn't seem to hear. She was grumbling, 'Finn, you're impossible! I tidied these last week.'

But Finn heard. He hugged me against the crackling jacket and said, 'Truly we are pleased to have you. And *kondolere min kjaere dig*, which means "Deepest sympathy, my dear". I am so sorry about your Pa.'

Finn hadn't changed one bit from the time he used to come home with Stella from college and be nice to me, even though I was only a kid sister. Except for the top of his head, which was thinning, he still had the look of a teddy bear that has been washed and pegged up by the back of the neck to a clothesline and left to elongate in the rain. He was tall and stooped and furred all over with blond hair that even stuck up out of his collar. He had dark blue eyes that looked as though they had come from some deep part of the sea, and huge whorled ears with more hair growing out of them. 'Good to see you, Izzy,' he added.

I didn't mind the Izzy from him because I knew by the way he snuffled that he was just being affectionate. Finn used to make a snuffling noise at the back of his nose when he was saying something important; Stella said it was because he had permanent hay fever and was always telling him to blow the damn thing, but I liked it. It went with being a teddy bear hung out in the rain. So I don't know why it made me start to cry, really cry not just leak, bawling like a baby against Finn's silver-shanked bone buttons.

He hugged me tighter. 'Come now, aren't you glad to see me?'

I couldn't answer, just stood blubbering and trying to hide my face against him. Stella stopped crashing bottles and came over and put her arm round my shoulders, saying over my head as she tried to prise me off him, 'It's been hard for her, having everything happen so suddenly.'

Finn said, trying to make me stop crying by teasing, 'I think it's the shock of seeing my handsome face again. You're overcome with yustified emotion, ya, Izzy?'

'She doesn't want to be called Izzy any more. And Isabel's too long. We're going to have to think of something else.' Stella's fingers were biting into my arm.

'You'd better call me Nuisance,' I sobbed, holding on tightly. It felt so safe against Finn.

Stella gave a cluck of annoyance and jerked me away from him to face her. 'Stop that now! You're just being silly. Of course you're not a nuisance. One of the reasons I fixed up the spare bedroom was so we could ask you to come down and stay with us.'

She was lying, of course. Ma had come down to see Stella a few times, but she hadn't shown any signs of wanting to see me in the six years since she'd left home. I stood looking down at the floor with my hair hanging over my face, snivelling. It was awful the way Stella could reduce me to being a kid again.

'Look at me! I haven't made you feel unwelcome, have I?' She was getting angry with me, or maybe it was just some of the general anger always simmering beneath Stella's surface being let out. Living with her was like living near Mount Etna; you soon learnt that continual small eruptions at least prevented the big one.

I shook my bent head.

Finn said, 'Yently, Stella. It's hard for her.'

She went raging on. 'I've been the soul of sympathy ever since I picked her up, but she acts as though she's a bag of dirty laundry foisted on us.' I felt her hand grabbing my chin, and my face being forced upwards. 'What more do I have to do to make you feel at home with us? I can't make your sadness go away. Everyone has to face up to illness and death sometime.'

Platitudes. Why do articulate people like Stella start talking in platitudes when things get emotional? She had it all wrong, anyway. I wasn't crying for Pa; he was gone. Or for poor peeing Ma. I was crying because Finn was glad to see me.

When she first brought him home from college we were surprised because he was quite a lot older than she was. But he turned out to be much easier to talk to than the self-consciously arty students she'd brought home at first. He answered my faltering attempts at conversation with real interest, not the usual brush-off I was used to from Stella's friends.

Finn Rosholt was the only son of Norwegian missionary parents who lived and worked in a remote corner of Zululand, though he didn't seem to be the least bit holy. I think it was partly this anomaly that had attracted Stella; she loved para-doxes. He was also kind, affectionate and tolerant – she relaxed when she was with him, feeling no need to sharpen herself on him as she did with others. Then she fell pregnant halfway through her final year as an art student, and Finn was no longer a comfortable friend but an instant husband. When Pa threw her out of the house, he took his savings as a research chemist in a pharmaceutical company and a bank loan, and bought the pharmacy sight unseen instead of spending it on a honeymoon. A month after they went to live in Two Rivers, Stella lost the baby. Now she was trying to compensate for the art diploma she hadn't achieved by redecorating a house she disliked and teaching art at the local convent school.

She was entitled to a few platitudes, I had to admit.

A bell tonked over the door that led into the pharmacy from the street. Finn said, 'Yust a sec, now,' and went out. We heard him murmuring and sliding drawers in and out. Stella gave me a tissue and I blew my nose.

Then she looked at me hard and said, 'Let's just straighten things out a bit between us. If we're going to get along, I won't have you siding with Finn all the time. Or vice versa.'

'What do you mean?'

She rubbed at the back of her head with her hand, ruffling the copper spikes of hair. She always did that when she was concentrating. 'Listen, Isabel, try and understand. You're old enough. Marriage between two individuals isn't easy, but Finn and I have achieved a sort of balance now. I think we're nearly happy.' She didn't look happy. She had inherited Ma's bruised rings under the eyes and Pa's habit of worrying at things until they fell apart.

'I don't understand. Please, what are you trying to say?' A dread came over me that she would send me away in case I disturbed the balance.

'Men are like children sometimes,' she said, 'easily distracted. Finn hasn't an ounce of ambition or drive. Look at him.'

She pulled me over to the door and gestured at his tall silhouette stooping over the glass counter, patiently explaining the instructions on a bottle of pills to a fat woman in a green sari. 'Patent medicines for bloody hypochondriacs! And he's got a good brain, Finn has. But he won't use it without me pushing him. He always takes the easy way out. I don't want you to be his new excuse.'

There was an awful look in her eyes. I thought, Finn may not realise it, but he's married a missionary just like his parents were.

I burst out, 'You're always trying to interfere, just like Pa did! Why don't you leave Finn alone? It's his life.'

'My life too, remember?' Her face was the colour of candle-wax. 'We're married. I believe in marriage. It's all I've got that's fixed and good. Promise me you won't upset the balance?'

She looked so desperate that I nodded and reached out and clung to her, and at last it felt like proper sisters and having a family again.

Isabel

She puts her pen down on the desk to massage the cramp in her hand and looks out at the overgrown lawn, thinking, I must get Ralphie to mow it when he comes home on Saturday. The exercise will be good for him. And the paths need sweeping. I suppose I'll have to do that myself. There are so many damn things to do in a house with a big garden.

She and George have discussed selling it now that the children have gone – except for Ralphie at weekends, of course, but he is too preoccupied by his interminable dialogue with his computer to enjoy the garden. She doesn't think he'd mind if they moved to a smaller house, or even a flat. Ralphie seems to prefer computer games to people. He would rather pit his wits against death-spitting aliens and labyrinthine castles full of nasty surprises than summon up the huge effort a shy person has to make to communicate with others. Isabel insists that he comes to meals and talks to them, tells them what he is doing at college, but more often than not he just says, 'Oh, nothing m-much,' and eats his food in stubborn silence.

She thinks, The girls are old enough now to handle a divorce, but how can I abandon Ralphie when I know he's not coping with the circumscribed life he leads, let alone the outside world? She gives her head an angry shake. Kids bind you to a home and a marriage with such an intricate web of needs and demands that it's almost impossible to fight your way out. Or am I just being feeble? Using Ralphie as an excuse to put off the frightening decision to slice my old life away and leave?

She remembers what her lover said the last time they talked about it. 'You've got to realise that you're swimming against the strongest current in the world: the survival of the species. A woman is programmed at birth with a responsibility microchip that turns her into a zombie guard dog as far as her children are concerned. She can't see reason any more. She can't distinguish between manipulation and real need.'

'That's rubbish.'

'Think about it.'

Needing to hear his voice again, and some encouragement to keep up the momentum of her writing – the three chapters she has written so far have come rolling out of her memory with surprising ease – she picks up the phone and dials his number.

His voice crackles with static; he is staying in a friend's mountain retreat, working on a book about his recent travels in Central Africa. 'Hullo?'

'It's me.'

'Izzy. How good to hear you.'

'How's the book going?'

There is a tinny explosion of laughter in her ear. 'Slowly. A lot of turgid wading through statistics and notes, some of which are barely legible; I left two of my notebooks out in a downpour one night, and felt-tip pens run. Teach me to stick to ballpoints.'

'I wish I could stick to you right now. I miss you so much.'

She carries in her mind a colour photograph of his sleeping body sprawled across the white sheets, his grizzled hair still damp from a swim, his skin sparkling with fine salt crystals. She daren't keep an actual photograph of him because of George's inveterate snooping. In the civil service, people watch each other like hawks for signs of unearned credits given, unfair advantages taken. George is a camouflage expert, adept at hiding his real feelings and opinions from his superiors. Not from her, whom he considers his inferior. She gets the full blast. This morning before leaving for work, he berated her for ten minutes about her neglect of the house and garden, 'While you sit and scribble in your room all day. What's it for, anyway?'

'Just something I have to do.'

'Do you mind telling me what you're writing, or is it a state secret?' He gives her the tight sarcastic grin he reserves

42

for points scored on their daily tally-sheet. He loves scoring points; provokes arguments that sometimes go on for days, picking gleeful holes in her reasoning.

'I can't talk about it, sorry.' She thinks now, I'll have to find a better hiding place for the manuscript. I don't want him devaluing it for me with those prying boiled-sweet eyes. How could I have tied myself down to this man for so long?

Yet she hadn't known what she was missing until she met her lover again, more than thirty-five years after they had parted as teenagers. She thinks, One of the most restful things about him is that he never argues just for the sake of it; he's so comfortable with who he is and what he's doing that there's no need.

His voice crackling down the phone has gone serious. 'If you miss me, you know what to do about it.'

'I know.' She knows that a stronger woman would have walked out of her house without a backward glance and gone to him. Her excuses come tumbling out. 'It's just, well, Ralphie's floundering at college, and I'm worried about him. He doesn't live in the real world at all. He's lost somewhere in the computer jungle, so used to communicating by means of positive and negative impulses that he can't put words together without stammering.'

'I can't imagine a son of yours being inarticulate.'

'He is. I don't think he's ever looked at a girl either. I'm afraid he's going to end up like his father, so ignorant of women that he won't know how to communicate with them.' The fear has been hovering in her thoughts for months; this is the first time she has voiced it.

'A fate worse than death?'

'Don't joke about it. I'm really worried. Ralphie was a dear little boy, very shy but more loving than the girls. He needed a lot of reassurance and cuddling.'

'So do I.'

She thinks crossly, That's blatant manipulation. He knows damn well how much I want him. She says in the cool voice she uses to her husband, 'Ralphie needs me more than you do right now.'

'And who am I to argue with a mother's instinct?' His tinny laugh explodes down the line again. 'I've never been a

43

father, but I reckon I could teach Ralphie a thing or two about life.'

'You probably could, but the issue's not negotiable. Broken homes are bad for kids.'

'Unhappy homes are worse. And he's not a kid. He's nineteen, for God's sake!' He is growing impatient with her, impatient with her excuses. He is so certain about what he wants, so used to going after it, that he finds her dithering over her family obligations maddening.

She feels a surge of panic at his tone. He's getting tired of waiting! He'll stop wanting me, and then –? She says in a rush, 'Give me a few more months. The writing's coming along well. I've done three chapters already.'

'Will you send me a copy?' He sounds mollified.

'I couldn't yet. It's too private. Too new. If I showed it to anyone else, I feel that it might lose its magic and the thoughts wouldn't come any more. Do you understand?' Anxious to get her deep need for privacy across to him so that he won't see the denial as another rejection, she goes on, 'It's still vulnerable, as though it hasn't grown enough of a shell to protect it from criticism.'

'I wasn't going to criticise your work, just try and help it along.'

'I'll ask when I need help. Right now, I'm doing fine.' She is proud of what she has done and thinks it's good. Better than a lot of the stuff that gets into print, anyway.

Hearing her pride and her sense of purpose, he smiles to himself in the distant cottage, thinking, She's beginning to cut loose, even if she doesn't realise it. I'll get her away from that little nerd Ralphie yet. He says, 'Keep up the good work, then.'

'I will. I'm enjoying it.'

'I miss you, my dear love.' Is there any chance you'll be able to come to me here? The valley is very beautiful; I look out on rocky kloofs and aloes and range after range of blue mountains. And there's a stream near the cottage with an icy gin and tonic pool where I swim every day.'

He hears her sigh of envy on the other end of the line. 'Don't tempt me. I can't come now. In a month or two, maybe. Then I'll be further on with the writing and less defensive of it. Less like a mother hen.'

With the boy too, is his fervent hope. He says, 'I'll hold on to that thought.'

'And I promise I'll come soon.'

'For good this time?' He can't resist another tug.

'That I can't promise. But you know I want to.'

'I know your intentions are pure, but I worry about your will.'

She looks at the black and white photograph of Ralphie in school uniform on her desk, an anxious, pale little boy with his combed-back hair making his ears stick out, and says, 'You needn't worry, darling. I know what I want.' But she is not as sure as she sounds; this photograph is a relentless weight on her mind.

'Phone again soon,' he says. They can only talk during the day when she is alone in the house. 'I need to hear your voice.'

'And I yours,' she whispers against the crackling that measures the distance between them.

Extract from the official report of the Sandham Commission of Enquiry into the Easter 1952 Riot:

'. . . the labour requirements of the sugar cane process have a direct bearing on the existing state of friction in Two Rivers between the contract workers from Pondoland, local Zulus and Indian shopkeepers that led to the riot.

The Natal coast is ideal for sugar cane because of its subtropical climate and abundant labour of a strong, well-built body type. Though Zulu men are often unwilling to work in the canefields with the Pondos, they form a pool of reliable local labour from which a majority of the mill-workers are drawn.

The cane is still cut by hand, as the low rounded hills of the Natal coast make mechanical harvesting difficult. Cane knives (also known as pangas) are used, and a good knife is cherished by its user. Milling of the cut cane is continuous, operated by three shifts a day, seven days a week. This means that there are always two shifts off duty in the native labour compounds, and the numbers swell considerably when the cane-cutting teams return in the late afternoon.

Friction between men of different tribes is kept in check by housing them according to the district from which they come. However, there is endemic fighting of a historical nature between Zulus and Pondos, exacerbated by the fact that the more belligerent of the Pondos are quick to use their cane knives, and no Zulu will go anywhere without his brace of fighting sticks. Outside the mill premises, roving groups of off-duty workers often clash.

The Indian shopkeepers too are not without blame. Working long, difficult hours as they do, many are short-tempered with their poor or ill-educated customers. There is also a strong public perception that they are making inflated profits . . .'

46

4

Weekdays were heralded in Two Rivers by the pre-dawn clanging of cane trucks being shunted into the station sidings at the mill. Our house in the mining town had been near a station too, and when I woke the next morning I thought at first that I was in my old bed, hearing the familiar chuntering noises of a busy steam engine, the brisk let's-get-on-with-it toots it gave, and the rumble of heavy iron wheels on rails.

Then I noticed other noises. The coughing roar of a tractor crunching over gravel, and thumps which I later learnt were made by the chain-bound bundles of sugar cane it was unloading. The high wavering call of a muezzin calling Moslems to prayer. A bazaar squabble of mynahs outside the window. I opened my eyes on the misty whiteness of a mosquito net hanging all round me, and beyond it a strange room. For a moment I thought it was a dream until I remembered: this was Stella and Finn's house, and the room was my beautiful new bedroom.

I pulled the mosquito net out from where someone – it must have been Stella – had tucked it under the mattress, and stumbled over to the window to look up through its perfumed fringe of jasmine flowers at the sky. It was an iridescent pearly grey; the sun had not yet risen on the first day in my new world. Too excited to get back into bed, I put on shorts and a shirt and crept down the passage and out on to the veranda through the screen door, which banged softly behind me on its felt pads. The paving stones of the courtyard felt clammy under my bare feet, but there was a promise of heat to come in the humid stillness and the already-drooping hydrangeas. I sat down by the fishpond to watch the goldfish finning slowly between waterlily stems, coming up every now and then to gulp some air. Why should fish swallow air? Perhaps I could do a scientific study of goldfish and their habits during my holiday from schools.

'Morning!'

I turned round.

Finn was leaning out one of the windows. 'I'm yust getting ready to go fishing. Want to come?'

I wondered what Stella would say, but nodded anyway.

'You'll need shoes.'

I went back inside for my sandals and heard Stella say in a sleepy suspicious voice, 'Finn, where are you going?'

'Down to the river to catch some mullet. I'll take Isabel with me, seeing she's already up.'

There was a noise of bedclothes being pushed back, then she said, 'You can't go like that.'

'Why not?'

Stella's voice went up several notches. 'Do I have to keep on spelling it out? You're a professional man, practically a doctor to most of these people. You know you can't walk round town in an old shirt and ragged shorts and velskoens tied with string.'

'You mean, it's all right for you to go on playing the bohemian art student, but I must be Mr Prim and Proper for fear I might frighten off my customers? Come down off it, Stella. I'm sure they're aware of the fact that I'm a normal human being onder my white yacket.'

I had never heard Finn being sarcastic; I suppose he must have caught it from Stella. Are things like sarcasm contagious?

'The question of appearances is more complicated than that, and you know it.' The way she said it, I knew they'd had this argument often before.

'There is nothing complicated. I am going down to the railway bridge to fish. I will most likely get dirty. Therefore I am wearing my oldest clothes.'

'God, you can be infuriating!' I heard her bare feet thump on the floor. 'If you were a free agent, Finn, you could wear what you bloody pleased. But you're not. You're the dispenser of medicinal marvels in this awful little town we live in. If you're seen around looking like a tramp and stinking of fish,

48

don't you think that your customers might lose some of their touching confidence in you?'

'And don't you love to exaggerate, Stella.' I had never heard him sound like that: cold and angry. 'The fact is that nobody's perfect. Most other people besides you know this.'

'I wonder what else they know?'

Into the silence that stretched out like a sheet of rubber being pulled tightly on all sides, Finn's words fell like stones. 'What do you mean?'

'You needn't think I'm blind.'

I wanted to creep away but I couldn't. Standing in the passage where it was dark I listened as he said, 'Explain, please, what exact sin you are accusing me of this morning. I agree that I'm ontidy and onambitious and not attentive enough to the white customers who really matter. I plead guilty to sometimes wearing clothes that make me look like a tramp. Which of my many other failings and faults are you talking about?'

She said in a tired voice, 'Oh, forget it.' I heard her flop back on the bed again and pull up the bedclothes, and scuttled into the kitchen.

When Finn came in and saw my face, he forced a smile and said, 'Yust remember that your sister is at her most onreasonable in the early mornings. Her sense of proportion does not operate too well before breakfast.'

Finn's way of talking was part of what made him different and special, but it took a while to get used to. His voice went up and down in the lilting Norwegian way though his English was excellent thanks to all the books he read, except for getting his word order and idioms mixed up sometimes. Apart from pronouncing his j's like y's and some of his u's like o's, his th's were often close to being d's. He used occasional Norwegian words too, all of which I have forgotten except one that sounded like 'frickly', spoken with a long wait on the 'ck', which he told me once is spelt 'fryktelig'. It means dreadful, ghastly, frightful, but he often used it in a humorous way, to make light of a problem or an unpleasant customer. It was one of his ways of coping with his difficulties, to joke about them.

I said, 'You don't have to explain Stella. I grew up to the sound of arguments.'

'So. We get ready for fishing.' He gave me a relieved wink and went into the pantry, coming back with two bamboo fishing rods and a loaf of bread. 'We'll try the mullet on bread crusts seeing as I don't have any sardine guts handy this morning. You know something about fishing, I presume?'

'A bit.' What I'd read about it in books, actually. Pa would never have considered taking a mere girl fishing.

'You probably haven't come across mullet, then.' He went on to describe their appearance and habitat as he cut door-steps of white bread for what he called our fishermen's breakfast, slicing off their crusts, slathering on butter and marmalade, then clapping them together to make thick sand-wiches which it was my job to wrap in wax paper. Finn gathered up the crusts in a twist of newspaper which he stuffed with the wrapped sandwiches into a canvas tackle bag next to a tin of hooks, some reels of nylon line and a tangle of traces, corks, floats and lead sinkers. Then he gave me one of his rods to carry and we went down the passage and out on to the veranda. There wasn't a sound from the bedroom.

Through the door in the wall, the Coolietown end of the main road was coming to life in the silvery early morning. It was like the opening scene of a musical Ma once took me to, with people beginning to drift onstage as the lights went up. Some of the shopkeepers were already out yawning and tugging at their wooden shutters. Outside the Palm Café, a group of gumbooted labourers with sweat-rags knotted round their necks stood waiting for a truck to come and take them to work. One of them, a Zulu with heavy round beaded plugs in his earlobes, was rolling shaggy-looking tobacco into a spill of brown paper. He licked the edge and smoothed it down with his forefinger and gave the open end a twist before he stuck it on his lower lip and began searching his ragged trouser pockets for matches. As we passed him, he lit it, drew deeply and let out a puff of pungent smoke before passing it on to the man next to him.

'Dagga,' Finn said when we were out of earshot.

The gardener at home had smoked cigarettes smelling like that, and I had thought it was just the cheap tobacco that black people had to buy because they couldn't afford anything better. I gasped, 'Are you going to tell the police?'

50

Finn looked amused. 'Tell on a man who is yust having a quiet smoke? Of course not. The Zulus have been growing and using dagga for centuries, and who am I to deny a working man his few pleasures? It would be different if I caught you at it.'

I looked up at him sideways under my eyelashes, without moving my head. He couldn't possibly know that I already had dagga on my list to try one day if I could get hold of some, just the merest puff of course, to see what it felt like. I was kicking myself for not having twigged about the gardener.

A water cart came rumbling past, pulled by a lazily clopping mule. Walking next to it was a very tall, very thin Indian man in a khaki municipal uniform, army boots and puttees. His mouth and chest were hidden under a flowing grey beard streaked with brown and pink stains.

'Morning, Mr Padayachee!' Finn called. 'How's business?'

'Morning to you, Master! Business is OK.' Mr Padayachee tugged the reins and the mule stopped at once, stiffening its legs so that its shod hooves slid along the tarmac throwing up sparks as the water cart rocked to a sloshing standstill.

Finn said, 'This is Isabel, my wife Stella's sister.' We nodded shyly at each other. He went on, 'I wish you wouldn't call me "Master".'

Mr Padayachee shook his head. 'I thank you for this, but I cannot make an exception, you know? It is too much confusement.'

'Mustn't rock the boat. Always the besetting sin.' Finn gave him an ambiguous smile. 'Cannas by the station are looking good.'

'Indeed! Indeed.' Mr Padayachee's voice had a gentle hairy sound. He was so thin that the cartilage in his nose stood out like a picked chicken breastbone, and the hollows at his temples were as deep as egg-cups.

'Mr Padayachee is our municipal water carrier,' Finn told me. 'He has nine children, and at the Mariamman festival he can take six needles through his tongue at once and walk over a bed of red-hot coals without getting a mark on his feet. I am lost in admiration of Mr Padayachee.'

The beard wagged as Mr Padayachee chuckled. 'I think you exaggerate, Master.'

'I think not. I've watched you do it.'

'Where? Can I watch too?' The questions tumbled out before I could stop them. To watch a fire-walking ceremony would be amazing; it would far surpass anything Evelyn Simpson had seen.

Mr Padayachee looked reproachful. 'The ordeal by fire is not meant to be a spectacle, Missy.'

I felt one of those overwhelming blushes climbing up my throat and face. My runaway tongue (a constant trial) had offended this dignified man of awesome talents. I blurted, 'I'm sorry. I didn't mean to be rude.'

Finn said, 'Nay, of course you didn't,' and turning to Mr Padayachee, 'This is Isabel's first visit to Two Rivers, so she's interested in everything.'

'Ah.' His black eyes seemed to be trying to plumb the depth of my interest. 'You are wishing to see the fire-walking in a spirit of enquiry? It is a religious ceremony, you understand.'

My cheeks felt like the red-hot coals Finn had talked about. 'Of course I understand. I'm sorry.'

'No need to be sorry. We are welcoming sympathisers like Mr Finn Rosholt, you see. If you are also a sympathiser –'

'I am!' At that moment, I was probably the most fervent sympathiser in the whole world.

'Then we would be very pleased to welcome you to the next ceremony, Missy. Goodbye, please.' And Mr Padayachee clicked his accomplished tongue at the mule and they clopped on up the street.

'You made a hit there,' Finn said.

'Gosh! Will he really let me go and watch?' I could hardly believe my luck.

'They hold the Mariamman festival on Good Friday, yust before Easter. It's our local version of a ceremony the Hindus call Kavady, when people do religious penances like fire-walking and also bring thanksgiving offerings to the gods for favours granted.' He smiled down at me. 'You'll be able to watch for sure, if you're still here with us.'

I crossed my fingers behind my back and wished, hoping it would work without delaying Ma's recuperation.

We turned right on to the gravel side road that led down to the railway bridge over the Umsindo river, walking on the edge of the pathway to avoid yesterday's swept-out rubbish and the piles of rough wooden crates heaped with discarded leaves and shrivelled vegetables and fruit that had gone bad. Where the shops ended there were rickety wood-and-iron houses crowded together in groups of four, each front door opening on to a small dark stoep and exhaling its own bad breath: things frying in hot oil, urine, smoke, mould, staleness – a compendium of the smells of poverty. Dirty little kids with snot running from their noses were brawling on the steps; stringy fowls pecked and scratched; an old man sat in a sagging armchair with his eyes closed, singing to himself in a quavering voice.

Finn said, 'Stella's a contradictory soul. She believes most passionate in the dignity of mankind, votes for all, down with the new apartheid laws, yet she so much resents having to live close to all this squalor. "Coolietown". It's a rotten word, but the one that everybody uses.' His tongue lingered on the double 't' in rotten.

I was quiet for a bit, then said cautiously, 'She often says things she doesn't mean when she gets worked up.'

He looked down at me. 'Poor Isabel. I'm sorry you had to overhear our quarrel this morning. Stella is, you know, more opset by your father's death and your mother's illness than she lets on. She's been very tense all week.'

He felt sorry for me. I felt sorry for him. All because of grumpy old Stella. I gave my celebrated shrug. 'We're probably all nutty in our family.'

'Ya?' A bear's rumble of laughter. 'You too?'

'It's not funny.' It wasn't, when you thought about it. Death and madness had struck those closest to me in the space of a few days, and now there were Stella and Finn to worry about. I could feel quite sorry for myself if I worked at it. I said, 'It's never been funny, dangling alone at the end of the family with old parents and nobody else at home.'

Finn shifted his rod to the other side so he could put his bear's paw on my shoulder. 'I know how it is. My parents were old also when I was born, and aging seems to do different things to people. It gives some the confidence to stand op and be themselves without apology, but in others it gradually erodes even their foundations. In the pharmacy I get a lot of people soffering this way. When they feel things changing or dissolving around them, they put their faith in remedies that have a predictable effect, like aspirin and Eno's Fruit Salts and laxatives. Alcohol too.' His voice got softer. 'I wonder, taking the analogy further, whether it is ever possible to build new foundations onder an existing house?'

I didn't fully understand what he was saying, but that was one of the things I liked about Finn. He never talked down to you, or underestimated your intelligence. I thought, Is he telling me about Stella or old parents or what? They seemed sombre words for a fishing expedition. I still had to learn that escaping from the precise measurements and obligations of the pharmacy to the freedom of doing as he pleased always put Finn in a contemplative mood, during which he teased out the ideas he had little time for otherwise. One of your duties as Finn's fishing companion was to act as a sounding board for them. He should have been a rabbi or a philosopher, the way he loved bending ideas and concepts into different shapes.

Another one we got on to that morning was personal freedom. When I started complaining about how old parents were stricter than younger parents and mine never let me go anywhere by myself, he gave a sympathetic nod. 'They imagine all the bad things that can maybe happen, ya? And they bring out horror stories from years back to support the saying of "no".'

'Exactly.' I was feeling quite sorry for myself, having been under a geriatric regime for so long.

'If it was op to me as a father – if, of course,' he slid me a sideways glance to make sure I appreciated that there was no certainty in the matter, 'I would try to give my children personal freedom, but make sure they knew that it carries responsibility to others.'

'How do you mean?'

'I believe very strong that people should make their own decisions from the time when they are quite yong. It is for you alone to choose how your life goes along, and nobody else. But in making your decisions, you must always consider how they will affect other people. "No man is an Island, entire of itself" the poet John Donne said.' I got a sideways smile now. 'Or woman, of course. It is a shame, I think, that women have still to fight for the right to make their own decisions.'

I was thinking, I wish Finn had been my father, when he turned away and said, 'Ah, now. There's the river.'

Ahead of us was an iron railway bridge, rusty in parts, with a metal mesh catwalk along one side for pedestrians. I ran ahead with my fishing rod and hung over the catwalk railing, waiting for him to follow. The river was muddy, its reed beds partially flattened by flooding after heavy inland rains; they gave off a smell of decaying vegetation that came up off the river in warm gusts as though it had bad breath. Plump grey-and-white seagulls bobbed on the water. On the far bank some cows had been driven down through the market gardens to drink, heads lowered for a long slow slurp and then up for a heavy-lidded look around before drinking again. They had trodden a sloping mud wallow down to the water and two herdboys were cavorting in it, their slick brown bodies wriggling in the mud like eels.

Finn came up and said, 'Tide's in.'

'How do you know? We're not near the sea, are we?'

'It's half a mile downstream. But you can see when the tide's in because it fills the lagoon and the water starts backing op – look.' He pointed down. The muddy water was sliding very slowly upstream under our feet.

'It must be salty, then.'

'It is. This is one of the best places for mullet, here and at the lagoon mouth. If you watch careful, you can see them.'

He pointed downwards before squatting over his tackle bag, and when my eyes had adjusted to the brown translucence of the water, I saw black fish shadows flitting past one of the bridge bastions. I also saw a khaki pith helmet with a pair of legs sticking out from under it; next to them was a second, browner, pair. Tied to each big toe was a length of fishing line with a cork bobbing at the end.

'Whose legs are those?' I asked Finn.

Without looking up he said, 'They can only belong to Titch and Kesaval. They must have beaten me to it again.'

So Finn met other friends on his fishing expeditions. I felt the silver morning taking on a slight tarnish. 'Who're Titch and Kesaval?'

'Two boys on the verge of becoming yong men. Impossible to describe. You'll have to meet them.'

'I don't like boys.'

Finn had broken the rubbery part of one of the bread crusts into pieces and was threading them on to three small hooks on nylon traces joined to a wooden float by wire spreaders. 'I'd reserve my yudgement in this case if I were you.

'Which one wears the ridiculous hat?'

'You'll see when you meet them.'

'I don't think I want to.' The few boys I'd met had been so defective at sensible conversation that I'd been bored after a few minutes. I mean, who wants to talk about motor bikes and guns and rugby all the time? In the interest of my sex-versus-love research, I'd tried hard with a boy called Martin who was quite nice looking with only a few pimples. It hadn't been a success; when I mentioned a rather good book I'd just read, he looked incredulous and went away. Evelyn Simpson never had any trouble talking to boys, she just giggled at everything they said and was asked out every single Saturday night. She wore a black velvet ribbon round her neck (the unmistakable sign of a fast girl) and a Merry Widow waspie to pull her waist in and a white angora bunny jacket that shed fluff all over their school blazers; and she would tell us in breathless detail on Monday morning at school how far she had allowed each one to go. Though I was impressed by her daring, the actual encounters didn't appeal to me much. French kissing meant getting someone else's spit in your mouth which didn't sound hygienic at all, let alone pleasurable; the same went for boys groping down your bra. I was beginning to suspect that besides being a teenage pervert I was also a frigid social misfit who'd end up talking to myself for company.

Finn said, 'Bring me your rod and I'll show you how to bait up. And don't worry about those two; I'm sure you'll like them when you get to know them.'

'Who says I'm worried?'

'I recognise the tone. Boys go through their own agonies – maybe worse ones, ya?' He took the end of my line, threaded it through the eyes of the rod and started to tie on a wooden float with spreaders and hooks like his. 'I never dared to kiss a girl ontil I was nearly eighteen. Living on a mission station, I didn't come across many willing candidates. Have you thought how hard it is for a boy without any experience to have to make the first move, impressing an alien creature wearing red stuff on her lips enough to get her to hold them still for him to kiss?'

'But we're not alien creatures.'

'To a boy in this country you are, onless he has sisters. It's the frontier ethos at work. Boys must be toughened up yong and turned into men able to take their place defending the laager from the marauding hordes. The European niceties of culture and the social graces women admire are considered unimportant.'

'You're not like that.' Finn read more than anyone she knew, Stella had told me.

'I have my dear old-fashioned parents to thank. They were determined not to bring up a barbarian.' He threaded a bread crust on to my last hook and smiled up at me. 'We Vikings have our pride. So. Let's see if we can still catch fish.'

I stood next to him by the rail watching how he cast his float in front of a shoal of mullet shadows. 'You must put it far enough away so the splash doesn't frighten them, and not throw too hard or the crusts will come off the hooks,' he explained. 'I've made them small because mullet have very small mouths which they use to feed on tiny organisms on the surface of the water and in the bottom mud. See, you have to entice them to the bait, wait ontil they begin nosing it and then watch for one to swallow it.'

He leaned out, using the tip of his rod to coax his float into position. I leaned out to look for another shoal of mullet shadows to throw my bait in front of and saw one immediately below, close to the legs. I lowered my line and let the hooks dangling from the float drop gently into the water several feet in front of the shoal – well positioned, I thought.

One of the legs jerked sideways and a cork flew out of the water with an empty hook at the end of it. The pith helmet began to turn upwards and an indignant voice called up, 'Hey, Finn! You frightened off my fish.'

'I'm not Finn, and I did nothing of the sort. They're still swimming along quite peacefully,' I called down.

57

'Who're you?' The face under the pith helmet was scowling.

'Titch, I introduce you to Isabel, Stella's sister,' Finn said. 'She came down from the Transvaal yesterday to stay with us for a while. Isabel, this is Titch.'

'I should have known it was a girl. Can't trust them around fish.' He began to untie the fishing line from his toe, grumbling.

A second head appeared with an upturned face, milk chocolate this time: an Indian boy with a startling flash of white teeth. 'I'm Kesaval. I trust girls.'

Titch kicked him. 'Don't be a shloep.'

I turned to Finn. 'Barbarians.'

'You will find that these two are different.'

'I doubt it.' I turned back to see what my baited hooks were doing. The mullet shadows were swimming towards them and, as I watched, one started to nuzzle at a water-softened crust. 'Finn, look, they're beginning to bite,' I whispered. 'What do I do next?'

'Wait ontil one of them sucks hard enough at the bait to take it into its mouth and starts to turn away. Then strike yently; too much of a pull will only tear the hook away from the mouth. You'll find that the resistance of the float is usually enough to drive a hook in.' He was leaning right over next to me. 'Careful, now.'

I was concentrating so hard that I didn't notice the legs disappear. The mullet nosed cautiously at one of the bread crusts, backward-finning against the current. The other mullet appeared to have ignored my bait and were swimming on. If they went much further, my mullet would let go and follow them. I held my breath and willed it to suck the bait into its mouth so I could catch my first fish with my first cast. That would be something to show Finn what his alien creatures were made of.

The mullet spat the crust out and flitted after the others.

'Nay, you've lost him. Never mind. Keep trying.' Finn turned away to check his own baited hooks.

My bid for glory thwarted, I began to look for another mullet shoal to tempt. There wasn't one. The water slid slowly upstream looking like watery cocoa. A seagull floated towards the bridge and I began to worry what would happen if it took a fancy to one of my bread crusts and tried to fly off with it. To hook a seagull would be extremely embarrassing and probably bad luck. If it plummeted out of the sky at the end of my line and killed itself, would its ghost come and haunt me, squawking piteously night and day on the windowsill of the beautiful bedroom until it drove me demented (not unlikely since the family was already tainted with madness)?

I jerked my line and its float out of the water, out of reach of the seagull, and it flew over my shoulder with the bread crusts going one way and the hooks another – straight towards the figure of a nonchalant boy in a pith helmet who was walking along the catwalk railing with his hands in his pockets. 'Look out!' I shrieked. To hook a boy would be infinitely worse than hooking a seagull, specially if he fell over the edge and hit his head on one of the bridge bastions and died. I dropped the rod and called, 'Finn! Finn!'

But the boy swatted the flying hooks away as though they were pesky mosquitoes and jumped down on to the catwalk with a double thump of his bare feet. 'Didn't anybody teach you to be careful with hooks, Isabel-Necessary-On-A-Bicycle? You could have taken my eyes out.' His eyes were the same colour as those extra big greeny-blue glass marbles called ghoens that you can see right down into, starred round the pupil with a thin scribble of brown.

The rod clattered to a humiliating standstill at my feet. Clammy with fright I blurted, 'I'm sorry.'

Finn, who had swung round, began to laugh. 'That'll teach you to walk on the railing, Titch, ya? Next time she might yust hook you proper.'

'Rubbish. Girls can't cast for toffee apples.'

My fright dissolved into annoyance. 'I'll show you how girls can cast!'

He cowered in mock fright. 'Please don't until I can take cover. I beg of you.'

Finn said, 'Where's Kesaval?'

'Having a pee. Can't do it in present company.'

He was trying to make me feel as though I was an intruder, spoiling their all-boys-together fun. And it wasn't fair, not on

59

that pristine silver morning when I had Finn to myself and was just beginning to get to know him again. I've learnt a lot since then about the subtle ways men have of shutting women out of those parts of their lives they consider sacred to their manhood – and I suppose we do it to them in reverse – but I wasn't going to be sidelined on the first day of my heady new independence.

I slitted my eyes and said, 'Kindly don't call me Isabel-Necessary-On-A-Bicycle. It's mocking.'

'You've got to admit it's a good name to mock.' He had an infuriating grin.

'And yours isn't? Titch, rhymes with itch, bitch, witch, snitch –'

He held up a muddy hand. 'You don't have to run through the entire list. I've heard them all. The one I like best is nouveau rich, which I intend to be one day so I can insult anyone I please and they'll be too intimidated by my immense wealth to object.'

At least he was literate, this boy. About my age and height but square-cut and restless as the young bulls you see at agricultural shows, always butting each other. Titch was never still for more than ten seconds; he had a pent-up energy that kept breaking out as though he couldn't contain it – not only physically but in great bursts of curiosity. He wanted to know how things were made and how they worked: animals and plants, machines and crystals, stars, rocks, bridges, insects. Girls weren't included until I changed his mind about their worth relative to the exclusively masculine world most schoolboys lived in then. Titch had a researcher's mind but little of the necessary patience. And few social graces, though his mother tried hard to turn him into one of those polite boys who handed round plates of snacks and asked wallflowers to dance.

But getting to know Titch came later. That morning he was just a pith helmet and a faded khaki shirt and shorts held up by a belt with a snake clasp. And a scowl.

In my experience, people with nicknames generally allow them to be used because the names they were given at birth are either embarrassing or inappropriate or twee. I wondered which was the case here, and said, 'Your mother can't

possibly have looked down at her newborn son and said,
"This little titch shall be called Titch, and nothing else."
What's your real name?'

A pained look crossed his face. 'I'd rather not say.'

'You know mine,' I pointed out. 'There can't be many
worse names than Isabel.'

'Don't you believe it. I've got a string of real buggers.'

One bare foot was rubbing the other. I had him cornered.
'Tell me.'

'Only if you promise on your honour not to divulge them
to a living soul, so help you God.'

'Why should I?'

'You want me to be crucified?'

This boy had no small opinion of himself. I said, 'Don't tell
me everyone chucks down palm branches when they see
you coming.'

'Ha bloody ha. Very funny.'

He was hedging. I said, 'Your full name, fair's fair. Promise
I won't breathe a word to anyone. I don't know anyone to
breathe it to anyway, besides Stella and Finn.'

'On your solemn oath?'

'Cross my heart and all the way up to heaven.' I spat on
my thumb and sketched a cross over my heart.

He looked away up the river and said, 'Timothy Montague
Wotherspoon McFadyen.'

I was impressed. It was the second to worst name I had
ever heard. The worst was Eeufesia Magdalena Salomie
Vosloo, an Afrikaans girl I knew. I whistled through my teeth
and said, 'Hell, not bad.'

'Are you kidding? It's ultra double purgatory. How could
two normal, quite decent parents do that to me?'

'People who've just had babies do funny things.'

'They knew there'd only be me, so they saddled me with all
the family names put together. It could blight my life.'

I couldn't help it. I said, 'Shame, hey, Timothy?'

That made him really mad. The pith helmet joggled as he
shoved his head forward and said, 'Don't you bloody ever
dare –'

'Got him!' After watching us for a while, Finn had turned
back to his fishing, and now he shouted as he jerked his rod

61

backwards, striking twice. Titch abandoned me at once and ran towards him; the Indian boy came running up from the river bank. He was taller than Titch, with black curly hair and a humorous face and a kind of slender elegance that extended to the clothes he wore: a white shirt and blue jeans rolled up to his knees. After a good look at him (his back was turned and I'd never met a black – well, brown – boy of my age), I leaned over the railing to watch too.

The float at the end of Finn's quivering line bobbed and jerked as the mullet took off through the muddy water, arrowing against the current and leaping up again and again to try and shake the hook. It was so beautiful as it arced and twisted and fought for life, catching the first pink light of the sun on its glistening torpedo body, that I felt a growing anger. Why did we feel this compulsion to kill the beautiful things of the earth and sea and air? To dangle hooks in front of them hidden in innocent bread crusts so we could catch them and cut them into bloody pieces to use for bait to catch other creatures? Even Finn, gentle Finn, had a look on his face now of fierce glee, his hands moving like two predatory blond-furred rats as they worked rod and reel in unison to play the fish – play, that gambolling word that really meant to pit your human strength against a fish a fraction of your size until it was too exhausted to resist you any more.

'See, Isabel, how I keep the rod well op so that it acts as a shock absorber for the line,' Finn was crowing. 'Yust watch the expert at work.' He began to play the fish towards the river bank.

I turned away, sickened. Walking behind me as he and Kesaval followed Finn to watch him land the fish, Titch muttered, 'Girls are so predictably squeamish.'

I flared, 'We don't like killing, that's why!'

Titch made a rude noise and went on, but Kesval stopped and said, smiling, 'It is sometimes necessary.'

The pleased smug look on his face made me even madder. 'Killing dumb animals for sport is necessary?'

He said, and I've always remembered it, 'This is maybe the difference between men and women, nè? We accept the fact that violence is part of life's pattern. You wish it wasn't. Who is being more realistic?'

62

I looked at him, flattered that he'd said 'women' instead of 'girls' and, to be honest, surprised that an Indian boy should speak such good English. 'It's not a question of being realistic. Men just seem to be naturally violent. Even Finn.'

I turned back to look at him. He and Titch were bending over the fish which was struggling and gasping in the grass on the river bank. As we watched, he held its body and Titch wrenched the hook free of its bloody mouth.

Kesaval said behind me, his consonants making soft explosions in the Indian way, 'Violence is easy to condemn, impossible to predict. You'll understand better when you've been in Two Rivers for a while.'

I felt a shiver run across the silver morning, now turning pink and orange as the sun rose above the reeds.

Isabel

Violence, she thinks as she staples the newly copied pages of the fourth chapter together and tucks them under the first three. Will we ever understand it? Understand why one person deliberately kills another, why men rape and hit defenceless women and children, why people who truly believe in God can resort to torture and war over theological differences? How ordinary, pleasant human beings in crowds can turn into a pack of ravening beasts?

The cheerful morning sunlight slanting on to her desk dissolves into a blazing memory of the shouting, sweating, furious bands of men roaming Two Rivers on the unforgettable night of the Mariamman festival. It sweeps over her in a flood of horror that she had thought was long suppressed. She knew many of the faces from her walks round the town, but that night they were distorted with hatred and rage, howling faces out of a nightmare. Strong brown muscular arms rising and falling, smashing glass, splintering inadequate shutters, bone-crushing blows thudding down on the bodies of people trying to flee. Frantic, desperate, hideous screaming. And the looting lust she had witnessed: the furtive greed mixed with triumphant revenge on the looters' faces.

The tumult and the shouting. Where did that phrase come from? Shakespeare? The Bible? Did they have riots then, or was it describing just another skirmish in one of the endless, mindless wars? Nothing to make a fuss about, only a few thousand dead, ten thousand wounded, a million homeless refugees. Another ordinary day in the life of a world that seems unable to comprehend the meaning of peace. Another –

The telephone rings several times before she can unclench her hand enough to pick it up.

'Izzy?'

It's him, thank God. Not the carping voice that phones from the office at odd moments during the day to check up if she is at home like she said she would be. George loves to catch her out in inconsistencies.

'Is that you?' The tone is guarded.

'Yes, it's me.'

'You sound strange. What's wrong?'

'Nothing. I was just –' She falters. Dizzying black shapes are still swirling in her head.

'Just what?' He is alarmed now. His voice drops at least two octaves when it is worried. 'What's happened? Is there someone in the room with you?'

'No.' She thinks, I must reassure him. This emotional cat and mouse game I'm playing must be hell on his nerves. He's such a direct person, with no kinks, no need to camouflage everything with lies. She says, 'I've been having a daymare.'

There is a relieved chuckle. 'What about?'

'The riot. I've managed not to think about it for years, but it all came pouring back this morning.'

'You've got that far already?'

'No,' she says again, quickly. 'I'm not even past the first morning in Two Rivers. It just came back as I was sitting here thinking about violence. Every time you pick up a paper today, there are reports of violent attacks on train passengers and old people and schoolkids and shopkeepers. What's happening in our country? Are we all going crazy?'

'Have been for decades. It's nothing new.'

He is not often sarcastic. When he is, she finds it hard to respond to because her sympathies give him the moral edge. She says in reflex defence, 'Well, it worries the hell out of me. Mainly because of the children. We're messing up everything for them.'

His laugh has no mirth in it. 'You really should stop using your children as excuses, my love.'

Oh bugger, she thinks, I've said the wrong thing again. I bet he's got that look on his face: what the hell am I doing getting involved with a middle-aged married woman with greying hair and wrinkles and wriggling silver stretchmarks everywhere? She is silent, afraid of saying anything that will make things worse between them.

'Izz?'

'I'm still here.'

'Sorry. That was uncalled for. I'm being a bastard.' His apologies are always handsome. 'I've just had a morning that started at four and has been fraught with logistical problems. Not to mention a few epic encounters on the motorway.'

She suddenly realises that the line is not crackling as it usually does. 'You're not in the mountains?'

'No.' Good humour seeping back into his voice.

'Where are you?'

'Guess.'

He's here! she thinks. And my hair needs a wash. I could have a quick shower, use the hairdryer ... What shall I wear? Where is he phoning from? She gasps, 'I can't believe it. You're in town. Why didn't you tell me you were coming?'

'It was very last-minute. Had to come up to talk to Vince about an extra chapter suggested by the American editors of *Ethiopian Enigma*.' Vince is his publisher. 'Some of the places I wrote about five years ago have gone through drastic changes since Mengistu was overthrown, and they're suggesting that I pay another visit and write an epilogue.'

'And will you?' She dreads him going away, specially now that she has become so involved in writing her own book. His voice caressing her over the phone keeps her courage up and her motivation soaring.

'Probably. It's a sensible idea, means the American edition will be bang up to date.'

'How long for?'

'Not sure. A few weeks, maybe. I can't afford more. Have to have the Central Africa book finished by the end of the year. Talking of which, are you ready to show me what you've been writing?'

Not yet! she thinks, panic-stricken. I haven't had time to polish it. I want it to be as good as I can manage when I give it to you, so you'll be impressed rather than disappointed with me.

She dreads the moment when he, the professional, picks it up to read. She dreads being found wanting by this man she

66

wants so much. But she knows that she can't go on hedging with him and struggling to steady the tremor in her voice, says, 'When?'

'Midday suit you? I have another short meeting, then I'm free.'

She glances at her watch. Over an hour. Plenty of time to wash and dry her hair and get ready for a lovers' tryst. George, she knows, is going out to lunch with business colleagues today and never gets back to the office before four on the days he lunches out, so she won't have to think up an excuse for not being in the house if he phones. 'Midday will be perfect. Where?'

He names a quiet hotel twenty minutes' drive away. 'Room 220. I'll have the champagne on ice.'

Her laugh is pure joy. 'No need. I'm high already on the thought of seeing you.'

'So am I, my dear love.'

After he rings off, she treads air down the passage to her bedroom thinking, Why didn't anyone ever tell me what it's like to be head over heels in love? I'd never have settled for George if I'd known.

She has forgotten the hard lesson she has had to learn where her children are concerned: People don't want volunteered advice. As Chryssa, the headstrong teenager, used to insist, 'We've got to make our *own* mistakes, Mum.' Looking at her daughters, Isabel has often thought, I hope they're better choosers of husbands than I am.

Until she wrote it in this chapter she has just finished, she had forgotten too what Finn had said about personal freedom. His words ring through her head as she prepares to meet her lover. 'It is for you alone to choose how your life goes along, and nobody else.'

5

That morning was the first time I saw the Hindu temple.

Titch and Kesaval had gutted the mullet while Finn tried to catch another and I tried without success not to look; fishes' guts are undeniably fascinating however much you may loathe the way they're caught. They fit into their cavity so neatly, the intestines convoluted like brains and the liver gleaming like an angled glob of dark blood and the bright red feathery gills in looped rows. Titch held the mullet's heart out to show me and it lay convulsing on his bloody upturned palm, still alive, still trying to pump non-existent blood when its owner lay already dead. Seeing a heart beat like that out in the open air, naked and doomed yet carrying bravely on with its task, makes you wonder what life really is. What is it that makes your physical body move and breathe and grow and think, yet can abandon it in a split second – in an accident, a heart attack, a knife slicing up your belly – leaving just a lump of bloody meat? Finn used to talk sometimes about 'the life force' being what people really mean when they say 'God', and it would be nice to think that we all had a little bit of God in us. But it still doesn't explain what life is.

By the time they had finished the gutting, Titch was late for breakfast and Kesaval said he had to go too, so they ran off together along the river path.

Watching them go, Finn said, 'Very different, those two, but old friends.'

'I'm surprised.'

'Why?'

'Well, I mean –' What I meant was, Titch is white and Kesaval's an Indian. What I said was, 'It's sort of unusual, isn't it?'

Finn knew exactly what I meant. 'Not really. This town is quite a bag of mixtures, you know. Indians and whites and Zulus have lived parallel lives here for yenerations. The government's never going to be able to separate us all.'

I heard people say things like that often during my time in Two Rivers. It took years for English-speaking Natal to take the Nationalist government and its dream of strict apartheid seriously. It was assumed that things would go on as they always had in the Colony: the old white families would turn a blind eye to minor interracial mingling (there's no accounting for taste, is there?) as long as they were left to run the show. Which of course they weren't. But in the early Fifties people in small towns like Two Rivers still lived physically close to each other, and it was possible for a white boy and an Indian boy to be friends though their parents were unlikely to progress further than nods and possibly a polite greeting as they passed each other in the street.

I watched them running along the river path until they disappeared, thinking that maybe all boys weren't barbarians.

The fish had stopped biting and Finn began to pack up. As it was Saturday and his assistant Govind Desai would be opening up the pharmacy, he decided that we should walk back home the long way, along the river bank towards the temple.

From the railway bridge where we'd been fishing, the Coolietown part of Two Rivers ran for half a mile or so along the Umsindo river, a maze of old wood-and-iron houses bursting at the seams with the number of people living and working in them. Every other kitchen and back yard seemed to have a family business going: mother and grandmother and aunties making samoosas or chilliebites, father and grandfather and older sons selling bait or vegetables or upholstering or mending cane chairs, and the children acting as runners. The small yards between the houses were of red earth trampled glassy-smooth; mango trees strung with coloured light bulbs shaded tables and chairs where old women sat during the day and men sat after work during the hot evenings. The only large building was the Reddy Steam Laundry, which was brick with a tin roof and a tall black chimney that purled smoke all day, looking like the Sobranie Black Russian cigarettes that Stella so loved to flaunt when she could afford them.

Towards the main road there were more affluent houses painted in blue and yellow and green and hot pink distemper, with fancy mouldings picked out in silver and gold. Rearing up from their midst were two austere Spanish-style mansions with tiled roofs and towers and curvy wrought iron grilles over the windows; they could have been haughty señoritas at a gypsy gathering.

Spanish houses were all the rage in Durban in the Fifties, and these two were huge. 'Who lives there, Finn? Rich brothers or something?'

He laughed. 'Rich rivals, more like. When Mr Reddy built the one on the left, Mr Pather who owns the yewellery shop opposite the pharmacy – you've seen it? – built the bigger one with more rooms on the right. They have been competing for the honour of leader of the Hindu community in Two Rivers for years, though neither would admit it.'

'Stella says Mr Reddy's a mogul.'

I got a considered nod. 'Mogul on a Natal scale, I would rather say. Not compared with the Oppenheimers.'

'Did he get rich from his laundry?' I couldn't help being envious. My family never stopped worrying about money. Pa was forever going on about not using too much hot water in our baths and turning lights off when you left a room. He even used to make Ma boil chicken carcasses after we'd eaten off all the meat, and bottles of the thin grey stock used to fill up the fridge and go mouldy on top because Ma could never think what to do with it. She wasn't a very diligent cook.

Finn shook his head. 'Nay, you fall into a common trap there. Mr Reddy got rich from working day out and day in for forty years, starting with two baskets and a tin tub with a scrobbing board down by the river. He told me about it once. He would collect the dirty clothes and household linen and wash them, then Mrs Reddy would iron them with one of those heavy old flat-irons heated on a coal stove, after which he would put them in his baskets and carry them back to his customers. My mother used to do her ironing in yust the same way; it was terrible hot, heavy, backbreaking work. See, my feeling with rich people like Mr Reddy and Mr Pather, who started with a stall selling coloured glass bangles at the Indian market in Durban, is that it's wrong to envy them if you aren't prepared to put in the same amount of effort as they did.'

'I'd work hard if I knew I could get rich by it.' I couldn't see myself using a flat-iron exactly, but there were plenty of other things I could do to make money, I was sure. 'But how can you tell if it's going to have results? Ma and Pa worked hard and they never got rich.'

'That's yust the problem, you don't know.' Finn was snuffling. 'There are no guarantees in life. Nothing is certain. And ontil you learn to face this central fact as a good Hindu like Mr Reddy does, accepting the element of chance, you will not be content. Stella has not accepted it; she still thinks she can control what happens.' He looked down at me with a sad smile. 'Me, I live from day to day. It drives her round the bend. But I try to appreciate what's happening around me, to enjoy the moment, as they say, not dream all the time about what could maybe happen in the future.'

I had enough of Stella in me to be horrified. 'But it must be so boring! I dream all the time. I *love* dreaming.'

He put a bait-smelling hand on my shoulder and shook it gently. 'Ah, Izzy, I'm not saying don't think of the beautiful things that can happen. All I'm trying to tell you is, if you live all the time in dreams you won't see what's onder your nose. Promise me that in these months you spend with us, you will keep your eyes open and look around. There is much to see and learn in Two Rivers.'

The conversation was turning serious again. I wasn't sure that Finn was entirely right either; I could still hear Stella's voice saying, 'He always takes the easy way out.' But he was looking so earnest that I hadn't the heart to argue as I may have at another time. So I said, 'I promise, cross my heart,' and gave him my most reassuring smile so that we could walk a bit faster again. Despite the sandwiches we had eaten, my stomach was demanding breakfast.

The river path swung away from the houses, bordered on one side by tangled trees and bamboos. To our right the river had stopped sliding upstream and seemed to be motionless, as though holding its breath poised between tides. Across it was a vegetable patchwork of market gardens, and looming beyond them the bulky corrugated iron mill buildings. Even here on the riverbank where the smell of rotting reeds was strong after the recent flooding, there were whiffs of the sweet caramel scent of boiling sugar that always hung over Two Rivers, so constant that you hardly noticed it unless you went away and came back.

'We go onder the main road bridge, and there is the temple,' Finn was saying. 'Mr Reddy's grandfather, Kesaval's great-great-grandfather, built it. He was Kristappa Reddy, a famous temple builder who came from India over a hondred years ago.'

'Why did the Indians come to South Africa in the first place?' I hadn't thought about it before.

'To provide cheap labour for the Natal sugar farms. It was a very cynical transaction.'

'But why Indians? Weren't there enough natives to do the work?'

His eyes looked as though they had come from the very bottom of the sea as he glanced sideways at me. 'So. It is always black people who do the work?'

He was making me feel uncomfortable. 'I didn't mean it like that. I meant, well, surely there were enough Zulus living in Natal to –'

'I know what you meant. Why import more racial problems when we have enough of our own? Two reasons, I think. Because the Zulus didn't want to cut cane, and because those Victorian colonists were both greedy and stupid. They thought they could move poor people around the world to work for next to nothing on their farms and in their factories, then send them home afterwards with a few shillings and a pat on the head. It didn't occur to them that the yeneration born in a new land wouldn't want to go back to a life of poverty. They tried to keep women out, mind you, except for the prostitutes they imported to keep the men happy. You know what is a prostitute?' He stopped and looked down at me.

'Of course I know.' Evelyn Simpson had seen it as her

72

pleasant duty to inform ignoramuses like me on all aspects of sex. I added, 'I'm not a kid any more.'

'Nay, you are not. But women came anyway, wives and sisters and promised brides, and when their indentures were up these hardworking people bought land and shops and settled in like all good immigrants to work for a better future for their children. Like my own mother and father did. And they began to build temples. Look.'

I stopped and looked across the river to where he was pointing and saw a lovely white building half-hidden by mango and syringa trees, with a tall flagpole in front. Nearest to the bridge was a square tower built in diminishing tiers and surmounted by a studded dome shaped like a sea urchin shell with a gold urn rising out of the top. Linked to the tower by a narrow veranda with pointed arches that Finn called the portico was an oblong section with several smaller domes. Intricate plaster decorations made the temple look like an ornate, iced wedding cake. It had been thoughtfully sited too: close enough to their homes to be easily accessible to worshippers living in Two Rivers, yet separated by the tranquil river from the noisy commerce along the main road.

'You like the temple?' Finn was smiling down at me. 'It's even better on Hindu festival days when people gather for the processions. Then it comes alive with colour and noise and smells: women in their best silk saris, men chanting, camphor smoke, drums, fowls squawking when the priest grabs them by the neck to sacrifice –' He looked sideways at me. 'Apart from the bloody bits, I like the Hindu religion. It's conducted on a much more human scale than Christianity.'

'But your parents are missionaries, aren't they?'

'Yust so. But it doesn't mean to say that I must believe what they believe.'

I was shocked. Everybody I knew went to church, even if it was only to Sunday school under duress from parents like mine – insipid Anglicans who went twice a year, at Christmas and Easter, and thought they'd done their duty.

I said with a thrill of horror, 'Stella told us you were a Lutheran. Don't you believe in Christianity at all?'

Finn was looking serious again. 'I am not sure now, Izzy.

Living in Two Rivers gives you a different perspective on how the gods operate.'

'But you can't –'

'Take pot shots at Christianity? Let's sit here for a while and consider why not.' He moved towards the concrete picnic table and benches set in a clearing to one side of the river path. 'You're not ready for breakfast yet, are you?'

'No,' I lied, and set my fishing rod down next to his, leaning against the table. I was riveted by Finn's questioning of our taken-for-granted religion, and it seemed churlish to cut the expedition short because of mere hunger pangs when he was clearly enjoying himself.

He took a pipe and a pouch of tobacco out of his shorts pockets and began filling the bowl, tamping the tobacco down with his thumb. I hadn't known he smoked a pipe; it made him look older. When he had lit it and puffed a few times to make it glow, he said, 'The troble with churches is that they are divorced from the life going on around them. Inside, the atmosphere is hushed and people talk in whispers. Except for the stained-glass windows, everything is sombre – even the priest. He will have cold pale hands and if he's Anglican, most likely an affected English accent. The services happen at fixed hours, with fixed prayers and responses that people gabble so they can get home early to their Sunday dinners, smugly certain that God will provide.'

He stopped to take several gurgling pulls at his pipe, letting the smoke out the side of his mouth in little pops. His description perfectly fitted gloomy old St Agatha's in the mining town, where the Reverend Mundy's hands had been the palest you could imagine, but it didn't sound right coming from a missionary's son, and I said so.

'Nay, there you are wrong, Izzy,' he said. 'Being a believer shouldn't make you oncritical, and I am a believer in the concept of God. It is yust that I am less sure now of the best way He should be approached.

'Hindu temples like the Mariamman over the river are more like the old Christian churches. Inside they are small and homely and colourful, with familiar gods and symbols that can be recognised even by people who can't read. Temples are an everyday part of the community they serve,

74

not separated from it by spiked railings and graveyards of the dead. In the smaller ones, the priest – the poosalie – will work at another yob during the day. People come to pray at any time that suits them, bringing whatever offerings they can afford, and then sit gossiping on the steps outside. See, there is no line of demarcation between religion and daily living: the one is part of the other. It is more sensible to me, this way.'

He fell silent again, puffing at his pipe in that imperturbable manner pipe smokers have, looking as though they are thinking great thoughts while they stink up the atmosphere for everyone around them.

My eyes were beginning to prickle from the smoke. I said, 'The girl who used to work for us sometimes was a Lutheran, like you.'

That brought him out of his trance. Taking the pipe out of his mouth he asked, raising his eyebrows, 'Girl? She was a child, then?'

I'd never thought about it in terms of age like that. Everyone I knew called their servant women 'girls' and their gardeners 'boys'; those were just the words you used then, they weren't supposed to be insulting or anything. But when Finn questioned it like that, I could see that being called a 'girl' could be infuriating for an older person. I felt myself going pink and said, 'She was quite old, actually. She used to go to the Sunday afternoon service for black people at the Lutheran church.' I didn't add that it was generally known in the mining town as the 'kaffir church'.

Finn nodded. 'We Lutherans are not as encrusted with tradition as the smarter Christian churches. Yet even in our simplified liturgy, holiness is a favour conferred on poor sinners only after enough penance has been done. If you don't make it to heaven because you didn't try hard enough, tough luck, you've lost your chance for all eternity.' There is remembered pain in his eyes as he looks at me. 'I truly hate the frickly concepts of hell and original sin, Izzy. They are my main problem with Christianity. How can it be possible for an innocent baby to be a sinner? The Hindu belief in reincarnation gives people a much better incentive: if you don't make it to nirvana this time, you can try again in your next life.

'But I can see your expression glazing over. Time for breakfast.' He got up, putting his still-smoking pipe into his shorts pocket from which it kept sending out wisps of smoke all the way home. I was to hear ad nauseam from Stella how all his pockets had holes burnt through them.

I made a show of protesting, though my stomach was making noises like a runaway road grader by now, but Finn saw through it, of course.

'I'm away on one of my favourite hobbledy horses, paying no attention to my guest. Come, let's go. I'll take you to the temple one day and show you what I mean. I meet there with Mr Reddy sometimes. He's a very interesting man.'

I nodded, trying to look keen but obviously failing because Finn laughed as he picked up his fishing rod and the canvas bag which had a discoloured wet patch where the gutted mullet's blood was oozing through. 'You'll be surprised by the Reddy family,' he said, and led the way towards some steps up the side of the bridge to the main road and home.

Well, temporary home. Trudging along behind him I thought about Pa dying and Ma in the loonybin, and the silver morning dulled to pewter.

Isabel

She has not met him in a public place since their first meeting nine months ago. She had been sitting, envious and bored, over a solitary cup of coffee in an airport café after having seen a friend off on the plane to England, when she heard a voice saying, 'Can it be Isabel?' And looking up, had seen the now-famous friend from her time in Two Rivers who had swept her off to a lunch that had lasted a whole glorious, laughing afternoon, after which her life had exploded into new joy.

She feels like a conspirator walking into the hotel. In an attempt to look like a businesswoman on her way to a meeting with an out-of-town client, she has dressed in a subdued grey suit, white blouse with a bow at the neck and sensible-heeled shoes, and is carrying George's black leather briefcase. Inside, in a cardboard folder, are her first attempts at writing about Two Rivers, her brush, makeup bag and a box of bitter chocolates. They are always ravenous after making love.

I ought to have worn a broad-brimmed felt hat and my raincoat with the collar up, she thinks, trying to look calm and businesslike as she goes up to the desk and asks for her lover under the name they had agreed on.

'Room 220, Madam,' the desk clerk says, not even glancing up. 'He called down a moment ago to find out if his twelve o'clock appointment had arrived.'

Good move, she thinks. I wonder if he's done this before? Maybe he has other women friends coming on the hour. Izzy at twelve and Angela at one and Farida at two and Zoë at – no, of course he hasn't.

She still finds it hard to believe that he has never married, and even harder to believe that he should have chosen her, a shop-soiled wife, when he could have his pick of younger and more interesting women. He says he's spent his life living out of a suitcase and never had time to marry, and anyway he's always been too damn impatient; it's his worst fault. But she is sure there must be another reason. It doesn't make sense that such an intelligent, capable, worldly man should have gone unsnared. She is yet to learn how badly skewed a foreign correspondent's life becomes, and of the long despair before he finally came home from exile.

Going up in the lift to the second floor and walking along the quiet carpeted corridor with its recessed lights and muzak – faint smoochy violins – her heart slows to a thick, heavy beat. Despite the business disguise, she feels as awkward and gauche as a teenager. It's like going to a party held by people you don't know very well, she thinks. You know you'll enjoy it, but dread going in and having to get through the first few minutes. I don't know him in his city clothes. I hardly know him at all, come to think of it. Who is this man I've been meeting at the cottage? What am I doing here, a housewife with an unhappy marriage coming to meet a stranger in a hotel room where she intends to take her clothes off in the middle of the day and –

She is in a mild panic when she knocks at the door marked 220, and startled when it opens at once. He has trimmed his usually full grizzled beard and looks unfamiliar in a business-man's white shirt and discreet striped tie. His mouth breaks into a broad smile as he reaches for her. 'My dear love.'

'Not here!' she says in a fierce undertone. 'Someone may see us.'

He leans forward for a quizzical look up and down the empty corridor. 'Hotel ghosts, perhaps?'

'Someone,' she insists. 'I'd better come in.'

His smile fades and his hands drop to his sides as he steps back. 'Be my guest.'

Oh, hell, I'm doing this wrong, she thinks, walking past him into an air-conditioned room with twin beds, decorated in shades of beige. She had no idea there were so many. The only visual relief is provided by white net curtains drawn against the harsh midday sunlight outside. She whispers, 'Please don't.'

'Don't what? Lay an infidel hand on you?'

He is standing close behind her, his sarcasm scorching her neck. She feels her eyes starting to swim and thinks, What am I doing?

She falters, 'Sorry. I'm –'

'Having second thoughts?'

'No. Oh, no.' Tears are beginning to fall on her pale grey lapels, dark splotches of anguish. 'I love you so much. You'll never know how much. But it's hard learning to trust what we have growing between us over what I've accepted as normal and natural for twenty-five years. My great big suburban nothing of a life.'

Head down, desolate with self-pity, she feels both his arms coming round her. He holds her for a long contrite minute before he says, 'I'm the one who should be saying sorry. I'm an insensitive bloody idiot. Of course this is hard for you.'

A calming flood of relief stems the tears. She turns her face into his muscular shoulder, warm and familiar under his shirt, oblivious of the damp smudges of lipstick and eye-shadow she is leaving there. And in a few minutes she drops the briefcase and fumbles off the grey suit and the glamorous new underwear she bought after she met him, and they are pulling back the covers on one of the twin beds and reaching for each other.

At midday, in a beige hotel room, she thinks. What would the neighbours say if they knew? And smiles unseen into his beard.

6

It was a few weeks before the Michaelmas holidays when I
arrived in Two Rivers, and I hoped to stave off the horrors of
school at least until after Christmas. I had done well enough
at my school in the mining town for the headmistress to tell
Aunty Mavis that there shouldn't be any problem, considering
my family circumstances, in getting me accepted into a
higher class in the New Year despite the fact that I wouldn't
be writing the usual end-of-year exams. But Stella thought
otherwise.

She was already looking sour when we came in from our
fishing expedition because she'd got up and made bacon and
eggs as a special treat, and the eggs had gone hard with
waiting. She slammed the hot dishes down on the kitchen
table. 'What kept you so long?'

'We walked home along the river bank. Finn wanted to
show me the temple.'

'Seeing the sights already. Lucky girl.' She used tongs to put
the hard curls of bacon and fried bread on our plates, then added
the rather solid eggs and fried tomatoes and a little mound of
fried onions with an egg-lifter. My mouth was watering; bacon
and eggs with all the trimmings, even when they're a bit dried
up, is the best breakfast in the whole world when you're hungry.

'I wish you had come. It was such a beautiful morning,
and I caught a mullet.' Finn poured a little pyramid of salt on
the edge of his plate, then shook tomato sauce and pepper
liberally over everything. His ability to taste and smell had
been dulled by his years working with volatile chemicals at
the pharmaceutical company, and he liked his food strongly
flavoured and well-spiced. He could eat the fiercest curries
without showing a bead of sweat.

'I wondered what the pong was when you came in.'

As she jerked her chair back and sat down to her plate, he put his furry bear's paw on her arm. 'Don't be so cross with us, Stellen.'

It was his pet name for her, but only seemed to make her crosser that morning. 'You could have got back at a decent time. The food's ruined.'

'Of course not, it's delicious.' He took another mouthful and chewed heartily. 'Anyway, how were we to know you'd be cooking for us? You never cook breakfast.'

'I made a special effort for Izz – Isabel – for her first morning with us.' I could see her lower lip trembling.

That was the trouble with Stella. She was always making special efforts for people, then holding it against them when they didn't appreciate what she'd done. It made her difficult to live with because you were on tenterhooks all the time in case you hurt her feelings by not noticing the flowers she'd picked and arranged, or the artistic way she'd laid out a plate of food, or a side table she'd bought at an auction and spent hours sanding down and re-finishing. She was intense about everything she did as though there was a fire burning inside her that could only find release in a concentrated form, like a blowtorch. Now I realise that it was frustration at being trapped too young in an over-hasty marriage, at a time when wives were expected to do nothing more substantial than keep house. Stella had dreamed of making her mark on the art world, and now she was beating her head against small-town convention and a genuine fondness for Finn that had never gone as far as love.

I swallowed a mouthful of bacon and egg and said, 'You couldn't have done anything nicer, Stell. This is the best breakfast I've had for yonks.'

'You don't really mean that.' Her lip was still trembling.

'I do! Ma can't cook to save her life, you must remember. It's always cornflakes and toast and jam for breakfast, with a boiled egg if you're lucky.'

There was a faint smile. 'I do remember. Hard meatballs. Haddock in white sauce. Macaroni cheese. And roast chicken and potatoes with peas and gravy *and* bread sauce on Sundays, the big treat, followed by tinned peaches and icecream from the shop.'

'I hope she's all right in that place.' I'd woken up that morning worrying about Ma, wondering whether she understood where she was yet, and why. The room I had seen her in before I left had been painted a cold clinical green, with bars on the windows.

'Aunty Mavis says it's a good hospital. The best. You mustn't worry.' Stella picked up her knife and fork and began to eat her breakfast. From where he sat next to her, Finn gave me a grateful smile. We'd weathered the second storm of the day.

The respite didn't last. As she was finishing her second cup of tea, Stella said, 'I'd better take you along to the convent this morning and get you registered.' I must have looked blank because she went on, 'I'm talking about school, Isabel. The necessary evil that's supposed to equip you to go out in the world and earn a living, but seldom does. Besides spelling and my times tables, I can't remember a single useful thing school taught me. However, the law insists that each white child be put through the education grinder until the age of fifteen, which you haven't reached yet. So I asked the convent if they'd take you.'

I felt the whole lovely breakfast do a churning flip-flop in my stomach. 'But you didn't ask me!'

'Ask you what? As I just said, school is a necessary –'

'Ask me where I want to go! I'm old enough to choose. At least let me choose. At least.' My voice petered out. This was what I had been dreading most, having to go to a new school. I'd done it five times because of Pa being moved around to different mines, and I hated it. The worst is the first week when you're completely alone, surrounded by people who know each other, who know what to do and where it's OK to go and what it's OK to say, and who keep looking at you out of the corners of their eyes, measuring up your potential OK-ness. In my experience, girls' schools were worse than co-ed schools, and convents were the pits.

'There *is* no choice.' Stella was starting to get huffy again. 'In this dorp there is the government school and the convent, and the government school is dual-medium and full of Afrikaans railway brats whose parents can't afford to buy them shoes every year, let alone proper uniforms. You'll have to go to the convent.'

82

She seemed to have forgotten the grim Reef mining towns we came from where everyone spoke Afrikaans. Was it marriage that had done this to her, or coming to live in Natal which had a reputation for being snobby? I said, 'Can't I go to Durban? It's supposed to have lots of good schools.'

She looked annoyed. 'And how do you propose getting there?'

'I could catch the train.' I saw myself clickety-clacking into the city and walking down palm-lined streets to my school, which would be a stately building overlooking the harbour. Rigorous teachers in pince-nez and black gowns would teach us French and botany and history, and we'd have debates and discuss world events at break and play hockey and lacrosse in the afternoons. Whatever lacrosse was, it sounded glamorous. My image of the ideal school at that time was heavily influenced by some old Angela Brazil books of Ma's that I'd discovered in a storeroom at home. It seems ridiculous today that in our distant corner of the Empire we should so slavishly have tried to emulate the British way of life – particularly its rigid, cane-wielding, stuffy schooling – and considered ourselves better than non-English-speaking people because of it.

'Out of the question,' Stella said. 'Girls your age can't go running around on trains. They're not safe.'

'But I came down from Johannesburg by myself.'

'You travelled under supervision, don't forget. And let yourself get picked up by an old tramp the moment I took my eyes off you.'

'I didn't! He just followed me.'

Finn, who had been gathering up the breakfast dishes and putting them in the sink for the Zulu maid Eslina to wash when she came in, stopped and said, 'You didn't tell me about this, Stella.'

'Oh, there was some bother with an old tramp on the station yesterday. But that isn't the point I'm trying to make. Isabel must know that there's not much of Pa's pension left after Ma's hospital bills are paid, and we can't afford to subsidise an expensive school plus train fares.' Her teacup rattled down into its saucer. 'So it's the convent or nothing, kiddo.'

83

'Don't call me that!' I was furious. Nobody had thought to mention the lack of money to me, and now I had another horror to cope with: that I should become dependent on charity as well as a semi-orphan. 'I hate being called kiddo! I hate being shunted around the country as if I'm some sort of bloody parcel! And I know I'm going to hate the bloody, bloody convent!'

I ran out of the kitchen and down the passage to the bathroom and threw up the whole lovely breakfast into the lavatory, bits of bacon and egg and tomato and fried onion in a horrible yellow witches' brew at the bottom of the bowl. To make things worse, I could hear Stella shouting at Finn in the kitchen, 'Every time I try to help that child, I get tantrums. She's spoilt rotten. Ma never disciplined her properly –'

And so forth. After I'd rinsed my mouth out and cleaned my teeth to take away the foul taste, I crept along the passage to my room feeling like a carbuncle on everyone's life. Stella hated me, Finn humoured me, and my dead father and mad mother had abandoned me to loneliness and poverty. All I had in the whole world was temporary possession of a beautiful bedroom, a half-full suitcase of schoolgirl clothes and a worn teddy bear called Edgar in a too-short blue knitted pullover, who had been my constant companion in bed at night since the age of three. I got him out from under my pillow and sat in the wicker chair and hugged his embroidered nose and kind brown glass eyes against my chest while I cried. It was only the second time I'd cried since Pa's funeral, and I still had a lot of grief to let out. The top of Edgar's head got soaked.

When the storm had subsided to occasional sobs, I heard a knock at the door and it clicked open.

'Isabel?' It was Stella's voice, wobbly with remorse. The usual pattern from six years before. After she'd had a good shout, she would simmer down and be charming for hours; it was her way of being sorry without actually saying it.

'Yes?' I raised my swollen eyes to reproach her; no harm in twisting the knife.

She came towards me saying, 'You must realise that I'm not used to your being older, with opinions of your own. When I left, you were still a kid.'

'Well, I'm not now. And I don't like being pushed into things without being asked.'

She stood by the chair and put a tentative hand on my shoulder. 'It's not a question of being asked in this case. The convent's the only decent alternative, and you'll get a fee reduction because I work there. But I apologise for springing it on you like that. I could have been more diplomatic.'

Wonders would never cease; Stella apologising! Marriage to Finn had definitely smoothed some of the sharp edges. I mumbled, 'Thanks. And I shouldn't have got so upset. I know it's hard for you, having to have me around.'

'Shush, now.' Her hand tightened on my shoulder. 'We went through all that yesterday. Finn and I are glad that you've come to stay with us. You're my only family while Ma's not – not her usual self. We're going to learn how to be proper sisters, remember?'

I nodded.

'And we can start by giving each other a proper hug and then having a sensible talk about school. I promise you the convent isn't such a bad place. Most of the staff are excellent teachers and the girls are a nice bunch. I enjoy my art teaching; it's not as creative as I'd expected, but it's interesting learning how to –'

She rattled on for a bit to cover the awkwardness between us, and then we hugged and negotiated a deal about school: if I used my time constructively for the remaining few months of the year ('Read improving books and learn some cooking from Eslina and help Finn now and again in the pharmacy,' Stella said), and if the Mother Superior agreed to accept me into the higher class, I needn't start again until the first term of the new school year began in January. 'You could come with me to auction sales, if you like, and learn how bidding works,' Stella said. 'It's fun.'

I didn't see how smelly old auction sales could be fun, but she was being so nice that I said, 'I'd like to do that. I've never been to a sale.'

'Bidding and bargaining are essential life skills you'll never learn in school.' She gave me what I always thought of as her foxy look: an eyes-narrowed grin that made her nose look sharper. 'I've had to learn them in Two Rivers. The shop-owners think there's something wrong with you if you don't haggle. And I get a hell of a kick out of beating prices down. Unlike poor old Ma, who would rather die than dispute the price of anything.'

I had to laugh because she was right: people could foist any rubbish on Ma and she'd be far too intimidated to complain. Stella wasn't such a bad sister when I came to think of it.

She was saying, 'To get you orientated, we'll walk up to the better part of town. I've got shopping to do.'

The quiet silver morning could have been a dream by the time we closed the door in the garden wall and plunged into a hubbub of people, bicycles, rickshaws, delivery vans, buses, top-heavy cane trucks and main road traffic trying to squeeze through a small town's busy single shopping street. Before we reached the end of the stone wall, one of the rickshaws pulled on to the sandy pathway in front of us, its wheels making twin tracks on either side of the Zulu puller's splayed footprints. As he slowed down to a stop he leapt up in the air rattling the gourds on his ankles, laughing and tossing a beaded horn headdress so that its black plumes shook. His passenger, an old Indian woman surrounded by parcels, was thrown back in her seat and shouted at him with the tiny rubies in her nose flickering an angry red, 'You stop that now!' But he just laughed again and lowered the pulling bar to the ground and stood with his arms folded across his huge sweating chest as she gathered her parcels and climbed down.

'That's the widow Soobramony,' Stella said, 'mother of Mr Soobramony who runs the vegetable shop next door to the pharmacy. She's a disagreeable old bag, always nagging her daughter-in-law and shouting at the kids.'

There were similar sharp comments about the people in all the shops we walked past and I thought, She's trying to keep her distance from them, not wanting to be included in the shop-owning class. Poor Stella.

Further along the street as the noise and smells of Coolie-town faded, there were proper pavements linking the flamboy-ant trees and smarter shops with display windows and canvas awnings. At Stella's insistence we stopped for a while in front of a window with a sign saying LATEST TEENAGE WEAR.

'You probably need some new stuff to wear.' She gave my old shorts a disparaging sideways look.

But I hardly noticed. My eyes were riveted on the creation draped on a white-painted ladder, labelled 'For That Special Evening'. It was the most beautiful evening dress I had ever seen: a dreamy pale pink ballerina with a strapless taffeta top and layer after layer of tulle skirts. Pinned up on the partition next to it was a fluffy white angora bunny jacket just like Evelyn Simpson had, an artificial silk rose and a pearl-beaded evening bag; from under the froth of tulle peeped a pair of matching pink satin shoes. I stood entranced by a vision of myself gliding down a spangled staircase in all this finery with a posse of tail-coated Fred Astaires poised to swoop me off into a dance. It sounds corny now, but the Hollywood musical reigned supreme then.

Stella was saying, 'I think we could run to a pair of jeans.'

Remembering that I was dependent on charity, I tore my eyes away from the pale pink vision. 'Honestly, I've got enough things to wear.'

She let out one of her sudden barking laughs. 'You haven't *arrived* at your age until you own a pair of jeans. I'll talk to Finn about it.'

'Please don't.' Couldn't she see? I didn't want to be any more obligated to them than I was.

'No harm in talking.' She turned to walk on, impervious as usual to the unspoken plea.

The road widened into a square with a green lawn in the centre edged with beds of cannas, and more flamboyant trees shading parked cars. Old Man Herald's obelisk reared up from the middle of the lawn, a giant granite finger admonishing the current residents of Two Rivers to behave, or else.

Stella pointed to the colonnaded white buildings on two sides of the square. 'Town hall and post office, both built by the Herald Company from whom all blessings flow. The hall has rows of extremely uncomfortable flap-down wooden seats for the bioscope on Wednesdays and Saturdays, when Indians are allowed to sit behind a railing at the back if the film is considered suitable, but not natives. Don't ask me why.' She gave me a sarcastic smile and went on, 'Cosy Hotel and Bottle Store on the third side of the square, making this the official social centre of Two Rivers. Of course, the *real* social centre is the company club whose membership is restricted to salaried staff. Ordinary workers aren't permitted to sully its portals.'

She was at her most acid that morning, and I wondered how many snubs she had had to endure in this town during the past six years. She was such a contradictory mixture, wearing outrageous clothes and saying things that often offended people, yet being furious because she wasn't accepted. I suppose, looking back, that she was born twenty years too early. She would have fitted much better into the Seventies when people were admired for having strong opinions and blurting out exactly what they thought, but the early Fifties was a time when women mostly conformed. They wore hats and gloves when they went shopping, and frocks with long full skirts and waspies to pull in their waists, and pancake makeup with bright blue eyeshadow for the daring. They baked and cooked and gardened and held tea-parties; husbands who could afford it gloried in the boast that they wouldn't allow *their* wives to go out to work. But Stella was a misfit: trapped between her need to be taken seriously, her longing to be someone in the community, and her sense of style.

I brushed the uncomfortable thoughts away and asked where the convent was.

She looked pleased that I'd broached the touchy subject. 'A bit further along, three blocks off the main road. You won't find it too bad, you know. Sister Kathleen Killeally's a bit of a pain but the Mother Superior, Mother Beatrice, is a nice brisk woman with a good sense of humour and a passion for English history and literature. You'll be able to indulge your reading habit, at least.'

I remember thinking, How bloody exciting, I can't wait to go. But I was wrong in imagining that I'd be bored at the convent. I didn't know that it would become a raging theological battleground between me and Sister Kathleen, whose horror of the heathens of Two Rivers and their graven idols had begun to cloud her brain. Or that my stay in this peaceful-looking little town would end in terrifying violence and death.

We walked past the shops and a stone church to the Herald bridge over the Umlilwane, where you could stand looking down on the company estate. Its matching offices and research laboratories and clubhouse were in curly-gabled Cape Dutch style, linked with colonnaded walkways; its terraces and pergolas and lily ponds and lush gardens and gracious homes and palm-fringed golf course breathed old money and gentlemanly commerce. Stella said, 'Old Man Herald would have scorned all this. He started in a tin shack and said people got soft living in luxury. I sometimes think life was a lot simpler then.'

'But you love beautiful things.'

She gave me her foxiest look. 'I admire achievers too.'

We walked home via the Paradise Milk Bar and sat on swivelling stools to order lime milkshakes from the pimply youth behind the counter, who spoilt the treat by leering at me from behind the buzzing chrome mixer. He had slicked-back hair with a quiff in front that made me think of the jingle being played ad nauseam on the new Springbok Radio: 'Brylcreem, a little dab'll do ya, Brylcreem, you feel so debonair.'

Stella said as we went out on to the hot pavement, 'You won't have to look very far for a boyfriend. Percy Smuts seems to have taken a shine to you,' and laughed.

'What a drip. I'd rather die!'

'He wouldn't be a bad catch. He's got a job and a motor bike and a white tuxedo for dances.'

She was enjoying teasing me and I didn't want to spoil our sisterly time together, but the idea of having an actual boyfriend was still as tenuous as a soap bubble. So I said, 'Drop dead, Stella, man,' and laughed too, and we walked home in lime-burping amity.

Isabel

They are lying with their heads on the same pillow and their spent bodies touching all the way down. He is stroking the soft cushion of padding on her hip that she hates so much.

'I've put on weight these past few years, since my periods began to tail off,' she murmurs.

'You're gorgeous. Women should be round.' His voice is fathoms deep.

'Not this round. I must try and lose weight.'

He moves his hand upwards to cup one of her breasts. 'If you do, these will shrink like old goatskins.'

'Hey,' she protests, 'you're not supposed to say things like that. Old goatskins!'

'It's not a bad analogy, you've got to admit. People drink from goatskins.' He pulls the breast towards his mouth and runs his tongue round her nipple. 'May I sup from your fair tit, dear lady?'

She laughs and says, 'Bad luck. There's nothing there any more.' But he takes her nipple into his mouth and sucks it gently, and as it hardens she feels a delicious warmth spreading through her body.

She thinks, Being properly loved – being cherished – is wonderful. George never did anything like this. Their sexual encounters were always brief and silent, and when he rolled away she would be left wondering what everybody made such a fuss about. In guarded conversations with other women, she learnt that sex took up a very small proportion of most people's lives and that it was often unsatisfactory. 'So tell me, what's an orgasm anyway when it's at home?' one friend had joked bitterly. When Isabel read the startling sex scenes that cropped up more and more often in books and watched the now-unbanned writhings of beautiful bodies in darkened cinemas, she had begun to wonder if mutually enjoyable sex was just a figment of men's imaginations, conjured up to make them feel better about what was too often almost-rape.

But of course I was wrong, she thinks, exultant. They are making more leisurely love now, and afterwards they both fall asleep.

She wakes half-covered by a sheet to a knock at the door and the sound of it opening, followed by a murmur of voices. Her first panic-stricken thought is, George has followed me! Or had me followed. It's a photographer with a flash. He's going to burst through and catch me naked and there'll be lurid headlines in the newspapers and . . . She pulls the sheet over her head and lies doggo. The door is out of sight down the short passage next to the bathroom; she hears it close, and the sound of clinking. She risks a peep from under the sheet and sees a hotel trolley appear round the corner bearing champagne glasses, a green bottle chilling in a silver bucket and a platter of sandwiches which turn out to be smoked salmon.

Shedding the hotel towel wrapped round his waist, her lover is saying, 'I arranged a small mid-afternoon repast. Thought we might not have much time for lunch.'

In gratitude for the concerned tenderness of this man she has rediscovered so late in her life, she reaches her arms up towards him and he kneels to embrace her.

After a while he loosens his hold and says in her ear, 'Aren't you starving?'

Dizzy with sleepy joy, she whispers, 'I could live on nothing but love for the rest of my life.'

'An admirable sentiment, my darling. I'm extremely flattered.' He lets go and sits back on his heels, smiling at her. 'But you will forgive me if I stoke the fires of passion with fuel? I haven't had a thing to eat since the repulsive hamburger I had for breakfast on the motorway early this morning.'

Guilt jackknifes her upright, the sheet falling away. 'Heavens, I'm sorry! How thoughtless of me. You must be starving.'

'Moderately peckish.' He gets up and reaches down for her. 'Will you join me?'

'Just a sec.' She tugs at the sheet to loosen it so she can wrap it round herself.

'Do you really need that? It might be fun if we sat and ate with nothing on,' he suggests. '*Déjeuner sur le* hotel bed, you know?'

She laughs and drops the sheet. 'Of course. What am I thinking of? A love feast needs no clothes. And now you come to mention it, I'm moderately peckish too.'

Sitting facing each other, chatting about what has been happening since they last met, they devour the sandwiches and the champagne, then she brings out the box of bitter chocolates and they demolish most of the top layer before he slaps his stomach and says, 'Enough. I couldn't eat another morsel.'

'Me neither.' She leans back against the padded beige bedhead. 'You're a pernicious influence, you know? I've been trying to diet.'

'Why?' He leans over to put the box of chocolates on the other bed, then shuffles closer until his legs are arched over hers, his vigorous bush of pubic hair dark against the sheet beneath them. 'I've told you that you're perfect as you are. If I'd wanted a social X-ray, I'd have found a nice skinny model to cuddle up to. They're two a penny here in town.'

'Oh really?' She feels a pang of alarm.

He laughs. 'You're so transparent, Izzy.'

'What can you see now?' Jealousy, she thinks.

'Your concern about my potentially wicked past. But I keep telling you that I haven't got one. I've been living in an emotional bloody desert for years.'

'You've never had girlfriends?' She has not asked him directly before.

He shrugs. 'Of course. Ships passing in the night. I'm not a saint.'

'Never anybody serious?'

'Not since –' He stops himself. 'You really don't want to know.'

She says, 'But I do. I want to know everything about you since Two Rivers. I *have* to know.'

He shakes his head in brusque dismissal. 'Nobody can know everything about anyone else. Nor does one have a right to know. We all need our privacies.'

She pleads, 'But you know all about me. I've blabbed out my whole life to you, such as it is.'

'No, I don't. You've told me what you want to tell me. And I've done the same.'

She feels a familiar dread and her voice is shaky as she says, 'I just want to know if there's someone who's been really important to you. I've only ever had my kids.'

He looks away towards the drawn curtains at the window. 'There was a girl once. We were going to be married. Then she found someone else and dumped me. That's all.'

'Oh.' The word is barely audible.

'It wasn't a big deal. More my fault than hers.'

'But you stopped trusting women.'

'Bullshit! That's Mills and Boon talk. I just had my head screwed on wrong.' His anger at his wasted years comes boiling out. 'You've no idea what it's like to be a journalist who specialises in catastrophes and wars and general human ugliness. To be forever on the move, living out of suitcases and backpacks year after stinking pointless year. Never stopping anywhere long enough to put out feelers, let alone roots. Living on your wits and your ability to manipulate words that conjure up horror. Constantly on the alert to ferret out the sort of mayhem that makes headlines, and ejaculate it in copy that will impress editors enough to keep paying you. I tell you, if I hadn't been called back home when my mother was dying, I would have self-destructed.'

She reaches out her hands to cover the fists clenched on his knees. 'I'm sorry. I didn't mean –'

He breaks in, 'To agitate my can of worms? At least they've squirmed out now. At least you know that I was too busy fucking up a large chunk of my own life to fuck with hordes of *femmes fatales*. Thank God I discovered in time that I had a talent for writing books people actually want to buy. These last few years have brought me peace at last. And you.' He unfolds his fists and turns them upwards to enclose her hands. 'I hope permanently soon.'

'You really mean that?'

93

'I wouldn't say it otherwise.' He rocks her hands from side to side. 'Why do you sound so doubtful, Izz?'

She looks down and mumbles under the fall of greying hair, 'Just can't believe my luck. It seems so amazing: you, a well-known writer whose books everybody talks about, choosing me – at my age.'

The remains of his anger dissipate as he laughs. 'Thus spake Methuselah. I'm no spring chicken myself.'

'But you're so accomplished. I've done nothing with my life.'

'Bringing up three children isn't nothing.'

She has said exactly this to herself in her darker moments, but it doesn't help. 'Nothing outside the usual family things, I mean.'

He recognises the sense of desolation at wasted opportunities; it is a route he has travelled too often himself, only to learn that it leads nowhere. He gives her hands a gentle shake, and says, 'But didn't you say you had some writing to show me?'

She shrugs uncomfortably. 'It isn't much good. I'd rather not. It'd just be wasting time for you to –'

His voice cuts in. 'Did you bring it with you?'

'I –'

'Did you?'

With her courage failing, she debates briefly whether to lie and say No, then pushes the idea away. She will not put this relationship in jeopardy by lying. She looks up instead and says, 'I did, but I'm sorry now. You'll think it's useless. Just scribbles.'

He drops her hands and holds out a demanding palm. 'I want to see it. Hand over.'

'You'll think it's rubbish.'

'I'll be the judge. Give.'

'Now you're bullying me.'

'And you're being coy. I thought we'd got way past that?' He has mastered the journalist's trick of persuasion wrapped around accusation.

'I feel funny showing it to you.'

'Promise I won't laugh.' But he is smiling.

'I'll be mortified if you do.' She succumbs, extracting her

94

legs from under his so she can reach for the briefcase. 'Even though it's probably the worst rubbish you've ever seen.'

'I'm sure it won't be.'

She takes out the bundle of handwritten pages and turns to face him. 'I don't know whether this is worth going on with, or just nostalgic junk. You've got to be completely honest with me. If it's not up to scratch –'

'What then?'

'If I'm having delusions that I can write something worthwhile, I want to know, OK? I want to know!' She makes a fierce double thumb-slash in the air over her left breast. 'Cross your heart and all the way up to heaven.'

'I'll try and give you an honest opinion. But –'

'No buts! I want to know. If it's no good, if it's lousy, then I've got to think again.' Until she hears what he has to say, she will not give even a hint of the dream she has begun to construct around these hard-won pages.

He nods, unsmiling now, and takes them from her. She gets dressed and goes and sits on a chair looking out through the beige curtains at her reflection in the window while he reads.

7

A term and a bit off school when others of my age were beginning to worry about their exams, and a new town to explore ... Looking back now at those first months in Two Rivers is like moving from one stained glass window to the next inside a dark church: the colours glow unnaturally bright, lit from behind by the knowledge of what came later.

Finn and Stella had a major argument about whether I should be allowed to walk around town alone. He said it was a small place where everybody knew everybody else's business, and I was old enough at fourteen-and-a-half to look after myself. She said it wasn't safe.

'Nonsense, Stella. Sergeant Koekemoer keeps a close eye on everything that goes on in this town. I can't see what harm can come to her if she stays in the shopping section of the main road.' He turned to where I sat glowering on the other side of the kitchen table. 'You'd be sensible I'm sure, Izzy.'

'She can't just run about on her own,' Stella argued. 'Anything could happen.'

'Like what?' I was furious at the implication that I couldn't look after myself.

'Do I have to spell it out?' She was getting upset again. 'Like being attacked. Like being run over by a car with defective brakes. Like disappearing into one of those spooky little muti shops down near the bridge and never coming out again. It happens, you know.'

'Do you think I'm that stupid? Attacked by who, anyway?' I thought, She's turning into Aunty bloody Mavis.

'A dirty old man like that tramp at Durban station. A gang of millworkers. Drunk natives – you name it. This place is a racial maelstrom. White girls don't go walking around alone.'

Finn gave me a warning glance to stay quiet and said, 'Maelstrom's a strong word for a plain hardworking little town like Two Rivers don't you think, my dear?' He only ever called her 'my dear' when she got into one of these hot-balloon moods, blowing things up out of all proportion; it was his way of trying to be reasonable. I'm sure he got it from his parents. I could just picture them tottering around (they were both well into their eighties by then) calling each other 'my dear' in the same lilting Norwegian voices.

But Stella *hated* being called 'my dear'. It would needle her into even worse outbursts. 'It's not strong enough! This end of Two Rivers is completely black. Most of them are poor. The whole place is a rabbit warren. It's just not safe for a young white girl on her own.'

'It's where we live,' Finn said in his quietest voice. 'So-called Coolietown, like it or like it not. These completely black people are our neighbours and very good customers.'

'Worse luck! I hate this place!' The furious words lashed out before she could help herself, and you could see she regretted them because she said quickly, 'I don't mean that. I love our home. It's just this part of town. Everybody looks down their noses at us.'

'Everybody?'

A red stain was rising up Stella's neck. 'You've got to face it some time, Finn. We're considered more than a bit peculiar because we choose to live among Indians.'

'But where we live has nothing to do with choosing. The house goes with the business. You knew that when we bought it. Everybody knows. It is not, surely, a shameful thing to live here?' Finn had the deep sea look in his eyes again.

It was shameful to her, but she couldn't admit it to this son of foreign missionaries for whom life contained a rainbow spectrum of God's children, not just black and white. I saw her sigh and turn away saying, 'Oh, forget it. I just don't think it's safe for Isabel to go walking around by herself. She doesn't know a soul.'

'Then I will introduce her,' he said in an end-of-the-argument voice. 'And she will promise not to set foot off the main road, and not to go further than the bridges at either end.' He raised his eyebrows at me. 'You agree to this, Izzy?'

97

'Madam desires to be called Isabel,' Stella said, capitulating, but with bad grace.

I agreed.

That morning Finn left Govind Desai in charge of the pharmacy and we retraced the route I had gone with Stella: all the way up one side of the busy main road, right past the town square to where the white shops ended and then down the other side, taking me into each one to introduce me to the owners. Only he went on to include all the Indian shops too. He'd say, 'This is Isabel, my sister-in-law. She's yust come to stay here with us for a while. So. You keep an eye on her while she's walking around, OK?' And then he'd ask after their families and they'd give me a sweet or offer us a cooldrink, and we'd go on through the lacy shade thrown by the flamboyant trees to the next shop.

Apart from Pather's Jewellers diagonally opposite the pharmacy, which had its own smart striped awnings and specially lit windows lined with black velvet, and Ismail's General Dealers which took up half a block, the Coolietown shops were dark little caverns squashed into a long raucous bazaar running down both sides of the road. All manner of goods spilled out on to the sandy pathways, piled in cartons, on rickety stands and rails dragged out every morning after the shutters went up. There were dress shops and gents' outfitters and household linen shops with permanent SALE SALE SALE signs slapped across windows heaped with bolts of material, cheap clothes, snarls of net curtaining. Doorways fluttered with sari lengths and glittering gauze scarves hung on wire coat-hangers. Outside on trestle tables would be piles of shoes and plastic handbags going limp in the hot sun.

People strolled and pushed and shouted and pawed with greasy fingers that plunged alternately into packets of hot chips and chilliebites. Shop touts called out things like, 'Come in for best bargains, Madam and Sir,' and, 'Here, please! Sale prices, please!' Down side alleys, flyblown native eating houses sold bunny chow (a ladle of stew slopped into half a hollowed-out loaf of bread) and mealiepap with curry on dented tin plates, with dollops of free atchar.

Music blared in a dozen different keys and styles: sitars and saxophones and Mantovani violins moaning from café jukeboxes, Zulu men playing hypnotic repetitive phrases on tinny guitars as they walked along. Halfway down towards the river was the Delhi Palace bioscope, where eerie wailing seeped out past the shabby velvet curtains that hung in its doorways. Though I never saw a Hindi film – I wouldn't have dared go in there – Finn told me about one he had gone to. 'It was wonderful exciting, Izzy, six-armed blue gods and flying monkeys and demons with three heads and voloptuous princesses, but no kissing allowed.'

'Why not?'

'It wouldn't be seemly, Mr Reddy says.'

The vegetable shops had dazzling geometrical displays of fruit and great mounds of vegetables with earth still sticking to their roots. In season, there'd also be tall bundles of sugar cane that you bought by the stick to peel with a penknife and bite off chunks to chew the sweetness out before spitting the left-over wads of white fibre into the dust. The spice shops had rows of finely plaited round baskets heaped with gold and ochre and russet and yellowish-green curry spices, all giving off nose-tickling smells. Wreathed round the doorways and hanging from the dark ceilings would be bunches of dried leaves and twigs and seeds and aromatic bark.

Finn had some curry spices mixed by fat Mr Moodley who wheezed, 'You want the Dynamite Special again, sir?'

'Of course. It must blow my head off.'

Mr Moodley must have seen the expression on my face, because he said, 'And for the Missy? Something not so strong?'

Finn looked down at me. 'Do you like curry?'

Ma had never made it because Pa got indigestion if he ate spicy food. I said cautiously, 'I don't know.' The idea of having my head blown off didn't appeal.

He chuckled. 'We'll soon find out. Eslina and I make a very good chicken and coconut curry. So. One of your milder mixtures too, please, Mr Moodley.'

Jeepers, I thought, what have I let myself in for? The spiciest thing Ma had ever cooked was gingerbread. But as the fat man made up the mixtures, using tiny scoops to measure and add the different ground spices to the bowl of his brass scale, stirring them together then tipping them into small brown paper bags, with a bigger one for the seeds and bark and dried leaves, Finn explained. 'See, a curry works this way –' And I learnt another surprising thing about him: he enjoyed cooking, which wasn't something men did then.

Finn was a magical person to walk with, interested in everything. Being with him was an introduction not only to a new world of sights and sounds and smells but also to a mind that sought reasons and explanations, yet could still marvel. On the first silver morning's walk to the river he had been philosophical; now he was a fount of local knowledge and folklore. I think I came to love Finn a lot more than Stella did.

Our second-to-last port of call was the red-brick police station just off the town square. Here I was introduced formally to Sergeant Koekemoer, the station commander, who had covered himself in sporting glory in his youth by being chosen for the Natal rugby team. His predilection for meat three times a day had taken its toll, however; in middle age he was a flabby ex-athlete with a paunch and a flushed red face.

When Finn explained about my wanting to walk around town on my own, and the limits he had set, the sergeant leaned forward over the charge-office counter with the brass buttons of his navy-blue uniform clicking one by one against the wood. 'You got some sense, you'll stay nice and quiet at home, my girl.'

How could I explain to this disapproving policeman the joy of being able to find things out by yourself when you've had a reprieve from an over-fussy older mother? I stuttered, 'But – but I want to explore.'

He gave me what Evelyn Simpson always called 'the fish eye'. 'For why, hey? Two Rivers is just a town like other towns. We got it mostly under control, but there's sometimes trouble.' He turned in his ponderous way to Finn. 'White girls this age shouldn't be allowed to go walking around on they own in non-European areas.'

It was almost exactly what Stella had said. Finn said heartily, 'Nonsense, Sergeant. She's a good sensible girl and she'll be quite safe if she sticks to the main road between the bridges. I've taken her into each shop so that all the owners know who she is. They'll keep an eye on her.'

100

'I doesn't like it.' The massive lower jaw had an ominous jut. 'Telling you, I wouldn't let my kids just walk around Coolietown. It's not the charras themselves so much, it's the way they treat the coons. Overcharging and stuff. Makes for trouble, man.'

'Common perceptions aren't necessarily the truth, Sergeant.' Finn could get pompous when he was offended. 'I've lived here for four years and I know these people.'

The sergeant's look was a mixture of pity and contempt for such naivety. 'You people from outside come to our country and think you know everything. Let me tell you, Mr Rosholt, you'll never get to know these people. They too different from us.'

Finn said in his softest voice, 'I am not from outside, Sergeant. I was born in Zululand. I'm an African yust like you and most of the other people in this town.'

'Don't you dare to call me a bleddy African!'

'It's what you are. What I am. What my customers are. Natives of Africa.'

Finn was goading the sergeant now, calling him a native as well as an African – a word that liberals were only just beginning to use then. I'd never heard it used in the geographical sense. By this time they were nose-to-nose across the counter, the sergeant turning redder in the face as Finn grew paler.

Then someone came into the charge office and they both drew back, looking embarrassed. Finn said, 'Well, at least you know who Isabel is,' and the sergeant said, 'If you really going to let her run around by herself, get her a police whistle to wear on a string round her neck,' and my introduction to Two Rivers was complete.

The last place Finn took me into was the Palm Café. In its bleared windows stood jars of nameless things floating in oil and trays of bosomy cupcakes iced in the colour known as coolie pink and rows of dusty cooldrinks. Mr Chetty, the café owner, gave me a Twistee icecream and said, 'Greetings to a new customer, hopefully, please.'

When we got back to the house Stella was painting the pantry with a dishcloth tied over her hair, and ignored us.

In those months of freedom from school I prowled the

101

Coolietown shops until I knew all the assistants. When I grew tired of wandering, the mango tree that leaned over the stone wall served both as a private place to read and as an observation post for watching the people who passed by. Zulu women from the reserves come to town for supplies, their joggling hips padded for extra fullness under voluminous skirts, their hair built up with red mud into stately Nefertiti coiffures. Groups of swarthy young Indian men with slicked-back hair. Demure Moslem women in narrow pastel tunics and trousers, their heads wrapped in white silk scarves whose ends floated out behind as they walked. Bargain-hunting housewives from the company estate in Horrockses cotton frocks and shady straw slumming hats, picking their fastidious way between the spat-out wads of chewed sugar cane. Hindu women with their oiled hair in heavy buns and tiny jewelled studs winking in their noses.

If I turned the other way and looked down into the yard of the vegetable shop next door, I could watch the Soobramony family. The father reminded me of a piece of biltong: he looked as though he had been hung up for years on a hook to dry out. His skin had shrunk against his bones to dark sinews, and his mouth had twisted into a sour parabola under a ragged grey moustache. Besides the two Mrs Soobramonys, his wife and his mother, there were eight cinnamon children with deep-sunk eyes and lustrous hair who were often beaten for stealing food.

They would gather in an anxious knot in the yard to watch the eldest, Jantu, slide into the rotting darkness at the back of the shop and come back with bulging pockets of stolen fruit which he unloaded in the grain shed at the back of the yard, where they could hide among sacks of peanuts and mealies and dried lentils. Their father kept a mongoose in there because of the rats; they were teasing it one day when it bit into an unwary finger and the younger ones ran howling off to their mother. Jantu and the biggest girl stayed behind to gather up the spoils but their father came storming out and hit them with a tomato box plank, leaving bloody weals on their arms and legs. They just stood there as he lashed at them, not trying to turn or run away. And I realised, for the first time, how privileged my dull life in the mining town had really been.

102

I had to share the mango tree with the resident mynahs. When their jabbering got too much, I would climb down and sit where I could watch the goldfish navigating through the furry green stems of the waterlilies in the fishpond, breathing in the heavy scent of frangipani flowers, enjoying the garden quietness after the street bustle. Or I would wander through the house to the kitchen to see what Eslina was cooking.

She was a Zulu woman who came and went morning and evening by bus, the second wife of a man who was away working on one of the Reef goldmines for fifty weeks of the year. She and the first wife had divided their duties amicably, the first taking care of the fields and the children, and Eslina working to bring in extra money. 'But I never leave my kids to be with her at night. Aikona!' she said by way of explaining why she preferred the long daily bus journeys to living in. 'You must watch your kids so they don't go wrong.'

Eslina hummed and sang round the house all day. She was shaped like a feather pillow pulled in at the waist by the ties of her white bibbed apron, round-faced, shortsighted and moon-spectacled. Her hair was hidden under a doek as neatly wrapped as a Red Cross bandage. From the earlobes that peeped out beneath it hung her only visible indulgence: a pair of imitation pearl drop earrings that jiggled about as she rubbed and scrubbed and polished with strong brown forearms. Endlessly patient and kind, she taught me how to make scones and crunchies, and in her lunch break when she sat on a kitchen chair in the back yard with her needlework, how to sew beads in looped patterns on to net circles to make milk jug covers that kept the flies off. The sound of beads clashing on china always takes me back to Two Rivers and having tea with Stella, after which I would carry a cup across to Finn in the pharmacy.

Then I would drift out into the mysterious green light on the back veranda where the jasmine creeper hung in a curtain across the heat of the afternoon, or curl up in the wicker chair in my lovely bedroom to think.

Now that I have children of my own, I know that aimless activity is an essential part of growing up and finding out who you are. Children need time to themselves, time to lie in the grass looking up at the clouds or to walk in no particular direction or to sit by a window dreaming. Yeats put it so well in his poem: 'Like a long-legged fly upon the stream, her mind moves upon silence.'

Stella called it 'mooning'. 'What are you mooning around the house for? You were so keen to run about on your own exploring the town.' She was up a ladder in the passage, painting it a creamy yellow because she said it was too dark. She always got grumpy when she was painting; the trouble was that she didn't see it as a self-inflicted obsession for decorating, but as a labour of love which nobody appreciated.

I said, 'I've explored all the shops already, and you won't let me go off the main road or past the bridges.'

She swung round. 'For heaven's sake, Isabel, you act as if I'm deliberately trying to restrict your freedom. I just want you to be safe.'

'You treat me like a child, and I'm not!'

One eyebrow went up. 'You're not an adult yet, that's for sure. They don't have time to sit around.'

'You don't understand! I'm – I'm recuperating.' How could I put it so it didn't sound self-pitying? 'I've got a lot of things to think about, with Pa dead and Ma gone dippy. It's like my whole life changed so suddenly, I haven't had time to catch up.'

That brought her down the ladder, and she hugged me and said, 'You're right. I'm not being very sympathetic, am I? Maybe what you need is to meet a few people of your own age.'

'They're all in school.'

'Not at the weekends.' Her face began to get a considering look. 'I should give Lilah McFadyen a ring. She has a son called –'

'Titch. I've met him.' The last thing I wanted was to be dragged around town to meet suitable boys.

'When?'

'The first Saturday morning when I went with Finn to the river. Titch was also fishing there. I thought he was quite rude.' I didn't mention Kesaval Reddy, afraid that Stella might veto future fishing expeditions. She may have been on talking terms with his grandfather, but from the way things were in Two Rivers, I guessed she'd feel different about my having conversations with an Indian boy of my own age.

The considering look intensified. 'Titch must have been home from boarding school for the weekend. He's very bright, you know. One of the top scholars at Michaelhouse. A much better catch than Percy Smuts in the milk bar.'

I flared, 'Spare me the sales talk! I'm not interested in boys, however bright. And I'm quite capable of making my own friends.'

'God,' she said with one of her rare foxy smiles, 'you're so like me when I was your age.'

I thought, Proper sisters. It's what I wanted, isn't it? Then why did we always seem to be arguing?

The lazy days went by. I didn't notice anything out of the ordinary because I was still a wet-behind-the-ears adolescent, too busy exploring the new town I found myself living in to realise that it was on a fault-line between racial groups that were grinding against each other accumulating stresses, and ripe for an earthquake.

The build-up is all there in the Sandham Commission report that lies on my desk: the growing tension, the local animosities and historical hatreds – all documented in the voices of the townspeople who came forward to try and explain what happened. To try and expunge the memory of a night when the veneer cracked and the real ugliness of Two Rivers showed through.

Isabel

She is watching him read the last page of her manuscript. Outside it is late afternoon and the traffic noise in the road below has risen to an aggressive growl. She will have to leave soon, to get home with the briefcase so George won't smell a rat. On days when she is late, there is a tedious gauntlet of questions to run. Today especially she does not want to have to answer questions; she is afraid that happiness will bubble up through her usual bland housewifely facade and give the game away.

Her lover puts the page down and looks up. Her hands tighten on the chair's padded beige arms.

'This is bloody good.' His frown of concentration is fading to a look of appraisal. 'Have you written anything else?'

She blushes and looks away. 'Just journals. Nothing serious.'

'How many journals?'

'One every few years.' She had started them when the children were small, for mental escape from the deep litter of nappies and toys and food messes she found herself living in. Now she says, 'I felt I'd grow into a boring suburban cabbage if I didn't do something that made me use whatever brain I had left, so I got into the habit of jotting things down.'

'What things?'

She thinks, How can I even talk about my scribbles to a serious writer? It's embarrassing. And says, trying to make it sound offhand, 'Oh, just things that came into my head, descriptions, ideas for stories. And I'd copy out pieces of writing I admired. I've always read a lot. We have a good library just down the street.'

This is the first time in years that she has admitted to

writing journals. She has always thought of them as a private indulgence – addiction, even – though there have been days when she has allowed herself to dream of culling the best pieces and submitting them to a women's magazine under a title like *The Diary of a Suburban Nobody*. There must, surely, be thousands of suburban nobodies out there who would appreciate her thoughts on problems faced and overcome, on the joys and pains of family life, on gathering your rosebuds while ye may . . .?

'Where are they? I'd like to see them.' He is behaving like an interrogator, firing impatient questions at her.

She shrugs. 'Packed away at the bottom of a trunk in the store room off the garage. I had to hide them from George. He found one of my early ones and read it out loud one long dreary evening, mocking what he called my delusions of intellect. Since then I've been more careful, only writing in them when nobody's at home.' She is still blushing. Her life sounds so feeble when she talks about it.

He stands up and goes to her, bending over the chair with his hands braced next to hers. 'What I don't understand is why you've never developed this talent. You're a strong character with a good sharp mind, yet you married that egotistical fart and kept house for him and had his kids when you should have been giving birth to words.'

'I love my kids.' As she says it, she thinks, Why am I being so defensive?

'Of course you do. The mother instinct is imperative, and you are a loving person. But kids aren't everything. Life has other dimensions. You talked about finding your self-respect down at the cottage; how come you lost it in the first place?'

She feels herself shrinking away from his insistent demand that she face the conundrum her life has become. 'George failed me. The kids were all I had.'

'Excuses!' He is almost snarling. 'You're too resourceful to get caught in that trap. There must have been other things in your life.'

She thinks, He's asking for an inventory, and what have I got to show? With her head down, she says, 'I garden. I cook. I read a lot, go to movies with my friends, belong to a discussion group and a book club. All the trivial things

107

housewives do to justify their existence and pretend that they haven't got completely lost in the domestic jungle.'

'Izzy, look at me.' When her eyes rise to meet his, he says, 'What I see when I look at you is an intelligent woman who has kept her head buried in the sand for more than half her life. I ask again: why have you been martyring yourself?'

Martyr, she thinks. He's right. I've been acting the martyr's role all these years, sublimating what was important to me to some muddleheaded notion of what a wife and mother should be. Another legacy of the Fifties: nice girls get married and have kids and live happily ever after. Nobody warned you that life never turns out the way you expect it to, or taught you how to handle failure. We were fed a lot of sanctimonious bullshit.

She shrugs again and says, 'You lead your life as it comes, and if it doesn't turn out too well you think, So I got short-changed. I've always been easily hoodwinked. Too gullible and easily persuaded when I was younger, a sucker for smooth talkers like George. And when I grew older and realised that I had made mistakes, not brave enough to admit them and cut my losses.'

'That's just not true.'

'How do you know?' She feels a live-wire prickle of anger. What right does this insistent bearded man have to cross-question her? To lay siege to her carefully constructed defences? Specially when by his own admission he has squandered a large chunk of his own life.

'After nine months of loving you, I have a damn good idea who you are.' He pulls back from the confrontation over her chair to sit on the low table in front of it, picking up her hand. His naked body is a fugue of burnished accents and shadows in the late afternoon sunlight muted by drawn net curtains behind heavy beige brocade window drapes.

'You don't! You don't know me at all!' She is furious now, trying to pull her hand away. 'You've been footloose for so long that you've manufactured an ideal woman in your mind, and you're seeing her, not me.'

'You're wrong.'

'I'm not. Can't you see?' She is sobbing with rage, wrenching at her hand which he is holding tightly in both of his. 'I

108

don't *want* to be anyone's ideal. Or anyone's doormat or punchbag or skivvy. I want to be free and equal and allowed to choose for myself who I want to become.'

He smiles. 'Bravo.'

Enraged, she thinks, He's manipulating me. All men are the bloody same. I should have known.

Trying to soften her baleful glare, he says, 'You think I'm being manipulative and condescending. Wrong again. I'm just trying to make you see your situation more objectively, unclouded by the family demands that you still respond to because you're programmed that way, but are no longer valid.' There is a sudden grin. 'I have a powerful ulterior motive, of course.'

As he has done since they met again, he is picking up her thoughts. Invading. Disturbing. She says childishly, 'But it's *my* situation, dammit! My life.'

He nods agreement. 'Yours alone, and I wouldn't dream of telling you what I think you should do with it. I want things between us to be free and equal, like you said. Just be clear about what you want, my dear love. And when you are, go out and fight for it. I hope to God that it includes me.'

There is a long silence between them. They are leaning towards each other, she from the chair and he from the table, tense hands clasped. She says at last, 'No strings attached?'

'None.'

'You won't start bullying me the way he does?'

Her eyes catch the last orange gleam of sunlight coming through the net curtains. He shakes his head. 'No. It's not my way.'

'You haven't done too badly this afternoon.'

'I've been trying to help.'

'Then you haven't heard a word I've been saying.' She tightens her already fierce clasp. 'I have to do these things alone. Write this story to my own satisfaction. Break away from George. Settle my debts as a mother. Then I can consider what comes next.'

He looks at her, seeing the change that has already happened and of which she is not yet aware: she is beginning to take charge of her life again. He also sees a less pleasant reflection, that of himself trying to take charge. Nobody is lily-white, he thinks, even cocky know-it-alls like me. He says, 'You're right, of course. I apologise for stepping out of line. May I make one more observation?'

She nods.

'From what I've read this afternoon, you have a lot to say and the ability to say it well. It's a rare talent. Whatever you feel about me now, you must go on.'

'You know how I feel.'

There is a ghost of his previous grin. 'I know you're angry with me.'

She closes her eyes to blot out the rueful schoolboy's look on his face. She needs a clear head now, unclouded by sentiment. 'I'll get over that. You also know that I love you, and it is a wonderful thing for me to be loved too. But you must understand that I need to do things in my own time. My own way. It's not going to be easy.'

'Nothing ever is. And that's a cliché I've learnt the hard way.'

His face is seamed with remembered pain. She thinks, I keep forgetting he's had bad times too, and bends forward until her forehead is resting on his shoulder and his beard is tickling her ear. 'I'm sorry if I've acted like a self-centred bitch.'

'You were standing up for yourself. I was the one at fault.'

She begins to smile into the skin-warmth under her lips. 'Don't let's start competing in the sorry stakes. You're going to have your time cut out keeping me reassured.'

'I'll keep phoning.'

'I'll keep writing. You can't begin to know how encouraging it is to be praised by someone who actually knows what he's talking about.' There is anger in her voice; George is one of those men who thinks he is an authority on everything. 'And now I've got to go.'

Her lover turns his mouth to beg in her ear, 'One last cuddle? It's a long drought between assignations.'

She lifts her head and laughs, knowing how long his cuddles take. 'No time. But I'll think of you every waking minute. When I'm not writing.'

'And I of you, my dear love.'

They stand up and embrace, two middle-aged people stealing happiness in a beige hotel room.

Extract from the official report of the Sandham Commission of Enquiry into the Easter 1952 Riot:

'... It is the opinion of this Commission that the Herald Sugar Company bears a portion of the responsibility for the riot.

Members of the Herald family who are major shareholders no longer live in the town, and appear to take little interest in Company affairs as long as their dividends are maintained. This indifference has clearly had a deleterious effect on the Company's relationship with the community which it dominates.

Mr Leonard Frampton, recently retired Chief Clerk, testified: "None of this would have happened in Old Mr Herald's time. He cared about this town. He kept an eye on things. People wouldn't have dared to lift a finger if he was watching."

Major Harold McFadyen, General Manager, made strenuous efforts to defend his action in calling out the army as well as the police. He testified: "I was guided by military logic. The police force in Two Rivers is hopelessly understaffed."

In the opinion of this Commission, however, the appearance of army vehicles and heavily armed soldiers exacerbated the already ugly situation.

Finally, labour relations within the Company appear to have been strained. Mr Jimmy Singleton, Compound Manager, testified that there had been complaints for months over the poor quality and paucity of the food in the millworkers' canteen.

"We didn't believe them at first – you know these coons, never satisfied with what they get. But they went on moaning and when we finally checked, we caught one of the cooks pinching bags of mealie meal and selling them

111

on the side. Also, he and the butcher who supplies the meat had got together and were using the cheaper boys' meat that was sometimes off instead of the better stuff, so they could split the difference. We fired the bugger and changed butchers but even then the coons weren't satisfied: they wanted us to sack the whole kitchen staff and increase the meat ration because they weren't getting enough for the heavy work they do. It was bloody unreasonable, man. Our dietician is an expert on minimum daily requirements and she reckoned the rations were OK so we told them nothing doing, that's what you get, take it or leave it. You've got to be firm with coons or they play up all the time.''

When questioned about this, the Bantu headman, Lucky-boy Mbabala, said, "The food was not enough. But Baas Singleton, he shout at us when we go to tell him. Why we must buy food for work out of our small money? The men fight because they are hungry and the coolie shops charge too high.''

Moving on to . . .'

112

8

For all her alleged outspokenness, Stella could be damn
sneaky sometimes. I suspect that she engineered the meeting
with Mrs McFadyen in the Cosy Hotel tea lounge where we
went for cream scones after a Saturday shopping expedition,
loaded with brown paper parcels containing what she called
'your absolutely basic teenage necessities'. These were a pair
of the jeans we'd seen in the display window, several T-shirts,
a boat-neck blouse, a wide black elastic belt that clasped in
front and a swirly red square-dance skirt. Not that I knew
anything about square dancing, but she said I'd need it in
case I was asked to a party.

Talk about wishful thinking. I moaned, 'But I don't know
anybody in this town.'

'That'll change.'

'I hate parties anyway.'

'That'll also change.'

You couldn't argue with Stella; she always knew better.
Anyway, I was having to concentrate on clenching my toes
with every step so my new Indian sandals wouldn't fall off.
They were brown with narrow leather straps only in front that
came up in the gap between my big and second toes, and were
chafing the tender skin there; besides a good clenching technique, you need tough big toe gaps to wear Indian sandals.

While I'd protested about all the money she was spending,
I had to admit that the teenager looking back at me from the
changing room mirrors with her darkish blonde hair pulled
back into a stubby ponytail was an improvement on the
mousy schoolgirl who had arrived on the train a few weeks
earlier. Stella stood nodding behind me. 'That's better. You
look more your age in those jeans, and a ponytail suits you.'

113

'I feel like a real dweet. They're so stiff and starchy and new.' I plucked at the rough dark-blue denim, hoping it didn't look ungrateful.

But she just laughed. 'Eslina can easily fix that by beating them on the rocks by the river where she does her family's washing. We'll get you looking right, Izz, never fear.'

We'd settled on Izz for my name, which I didn't mind too much – at least it was better than Izzy. I said, 'I keep telling you and Finn, I don't *care* what I look like,' but I was lying through my teeth. I'd been sick with envy of Evelyn Simpson's modish pedal-pushers and full-circle skirts that flared out like morning glories when she did the London Jive, and convinced that she owed most of her popularity to them. Now that I had some proper teenage clothes of my own, of course, the onus was on me. My feet were starting to get cramp by the time I clenched into the tea lounge behind Stella.

She pretended surprise at the sight of the woman sitting by herself at a table near the window and went towards her saying, 'Hullo, Lilah. May we join you?'

The woman looked up, first at Stella then at my reddening cheeks (I'd known at once who she was), and said, 'Of course, my dear. Have a pot of tea with me.'

'Love to.' Stella shot me her foxiest look. 'This is my sister, Isabel. Izz, this is Mrs McFadyen, Titch's mother.'

She had his greeny-blue transparent eyes under a broad-brimmed straw hat; her chiffon afternoon frock was splashed with roses and she wore a double strand of pearls. Mrs McFadyen did an impeccable impression of a general manager's wife; I often saw her willowing along the pavements outside the white shops greeting people and patting little heads. But her passion was gardening and when she wasn't on show, she was up to her dungareed knees in compost – 'Exceptionally potent stuff, made from racehorse shit,' she'd say in her posh English accent (you can say *anything* in a posh English accent) – or bullying some reluctant plant to do what it was told. She was ruthless with pests and would grab trespassing grasshoppers and crickets and rose beetles and twist their shrieking heads off without a qualm. Titch told me after we became friends that she had once bent over a snake lying in her path with both ends hidden in the long grass on either side, and chopped it in half with a sharp spade she was carrying before walking on.

The hand she held up to me now was covered in scratches, though well creamed. I took it and said, 'Pleased to meet you,' then remembered that Stella had said that our mining town 'Pleased to meet you' was common and stammered, 'I mean, h-how do you do?'

She said, looking amused, 'And I am very pleased to meet you, Isabel. I gather that you've already encountered my Titch.'

'Yes.' What else could I say? She had hung on to my hand and was giving me a good once-over. I wondered if this was normal practice for Two Rivers mothers of eligible sons, or a kind of company test to see if we were worth having tea with. If it was the latter, I wasn't going to –

She said unexpectedly, 'You managed to impress him in some way. Perhaps my little barbarian is growing into a young man at last.'

I blurted, much too loudly (several permed heads turned), 'That's what I call boys – barbarians!'

Mrs McFadyen let me go with a laugh as blunt as a butter knife. 'The little buggers usually are. But they change. Some of them, anyway. One only hopes that one can counteract the forces of barbarism they are subjected to at school and turn them into sentient beings one day. Sit down, dear. Would you like tea or a milkshake?'

She knew how to prompt teenagers. As my cheeks cooled over my double-thick chocolate malt, I told her about Pa and Ma, the books I'd read, the morning I'd gone fishing with Finn and met Titch, and the clothes Stella had just bought me. She insisted on our undoing all the parcels and showing her, saying wistfully, 'I could never manage a daughter to buy pretty things for. You're lucky to have a younger sister to spoil, Stella.'

I looked across the table at Stella, wondering what she'd say. If she was being honest it would be, 'This particular sister has never been anything but a drag and a nuisance to me.' But she didn't. She said, looking quite surprised at herself, 'Yes. Yes, I am. We've had fun together this morning.'

115

'Perhaps you'd like to bring her to tea next Saturday afternoon, when Titch will be home for the weekend,' Mrs McFadyen said. 'She'll need an opportunity to wear that lovely skirt.'

I burst out, 'Oh, but I can't –!' at the same time as Stella said with a missionary gleam, 'I'd love to. She doesn't know anyone of her age in Two Rivers yet.'

Mrs McFadyen leaned towards me, pearls clicking. 'I'd really appreciate it if you'd come, Isabel. Titch needs to enlarge his horizons from the exclusively male. I was thinking of holding a party for him in the Christmas holidays, and perhaps I'll go ahead now –'

She drifted off into a train of thought I knew well: that of the scheming mother. Unlike today, in the Fifties we were very much at the mercy of our mothers until we were able to get away from home. We rebelled, of course, by arguing and shouting and turning up the wireless and the radiogram to excruciating levels and flouncing out of rooms slamming doors, but in general we ended up doing what was expected of us. With a sinking heart I recognised a mother hen determined to chivvy her only chick into the social arena. There would be an embarrassing afternoon tea with a press-ganged and therefore hostile boy, followed by a painful party where I wouldn't know a soul except him – already maddened by having had to make polite conversation with me. All I could think was, Jeepers! What has Stella got me into now?

Even though it was less than half a mile from the pharmacy, Stella and I drove to the McFadyens' house in the Ford so we could sweep past the imposing pillared company gates and through the estate and up the gravel drive in style. It was one of those rambling old red-brick colonial bungalows with a steep tin roof and wide verandas and green rain tanks at each corner, and must have been one of the Herald family homes, built to command a vista of canefields but now simply the big fish in a shoal of company houses. Tall hedges gave it more privacy than the houses of lesser officials; the garden inside was a pastoral dream of stately trees and lawns and rose beds and perennial borders – a little piece of England except for some subtropical palms. It wasn't all Mrs McFadyen's

116

work, of course. The company had an army of Zulu gardeners to keep the estate looking like paradise regained.

She came to greet us down a flight of steps with marble lions crouching on both sides, elegant in a striped silk blouse and a white linen skirt. I was grateful that Stella had made an effort for me and abandoned her dog's breakfast clothes for a yellow shirtwaister she had picked up at a sale: it was a bit floppy from being a size too big but at least it wasn't purple. I was self-consciously wearing the new blouse and skirt and elastic belt and the Indian sandals; my big toe gaps had toughened up and my clenching technique had improved, though the sandals still had a tendency to drop off in mid-stride if I didn't concentrate.

Mrs McFadyen led us down a passage and through a drawing room (you could never have called it a lounge) with plump sofas standing around on Persian rugs, to a veranda with deck chairs. Tea had been laid on a low table: a daunting display of silver, fluted porcelain, starched linen and plates of tiny triangular sandwiches, biscuits and cake. If she wanted to impress, she certainly succeeded with me: my hands began sweating at once. What if one of the almost translucent cups slipped through my fingers and shattered on the tiles? What if I knocked over the sugar bowl?

She called out, 'Titch, dear? They're here,' and he appeared wearing a clean khaki shirt and shorts and the familiar scowl under wet combed hair in which the toothmarks still showed. At the look on his face, I dropped the 'Hullo, Timothy' I'd decided would make a good opening gambit and mumbled, 'Hi.'

He nodded back looking past me and began handing things round for his mother in the clumsy way boys do, slopping tea into the saucers and dropping all the cake forks which made a silvery noise bouncing on the tiles. (Finn always used to say that cake forks were expressly designed to confuse men who are foolish enough to get trapped in a tea ritual.) Titch's scowl deepened. When he offered me a plate of biscuits, nearly decanting the whole lot in my lap, I saw that he had thin rims of mud under his fingernails. If he'd been hauled back from the river for this ordeal, no wonder he was mad.

117

The veranda was hot and my new skirt felt scratchy. I sat swinging a sandal on one toe and looking out at the garden because I didn't want to look at Titch, who was making his deck chair creak and gazing in the opposite direction. Neither of us said more than 'Please' or 'Thanks'. Even if we'd known what to say, we wouldn't have got much of a word in because Mrs McFadyen and Stella were having a boring gossip about someone whose husband had just left her.

I was just beginning to calculate how long the agony would last when Mrs McFadyen said with a hearty smile, 'We'll leave you young ones to it, then,' and hustled Stella out into the garden to admire her bearded irises.

When they got out of earshot I heard Titch mutter, 'Jesus H Christ.'

I thought, He thinks he's suffering! and said, 'Ditto. With knobs on.'

That made him actually look at me. 'So you'll be glad too when this latest farce is over?'

'What do you mean, latest farce?'

He had a brown sugar spill of freckles across his nose like I had; I wondered if boys also examined their faces in the mirror every morning to try and imagine how other people saw them. Did they worry about their looks too, and getting pimples, and showering everyone with bad breath they didn't realise they had? Bad breath was the most dreaded form of social death then, closely followed by BO.

He was saying, 'My mother has been setting up these excruciating encounters with girls for the past year or so, because she maintains that boys' boarding schools turn out social barbarians. It's just a bloody waste of my time. I've got better things to do.'

I felt a momentary pang of disappointment at knowing I wasn't the only girl Mrs McFadyen had tried to dangle before her son. I'd thought that I'd impressed her with my wit and sparkle in the Cosy Hotel tea lounge. But I wasn't going to let him get away with insults, specially as I was damn sure I'd been more reluctant than he was. 'What about the waste of my time?'

He didn't hear me. 'I've got exams to swot for. I've got my aquarium to clean and my snakes to feed.' He stood up so abruptly that his deck chair rocked and collapsed with a bang on the tiles. 'And she forces me to sit around drinking *tea*. With a *girl*.'

I used to have a temper that flared like petrol thrown on a fire; it was scary sometimes. I zoomed up out of my chair hissing, 'So what's wrong with girls, might I ask? And what makes you think you're the only one who's been dragged here?'

That got his attention. He blinked.

'What makes you think, Timothy Montague Wotherspoon McBloodyFadyen, that I am even the tiniest, weeniest bit interested in how your time gets wasted? I've got my own problems. So drop dead, OK?'

I was flouncing through the door into the house when one of the Indian sandals began to slide off and snagged on the edge of the doormat. With the suddenness of a judo throw, I was sprawling flat on my face with my nose buried in a Persian carpet and my bum in the air and howls of cracked adolescent laughter coming from my host.

So are friendships born. When he stopped laughing, Titch helped me up and found tissues to stanch my copious nose-bleed – all over the new boat-neck blouse, needless to say. I sponged off as much of the blood as I could in a bathroom the size of an indoor swimming pool with black and white tiles and complicated brass taps, and when I came out found him hovering in the passage saying, 'Are you OK now? I could get you some more tea.'

I said hopefully, 'Could I have a Coke instead?' The universal teenage panacea was still a treat for me; my sort of family couldn't afford to keep it in the fridge all the time.

'Of course.'

He led me to the kitchen and then, sipping our Cokes through straws, out into the back yard where he kept a salt water aquarium designed like a rock pool. Because I was genuinely interested, he took me to see the two red-lipped herald snakes in a glass terrarium in his bedroom, then the aviary next to the garage. By the time Mrs McFadyen and Stella came in from the garden (and I'm sure they prolonged the visit to the bearded irises as long as they could), we were so busy comparing biology teachers that I think he had forgotten I was a girl.

119

In the Christmas holidays, Titch would take me to parts of Two Rivers that I'd never have been allowed to go to on my own. We often hitched rides in Ram Pillay's *Sweet-Smelling Jasmine*, sometimes with Kesaval but more often not. He didn't have our comparative freedom; his grandfather kept a stern eye on him and there were many obligations in his Hindu family. I only realised how many when Finn and Mr Reddy took me to the temple.

Isabel

She lies in bed in the early morning alternately dreaming about the afternoon in the hotel, and wondering how to start her next chapter.

The writing is going more slowly now that her lover has gone away for a few weeks. The rush to get everything written down has become blunted by a growing need to do it well. She is writing this story (this book? she hardly dares to think of it as such) for herself, trying to create something worthwhile to build up her lost confidence, and it must be done to the very best of her ability. Not because she needs to impress people – to impress him in particular, although of course she wants very much to do that – but because she needs to silence the exacting critic looking out through her eyes saying, 'This is not good enough.' She remembers the Archbishop saying so long ago, 'You write like an angel, Isabel,' and feels a sudden overwhelming need to vindicate that early promise. To create something of value to take away the acid taste of the wasted years.

There is desperation in passing fifty when life hasn't come up to scratch. The high hopes dwindle as the likelihood of success fades. Thoughts dwell increasingly on the past, sifting through regrets and betrayals and failures, searching for clues as to where everything started to go wrong. The seductive concept of a turning point takes hold: it is so tempting to think, 'If only such-and-such hadn't happened, if only I had chosen so-and-so, my whole life would have been different.' But it's a futile exercise, trying to lay blame on adverse circumstances. Most lives are lived in a feckless muddle; there are many turning points, many mistakes, many unavoidable tragedies.

Isabel is very conscious of the second chance she has been given, but everything hinges on this story she is trying to write. If it succeeds and helps her to regain her self-respect, she can abandon the farce of a marriage and begin a new life in which she, as an independent individual, will be free to choose to live with a man who loves and cherishes her. If it fails, she is lost. She will not go to her lover with empty hands, sour with unfulfilled ambition. She is too proud. She wants to go to him on equal terms, not as a supplicant.

With these high-minded sentiments buoying her up, she pushes back the bedclothes and swings her legs out and feels for her slippers. It is time to shower and dress and go downstairs to make the breakfast George insists on every morning: half a cup of oatmeal porridge (not too runny, served with skim milk and brown sugar), two slices of wholewheat toast and margarine, and a cup of decaffeinated coffee.

She has made the same breakfast for him for the past ten years, ever since he stopped eating bacon and eggs and butter out of concern for his cholesterol level. It is one of life's little ironies that he should have ended up suffering from high blood pressure rather than the raised cholesterol he took so many precautions to prevent. But it would be a loss of face for him to go back to bacon and eggs now, after so many years of pernickety insistence on a low-fat breakfast. Instead he indulges in hamburgers and fried chicken takeaways and greasy chips at lunchtime, and takes a huge delight in scoffing them in the house when she is away. He is careful to conceal the evidence in the dustbin, wrapped in several layers of plastic bags, before she gets back.

And he is unaware of her indifference as to the state of his health. She is The Wife, an appendage who depends on him for support and a decent pension to bolster her inevitable decline into old age. He dreads retiring and the prospect of being at home all day with no office minions on call; he plans to take up bowls so that he will have male companionship and a club to go to. He sees himself aging gallantly like a latter-day David Niven, with interesting crows' feet and a debonair moustache and a twinkle in his eye; if Isabel chooses to be a dull house-bound scribbler, that is her affair.

The marriage was not a bad one in the beginning. George was handsome as a young man, a natty dresser with a good technical-college diploma and a promising job in government service. Isabel was enchanted by his navy-blue blazers and silk cravats and the way his fine blond hair broke into a suggestion of curls behind his ears. In the excitement of the courtship, dazzled by flowers and chocolates and picnics and dinner dances, she did not notice that he looked into mirrors more often than other men, and she mistook his narrow-minded ideas for firm principles.

Isabel had recently left school and hated the secretarial course that was all her mother could afford; the English degree she had dreamed of was out of the question. They were living in a cramped city flat on a widow's pension, and it seemed as though the world had shrunk to a small grey wasteland. To be offered marriage by a good-looking man with prospects like George seemed the answer to a prayer. She married him at nineteen, and there were some happy years when the children were small. But George was not what he had seemed. Under the surface charm he was intellectually limited and a poor lover, and as the scales fell from her eyes and she began to assert her contrary ideas and feelings, he grew domineering to keep her in her place.

In her more honest moments she admitted to herself that she had misled him too, by appearing to have no other ambition than to be a traditional wife and mother. When she had imagined herself in love with him, she had suppressed so much of herself in wanting to please him.

It is another of life's ironies that neither he nor she has the faintest idea that the dissolution of the failed marriage will be a relief to all involved – not least the three children, who come home reluctantly because of the chilly atmosphere.

9

Finn said I would be surprised by the Reddy family, and I was. We walked together to the side-by-side Spanish mansions one Friday after the pharmacy had closed; he had told Mr Reddy that I had an enquiring mind and wanted to know more about the Hindu religion, and Mr Reddy had invited us to accompany him to the temple during his devotion hour.

The thought of going into a totally different kind of church is scary. You're afraid you'll do something grossly offensive without realising it – walk into a holy place where people aren't allowed, for example, or not take your shoes off when you're supposed to. The problem for me then was, although I'd stopped believing in God because evolution seemed to be a more logical idea, I couldn't be a hundred per cent sure. If I was right and one big major God didn't exist, the idea of a whole panoply of lesser gods like the Hindus and Greeks and Romans believed in was quite attractive. If I was wrong, I'd only know when I died, too late to change my mind and repent. On the way to the Reddy house that afternoon I was thinking, If the temple's a holy place, maybe I'll learn the truth there – have a sudden revelation or be struck by a blinding flash of light. It would be nice to be sure.

Both mansions had high white walls all round them, and important wrought iron gates with a nearby chain hanging down from a bell that tonked when you pulled. Finn pulled the one on the right saying, 'This is the Reddys' bell. The other one belongs to the Pather family.'

'Do you know them too?' It was still surprising to me, Finn and Stella knowing Indians well enough to visit their houses.

He shook his head. 'To say hullo to, only. Mrs Pather runs the yewellery shop like a real old dragon, one claw on the till and no credit allowed.'

'And Mr Pather?'

Finn said, 'Mysterious. He's often away.'

I didn't have time to ask more about the Pathers because a girl in an iridescent pale turquoise sari was gliding towards the gate where we stood, looking as though she was lapped in tropical seawater. When she saw who it was, the serious look on her face melted into a demure smile. 'Oh, Mr Rosholt, hullo.' She slid the bolt back and swung it open.

Asha was only three years older than me but she acted about thirty, composed and sedate. It was her upbringing, Finn explained later. 'Indian girls from good families are still taught at home in many cases – schooled in women's duties to make them worthy wives. They often marry yong and have, you know, prescribed responsibilities towards their husbands' families.'

'How young?' I remembered reading about child brides in India, and shivered. Imagine getting married at nine or ten and having to submit to regular assaults by the giant organ Evelyn Simpson had so vividly described.

He laughed. 'Nay, not so yong as you are thinking. Asha's about the age now to be considered ready for marriage. I'm sure her mother and grandfather and aunties have already canvassed their friends' eligible sons and settled on a shortlist. She's very beautiful and has a talent for classical Indian dancing, I'm told.'

Finn was a great appreciator of beauty; he would often talk about grace and pleasing forms and the way a good painter could show you the beauties of nature in a new way. On our walks he would point out the curve of a grass stem or an archway and the rust patterns on old corrugated iron; he would talk about refracted light and why it differed going through a prism from shimmering off water. Looking back, I realise that he was a frustrated artist trapped between an uneasy marriage to a woman who was battling her own demons and a mundane job that demanded the chilly calculations of science.

Asha was beautiful, I had to admit. She looked like the girl in a Persian miniature I had seen in one of Stella's art books: her face a pale oval, her features small and fine, her nose delicately flared, her eyes dark as the centres of pansies. Her

125

fine black hair divided down a ruler-straight middle parting to be drawn back in glossy swoops on either side of the red dot on her forehead, into a sleek bun at the nape of her neck. Her skin was the colour of creamy iced coffee, her fingers cool when she touched mine in greeting.

Finn said, giving her his gentle teddy-bear's smile (and me a pang of jealousy; I had thought it was reserved for me), 'Hullo, Asha. This is Isabel, Stella's sister, who is staying with us. Izzy, this is Kesaval's older sister, Asha.'

The girl nodded, joining her hands palm together under her chin as Mr Reddy had done. 'Welcome, Mr Rosholt. My grandfather is waiting for you.'

As we followed her up the brick path, Finn explained in a quiet voice that the red dot on her forehead was vermilion powder, called kun kum, placed there to simulate the third eye.

'But what's it for? The idea of a third eye is –' what was the Norwegian word he kept using? '– frickly.' It made me think of the horrible drawing of Cyclops in my book of Greek myths, with the big angry bloodshot eye bulging out in the middle of his forehead and blank skin where eyes usually are.

'Nay, it's not really so. A third eye is supposed to help you penetrate what cannot be seen, so that one day you may attain the ultimate truth. I think it's a lovely concept.'

His eyes were on Asha as he spoke. Under the fluttering silk hem of her sari, I saw that she was wearing identical Indian sandals to the ones I was still having trouble keeping on, only she was walking smoothly without any obvious clenching. There must be a trick to Indian sandals. Maybe they were designed for elegant narrow feet like this girl had, not clodhoppers like mine? She whispered along in front of us, up a flight of steps and through a heavy wooden door into an entrance hall floored like a sheik's tent with overlapping Persian carpets. Ranged round and up the walls were enough brass ornaments to stock a bazaar: tall jugs with slender necks and fat bellies patterned with incised designs, trays and plaques and inlaid chests and mirrors whose frames were studded with shards of coloured glass. In a decorative niche was a brass statue of a four-armed dancing god with rays coming out from behind his head; in front of him were several small brass bowls and a scatter of wilting marigolds.

126

'That is Shiva, the most worshipped god of South African Tamil families like the Reddys,' Finn said into my ear. 'Hindus believe that he created the universe and dwells in the Himalayas ÿenerating the spiritual force that maintains the cosmos, keeping the world spinning by his dancing. He is quite a fearsome god, with black skin and four arms and a blue throat, and he has a wife called Parvathi who –'

'How do you know all these things?' Finn amazed me often with odd and fascinating facts fished out of the boundless storage bin behind his high forehead. He had a mind that gathered all sorts of information and kept it tucked away for future use, but he did it for his own pleasure, not to educate himself further or to be more successful or rich or socially acceptable. Stella could never understand this; she called him a magpie-brain and said it was a pity he didn't take more interest in accounting, because maybe then the pharmacy would make a decent profit for a change.

He gave me one of his deep sea looks. 'I like to take an interest in what goes on around me.'

Above our heads, the entrance hall soared up into a square tower with slit windows. When I looked down again, a stout woman in a spangled purple sari was bustling through an archway towards us. Mrs Reddy had oiled black hair and a sharp nose and no visible neck, like a seal, and her arms and hands glinted with an armoury of bracelets and rings. She rattled out a hail of words as she advanced.

'Afternoon, afternoon, Mr Rosholt. You have come most carefully upon the hour. My father-in-law is waiting in his study. This way. This way. Follow me to the study, please. Your wife is keeping well, eh? And this is her sister?'

I opened my mouth to try and say hullo, but she didn't even stop for breath as her round black eyes scanned me like twin lasers from top to toe, missing nothing. Mrs Reddy was the most thorough person I've ever met; not a speck of house dust escaped her, and all but the hardiest shopkeepers along the main road would quail when they saw her coming, melting into the gloom at the back of their shops in the hope that if they looked unoccupied, she would pass by.

As the scan progressed, she was chattering on, 'Yes. I see. Yes. They look like sisters. Not in the hair maybe, but in the

127

features. That is often the way. It's the genes, you know? Very strong in some families. With us it is the nose and the mouth and the fore-head. A noble fore-head, my father-in-law says. Even though we are not Brahmins.' She broke off for a brief grimace to show she was making a joke. 'No, indeed. So. You come this way, eh? This way. To the study where he is waiting. Come.'

Asha said, 'Mr Rosholt –'

Finn stooped towards her. 'Yes, my dear?'

'I –'

'Come! Come! This way, please. This way.' Mrs Reddy was commanding us to follow her down a passage. 'He is waiting in his study. Longtime he is waiting. You must come with me now, please.'

Finn said to Asha, 'Did you want to ask me something?'

She shook her head and said in a low voice that I could hardly hear, 'Never mind. Another day.' Her hands came together under her chin again. 'Go in peace.'

'He is waiting. You must come!' Mrs Reddy chivvied us down a tiled passage into a study with a large dark desk covered in papers and walls lined with austere leatherbound books. The only frivolous note was a red velvet and gilt couch shaped like a double throne. Sitting on it was the old man I had last seen talking to Stella in her kitchen, shiny-bald without his cap and dressed as before in the long grey jacket with a high neck and buttons all the way down the front. He was reading to a girl of about ten who was the image of Mrs Reddy, only fatter: her skin looked as though it would pop juicily in your mouth like a frankfurter if you bit into it. She glared up at us, demanding, 'Who are you?'

Mr Reddy began to close the book he was reading from. 'You know Mr Rosholt, Violet, and this is Mrs Rosholt's sister, Missy Isabel. They are coming with me to the temple.'

'Why? They're white. They can't go to our place. I don't want you to stop, anyway. Keep reading to me, Grandpa.'

He shook his head. 'I must be going, child. I have promised.'

'But I don't want you to.' She made a grab for the book. 'Read to me. Don't stop. I like this story.'

He relinquished the book and got up saying, 'Ask your mother to read. I cannot any more.'

On cue, Mrs Reddy came bustling forward. 'I will read to you, Vi-Vi baba. Come, let me sit. Your Grandpa must go now. I will read the story, and then we will have some tea and some nice cakes together, eh?'

'Go away, Ma!' the child shouted rudely. 'I want Grandpa to read! You can't do it nice! Grandpaaaa –' She began whining. 'Grandpaaaa, sit down. Don't go with these pooffy white people, stay here with me. I want you to read.'

The old man said something sharp in Tamil to Mrs Reddy, who made an agitated lunge at the child to try and shut her up. Then he turned to us and said, 'I am sorry for the unpleasant scene. Revaghie – we call her Violet – is spoilt, being sickly. Her kidneys, you know? We are maybe too concerned to be sensible with her.' He reached for the round white cap on his desk. 'Let us be going now.'

With Violet's furious screams fading behind us, we followed Mr Reddy out into the entrance yard and through the iron gate; Asha watched us go from the shadow of the front door. Or rather, watched Finn. She had wanted to ask him something, but not in front of me or her mother. I wondered where Kesaval was; I knew that he at least went to school, because Titch had told me he was clever and won prizes. And I wondered how he and the beautiful Asha could have such a pig of a little sister. The Reddy family had certainly been surprising. You expect people from another race to live and behave differently to you, yet the difference between their home and mine and Stella's was the difference between rich and just-managing, not between brown and white.

I bet Evelyn Simpson never went into an Indian temple, I thought as we walked past the shops on the main road towards the bridge. Look how daring and open-minded I am, visiting Indians and trying to understand their religion. Pa will be turning in his grave.

God, I was a smug little crypto-liberal. Finn, forgive me. You never saw the dividing lines, only the people.

The cement treads of the steps from the far side of the bridge down to the temple were worn in the centre from constant use and littered with cigarette butts, sweet papers, fruit peels and greasy crumpled food packets. Many people went there during the lunch hour and after work to make their devotions, eating on the way.

Mr Reddy stopped us before we went down, saying, 'You can see the tower best from up here. I am afraid that my grandfather was building it too close to the road – which of course was only a small dirt track then, on either side of the wagon drift across the river. I remember as a boy when they were laying concrete to make a causeway, watching the tin lizzies chugging across with water up to their running boards and sometimes higher so that they stalled in the middle. It was a local sport to hide in the bushes and spy on the white ladies lifting up their skirts and wading crossly to the bank. You can see by this anecdote that I am a very senior citizen.' He gave me a pinched smile. 'If you can call a person who doesn't have the vote a citizen.'

There was a delicate pause for it to sink in before he went on, 'So then Old Man Herald was building the sugar mill here in our little village of Two Rivers because of the abundant water, and the track became the main coastal road. The new bridge was sited over the causeway, but now it is too small for the heavy modern traffic and the Natal Roads Department says that it must be widened. To do this, they will need the land where the tower stands and they say that it must go. Our temple is under threat, Mr Rosholt. After more than fifty years on this very spot we are fighting expropriation.'

'I hadn't heard. I'm sorry. Is there anything I can do?' Finn was stooping over him in distress.

'No, my friend, thank you. The matter is with Abjee's son, a lawyer in Durban. We are trying what we can.' He turned to face the temple, half-hidden in its mango and syringa grove. 'The tower is crucial to our place of worship. We will put up a fight before we lose it.'

'Surely they could widen the bridge on the other side?'

'Apparently not. It is a question of bedrock.' Mr Reddy's hands tightened on the bridge parapet. 'When engineers are talking like this, you know the fight will be a hard one. And it is not, after all, a Christian church, nè? Just a place where coolies burn incense and offer up sacrifices to many-armed gods. Graven idols.'

'I can't believe –'

But he cut Finn off. 'Let us be facing facts, Mr Rosholt. That is how coolies like me survive, by facing facts. We know that we are at the very bottom of the racial pile in Natal, disliked and envied by both Zulus and whites. Why? Because we are working hard for long hours, and some of us are conspicuously successful. Because we are the traders and shopkeepers to whom people owe money, and whom they accuse of profiteering when they cannot pay. Because we think it is important for families to stay together, and seeing our large family groups, people say we have too many children. But we are a self-supporting community, we look after our own. We are not a burden on anyone! We are criticised for our very virtues. That is what is so hard to take.'

Finn said, 'You're preaching to the converted.'

'I know. But I must say it nevertheless. It is a constant fire burning in my belly.' Mr Reddy slapped the lower buttons of his jacket. 'When we are educating our children in the professions, we are mocked for our presumption – why not admired, as the Scots are? It is ironical in the extreme, Mr Rosholt.' There was a fleeting return of the pinched smile. 'The English poet Alexander Pope said, "To be angry is to revenge the fault of others upon ourselves." I try not to be an angry man, following the teachings of the Hindu sages, but sometimes it is very hard.'

I saw Finn reach out and grip his elbow, but he did not speak again. What was there for a white person to say to this dignified and wealthy man who could not aspire to many of the things we took for granted because his skin was brown?

After a while he clucked his tongue and said, 'But I am being discourteous. Please, do not listen to the outpourings of an old man who does not always mind his manners. The Missy has come to see the temple. Let us begin by admiring the tower.'

He leaned forward over the parapet to point out how the tower's square base rose up in diminishing tiers to the dome shaped and studded like a sea-urchin shell. Every inch of the surface was decorated with symmetrical designs of shells and peacocks and feathers and flowers and crescent moons, broken at intervals by niches with statues of gods and goddesses in stately poses: standing, seated, dancing, riding on

131

cows, playing the flute – entrancing in their frozen whiteness. At each corner the figures would be fused together, facing in different directions. Closer up now, I could see that, far from being the pristine white wedding cake it appeared from a distance, the temple was growing old, settling into the landscape with dust in its crevices. The outlines of the original statues and decorations had become blurred by many layers of whitewash; flakes of gold paint were peeling off the urn on the top of the dome.

Watching the direction of my eyes, Mr Reddy said, 'Do you see that the gold urn is rising from a base of lotus petals, and has a flame coming out the top? It is intended to show the fusion of male and female energy, symbolising the essential life force. On the day a temple is dedicated, the urn is placed up there and joined to the main deity in the shrine below by a long chain of grass. If you look down you can see where the shrine is – that square part connected to the base of the tower by the arched portico. Over there is the entrance porch facing the river, and the courtyard with its sacred pool where people may wash themselves and the offerings they have brought, partaking of the holy water before they enter . . .'

After he had finished explaining, we walked down the worn steps into a world light years away from the company-run sugar town and my prim white life: noises and smells and sights as unexpected as the street markets you sometimes stumble across in foreign cities, busy with the commerce of daily lives oblivious of your tourist presence.

People sat in groups on steps and low walls almost hidden under the foaming jasmine creepers that grew everywhere in Two Rivers, chatting and eating and throwing their scraps to the grey vervet monkeys that scampered everywhere. Worshippers squatted by a rectangular stone pool with scummy-looking olive green water, scooping it over their feet; others walked round and round the temple with their eyes half closed and their lips moving silently. Smoke from several small fires drifted through the trees, mingled with the smells of warm oil and incense and camphor. At the back of the temple was a heap of old offerings that had been flung down an embankment: dead leaves and flowers and rotting fruit and coconut shells.

Beggars called in wheedling voices from the steps: nearly naked old men with grey ash in their straggly hair and squatting women in dirty saris with babies in their laps and listless children leaning against them. A small boy sat at the feet of a man who was rubbing a kind of violin with a softly-strung bow to make wailing Indian music. The boy was banging two tin lids together with his left hand to attract attention to his deformity: a withered little right arm ending in a claw that he kept thrust out and resting on his knee.

I stuck close to Finn, shrinking at first from the stares that followed us and the casual litter of a much-used public place. For me, religion had always been well scrubbed, hushed and serious, and worship conducted indoors at special times with strictly defined rituals. But that day at the Mariamman temple, I began to understand that beliefs shouldn't be tucked away into rigid compartments and taken out occasionally for airing. For these people gathered after work in the grove, temple visits were naturally woven into their daily lives. Despite the riot of noises and smells, it was cool and pleasant under the trees by the sliding brown river in the late afternoon. The earth trampled to a sticky gloss may have been littered, but it was also easy on work-tired feet. They had a choice of fascinating gods besides, not just one stern old hypercritical headmaster.

We climbed the steps to the entrance porch, past a tall flagpole with three cross bars ('Earth, fire and water,' Finn whispered) and a platform altar with a low round stone sticking up in the middle surrounded by a marigold garland; Mr Reddy called it a lingam. Another fire smouldered next to it, and to one side there was a smaller pole with a silver bell that a young man reached up to ting every now and again.

The priest, a harassed man in a plastic apron streaked with blood (he had been sacrificing chickens, Mr Reddy told us), would not let Finn and me into the inner shrine. But we were allowed to go inside the main part of the temple and peer through an archway while Mr Reddy explained the gods and goddesses in the pictures lining the walls and on the altar with its rows of little brass lamps. I forget now which ones they were besides Mariamma, but they must have included a dancing Shiva. Mr Reddy explained that, although Shiva's

133

wife was actually called Parvathi, Mariamma was one of her aspects. Sitting in the centre of the altar swathed in a chiffon sari with a pattern of red and gold squares, she was about two feet high and crudely carved out of blackened wood with a gold-painted face, red ears and mouth, and a conical hat with serrated sides. She held a gold trident in one of her four arms, and behind her was a wooden arch painted green, red and silver with a terrible carved face like a gargoyle's grinning from the top. At her feet, poking out of the chiffon, was a stone barely shaped into a head with staring silver eyes.

'Mariamma is a mother goddess, the benign aspect of Parvathi,' Mr Reddy whispered. 'At your Easter time, our Kavady, she presides over our temple's fire-walking ceremonies, sitting at the head of the pit full of hot coals, which is why she gets so black and has to be repainted every year.'

I broke in, 'Mr Padayachee says I can come and watch him doing it.'

Mr Reddy's mouth pinched in again. 'Everybody is wanting to watch the fire-walking because it is sensational. Few understand why it is undertaken. For this reason, the temple committee has decided to restrict visitors next year.'

'But –' How could I convince him I was different? A white person who cared, not a sensation seeker. I blurted, 'But I *genuinely* want to understand about Hindus, Mr Reddy. It's why I asked Finn to ask you if we could visit the temple.'

He stood looking at me in the incense-smoky twilight, his shadowy face defined only by the uncertain flames of some ornate hanging lamps. 'You are seeking the truth, Missy, or the exotic local colour?'

How could I answer him? I sought both. I was curious and fascinated but half-repelled too by the smells of the place and the lurid pictures and the crude wooden goddess on the altar. I wanted to hammer out my beliefs on the anvil of other people's to see if they rang true, but I also wanted to rush back to my bedroom and write an epic letter to Evelyn Simpson full of gory details like the sacrificed chickens, to make her jealous of me for a change. With a sneaking feeling that he could see right through me, so utterly unworthy of his respect, I hung my head and said, 'Both, I'm afraid.'

I didn't expect him to throw back his head and laugh, or

Finn to join in. It was one of the most embarrassing moments of my whole life, standing in that god-haunted place with people starting to cluster around us and peering through the entrance arches, wondering what I had done to cause the old man's mirth. When he finally stopped and took out a handkerchief to wipe his eyes, he said, still chuckling, 'Oh, I like people who are making me laugh. There is not enough laughter in our lives. Levity is the soul of wit, nè?' He looked round at the gathering crowd. 'Here is an honest girl, my friends. It is a rare quality.' To me he said, 'You are welcome here in our temple at any time, Missy.'

It was an honour to be asked, Finn told me as we walked home. I basked in the unexpected glow of approval and went back with him at other times, and with Kesval and Titch too. The monkeys were the attraction for Titch. A whole troop of them lived in the grove, a constant agile grey presence swinging through the trees, sleek with good living off the offerings of fruit and grains brought by temple-goers. You would see their shadows slipping among the statues on the temple tower so that it seemed as though a whitewashed hand moved, an eye gleamed and plaster drapery billowed in the still air.

If there are gods, they were there in that temple by the river. Perhaps it was they, enraged by its imminent destruction, who instigated the rioting. Perhaps they didn't like Finn and me and Titch going there, taking us for sensation seekers. Perhaps gods go over the edge too sometimes. Finn told me that Shiva created the universe and keeps the world spinning by dancing, holding his symbols in his four hands: the trident, half moon, serpent and sceptre. But he didn't add that Shiva is also called the destroyer.

Isabel

She is in the store room off the garage delving into the trunk where she keeps old stuff she doesn't want to throw away: special letters, school reports, things the children wrote or made when they were small, her journals (tucked well out of sight so George won't find them) and the few remaining family things she couldn't bear to part with after her mother died. She is looking for the scrapbook she made so many years ago in Two Rivers.

Jammed down into one corner is a worn teddy bear and she thinks, Oh, Edgar! and picks him up. His body under the blue knitted pullover is emaciated and one glass eye is hanging by its wire loop. His mouth, a sweet curve of black stitches, seems to be saying, So you still remember me? I've been waiting here since that man threw me out of your bedroom.

She finds herself hugging him and thinking, Edgar was such a good friend. How could I have been persuaded to banish him? I've been so feeble all these years, not standing up for myself; the failure of this marriage is as much my fault as George's. He may be a self-centred bore, but I've let him get that way by living under false pretences, play-acting the role of wife while I kept my real feelings and needs to myself.

It is a moment of unwelcome recognition. Until now she has blamed him entirely.

She lays Edgar gently down on the concrete floor, thinking, He saw a lot of the things I've been writing about, sitting next to me up in the mango tree. If I hadn't had his familiar little body to cry into, I'd have been a lot more lonely and frightened in those first bad days after Pa died and Ma had her nervous breakdown. I must fix that hole and re-stuff him and wash the blue pullover . . .

136

Another memory of Two Rivers clicks into place: Stella hailing Edgar as an old friend when she saw him being unpacked, and saying, 'I knitted this pullover for him when you were four, do you remember? You said he was cold because it was winter, and I found some scrap wool and knitted it up. Very badly too; look at the uneven stitches. I think it's the only little woolly garment I've ever made.' Her face had gone still.

Isabel thinks now, How much damage that unborn baby did, being the cause of a hasty marriage that ended in such horror.

She shakes the thought out of her head and turns back to the trunk to unearth the scrapbook. She needs it because she is worried that, in concentrating on the people in her story, she is not giving it the feel of the Fifties – amassing enough background details to tie it securely into its time and place. She remembers starting the scrapbook as a record to show her mother when she went home; remembers sticking in sprays of pressed jasmine flowers, magazine and newspaper cuttings, her convent term card, letters from Evelyn Simpson, the label off her treasured little bottle of French perfume.

The scrapbook is lying right at the bottom of the trunk, beneath her journals. She recalls now burying it there before packing all the other stuff on top of it, hoping to lay the unhappy memories to rest along with Edgar Bear. She thinks, But you don't forget. You just coat them with layer after layer of defensive gloss in the same way as an oyster copes with a grain of scratchy sea sand by coating it in fine layers of pearl. The question is, can I unearth the scratchy truth of what happened in Two Rivers, and create something as beautiful and lasting as a pearl from it?

I hope I'm not romanticising what happened, she thinks. He'd spot that straight away.

She makes a pot of coffee on her way through the kitchen to her desk with Edgar and the scrapbook, then pours herself a cup, opens the first page and finds herself plunging back into the early Fifties.

Here is a Union Castle lunch menu from the time she and Stella had gone to see someone off on the Thursday mail-boat to Cape Town and Southampton. A page of photographs

137

taken with the Box Brownie Finn had given her for Christmas, the people in them all standing much too far away. A Boswell's Circus programme featuring Tickey the Clown. An eskimo pie wrapper. A pair of bioscope tickets: had they been for Esther Williams gliding across a jungle pool in a bathing cap of glistening rubber flowers, or *The Red Shoes* with Moira Shearer? She remembers when everybody stood to attention for *God Save the King* at the end of films – to no avail, because he was already dying of lung cancer.

She thinks, Stop turning the pages so fast. You've got to go slowly, take notes, immerse yourself. But she can't stop. There is so much of her younger self in here that she had forgotten. The insistent tug of awakened memory pulls her onwards through pages crackling with stiff brown stickytape, sometimes stuck together so that she has to get a knife and run it carefully down between the edges.

Here is an advertisement for the Studebaker Mr Reddy drove, daring because its boot was shaped like its bonnet: 'Pointing both ways,' people said. And a blurry photograph of her waving from the fold-out dickey seat of Finn's old Ford coupé, where she sat when Stella was in the passenger seat, wearing a black velvet headband to prevent her growing hair from whipping across her face. She closes her eyes at the memory and the exhilarating wind is there still.

She remembers windy days at the beach, and Stella building a magnificent sandcastle decorated with shells and seaweed and standing next to it to be photographed, laughing in triumph, her hair ruffled up into spikes. She had a polka-dot swimming costume with a modesty skirt and padded falsies that gave her an incongruous jutting bosom – Stella who was so flat-chested that she used to talk about her light switches.

Stella who lives in an expensive Durban nursing home now, alone with her oxygen bottles. After a long career as one of London's most innovative and controversial interior decorators, she has advanced emphysema and has come home to die. The doctors have given her a year at the most. It is another reason why Isabel feels able to resurrect Two Rivers on paper; Stella will soon be beyond hurt. She thinks of her as she saw her last: white-faced, brittle as this old newsprint, rail-thin, gasping, her hair dyed a fierce red to hide the grey, her foxy eyes lustreless, all her anger spent.

Isabel's eyes are full of tears as she turns the last few pages with their burden of yellowed cuttings from the national newspapers: screaming headlines and pictures of devastation, inset with photographs of Finn.

Needing a respite from the crowding memories, she picks up the phone and dials the mountain cottage to find out if her lover has returned yet. The phone rings for several long minutes. There is no reply.

Extract from the official report of the Sandham Commission of Enquiry into the Easter 1952 Riot:

'. . . Two-thirds of the witnesses questioned referred without prompting to a rising state of tension in the town for some weeks before the riot.

Sergeant Koekemoer, the South African Police Station Commander in Two Rivers, testified that there had been a number of racial incidents. He and his men had been called out on several occasions to deal with faction fighting in the Herald compound between Zulu and Pondo millworkers. Two young Bantu boys had been arrested for throwing stones at Indian children on their way home from school. During a drunken brawl outside the public bar of the Cosy Hotel which he had been called to break up, one of the fighters, a white man, had suddenly swung on a Bantu bystander shouting, 'You buggers are the cause of all the trouble around here! You should stay where you bloody belong, in the reserves.'

Mr K K Reddy testified that there had been indignation in the Hindu community over the fact that they had not been consulted about the upgrading of the main road and the consequent necessity to widen both river bridges, which would require the destruction of the temple tower. He said, 'To offer compensation is not enough. That is sacred ground to us. Our gods were angry.' Let it be noted that in the opinion of the majority of the members of this commission, Mr Reddy, a wealthy and cultured man, is using this apparently superstitious belief as an excuse to justify the violent actions of the young men known as the temple guardians.

Miss Dorothy Gould, retired librarian, testified that she had witnessed an incident in which a Zulu woman caught shoplifting had been slapped by the Indian shop owner's wife before the police were called . . .'

140

10

I read somewhere that your brain never forgets anything. It's all there stored in the brain cells for future reference, only your conscious mind can't handle the mass of information so it highlights the people and the events and the emotions that had the greatest impact on your life: happy times, achievements, loves, fears, hatreds. The strange thing for me, writing now about Two Rivers, is that the more I fossick around in the past, the more memories come tumbling out of dusty recesses. And as I pick each one up and dust it off, so others are revealed, hidden behind accretions of more recent memories. I wonder if they have been subtly altered by their long time in storage? Since experience is subjective, the memories which distil and concentrate your experiences must be even more so.

This morning, trying to remember how the chain of events that led to Finn's death had started, a picture of Dicky Gould shambling into the pharmacy came into my head, as bright and sharp-edged as a new playing card.

The Goulds were an elderly brother and sister who had never married and lived together in one of the sagging old wood and iron houses on Darjeeling Road – the first eccentrics I had ever met. People in mining towns are too intent on making enough money to get out of them as quickly as possible, to waste time on nonconformist behaviour. I remember with loathing my enforced visits to the Goulds' home with Stella, who had decided that I would benefit from seeing charity in action; she took them bottles of home-made jam and chutney bought from a local farmer's wife, which she pretended she had made.

The visits were a series of grim ordeals but they did teach

me one thing: how to block off the back of my nose by raising my soft palate and breathing through my mouth, so I wouldn't have to smell either the Goulds or their house. Each time, I swore to myself afterwards that I would rather die young than grow old and disgusting. Now I see that they were just two old people trying to cope with decrepitude and illness and poverty, and failing.

Miss Dorothy Gould had once worked in the Two Rivers library, but after years of puzzlement at the number of books that disappeared annually without trace, the chief librarian had discovered that she compulsively stole and hoarded them, and dismissed her. She had almost filled a room to ceiling height by the time she was caught, and when they took the books away she felt the vacuum so keenly that she began to steal from other libraries and second-hand book stalls and bookshops. She never read them, just accumulated them in tilting piles linked by generations of dust-clogged cobwebs. Bookshop and library personnel as far afield as Durban were trained to spot Miss Dorothy sidling in with her old leather shopping bag, and to frisk her well on leaving.

She got away with enough books, however, to have half-filled the room again by the time I was taken to meet her. She was secretive about what she called her book treasury, and kept the door locked and the key on a piece of string round her grimy neck. But Stella managed to persuade her (with a foxy glance at me) that the hoard could be in danger of bookworms, and she and I were let in several times to inspect it for contamination with Miss Dorothy hovering anxiously in the doorway. I don't know which was worse, the mouldy fungus smell of the looming books or the ripe cheesy smell of the old woman.

Her scalp showed through her thinning hair and she sprayed spit as she talked. The house was full of caged budgies whose constant twittering would have driven any normal person insane. They were let out twice a day to fly around ('Sstretch their poor lissle wingss,' Miss Dorothy would hiss through ill-fitting dentures) and there were toothpaste squirts of grey and white bird droppings everywhere, so you had to be careful where you sat. Her dislike of non-Europeans, a handy South African term then for anyone who wasn't white, was legendary. As far as she was concerned, natives and coolies were lying, thieving, devious, no-good skellums and she would not allow them through her garden gate.

Since the Goulds no longer had the strength to attend to it themselves, the garden was a jungle of rampant weeds; in the servantless house, the dirt and the bird droppings accumulated year by year along with the books and bundles of old newspapers. Their kitchen table would be a fertile source for future archaeologists researching twentieth-century eating habits, Stella said once as we battled our way back to civilisation through the weeds. All they'd have to do is excavate the cracks and they'd find evidence of meals going back fifty years.

The Goulds' tragedy had begun with a violent father whose beatings had made them grow up distrusting everyone except each other. Then middle-aged Dicky Gould, working as a clerk for the Herald Company at the beginning of the war, had joined the Natal Carbineers to fight Up North and come home a shell-shocked old man, seething with an impotent rage that only alcohol could quench. Now he was the town drunk and spent his time trying to hustle enough money to pay for half-jacks of cheap brandy. He was banned from the company estate and shunned by most of the other whites, but the Indians treated him as though he carried an invisible begging bowl and gave him food and small change when they could afford it. He encouraged these small acts of piety by playing the part of a holy man when not too drunk; he would cup his hands together and touch them to his forehead and bless people in a syrupy voice when they gave him anything. The company had tried to have him put away in a home for the indigent but Miss Dorothy would not hear of it.

I heard her spitting to Stella once, 'People forget what war doess to men. Dicky makess them remember.'

He came into the pharmacy during the afternoon of my second day in Two Rivers. Finn had asked me to hold the fort for, 'Yust five minutes, right?' while he went through to the house to make us both a cup of tea, and I was standing proudly behind the glass counter all on my own, dying for a customer to come in so I could show off what I'd learned. Govind Desai would normally have been in charge, but it was his temple hour.

The bell tinkled over the door as an old man in a black leather-rimmed beret, bush shirt patched with darns and baggy khaki shorts came shuffling in. The shirt had food stains down the front and the shorts hung past his knees, where they disgorged a pair of scaly purple legs like an ancient rooster's, ending in sandals. He stopped halfway towards the counter where I was standing and said with a glare, 'Where's the chilliecracker?'

'The what?' I hadn't heard the word before.

'The chilliecracker. Indian feller. He knows what I need. Where the bloody hell is he?'

The old man's skin was a mess of sprawling brown freckles and splotches and blotches and round papery scabs like silver-white coins. His face had collapsed into wrinkles that didn't take kindly to shaving; there were several little bits of tissue stuck over cuts made by a razor, and forgotten. I could see there was something wrong with him and guessed that he was drunk, but was too full of my temporary self-importance to be afraid. Pretending to be June Allyson as a humble young shop assistant who was about to be discovered and whisked off to Hollywood, I said in a poncey voice, 'I'm sure I can help you, sir. What is it that you need?'

'Bottle of Laxton's Embrocation and one of their cough mixture,' he wheezed, flinging a leprous arm in the air where it hung as though supported by invisible strings. 'Up on the shelf there.'

There were hundreds of Laxton's bottles and boxes and packets on the shelves; it was a popular brand of patent medicine. I also wasn't quite sure what embrocation was: did you drink it or rub it in? So I gave him June Allyson's sweet chummy smile and said, 'What were you thinking of using the embrocation for, sir?'

A pair of mud-brown bloodshot eyes fastened on my face. 'Not for mending leaks in my French letters, you can be sure. Ha?' His mouth made a noise that would have been a guffaw if he had had more breath; it came out as the dying gasp of a switched-off vacuum cleaner.

I was nonplussed, never having heard of a French letter, and blurted, 'I can't help you if you don't tell me.'

He took several staggering steps in my direction then

144

stopped and stood looking around, absently picking at one of the scabs on his arm, as though he had forgotten what he was there for. 'Where's the chilliecracker, dammit? He knows how to help me. Puts my things down on account and nothing said.'

I was beginning to wish Finn would come back. It's not funny being alone in a shop with an irritable old drunk who looks as though he's about to topple over at any minute. What if he crashed through the glass counter and a sliver of glass severed his jugular vein and his blood began to gush out and he bled to death at my feet? Or (worse) if he came round the counter and grabbed me and started to do unspeakable things to me – whatever they were?

To stop him from coming any closer, I said hastily, 'What if I point to the shelves and you say which one they're on?'

'Point away, girlie. Had a dog once, used to point. Used to sniff up women's legs too. Dirty bugger.'

I started to blush and turned my back so he wouldn't see, pointing to the bottom shelf. 'Are they here?'

'Eh? What? No.'

I pointed to the second shelf. 'Here?'

I heard him stagger a bit closer. 'No.'

'Here?'

'No.'

'They must be on the top shelf, then. I have to use the steps to reach anything up there.'

I pulled the small folding wooden stepladder for the high shelves into position and began to climb up, watching him out of the corner of my eye. You feel very vulnerable on a ladder. What if he came nearer and put his horrible old scabby hand up inside my shorts and touched me? I felt myself blushing down there too, a spreading warmth that made my knees feel shaky. Where was Finn? The old man's sandals were shambling closer and he was breathing through his mouth.

Slavering? I wondered, panic-stricken. Newspaper headlines flashed in front of my eyes. GIRL RAPED IN CHEMIST BY AGED SEX FIEND. SAVAGE ATTACK ON TEENAGER. BRUTAL MURDER IN TWO RIVERS – SENILE KILLER ON THE RUN. THIS MAN IS DANGEROUS!

145

There was a wheezing cough right behind me. I tried to scream but my throat seized up and wouldn't let anything out. I felt my mouth opening and closing like the mullet Finn had caught, in soundless terror.

'Come on, girlie, make it snappy,' he barked. 'I haven't got all day.'

I forced myself to turn round. He was leaning over the counter glaring up at me in rage rather than lust, and I had a small pang of disappointment. For a moment I'd thought I'd have something really impressive to write and tell Evelyn Simpson.

'Whereabouts on the top shelf, sir?'

'I don't know! Look for them. Can't you fucking read?' He was trembling with impatience, his fingers drumming on the glass.

I'd never heard that word spoken before, though I'd seen it scratched on the backs of public lavatory doors. Trying not to giggle, I turned back and looked along the shelf and there they were: round-shouldered brown bottles labelled respectively *Laxton's Soothing Embrocation* and *Laxton's Expectorant Cough Mixture* (15% Alcohol, 2% Codeine). I reached for them and began to climb down again.

Finn's voice said from near the door, 'Hullo, Dicky. Trying to slip onder the fence again?'

He was carrying two cups of tea and smiling, but I could hear that something was wrong. I explained, 'He asked for embrocation and cough mixture and I was just –'

'Miss Dorothy said no more credit.' Finn kept smiling but you could see he was angry underneath. 'I won't have you coming in here badgering my assistants.'

'Blast you, man!' Dicky Gould shook a trembling fist at him then swung round to me, standing halfway down the ladder holding the brown bottles. 'And blast you too! Slow-witted cunt.'

This word I didn't know.

'Get out,' Finn said, crashing the tea cups down.

'I got better service from your wog. The wily oriental gentleman.' The old man gave a wheezing laugh that turned into a cough, doubling his body over so that he had to clutch at the black beret to stop it falling off his head.

Finn waited until he stood up again, then said in his softest voice, 'In what way, better service? Govind was instructed not to put anything for you down on account.'

Dicky Gould shrugged. 'Chilliecrackers know which side their bread's buttered on. I scratch his back, he scratches mine.' He began shuffling towards the street door.

'Yust how does he scratch your back?' Finn blocked his path, and for a moment I could see what the Vikings must have looked like when they invaded England. His face had a sort of hot liquid look that could easily become fury, quite unlike the everyday Finn.

'Expect me to tell you? Bloody cheek.'

'You will tell me, Dicky, or I'll close Dorothy's account. And you know what that means.'

They stood confronting each other: my tall brother-in-law the personification of stern hygiene in his starched white jacket, and the foulmouthed, red-eyed old drunk whom I must admit I was rather sorry hadn't tried anything on me. It would have been interesting to see how Finn reacted; I was beginning to think that he wasn't as quiet and unambitious as Stella imagined he was.

Dicky Gould's eyes dropped first. 'Feller figured out how to put things down on the company's account. It's big enough. My piddling little purchases aren't more than a drop in the bucket to them.'

Finn said, 'No more, do you hear me? I'll speak to Govind about this. Now get out.'

'I'm going, I'm going. Officious bastard.' The old man gurgled and spat, sending a glob of green phlegm flying on to the face of a smiling model in a cardboard shampoo advertisement, where it clung for several minutes before beginning to slide very slowly down her cheek.

I watched that glob slide all the way down until it finally made it to the floor, long after he had stumbled out the door which Finn slammed shut behind him. Long after Finn had explained about the addictive nature of alcohol/codeine mixtures. And long after I had asked, 'What's a cunt?' and he had replied, 'A frickly word for women. Forget it.'

But I didn't. I stored it away for future use, and now all these years later it tumbles out of my memory dragging that

147

afternoon in the pharmacy with it. Because it was Finn's angry reprimand of his assistant Govind Desai when he returned from the temple that turned the young man into a sulky, watchful enemy. Finn, the white errant.

Isabel

The telephone rings shortly before lunch one day and he says, 'Izzy?' Cautious, as usual.

'Where are you? When did you get back?' she demands. 'You've been away much longer than you said you'd be. I've been worried. I missed you terribly.'

'Got back late yesterday and drove up to the cottage last night. Forgive me for not phoning before, but I've been dead to the world for ten hours.' His voice is still sleep-furred.

Disappointed, she says, 'Why didn't you phone me from the airport? We could have had a few more hours together.'

'Arrived well after seven. Didn't think your husband would appreciate my dulcet tones if he answered.'

'Couldn't you have stayed a night in the hotel? We could have met this morning.' She speaks with difficulty past the lump in her throat. She had counted on seeing him on his way back.

'Not possible, sorry. The trip took for bloody ever and my deadline's next week. I'm going to have to work round the clock as it is.' She has never heard him sound so grumpy. 'And you? How's the masterpiece coming along?'

Ignoring the sarcasm in his voice and eager to tell him how far she has come, she pours out a progress report, imagining her words speeding along the thin wires that dip between rows of white insulators on telephone poles giant-striding towards the mountains.

'I've just finished a chapter about the Goulds this morning. And before that I wrote about the first time I went to the temple with Finn. The incredible culture shock.' She is elated with achievement. 'I can't believe how easily it's coming, like opening a vein. I can't think about anything else. The house and garden are totally neglected – not to mention George. I've got to be careful there because I think he's smelt a rat.'

'He's found out about us?'

She hears the leap of hope in his voice and thinks, Oh hell, that was a mistake. I can't let him imagine anything's imminent when it isn't. She says quickly, 'No, about me always being busy writing something. He wants to know what it is and I have to keep fobbing him off. He's beginning to call it The State Secret, and I know he's been searching my cupboards and drawers when I've been out because things are in the wrong places when I get back. I had to rack my brains for a hiding place he wouldn't think of looking in.'

'And where could that be?' His tone is ironic; she can almost see his eyebrows going up in the middle. He has wonderful eyebrows, strong and well-defined, pleasantly wiry without being rampant.

'Guess.'

'No. You tell me.'

Is there a note of irritation in his abrupt refusal? We've been apart too long again, she thinks. He's getting tired of waiting for me, tired of my shilly-shallying.

She says, 'I'll tell you when I see you. Listen, could I come for the weekend?'

'You don't have to ask! That's great news. I should have finished the update by then.'

'I'm longing to see you.'

'Why didn't you tell me straight away that you could come, then?' The odd note is still there in his voice.

She says defensively, 'I've got all these memories still buzzing in my head. You know how it is when you've just finished writing a section. It's like giving birth: hours of effort and agony, time crawling, your body and brain shouting, Enough! Enough! I can't do it any more! Then everything seems to happen in a rush and there's this brand-new entity you've created, all squashed and wrinkled, but whole and complete. You feel so triumphant.'

'It wears off a bit when you've spent more than half a lifetime grinding out the stuff to make a living,' he growls.

'But don't let me chuck cold water over your enthusiasm. I'm just not in the best mood this morning.'

'What's wrong?'

'Nothing important. Forget it. How come you're able to get away for the weekend?'

Pushing away a niggle of worry at his bad humour, she says, 'George announced last week that he's going to a golf tournament at Sun City with office colleagues. They've been invited by one of their major suppliers. It's an all-boys-together thing. He doesn't actually play the game but enjoys trailing around with the crowd watching, and of course the jollifications in the evenings: the extravaganza and the naked showgirls and the lavish meals and the gambling, all paid for by someone else. It's his idea of heaven. Nothing but –'

He interrupts, 'Come as soon as you can. I must see you. I need you. I'm sick of this bloody machine that only brings me your disembodied voice.'

She says again, alarmed now, 'What's wrong?'

'Nothing. Everything. I'm just not a patient man, Izzy. I find this waiting for an indefinite period very difficult. If it were up to me, I'd have had you legally in my bed months ago.'

'Legally?' She can hear her voice faltering. They have not discussed marriage.

'Divorced from that bastard so you're free to be with me, in whatever capacity you choose. If you still want to.'

'Of course I still want to!'

'I have moments when I wonder. There seem to be so many obstacles, mostly of your own making. Whereas for me the situation is clear-cut. Having found you so late, I am overwhelmed by greed. I want you with me all the time so we can make up for the lost years. Life is moving on for both of us.'

She blurts, 'Don't I know it. But I'm trapped in obligations which –'

'What obligations could be more important than our feelings for each other?' The telephone line is crackling badly; his words come through in spurts. 'Your children are grown and gone. Your husband is an uncaring bully. And it is clear that your home has ceased to mean anything to you emotionally

151

but the place where you live. What the fuck are we waiting for?'

She hears the angry passion in his voice with despair and shouts, 'You know I can't break it off just like that!'

'Why not, for God's sake? Why not?' There is a prolonged crackle on the line, and when she hears his voice again he is saying, '. . . I don't want bits and pieces of you. I want all of you, my dear love, before it's too late.'

'What do you mean, too late?' She feels a surge of panic. 'Are you sick? Is there something you haven't told me?'

Her answer is a deafening sizzle, followed by a click as the phone goes dead. When she tries dialling his number, she hears only the long beeping out-of-order tone.

There follow two hours of frantic anxiety while she prowls the house, twitching curtains and plumping cushions as she resists the urge to rush out to the garage and get into her car and drive to him. At one point she makes a pot of strong coffee to steady her resolve; her hands are shaking so much as she spoons ground coffee into the paper filter that some of it spills on the kitchen counter, followed by the contents of the milk jug as she knocks that over too.

Grabbing a dishcloth to attack the mess, she thinks savagely, What sort of an unfeeling, selfish woman am I, worrying about stupid little domestic details when he could be seriously ill – dying, maybe? What's wrong with me? How can I be so indecisive when he's so sure? Why can't I just dump everything in this rotten place and go for what I want? I don't owe George a damn thing. I don't owe the kids either; I've done what I can for them. Maybe I'm just using Ralphie's problems as an excuse because I'm afraid to leave the nest I've created. The suburban prison. Or maybe I'm just too bloody useless to be a decent partner to anyone. Let alone lover. I've had a failure of a life, and now I'm buggering up my second chance too. Shit. SHIT!

But she can't drop everything and run. George has arranged a meeting the following morning with Ralphie's student counsellor, who has written to them saying, 'This young man is generating problems that I'd like to discuss with you both.' While she'd cancel anything to do with George without a qualm, she can't leave Ralphie in the lurch.

152

Not even for the love of my life, she thinks in despair. A mother has obligations. You take them on so blithely when you bring a child into the world, without the least idea of what you're letting yourself in for. If you knew half the anguish they cause, you'd probably never have children. But you can't abandon them when they need you . . . Thank God the girls are well away.

Unaware that one of them is about to present her with a problem worse than Ralphie's, she picks up the telephone to send an urgent telegram to the mountain cottage.

11

November came, and with it – simultaneously that year – Guy Fawkes and Deepavali, two festivals of light that symbolise very different events on opposite sides of the world. In Coolietown the children went dizzy celebrating both at once. In the white parts of Two Rivers, people hardly registered Hindu festivals except in a general way as yet another 'coolie Christmas'.

Finn told me about Deepavali as we sat sat in deck chairs out in the paved courtyard one evening, watching fireflies flitting like miniature Tinkerbells above the waterlilies. It was one of those sultry coastal nights when your skin still sweats if you move; the scent of the sun-warmed frangipani flowers in the tree above us, cloying and creamy-sweet, overlaid the spicy afterbreath of the chicken and coconut curry Eslina had made us for supper.

Stella was out at a protest meeting about the proposed widening of the main road, which would mean that some of the precious Two Rivers flamboyants would have to be felled. She was an enthusiastic protester. Mr Reddy and his temple committee would be there too, trying to gather support for a reprieve for their tower. I wondered if the Christians present would do anything more than give the Hindus a polite hearing. He had been right about the general dislike of Indians; the white people I heard on my walkabouts talked about 'charras' and 'currymunchers' as well as Dicky Gould's 'chilliecrackers', and I had seen Zulus bending over and spitting when they came out of Indian shops. At home in the mining town, the disparaged people had been Jews; they were called 'kikes' and 'yids' and 'Jewboys', and children sang in the gritty streets, 'Crikey Moses, King of the Jews,

154

sold his wife for a pair of shoes.' Was it the legacy of our
tribal past or just plain jealousy, I wondered, that made
people disdain more successful races? What did I really feel,
deep down inside where other people couldn't see, about
Indians and Jews?

As though getting a whiff of my thoughts, Finn said, 'It'll
be Deepavali next week.'

'What's that?'

'It's a very beautiful Hindu festival, the festival of lights.
The word comes from "deepa", which means lamp, and "oli",
which is the radiance of the lamp. Did you notice the clay
lamps in the temple?'

I shook my head.

'I've got one in the dispensary. It's a clay bowl yust smaller
than the palm of your hand, designed to hold a puddle of oil
with a wick in it. At Deepavali, Hindu homes are decorated
with rows of them along windowsills and verandas and
rooftops, all flickering with little orange flames.'

It sounded lovely, like church candles everywhere. 'What
are they for?'

'To celebrate the safe homecoming of the god Rama after
his battle with the wicked King Ravana of Ceylon – the
triumph of good over evil. The lamps are also supposed to
light the steps of Lakshmi, the goddess of prosperity, good
fortune and beauty. Hindus believe that she comes to visit
homes where she is made welcome during the two nights of
Deepavali.'

She sounded like a good person for a semi-orphan to have
visiting. 'Could we try welcoming Lakshmi too?'

He nodded. 'Why not? You could ask Mr Reddy how it's
done.'

'He's a bit, well, daunting.'

'I thought he was yust as friendly as can be when he took
us to the temple. He's a good man.'

'Oh, I know. Only he makes me feel guilty to be white
when I'm with him. You know how I mean? He talks about
the bad things people do to Indians and I feel responsible.
When I'm not, really. I think it's terrible the way white
people look down on people of other colours.' I was quite
proud of how that sounded; I wanted Finn to know that my

155

heart was in the right place, even if I did come from the Trans-vaal.

His answer was gently mocking. 'Of course we never feel even the tiniest bit superior, do we?'

Luckily it was dark, because I felt myself blushing. I was, after all, much better educated than all except a very few black people and therefore couldn't help being superior in some ways. I said defensively, 'You can't blame people for being born into privileges. Kesaval and Asha were, and they're Indian.'

He put out his bear's paw and patted my hand. 'I wasn't getting at you, Izzy. We yust have to be aware of our ingrained attitudes. You could ask Asha about Lakshmi and Deepavali, if you're so interested. She's coming into the pharmacy tomorrow, made an appointment for ten. Beautiful girl, that.' He looked up at the frangipani flowers starring the canopy of leaves above us, wearing the rapt expression he wore when he was pointing out something that he admired. 'Grace is a rare quality.'

A thought flashed through my mind, soon suppressed. No one would ever call Stella graceful.

Next morning, I made sure I was helping behind the counter when Asha came shimmering in, this time in a palest yellow sari with threads of gold. Both Govind Desai and Finn stopped what they were doing to watch her. What is it about beauty that so mesmerises men? I wondered. It's not fair. Beauty is just something certain people happen to be born with, a super-privilege to do with bone structure, not a virtue or specially praiseworthy. Yet it has an aura of inno-cence and purity; truly beautiful women are assumed to be embodiments of perfection, placed on earth for worshipping. Like bloody living goddesses, I thought, seeing the look on their faces. It's not fair.

When she went over to Finn, Govind's eyes followed her as though pulled by invisible nylon fishing lines. He was a tall – almost willowy – thin young man with a pocked skin and a jutting adam's apple and limp hair that flopped over his forehead. He moved like a secretary bird, stalking about in the same slow, deliberate, precise way as he measured things out. Finn said he was a good assistant, very hardworking, but maybe too solemn with those customers who liked a bit of cheerful gossip when they were buying medicines. Govind had hidden yearnings, though; beneath his white jacket he wore jazzy shirts and ties with palm trees on them and tight pants and pointy black and white two-tone shoes, all of which shouted, 'Look at me!' He would take the shoes off and hang them by their tied laces over his bicycle handlebars before putting on trouser-clips to ride home in his socks every evening.

When I'd confided to Finn that I felt uncomfortable with Govind, he'd said, 'He looks cross a lot of the time, I know, but it's yust exhaustion from going to night school. I like that he's so keen to better himself. Poor fellow, his life isn't easy with a widowed mother and eight younger brothers and sisters to support.'

Now he stood watching Asha curved like a drooping yellow lily over the glass counter where Finn stood, whispering something to him.

I heard the quiet reply. 'Come into the dispensary, my dear. We can discuss it there.' He raised his voice and said to Govind and me, 'Mind the shop, will you?'

'Yes, sir.' Govind swung away as if he couldn't bear to watch any more.

I started to follow them, saying, 'I want to ask Asha about –'

Finn said, 'In yust a moment, Izzy. This is confidential.' As they went through the doorway, he had his hand under her elbow.

After about ten minutes of murmured conversation, during which Govind and I busied ourselves trying to impress each other with the fact that we weren't straining to listen to what was being said, they came out again. Asha was carrying a small paper packet; there was a dull flush on her cheeks. She said to me in her demure way, 'Mr Rosholt is telling me you like to know about Lakshmi. Maybe you come by the house later, eh? My English is not so good. Kesaval, he will tell you.'

I turned to Finn. 'Will you take me? Please?'

He shook his head. 'I can't this afternoon. But go on your own, Izzy. I'm sure Stella will grant you permission to venture into the dangerous territory off the main road in this case.'

157

He often said teasing things like that about her. In spite of his apparent easygoingness, he got his digs in all right.

Asha said, 'Later, then?' to me and, 'Thank you, goodbye, Mr Rosholt,' to him, and went gliding out through the glass door. Govind crossed to the display window and stood watching her until she disappeared. When he turned back, his mouth looked as though he had been sucking lemons.

I was shy about going to the Reddy house on my own and tried to persuade Stella to go with me, but she was busy marking tests and setting end-of-the-year exam papers, and seemed to have forgotten about my dubious safety on the streets. Her hair stuck out when she was harassed, giving her the look of a ginger cat arching its back. 'Don't be so feeble, Izz. Go on your own. They won't bite you.'

'Mrs Reddy might. She looks as though she sharpens her teeth on a grindstone every night.'

Stella laughed. 'She's a formidable woman, I'll grant you. Knows everything that's going on in this town, and then some. But she likes Finn. You'll be welcomed, really. I wouldn't mind a spot of peace and quiet either so I can get these papers finished.'

I took the hint and went, and it wasn't such an ordeal after all once I'd run the gauntlet of Mrs Reddy's voluble welcome and Violet glaring at me from the depths of an archway. I had incurred her displeasure on my first visit and wasn't going to be allowed to forget it. Talking non-stop and propelled by her elbows, Mrs Reddy forged ahead of me down a long gloomy passage, breaking off as we passed a baronial sweep of staircase to call upwards, 'Asha! Kesaval! Come now, please, your visitor is here.'

'We're in the lounge already, Mama.'

The voice came from an open pair of doors at the far end of the passage, muffled by distance. The house must go on for *miles*, I thought, wondering just how rich Mr Reddy was. And it had an unfamiliar spicy smell, quite different from the house smells I was used to. Taking little surreptitious sniffs as I hurried in my hostess's busily slapping footsteps, I tried to identify the difference. Incense, of course. A lingering trace of

158

curry. Camphor wheezing from an open door. A waft of what must be sandalwood as we passed a carved wooden chest. And the heavy scent Mrs Reddy was wearing: could it be musk? I'd always wondered what musk smelled like, and had imagined sloe-eyed odalisques lounging about a harem in a perfumed mist sprayed by eunuchs from crystal bottles with fat netted squeeze-bulbs. Ma had an empty scent bottle like that on her Dolly Varden dressing table at home, and when I was small I used to creep under its chintz skirts and hold the bottle in front of my face and squeeze the bulb with its red silk tassel to make puffs of air all over my skin, hoping that the ghostly breath of the long-dried scent would somehow make me beautiful.

Poor Ma. Hurrying behind the Indian mother, I wondered whether she knew where she was yet. Poor Ma.

I was blinking as Mrs Reddy ushered me into a vast reception room where sunlight slanted through symmetrical arched windows on to a profusion of yet more carpets and brass ornaments. An impressive gathering of linenfold imbuia furniture stood around on ball-and-claw feet; the pale brocade upholstery on the chairs was still covered with sheets of plastic. One corner had been made cosy, however, with a facing pair of red and gilt sofas like the one in Mr Reddy's study. Kesaval and Asha were sitting side by side on one of them looking vaguely guilty, as though they had just slipped on their polite expressions.

Mrs Reddy came to a halt at last and propelled me forward with a plump clinking arm. 'Here we are now. So near and yet so far, eh?' I got a flash of teeth glittering with gold inlays. 'This house takes up all my time. The cleaning and so forth, it never ends. Never ends. Such is life. Sit down, please, Missy.'

I stumbled towards the sofas. Kesaval, unfamiliar in a school uniform of blazer and striped tie and long grey trousers, stood up and said, 'Hi.' He was more Indian than I remembered, his black hair thicker and curlier, his skin a deeper shade of milk chocolate. His eye sockets looked as though they had been smudged with soot; like so many boys, he had an unfairly generous sweep of eyelashes.

Not sure whether to shake hands or not, I kept my right

one dangling in a ready position and said 'Hi' back, directing it also at Asha who was sitting next to him. 'Hi' was a recent gift to our generation from American movies; it's a useful monosyllable when the teenage throat is paralysed by social angst.

He made no move to shake so I dropped my hand again, covering the move with a weak grin.

'You can all three talk now, eh? Sit down. Sit down. I will go and organise some tea.' Mrs Reddy bustled off, her sleek black seal's head thrusting forward in her haste to provide suitable hospitality.

Kesaval sat down again next to Asha. I tried to perch unobtrusively on the opposite sofa, but it gave way and I found myself toppling back into a warm red embrace as soft and squishy as a ripe tomato. I wondered wildly if it was going rotten inside. When you're growing up you have these weird thoughts at the most inappropriate times – or I used to, anyway. Right then I was thinking, What happens if this sofa bursts and I sink into a seething mass of sofa guts? Or maybe it's a trick sofa that suddenly closes up around unsuspecting guests like a Venus flytrap, imprisoning them against their will? Maybe Mr Reddy really got rich by being the South African agent for the white slave trade?

But then Kesaval cleared his throat and started telling me about Deepavali and Asha explained about Lakshmi, and for about ten minutes we were just three young people talking in the corner of a seldom-used room. What they said was really interesting too, once I'd manoeuvred myself forward into a less sprawling position. At this rate I'd be permanently one up on Evelyn Simpson, who may have been able to garner a few fag ends about the mysteries of sex but would never have a chance in the mining town of exploring the far more exotic mysteries of other people's beliefs and practices.

Then Mrs Reddy came in followed by a dignified old man in a white uniform pushing a tea trolley, and unleashed such a fusillade over our cups of sweet tea served with sticky pink coconut cakes that none of us got another word in edgeways. I left soon afterwards.

On the way home I passed several shops selling little red clay bowls like the one Finn had shown me, and I started to

160

think, If I do all the right things like they've told me, will Lakshmi come and bestow wealth on me even if I'm not a Hindu? I wouldn't mind more pocket money, for example. Stella always gave me a few bob extra if I asked, but I hated asking because I knew she and Finn didn't have much money of their own.

It sounds like I wanted to experiment with a Hindu goddess for a purely mercenary reason, but that was only a small part of why I wanted to join in what everyone else in Coolietown was doing. I wanted to belong in this new community I was living in, and even more, I wanted to be part of the magic of customs and ceremonies that had been happening for millenniums. Old customs carry with them a feeling that people have been honing and polishing them over the years, smoothing away roughnesses and inconsistencies until they must surely have achieved some essential form – a fine flowing shape basic to humanity. In allowing so many old customs to die now, are we gradually killing off the grace notes of living?

Finn helped me buy ten clay lamps and a stylised, highly coloured picture of Lakshmi as a beautiful Indian woman wearing a jewelled crown, standing on a lotus with one hand holding a full-blown lotus flower and her other hand raised palm forwards in what he said was a boon-conferring gesture. Two elephants on either side of her were pouring water from jars held in their upraised trunks, and in the background were swans on a blue lake. He showed me how to make cotton wool wicks for the lamps and gave me some sweet oil from the pharmacy to burn in them. He also went down to Moodley's and bought some saffron, saying when he gave me the little packet, 'Only a pinch, ya? It's expensive.'

His enthusiasm for my private ceremony was in stark contrast to Stella's dismissive, 'I don't know why you want to mess around with things that don't concern you.'

'I expect I'm going native,' I said. Sarcasm is definitely catching.

On the afternoon of Guy Fawkes, I swept and tidied my bedroom, lined up the clay lamps on my windowsills and filled them half-full of oil with a blob of cotton wool in the middle for the wick. Then I covered the commode with a lace-edged tea cloth sneaked out of the linen cupboard and pushed it in front of the window nearest my bed. One of my library books propped up the picture of Lakshmi with two brass-bowl ashtrays (polished to a high shine by Eslina) in front of it, one heaped with cold cooked rice from the fridge and the other half-full of milk. A small brass tray held a few copper and silver coins sprinkled with the saffron, a scatter of frangipani flowers and two Sharps toffees in lieu of sweet-meats. The only thing missing was camphor which Stella had refused to let me burn, saying that it would stink the whole house out for days.

Lying in a miasma of her bath salts which I'd begged for my ceremonial bath before putting on new clothes (the still-unworn jeans and a checked shirt) to go with Finn to the Guy Fawkes display, I thought, Probably I'm being silly thinking Lakshmi will come, but at least I've tried. At least I'm part of what's happening.

Officially the giant fireworks display put on by the Herald Company was supposed to be for employees and their chil-dren: the white families who lived on the estate, the Indian families from the staff cottages near the mill and several busloads of black workers from the mill compound. But because it was held in front of the company offices where the lawn sloped down to the Umlilwane river, fully visible to anyone standing on the bridge and the opposite riverbank, all the kids in town tried to drag their families along to watch as well. With Deepavali falling on the same date that year, there was an even greater incentive to be there as it would save on having to buy fireworks for the celebrations.

Finn and I walked up early and found a good position directly opposite the sloping lawn on the far side of the river where the fireworks had been set up, just off the path that ran along the riverbank. We had brought a rug and some old cushions, and were sitting with our backs against the trunk of a tree with sprawling branches and dark leaves and small red fruit that he said was a milkwood. Stella had refused to come, saying that fireworks were childish and she wanted to sand down a chair she had bought at a sale.

'Come with us,' Finn had pleaded. 'The company always puts on a good show.'

She had closed her eyes in exasperation. 'You know I can't *stand* fireworks. As far as I'm concerned, they're just men playing pretend war games – big bangs and pretty artillery tracers and rockets whooshing off. It isn't so long ago that people in England were cowering in terror when they heard a rocket coming. You've forgotten.'

'Nay,' he said, 'I haven't forgotten. Dicky Gould reminds me of the war every time he comes into the pharmacy. But you're wrong about fireworks, Stella. They're for celebrations, for happiness and fon.'

'Guy Fawkes trying to dynamite Parliament, fun?' she jeered. 'Come off it, Finn. Even a Norwegian can't be so naive.'

I saw how the muscle in his jaw tightened. 'You are yust trying to provoke.'

'Watch how the men scrap with each other to light the stupid things tonight, and you'll see what I mean,' she said.

'Stella –'

She flapped impatient hands at us. 'You'd better run off, you two, unless you want to miss the lovely bonfire where they burn the poor Guy at the stake.'

Contradictory as always, she had packed a small basket with roast beef and tomato sandwiches and apples and two small tubs of icecream well wrapped in newspaper so they wouldn't melt. Finn said, licking the last mouthful off his wooden spoon, 'That was good. Stella knows how to put up a picnic.'

'I wish she had come. It would have been fun all together.'

He turned to look down at me. 'You mustn't let Stella's fonny habits bother you, Izzy. That's yust the way she is. I have had to come to terms with it.'

'But does she –' I stopped.

'Does she what?'

I blurted out what had been worrying me. 'Does she love you? I mean, really?'

I got his gentlest smile in the growing dusk. 'Oh, yes, I think so. In her way. This is nothing for you to worry about.'

Before the display began, the different groups of company employees were treated to separate parties on the terrace above the lawn. Their delicious smells came drifting over the river to us: grilling meat from the braaivleis for the whites, which came with salads and puddings and drinks on trestle tables draped in long white tablecloths; spicy turmeric and hot chillie from the curry supper with sambals for the Indians; bubbling gravy from the cauldrons of steaming phuthu and stew set well to one side at the back for the black millworkers. One big party for everyone would not even have been considered; people knew their places in Two Rivers in the Fifties.

On the riverbank where we sat, the town families who had brought their own picnics were setting up folding chairs and delving into food baskets and trying to get excited kids to settle down. If you watched carefully, you could also see a surreptitious uncorking of beers and half-jacks of brandy and cane spirit and jerepigo; for some, the celebration on the riverbank would go on all night.

We sat watching the people gathering round us and up on the bridge, whites and Indians for once mixed together because this was public ground and the Whites Only/Slegs Blankes signs hadn't begun to go up everywhere as they would soon. The few Zulu families sat in a group well to one side, however, the silent children watching everything with awed eyes. Across the river I could see Mrs McFadyen dressed in pale blue linen slacks with a matching cardigan over her shoulders and her hair in a smooth blonde pageboy, standing next to a distinguished-looking man in a navy blazer and a maroon cravat. Both had drinks in their hands; he was talking to a small circle of people who were listening with deferential interest.

I turned to Finn. 'Is that Titch's father?'

He nodded. 'Major Harold McFadyen, yeneral manager of the Herald Company. They say he's a fair boss, keen on team spirit, oplifting his employees via education and so forth. But I find him much too pompous for my taste. He was a major during the war and likes to be called by his title.'

'He doesn't look much like Titch.'

'Nay, and I don't think they get along either, because the Major can't onderstand why Titch is such a poor rugby and cricket player. Calls him a boffin.'

'What's that?'

Finn chuckled. 'Scientist to us commoners.'

The crowd around us was growing, people packing closer and closer. Most of the Indians were wearing their new clothes for Deepavali; smells of soap and unfamiliar perfumes and coconut hair oil eddied around us, adding to the strangeness of the deepening night as they mingled with the smells of the different foods people were eating. Across the river, groups were beginning to move to the edge of the terrace and rugs were being spread for the children of the white staff to sit at the top of the lawn. The chatter all round us died down to a murmur of anticipation. Two Rivers waited for its annual free fireworks display, Company-bestowed like all its public buildings. Nobody could have guessed that it would never happen that way again; the Easter Riot wiped out years of trust between neighbours, making them afraid to sit together again in one place.

But that terrible night was five months away, and the crowd cheered as the bonfire blazed up with its guy made of sacking tied over crossed broomsticks gradually toppling over into the middle. True to what Stella had predicted, several young men had taken off their jackets and were vying with each other to light the fireworks lined up on the lawn. You could see their intent faces right across the river, lit from below by match flames held under the blue touch papers and then falling back and yelling with triumph as the fireworks exploded into a fizzing, whirling, sparkling dance of brilliant light. The crowd gasped as crackers and jumping jacks stuttered out salvos of bangs, and rockets zoomed up to climax in jewelled starbursts against the black velvet sky. The best firework was kept until last: a fat cardboard column that went on spitting out a succession of coruscating fountains and Roman candles that must have gone on for five minutes before it ended with a loud pop in a glittering silver *fleur de lys*. Its image glowed redly inside my eyelids long after people had shaken off the enchantment of the spectacle and begun packing up all round us.

The firework smell of phosphorus and gunpowder smoke was drifting over the water now as we began to walk home in the human river of townspeople. On the company terrace, the white children were being hustled to bed by their nannies while their parents strolled back to the trestle tables for more drinks; the Indian staff and the black millworkers were hurrying for their buses.

Along the main road the uptown shops were shuttered and dark as usual, but further down towards Coolietown it looked as though a fun fair had suddenly started up. Rows of glowing clay lamps lined the roofs and shopfronts and the houses down the gravel side-roads, their little orange cat's tongues of flame shuddering and licking upwards into the hot night. I couldn't believe the change. The shabby buildings and shacks that I passed every day, sometimes holding my breath so I wouldn't have to smell them, had been transformed into a lamplit fairyland where throngs of people shouted and laughed and greeted and kissed each other, hooters blared from inching garlanded cars and sinuous music wove in and out of windows and doorways. Finn and I lingered a while to enjoy this second spectacle, looking down from the pharmacy steps, but he said all too soon, 'We should go in now. Stella will be wondering what's happened to us.'

'Can't we stay and watch? Please.' It was unbearable to have to leave the cheerful open-air celebration effervescing all round us.

He shook his head. 'For me, nay. If I must be honest, I always feel like an intruder at other people's festivals. It's not that I feel onwelcome, it's yust that I know I'm standing outside what's happening and this must take something away from their enjoyment.'

'Oh.' I felt my eagerness subsiding. He was probably right. 'Would it be OK if I watched from the mango tree for a bit?'

'Of course.'

He went into the house and I climbed up to my favourite branch in the darkness and looked down unseen on hundreds of people enjoying themselves, but it wasn't much fun. Before I got down again, I looked over the wall into the Soobramonys' yard. The grandmother and parents must have been out somewhere, because the children were holding their own private ceremony on the back steps: a ring of intent cinnamon faces crouched over a single oil lamp, each holding out a piece of over-ripe fruit, praying for Lakshmi to bring them better fortune.

When I went inside, Stella was sitting on the back veranda

166

out of earshot of the noise in the road, listening to a symphony concert on the wireless. It was her protest against Guy Fawkes and Deepavali and having to live behind a shop in a part of town that embarrassed her. Finn had made tea and I sat at the kitchen table drinking it with him; he took her a cup and she looked up with a brief smile of thanks, but wouldn't join us. Pointing at her ears, she gestured, 'I'm listening.' The set of her shoulders as she turned away to sip her tea and gaze out at the back yard through the jasmine curtain said, 'I may have been here alone all evening, but I've been perfectly happy.'

Maybe Lakshmi visited her that night, because she certainly achieved prosperity in her lifetime and a stylish, gaunt beauty. I lay awake as long as I could keep my leaden eyelids open, watching the tongues of flame licking up from the ten clay lamps on my windowsills in the childish hope that they would illuminate the ghostly shape of a visiting goddess in the darkness. But my wishes were in vain, or perhaps I got the ritual wrong. Lakshmi did not come even after I fell asleep, because I was never to be either beautiful or rich.

Isabel

The phone rings a few seconds after she puts the receiver down from sending the telegram and Isabel snatches it up again, hoping to hear his voice coming down the restored line from the mountains to reassure her.

But it is her eldest daughter, Chryssa. 'Mum? How are you?'

Dismay robs her for a moment of speech.

'Mum? Are you there?'

She adjusts to her mother mode. 'Of course. I'm fine. How are you, love?'

'OK. Are you going to be at home this afternoon?'

From long experience she recognises the tone of voice: Chryssa is going to ask her for something. And today, of all days, she is not in the mood for other people's problems. Trying to fob her off, she says, 'I'm pretty involved right now.'

'Don't talk to me about being involved.' Chryssa sounds grumpy and harassed. She is a fashion buyer who travels a great deal, often to exotic places like Hong Kong and Brazil. She has been married for several years to a young accountant and they are both very ambitious. 'We want to make it to the top in our careers,' is how they put it, confident that success is simply a matter of aiming high and hustling harder than the competition. They live in an ultra modern townhouse in a high-security complex because it offers protection for their expensive toys: 'executive' cars, imported hi-fi, video and camera equipment, personal computer plus a laptop for business trips, and a kitchen bristling with appliances and gadgets. Isabel feels slightly nauseous when she visits them, thinking what they must spend on hire purchase payments every month.

She says, 'Have you been away a lot recently? We haven't seen you for ages.' Listening to her words – second nature for mothers of adult children in their critical twenties – she thinks, That sounds far too reproachful. She'll think I'm dropping hints when I'm not. What I'd really like to imply is that I don't approve of her lifestyle; it's far too stressful.

'I've been in Taiwan and Singapore, and there was a seminar in Cape Town –' Chryssa's voice trails off. She doesn't want to make a lot of lame excuses. The real reason why she seldom comes home is that she finds her parents' lives so boring.

Isabel can't resist saying, 'Do you and Tom manage to schedule the occasional night together at home?'

'Oh, for God's sake, Mum. I never was cut out to be a housewife, you know that.' Chryssa sounds more defensive than usual, and the faint prickle of warning her mother feels is strengthened when she goes on, 'I'd really like to come and see you this afternoon.'

Isabel bites back the impulse to say, 'What for?' and says instead, 'Aren't you working?'

'Got the afternoon off. I need some advice.'

She thinks, Oh, hell, it's important then. Chryssa hasn't asked for her opinion since she was sixteen. She says, 'Come around tea-time. I should be finished then.'

'Finished what?'

She hasn't told any of the children about her writing, not even Ralphie on his Saturday visits home. It's too new and too personal, but more importantly she doesn't want to have to admit defeat to anyone but herself if she doesn't finish the story. So far she has managed to keep her notes and the completed chapters hidden from George inside a pile of folded sheets in the linen cupboard, which he never goes near because he considers that making beds is women's work. She has stopped writing when he's at home, hoping that he will forget he saw her doing it. She couldn't bear to have him pawing through the memories that are accumulating chapter by chapter, calling them 'scribbles'. Her confidence is growing with the increasing pile of handwritten pages.

169

She says, 'Oh, just a project I'm working on,' and hopes that Chryssa will assume it is for her charity committee.

'I won't be a nuisance, coming then?'

There is an uncharacteristic note of uncertainty in Chryssa's voice and Isabel's prickle of warning turns into a jangle of alarm. 'No, of course not,' she says. 'See you around four.'

'I'll bring something from the bakery.'

'That would be nice.' Putting the phone down, she thinks, Unusually thoughtful of her. I hope there's nothing wrong – trouble between her and Tom, perhaps. I don't know what I'd do if she wanted to come back home.

Isabel has two friends with severe empty-nest blues which she finds hard to understand. Even before she met her lover again, she had begun to tire of playing the roles of wife and mother that can overwhelm, so insidiously, the women trapped in them. She loves her children, of course, but she had begun to feel that she had done what she could for them; it was time that they spread their wings and flew away into their own lives. She found herself thinking, I want to spend time on myself and have some fun and explore new avenues before I get too decrepit to enjoy them. She had intended to go to an adult education centre for training to equip her for what the women's magazines call 'a prime-time job' despite George's sneering, 'Who would want you now?' But then the miracle happened in the airport café and the new avenue became her new love.

All she wants to do now is reassure herself that he is not ill or in trouble, and to get to him as soon as possible; the thought of Chryssa coming to dump a problem in her lap gives her a feeling of guilty ennui. The trouble with being a mother, she thinks crossly, is that you can never resign the bloody job. Children expect you to be continuously there for them, dependable old Mum, always good for a shoulder to cry on even if her advice comes out of the ark. They never think of asking about your problems, or dream that you might want the same sort of independence that they fought you so hard for in their teenage years.

Age negates you as much as youth does, she thinks, remembering how angry she used to get when her parents didn't introduce her to other adults. You don't change inside – the emotions keep on seething away – but with the arrogance of their youth, your children perceive you as old and boring and past it. I wonder what they'd say if they knew their dependable old Mum was meeting a secret lover?

The thought makes her laugh despite the nagging anxiety about him that has begun to give her a dull pain in her lower belly. She is still chuckling when her second daughter, Janine, phones. There is a short hesitation before she says, 'Mum? Is that you?'

'Of course. How are you, love?'

'You're laughing!'

'Why shouldn't I be?'

'Is there someone there with you?'

'No.'

'Are you just sitting there laughing on your own?'

Isabel feels her brief moment of good humour draining away. 'Why shouldn't I laugh on my own?'

There is silence from the other end before Janine says in a hushed voice, 'Mum? Are you all right?'

'Of course I'm all right!'

There is a longer silence, then, 'Are you mad with me for not getting in touch for so long? It's just that I've been so busy. It's the athletics season.' She is a Phys Ed teacher at a large high school and lives with a divinely good-looking professional cricketer. She knows that he can't resist young blonde cricket groupies while on tour, but says she loves him too much to give him up.

Isabel can see much heartache ahead for this loyal, stubborn daughter who believes in the myth that love can conquer everything. But now she thinks, The self-centredness of children! Janine still assumes that my life revolves around her and Chryssa and Ralphie. She sighs and says, 'I am not mad with you. I am very pleased to hear from you. How is the Gorgeous One?' She always calls the cricketer that because she has watched him admire himself in every mirror he passes, just like George used to.

'He's been away in Bloemfontein the whole week.' Janine knows her mother doesn't like him, and why. She dismisses it as prejudice in an older person who doesn't understand

171

modern relationships. To herself she rationalises his infidelities as, Some Men Just Need More Space.

'Not much fun for you.'

'I've been too busy to notice.' She certainly won't admit to her mother that she has cried herself to sleep every night because he hasn't phoned. 'But I don't want to talk about me. Has Chryssa phoned? Did she say she was coming round?'

'Yes, a few minutes ago. She's coming for tea.' The alarm bells are positively yelling now; the fact that both her daughters have phoned within minutes of each other means definite trouble.

'Can I come too?'

'Of course. What's wrong?'

'Tell you later. I've got to run. 'Bye.'

The phone clatters down and Isabel is left with her double burden of worry. Despite all the mental big talk about being tired of her role as a mother, she spends the next hour in a state of dread, wondering what her daughters are coming to talk about while she tries again and again to get through to the mountain cottage. There is no point in trying to write; her thoughts and emotions are whirling in confused circles.

12

Christmas wasn't such a big deal in the Fifties in South Africa as it is today. Shops had not yet realised its full commercial potential, and only broke out their decorations a desultory week or so into December. Children could still believe in Father Christmas without having their faith continually tested by unconvincing placebos in moulting cotton wool; then, he was a benevolent old gent with a real white beard and attentive (if hairy) ears for whispering secret wishes into, usually installed in a department store grotto surrounded by cardboard towers of lucky-packet boxes. The aural affliction of non-stop smoochy carols still awaited the coming of muzak, though the more enterprising establishments in Coolietown had gramophones cranking out an eclectic medley of Indian music, Bing Crosby, mbaqanga and tiekiedraai that grew more frenetic as the climax of the year approached.

Since December is one of our hottest months, Christmas is a peculiar feast here anyway. Snowmen and holly and reindeer appear on our Christmas cards and cakes, but the holiday that evolved from the icy northern winter solstice via a child's birth in a stable is celebrated in the full blast of the southern sun. And tradition can be senseless to the point of absurdity when the weather is out of step: southern Father Christmases pour with sweat, the idea of a sleigh is ridiculous, roast turkey and gravy are too hot, and plum pudding too rich. Many older Natal people then did make a show of listening to the King's speech on Christmas afternoon, though I think it was more to reassure themselves of their pukka British origins than out of affection for the ailing monarch in distant Sandringham.

Finn and Stella kept some traditions, however. She told me

173

that they held their celebration on Christmas Eve in the Norwegian way, singing carols round a small decorated fir tree, then handing gifts out afterwards over coffee and Christmas cake. She and Eslina and I made the cake together the day after the convent term ended, Stella having said with a sigh at breakfast, 'We'd better get it over with.'

'Don't you like making Christmas cake?' I had always helped Ma and loved the whole process, from flouring the dried fruit and nuts to adding the sharp-smelling brandy to the knobbly cake mixture to lining the baking tin with five layers of buttered brown paper. My reward was sole licking rights over the huge scraped bowl, one of the few perks of being the only child at home. And then there would be the comforting spicy aroma of fruit cake baking for long hours in the oven, filling our too-quiet home with the promise, at least, of family celebrations.

Stella shrugged over the list of ingredients she had begun to jot down for me to go and buy at Ismail's. 'You know I'm not crazy about cooking.'

Over by the sink, Eslina gave what I always thought of as her molasses chuckle, because it sounded rich and slow and dark brown. 'Ai, Nkosazana. This cake you make so nice.'

She called Stella 'Nkosazana', the respectful name for an unmarried woman, when it should have been 'Nkosikazi'. Maybe it was prophetic. Eslina must have had some sort of window into the future because she could predict things that would happen – small things like a parcel coming in the post and thunderstorms and unexpected visits from people. Once she stopped ironing in the middle of the afternoon and said she had to run home quickly because one of her children was going to hurt himself, and sure enough he fell out of a tree just as she was hurrying up the path towards him.

'At least it's a foolproof recipe – even I can't mess it up.' Stella gave one of her deprecating barks of laughter. 'And the effort is worth it because fruit cake lasts. I get at least two months off before I have to worry again about what to give people I actually like when they come to tea.'

One of the banes of her life was the number of women with nothing better to do who got dressed up and went calling round town, even to the house behind the pharmacy on the shabby fringes of Coolietown, expecting to be offered tea and something to eat. She was too busy to play ladies and sit about making inane conversation, she said, and developed fobbing-off tactics that included serving tea in chipped cups, cheap brown government sugar and shop biscuits. 'I don't care if they call me a slut,' she'd say. 'I just can't stand having my precious time wasted by those patronising old bags who only come because they're quizzy about what it's like to live here.' The Christmas cake, she explained, would be saved for the people she really wanted to see, like Lilah McFadyen.

I kept quiet, not wanting to disillusion her before the cake was even made; I was a notorious secret nibbler of fruit cake and could guarantee it wouldn't last past the first week in January.

'Which reminds me,' she was going on. 'Lilah spoke to me after giving out the end-of-year prizes at the convent yesterday. She's organised a party for Titch on Saturday the thirteenth, the day after he gets home from boarding school, and wants you to come. He'll be bringing some of his schoolfriends home.'

I thought, Oh hell, here we go again. I'd only had one conversation with this boy – who'd been quite pleasant, admittedly, after the initial hostility – but I hardly knew him. Now his mother was cooking up another painful social occasion where I'd almost certainly make a fool of myself. In front of a whole lot of other boys from his snob school too.

I burst out, 'You can't make me go. I won't!'

'Aren't you lonely, mooning about by yourself all the time?'

'No! I'm perfectly happy. I love being able to explore on my own, and it's great to be with you and Finn after just Ma and Pa all those –' The words died on my lips. Pa was dead now, and poor Ma locked up in a place she couldn't get out of until the doctors agreed that she was better again. How heartless could a daughter be, criticising the life we'd had together? I turned away so Stella wouldn't see my eyes getting shiny.

She understood, though, and got up and came and put her arms round me from behind. 'It's all right to feel that way, Izz. Being alone at home with old parents can't ever have been easy for you. That's why I want to help you make friends of your own age here in Two Rivers. I'm not trying to meddle in your life or make decisions for you, just to smooth things a bit. Give this one party a try, please. I promise you that if you don't enjoy it, I'll drop the whole thing. Just try this once. For me. For Finn. He wants you to be happy too.'

How could I keep resisting? Specially after she went out and bought me, as advance Christmas presents, a pair of white shoes (my first high heels, only an inch-and-a-half – I measured them – but a long-desired milestone) and the white angora bunny jacket I'd been eyeing every time I passed the 'Latest Teenage Wear' window. They would dress up the red skirt and boat-neck blouse and give me confidence arriving at the party, she said. She noticed a lot more than you expected, Stella did.

My hands were clammy with terror as Finn drove me through the company gates and up the crunching gravel drive to the McFadyens' house on the sticky-hot evening of the thirteenth. Though Stella would have loved to come with us for a glimpse of the party, she had nobly declined so I could sit inside with the hood up instead of in the dickey seat at the back where my hair would get blown around. She had really entered into the spirit of the occasion, first helping me to wash and set my raggedly growing hair with wire-mesh rollers so that it brushed out into curls, then making me sit down on the bed when I was dressed so she could put on some makeup.

When I bleated, 'I don't want any. I'll feel like an idiot,' she laughed and said, 'Of course you've got to wear some. You don't want to be a mouse among the swans do you?' and started touching up my eyebrows with a brown pencil.

'You mean an ugly duckling,' I muttered, trying to see what she was doing in the hand mirror.

'Trust me,' she said, telling me to open my mouth and stretch my lips over my teeth so she could use a sample Max Factor lipstick from the pharmacy, chosen to match the red of my skirt. It felt like congealed blood.

'How can I? You don't wear lipstick.' I tried in vain to squirm away. Stella had a very strong grip.

'I'm not as pale and wan as you are,' she said, coaxing me to look in the mirror at the improvement a bit of colour made. 'Let's try some eyeshadow as well. Sit still and close your eyes.' She was dabbing at a round cake of glittery blue powder with a little brush.

'No! Sis! Pa says that blue stuff on girls' eyes makes them look like monkeys' balls.' The only time I'd tried a touch of discreet makeup (after a public sneer by Evelyn Simpson about kids who didn't understand what sophistication even *meant*), he'd ordered me to wash the muck off my face.

'Pa's not here any more, Izz,' Stella said gently. 'You don't have to abide by his prejudices; you can cultivate your very own. Just let me try a touch of blue, and if you don't like it I'll wipe it off. But see what it looks like first before you say no, OK?'

Goebbels would have rejoiced in her genius for persuasion. When she had finished and I was allowed to look through half-closed lashes at the palest blue skylids she had given me, I thought, Actually they don't look too bad. In my new curly hairstyle with a made-up face rising out of a floaty cloud of white angora, I looked quite different from the everyday Isabel. Almost – what was the word? – svelte.

'Does my handiwork meet with your approval then, madam?' Her expression was smug.

'I suppose it's all right.'

I tried to make it sound as if I didn't care either way, but I didn't fool her. As she hustled me on to the veranda where Finn was waiting, plopping at his pipe and jingling the car keys in his pocket, she was trumpeting, 'Ta-ra! Doesn't she look good? Despite extremely stiff opposition, I might add.'

He smiled round the pipe stem. 'Yust lovely. You'll knock dead all those smart boys.'

Stella shooed us off. 'Better hurry, or you'll be late. Have a wonderful time, Izz.'

Though I'd practised walking in the new shoes to get used to wearing heels, they felt wobbly going across the uneven surface of the courtyard. My fragile confidence lasted as far as the other side of the garden gate, where it faded to panic at the sight of the car waiting to whisk me up the road into Two Rivers society. I wailed, 'Jeepers, Finn, I haven't got a clue how to dance. And I'll die of embarrassment being up close to boys I don't know. I'll probably stomp all over their feet or slip in these new shoes and fall down with my broeks showing, and they'll think I'm just a green little kid. *Please* don't make me go.'

He stuffed his still-smoking pipe into his pocket to open the car door, and gave me a reassuring hug. 'You agreed to give this party a try, Izzy, and you know what? I think honestly that you might surprise yourself and enjoy it.'

'But I won't know a soul there.'

'You know Titch.'

'Hardly at all. I'm useless with boys, anyway. I never know what to say to them, so I end up just standing there like a dweet until they give up and go away. And I've got these stupid freckles on this stupid nose that goes up in a blob at the end. And I don't even know how to do the London Jive.' I was babbling my social nightmares out all at once.

He turned me to face him and put his tobacco-smelling hands on my shoulders. 'Have I lied to you ever?'

'No.'

'Then listen to me. You're an intelligent, special girl and I've never seen you looking lovelier. Stella has truly waved a magic wand. You can handle this party easy if you remember what I said about boys having the same problems. You're not alone, right?'

I nodded my bent head.

'And this I promise faithfully. I'll come by the McFadyens' house halfway through the evening at around ten to check that everything's going all right. If there is even the smallest problem, yust make me a signal and I'll bring you straight home.'

He repeated the promise as we went up the steps between the crouching marble lions and down the passage towards the sound of Theresa Brewer nasally belting out *The Tennessee Waltz*. 'I'll come by later. Courage, Izzy. You'll be fine.'

He squeezed my hand and we went into the drawing room, which had been cleared of furniture and carpets except for a radiogram piled with records and the usual table with cooldrinks and fruit punch and bowls of peanuts and chips. (No beer then; boys drank liquor, of course, but out of half-jacks in crumpled brown paper packets that they hid outside under bushes in the garden when they arrived. Just as the more daring of them carried condoms whose worn wrappings betrayed how long they'd been on display in the owner's pocket.)

Major and Mrs McFadyen were hovering by the door that led out on to the veranda trying without success to look genial and relaxed: she in a royal blue taffeta cocktail dress and he tall and moustached and eagle-eyed in a tweed jacket, his hair combed back in shining undulations. I wondered what it must be like for Titch who loved snakes and fishing and muddy riverbanks to live in such a formal household, and sent up a small prayer of thanks for my comfortable if undistinguished family.

Mrs McFadyen greeted me by wrapping her scratched hands warmly round my ice-cube fingers. 'We're so pleased to see you here, Isabel. Thank you for coming, dear.' She leaned towards me and whispered, 'The little buggers behave less like barbarians when they're forced to dress up and be civil.'

I managed to crack a feeble smile, but the first half-hour of that party remains a blur in my mind of introductions to strange boys in school ties and blazers, assured-looking girls whispering together and wearing much more makeup than I was, taking more sips of Coke than I'd had in my whole life, and the salty crunch of chips and peanuts which I kept reaching for to keep my hands and mouth busy. Several couples started dancing, twirling through steps that remained a mystery to me because I'd never tried them. I felt my Finn-bolstered confidence crumbling by the minute; how could I possibly last the two hours until he came?

Then I saw Titch being chivvied in through the door by his mother and he sidled round the room towards me and said under his breath, 'Could you help me out by having this dance with me? Though I'd better warn you first, I never know what to do with my feet.'

I stood there gaping at him. It was a revelation. Finn was right. This boy, unfamiliar in a blazer with slicked down hair instead of a pith helmet, felt the same way as I did: forced by the well-meaning adults in his life to play their social games.

179

He shifted from one black lace-up shoe to the other. 'Well? You don't have to if you don't want to, but Mum will be on my back all evening if I don't try at least once. And I don't know any of these other girls she's lured here. They look bloody terrifying.'

A flood of relief that I wasn't considered bloody terrifying released my tongue and generated a nervous giggle. 'I think so too.'

'You want to give dancing a shot?'

'Sorry. Can't dance to save my life.'

His tense scowl relaxed. 'Neither can I. But if we shuffle around for a few minutes with each other, we could get the agony over and done with.'

I nodded. 'I'm bok for a try. As long as you're not expecting Cyd Charisse.'

'Wouldn't have the first clue what to do with her. Watch out for your toes, hey?'

He took my hand in a fierce clammy grip and put his other arm gingerly round my waist, and we ventured on to the floor in an inconspicuous corner. I think we were both surprised to find how simple it was to copy what the others were doing – and it was made easier by the fact that we were learning to do it together. Titch was only an inch or so taller than me and he moved rather jerkily at first, but we soon got into a sort of rhythm and my feet in their new high heels did more or less what I told them to do without wobbling too much. It wasn't long before we'd shed the blazer and the bunny jacket and were attempting the London Jive (which turned out to be a piece of cake) and chatting away about our schools and Two Rivers. It wasn't even embarrassing being so close to a boy; Titch smelled of soap and clean cotton shirt, and his scowl faded as our steps became more automatic. Over his shoulder, I saw his mother give me a large wink before she and the Major went out on to the veranda to join some other parents for a drink, looking smug.

Titch and I launched ourselves simultaneously on to the social scene that night, and I hope he was as grateful to me as I was to him for making the awkward transition from wallflower to dancing partner so painless.

After what seemed like a few minutes but turned out to be

nearly half an hour, he let me go and said with a grin, 'Thanks, Isabel-Necessary. That wasn't so bad, hey? Want to try some grub?'

I found myself grinning back. 'Lead me to it, Timothy Montague Wotherspoon –'

The scowl came back. 'Watch it.'

'– McFadyen. Otherwise known as Titch. No, it wasn't bad at all. We should do it again sometime.'

I remember the rest of that evening in short vivid sequences like you get when you use the skip search button with a video:

The feast spread out in the banquet-sized dining room . . . my first Paul Jones . . . talking to several of the assured-looking girls, who turned out to be quite friendly . . . being introduced to Titch's friends, and finding that guys from posh boys-only boarding schools were different from the few I had met in the mining town. They didn't flinch if you mentioned Shakespeare, but their smooth party manners couldn't quite conceal an almost total ignorance of girls . . . Dancing in the increasingly muggy room until my feet ached and my new makeup dissolved in sweat and my blouse stuck to my back under my partners' hands . . . Sneaking out into the garden with a group of conspirators for an illicit swig – again, my first – of Old Brown Sherry, and just managing to avoid a posse of patrolling parents as we snuck back in again.

And most memorable of all, meeting the divine James Singleton.

He was the son of Jimmy Singleton, the compound manager at the sugar mill, an ex-merchant seaman with a gammy leg and a foul temper who kept the labour force under tight control. His wife, Rita, her henna'd hair frizzy with too-frequent home perms, worked in the bar at the Cosy Hotel. This unlikely pair had produced a young Greek god whose talent for maths and cricket had won him a scholarship to the same exclusive school as his father's boss's son.

Looking back, James must have led an unbearably schizophrenic life between the sooty company bungalow at the gates of the compound and the gracious creeper-covered red brick buildings of his school in the Midlands. Maybe it was why he seemed so cool and remote and superior; maybe his mechanism for coping with home circumstances that included alcoholism, rage and physical violence was to distance himself from what was happening around him. Whatever the reason, it was wildly attractive. Girls threw themselves at him, gathering around him at parties and begging him to come to their school dances and lying in wait for him when he walked down the main road so they could pretend to bump into him by mistake. I know, because I saw them do it – because I began to do it myself.

James asked me for the second-to-last dance at Titch's party, *I'm In The Mood For Love*, and when the lights went out pulled me closer so that for a few magic minutes we were dancing cheek to cheek. Bewitched by the music and the dizzy feeling of being a genuine teenager at last, snuggle-dancing with other teenagers in a darkened room, I fell instantly in love. After Finn came at midnight, a tall stooped silhouette standing in the doorway with a group of fathers as Titch and I swung confidently through the last dance together (it was always *Goodnight Sweetheart* in those days), I floated down the steps between the crouching marble lions and into the car.

Before he started up, he said, 'I came at ten, you know, but you didn't see me.'

Remembering my vehement initial opposition to what had become the most wonderful evening of my life, I blushed and said, 'Sorry. The party was OK, like you said it would be.'

'Yust OK?' His blue eyes were star sapphires in the car's darkness.

How could I convey the heady joy of being able to dance and actually converse with boys at last? I burst out, 'It was great! Amazing! I had a fabulous time.'

His warm hand covered mine. 'I'm so glad, Izzy. It's good to be growing up, ya?'

We drove home under a full moon reflected like shivering quicksilver on the river. Stella had hot cocoa waiting for us, and they listened smiling while I poured out what I could remember of the party through my besotted haze. I didn't tell them about James. He was my secret to hug to myself. Just getting him to say hullo to me when we passed each other on the pavement would be my goal for the next few weeks, and perhaps there would be more parties and dances in the dark . . .

Beautiful, unfathomable James. He dominated my dreams in Two Rivers from that night onwards.

Isabel

Chryssa is on the doorstep at five to four, carrying a briefcase in one hand and a square white box in the other. Isabel has always thought of her as her Huguenot daughter, because she has the dark eyes and dark brown curly hair and olive skin of Pa's family. She also has an eldest child's bossy impatience and drive; when she comes home she sweeps through their lives like a fast-moving thunderstorm, crackling with opinions and a fizzy energy that Isabel finds exhausting.

Today, however, she looks pale and tired and her rumpled linen jacket is carelessly slung over her shoulders. Chryssa as a rule is meticulous about her clothes; if you want to be a fashion trade executive, she says, you've got to look the part.

'Hullo, love.' Greeting her with a warm hug, Isabel tells herself, Put that non-ringing telephone out of your mind. Daughters in trouble take precedence over lovers. But the chiding is not necessary. When Chryssa leans into her and buries her face in her shoulder, a little girl again seeking comfort, her own worries are erased in an instant.

The words are pouring out. 'Oh, Mum. I'm in such a fix. I don't know what to do.'

Isabel murmurs, 'Come along and we'll talk. I've got the tea trolley waiting.'

'The geriatric panacea, tea and sympathy.' Chryssa's eyes are full of tears as she looks up through spiky eyelashes. 'As though they can help. This isn't just a little problem, Mum. I'm in deep shit.'

Isabel suppresses her usual irritated response: I wish you wouldn't use words like that. Instead she says, drawing her daughter in through the door with an arm round her shoulders, 'Go and sit on the veranda while I make the tea

184

and get a plate for this –' she peers under the white cardboard lid '– tart. Almond, too. You've remembered that it's my favourite.'

'Despite not doing home duty for so long, you mean?' Chryssa breaks away and slouches down the passage towards the veranda with its comfortable basket chairs, looking more like a miserable teenager than a career woman.

Isabel thinks, That remark is too much, and says, 'Home duty! For God's sake, what a repulsive idea. I'd hate to think that you and Janine and Ralphie only come home because you feel you have to.'

Chryssa swings round in the doorway with a guilty look on her face because it is close to the truth. 'I didn't mean it *that* way. I just –'

Familiar for over twenty-five years with the guilty looks on children's faces and the fear that lies behind them, Isabel forces herself to smile. 'Of course you didn't. Sit down, love. I'll have the tea ready in a moment, then we'll talk.'

In the kitchen waiting for the kettle to boil, she faces another unpleasant moment of truth. They've been cropping up with disturbing frequency since she started writing the story; digging around in one's past inevitably becomes a process of self-appraisal. She can't help comparing the dreams and hopes of her younger self – the bright, inquisitive Isabel who showed so much promise in her teens – with her dead-end marriage. She thinks, I've become someone my own children visit out of a sense of duty. A dreary old has-been. How could I have let it happen? How could I? Where's my sense of pride, dammit?

She surges on to the veranda pushing the loaded tea trolley, intent on saying, I will not be treated like an old dog you feel sorry for! But Chryssa is sitting on one of the chairs with her shoulders hunched, crying over the briefcase on her lap, her feet splayed like a bereft child's in their beautiful Italian leather shoes.

And the doorbell rings again.

13

While I dreamed every night of James Singleton, I spent my weekday mornings that December helping Finn and Govind with the Christmas rush in the pharmacy, and a good many of the afternoons with Titch.

Our expeditions began on the Tuesday following his party. I was walking past the town square with its admonishing obelisk when I saw a khaki pith helmet bobbing above a bed of red cannas. It could only be Titch. When I got closer I saw that he was gathering canna seeds: stripping them out of the spiky dry seed pods and dropping them into a small glass jar that hung from the snake-clasp belt of his khaki shorts by a piece of string.

I stood behind him and said, 'Hi.'

Turning round and squinting up at me to see who it was, he said, 'Oh, it's you. Narrow escape. I had to duck down because I've just spotted yukky Linda Todd walking past and she gives me the creeps.'

Feeling pleased that I didn't give him the creeps, I said, 'What are you collecting those for?' Since he was supposed to be such a top scholar, I thought he might be working on a special botany project.

But Titch was always surprising; he never did what you expected him to do. He stood up saying, 'They're for my pea shooter. A well-aimed canna seed stings like hell.' Before screwing on the jar's lid, he held out a handful to show me; they were round and black and hard like tiny cannon balls.

'Isn't it rather a childish pastime, pea shooting?'

'Maybe. But a silent missile is a useful weapon for pricking pomposities. I have a running battle going with some idiots at school who've been made prefects next year, and I need ammunition.'

186

'Jealous that you haven't been made one?' Since I had now been promoted from casual acquaintance to non-yukky dancing partner, I couldn't resist the dig.

The pith helmet gave an emphatic shake. 'Never. I'm allergic to school politics. Can't stand the way guys turn into little Hitlers when they're made prefects or head of house. Power goes to their heads the moment they put on their precious white blazers; they think they can lord it over the rest of humanity, specially the cringing little new poeps who have to scurry around fagging for them.' He was jiggling the bottle of seeds. 'I don't think I'm temperamentally suited to school. I can't wait to write Matric and get out into the real world and do something that matters.'

'Me too.' It was very much what I had felt on arriving in Two Rivers – maybe feeling like this was part of growing up? I remembered Stella saying, 'Besides spelling and my times tables, I can't remember a single useful thing school taught me.'

There was one of those short awkward silences that happen when you don't know someone very well yet, then Titch said, 'Hey, let's sit and talk for a bit. I've got enough seeds.' We sat on a nearby bench. Looking down as he untied the bottle from his belt, he said, 'Mum told me about your dad. I'm really sorry. Did you come down here because your mother went away on holiday afterwards?'

The casual assumptions of the well-off! My folks could hardly afford to go to the bioscope most of their lives, let alone go away on holiday. I felt my eyes pricking, but couldn't allow myself to cry in front of him and the Christmas shoppers crowding the hot pavements round the square. So I blinked hard to stop any tears sneaking out and said, 'No, she got sick.' I didn't feel ready to mention the loonybin yet. 'I'm just staying with Stella and Finn until she's better.'

'Lousy for you.'

I nodded, lifting a nonchalant hand to shade my eyes so he would think I was blinking because the sunlight was hurting them. 'But I like it here. It's different. Exciting, you know?'

'Two Rivers?' He looked sceptical.

'Better than a mining town, believe me.'

'Are you going to school here?'

187

'I'll be starting at the convent in January. Not my choice exactly, can't stand convents.'

'It's not so bad. I went to the kindergarten there when they took boys. At least you'll be living at home and not in a dormitory.' He jabbed a dusty sandal at the grass under the bench. 'Dormitories are bloody torture. Boarding schools should be abolished.'

There had been a time, thanks to Angela Brazil, when I had longed to go to boarding school and have midnight feasts and make apple-pie beds. It wore off after Evelyn Simpson told me the full unexpurgated version of *The Demon Headmistress* that she had found in the drawer of her father's bedside table. I didn't fancy being tied naked to my bed and whipped. I said, 'What's the Mother Superior like at the convent?'

'She's OK. Quite a nice old bat, actually. But watch out for Sister Kathleen Killeally. She's got a pair of X-ray eyes in the back of her head, hidden by her veil. If you watch the bottom of her skirts, you'll see that she runs on rubber wheels too. Nobody ever hears her coming. Some people say that she's a robot manufactured in a secret nun factory in the Vatican . . .'

He regaled me with nun stories until Dicky Gould went shuffling past on his way to the Cosy Hotel bottle store, picking away at the papery scabs on his arm, and we got on to the subject of eccentrics in Two Rivers. Titch had lived there all his life and seemed to know everyone. As he talked I began thinking, People have to be nice to him because of who his father is. The Herald Company was equivalent to heaven in Two Rivers, and the man who ran it was God.

But then he said of the people who lived on the company estate, 'Of course, we're a protected species.'

'Protected from what?'

'The teeming multitudes, of course.' The greeny-blue glass eyes went opaque. 'You'd better get one thing about this town straight if you want to survive here: the hierarchy is strictly defined by your relationship to the sugar mill and its smells and noises. The native workers who come in from the reserves live in single compounds right bang up against it. The Indians who don't live in the nearby staff cottages live across the first river in Coolietown. The town whites are one step further away on this side of Coolietown, and the white company employees live in the most salubrious position of all, across both rivers in a giant garden which drowns out any mill smells and noises with the temerity to venture that far.'

I was impressed; I'd never heard anyone actually use the word 'temerity'. 'Finn and Stella live in Coolietown. On the edge of it, anyway.'

'They're different. They don't seem to give a damn about the hierarchy, or the fact that they're in trade.' He wasn't smiling. 'You'll only begin to understand real snobbery when you've met the company wives. Not my mother, though. You've probably noticed that she's different too.'

I nodded, thinking, He's wrong about Stella. She gives a whole lot of damns. But this Titch is no stuck-up rich boy. He's someone I can really talk to at last.

It was wonderful to have found a friend. The idea for our expeditions began as we walked back towards Coolietown that afternoon. When I moaned about how Stella and Finn wouldn't let me go exploring off the main road on my own, Titch said, 'Listen, if you like I'll phone when I'm going anywhere interesting and you can come too.'

'Forget it. They wouldn't let me.'

'Of course they will. They know you'd be perfectly safe with me. We management kids are royal game in Two Rivers; people's jobs depend on our fathers, specially mine. That's another of the reasons why I can't wait to get out of this dump: I can never do anything private or daring. Some-one's always watching, ready to run and tell tales. The same goes for Kesaval and his grandfather. That's why we like to get away to the river when we can.'

'Hasn't he got a father?'

Titch shook his head. 'He died in a car smash two years ago and Kesaval's the only grandson. It's very important to a Hindu family to have a son or a grandson because he has to say a whole lot of special prayers and stuff when the old guy kicks the bucket. If there isn't a son, they often adopt one.'

'Really?' Titch seemed to know almost as much as Finn; they were very alike in the way they watched what was happening around them and teased ideas and theories out of their observations.

189

'Old man Reddy runs Kesaval's life, makes him study a fixed number of hours every day and go to tutors after school so he can take the English exams to get into Oxford. The idea is to add lustre to the family and give him a major advantage over other businessmen when he comes home to take over the steam laundry. I couldn't stand to have my life all mapped out like that.'

'Maybe Mr Reddy just wants to do the best he can for Kesaval.' I was thinking, Jeepers, I wouldn't mind being sent to Oxford. I saw myself striding past ancient stone walls with an armful of books and a black gown flapping around me, deep in intellectual conversation with an amazingly hand-some don who was hanging on my every word. He'd have dark curly hair and hands with long slender fingers, and when he took off his horn-rimmed glasses to kiss me, his eyes would be like polished agates . . . I wasn't quite sure what colour agates were, but they sounded romantic.

'It's Kesaval's life. He should be able to decide for himself, not have to do what his family wants.' Titch was scowling.

'Is he clever enough to get into Oxford?'

'Clever *and* works. Unbeatable combination.'

It was the ideal moment to ask Titch about the focus of my dreams for the past few days. I said in my most casual voice, 'Is James Singleton clever too?'

'Sure. The three of us have been friends since we were kids. We used to mess around together a lot, but Singles has changed recently. Doesn't seem to want to come along any more.'

'Why, do you think?' Damn! I'd counted on seeing him in Titch's company.

I got a sideways glance. 'He's discovered girls.'

As my heart began to plummet I managed to gasp, 'Any girl in particular? I mean, has he got a girlfriend?'

'Hundreds, I think. He's always hanging around where he thinks they'll congregate. It's a bloody boring occupation. I'd much rather be fishing.'

'Where –' How could I put it so he wouldn't suspect my interest? 'I haven't seen girls hanging around in Two Rivers.'

'They don't. They go to South Beach in Durban and lie around on towels comparing cozzies and tans. Haven't you noticed how brown James is?'

I shook my head in misery, thinking, Stella and Finn might well let me hang around Two Rivers with the general manager's son, but they'll never let me go to the beach in Durban. I'm doomed to lead a boyfriendless life.

Bravely hiding my forlorn love, I plunged into my pharmacy work and went on expeditions with Titch during which he took me into parts of Two Rivers I'd never have been able to go to on my own. Stella said with her foxy look, 'Don't let it put you off, Izz, but I couldn't have chosen a better friend for you.'

I wonder now what she would have done if she'd found out about our illegal rides on Ram Pillay's *Sweet-Smelling Jasmine*? Stella's good intentions were always in conflict with her distaste for the great unwashed.

As Christmas drew closer, the Coolietown shops bulged with bargain-hunting housewives, whole families buying new clothes, workers spending their bonuses and the desperate looking for last-minute gifts. The sandy pathways down both sides of the main road were twin rivers of bobbing heads and ankle-deep in litter. While the crowds were mostly good-natured, there were inevitably scuffles and arguments that sometimes turned into fights with passers-by clotting in silent groups around them.

One afternoon sitting in the mango tree, I heard shouting and saw a small native boy wearing only ragged shorts running out of Ismail's General Dealers in my direction. He had a loaf of brown bread under his arm and one of the Indian counter assistants was in hot pursuit, shouting, 'T'ief! Come here! Give it back! Stop, man!'

Almost under my branch a group of Zulu millworkers who were walking towards the running boy, without saying a word to each other, closed ranks after he had run past and slowed to a stop, blocking the assistant from following him.

He yelled, 'Let me t'rough! T'at boy is stealing!' He was a plump, clerkish-looking man who had often served me; sweat was pouring down his face and neck and ballooning in damp patches all over his shirt.

The millworkers stood unmoving in a sullen line across the pathway. Heavy passing traffic prevented the pursuer from dodging into the road.

191

He bent his head to wipe his face on his sleeve, then spread his hands beige palms upwards and said in a pleading voice, 'Let me t'rough, please, man. My boss is telling me to catch him. He's stealing t'at bread from under my nose. I have to pay for it myself if I don't get it back. Please.' He looked as though he was about to burst into tears.

There wasn't a twitch from the line of men. They were burly labourers dressed in company overalls, each carrying two short knobbed sticks; all but one towered over the agitated Indian. I sat as still as I could, afraid of what would happen if an odd noise from above set off an explosion in the tense shoulders under the overalls.

'Please, man.' I could hear from the way his voice was running down that he was losing hope. 'It's not for me, you understand? Me too, I work for small money like you. It's my boss, nè? He's telling me.'

But the men just stood there shoulder to shoulder looking at him until he shrugged and turned away and went back to the shop. One of them said something in Zulu, punching the air with his fist knotted round his sticks, and they all laughed and went on.

It was a disturbing incident that made me remember what Kesaval had said about violence on that first silver morning by the river: 'You'll understand better when you've been in Two Rivers for a while.' Was this part of what he meant, this simmering antipathy between people that kept breaking out in hot little spurts of anger as though it couldn't be contained? Mr Reddy had spoken of it too.

I didn't want to sit looking into the street any more, and got down from the mango tree to go and wrap my presents for Stella and Finn. I'd bought her an English *House & Garden* magazine with some of the money I'd earned, and made her a milk jug cover with blue and white beads to match the kitchen. It had taken hours of pricked fingers and a lot of patience from Eslina, but I knew that Stella would appreciate the thought even if the stitching was wobbly. For Finn I'd splashed out on an expensive American lure for river fish, guaranteed by the assistant in the tackle shop as, 'Top-hole for the fishing man.'

Christmas Eve was hot and close. After we'd given Eslina

192

and Govind their presents and food parcels and they'd gone home, we sang carols on the front veranda round a decorated fir-tree branch stuck in a tin bucket of sand concealed with wrapping paper. Though there were only our three voices floating out into the darkening shadows of the courtyard, it felt good to be sitting there singing the lovely old words together, like we were a real family.

I wondered how Ma was getting on in that faraway green-painted place, lost in her own shadows. Aunty Mavis had put through a special trunk call during the afternoon to wish me Happy Christmas and tell me that she would be going to visit Ma the next day, and not to worry because she was doing fine. But of course I worried. One of the worst things was that Ma seemed to be getting more and more remote, receding into some distant past that had nothing to do with the new Isabel that I'd become in Two Rivers. Life was so full and absorbing that it was hard to remember what she looked like. I had to keep checking on her face in the photograph by my bed.

When I'd voiced this worry to Stella, who was ratty because the frame of the bargain chaise longue she was re-upholstering had turned out to be riddled with borer holes, she'd just said, 'It's quite natural, for God's sake.'

Singing *Away In A Manger* into the sultry night, remembering how I'd loved Ma's wavery voice singing it when I was little, I sent her a mind message. Happy Christmas, Ma. I'm thinking of you. I haven't forgotten, really . . . Would it reach her?

Our voices died away and Stella said, 'Coffee before presents, I think.' She got up and went into the kitchen to make it, while Finn taught me how to say 'God Jul' and sing *Silent Night* in Norwegian.

Real coffee was a treat then, not so long after the war. Finn's parents had gone to a lot of trouble sending him a special packet of coffee beans that had come all the way from Norway so the exiles in Africa could celebrate Christmas properly. And Stella enjoyed the coffee ritual; I'd watched her making it before. She hand-ground the beans first, then percolated the ground coffee in an elderly aluminium percolator with a glass lid so you could check the strength of the coffee bubbling up. That night she served it in three of her precious porcelain cups, on a lacy tray cloth with a silver cream jug and sugar bowl. She spent hours scratching around in junk shops for these relics of gracious living; all the patterns would be different and often the cups would have a fine crack or a slight chip, but it didn't matter, she said. They were beautiful anyway. She kept them in the glass-fronted display cabinet in the lounge, where Eslina dusted once a week with her tongue clamped between her teeth.

The Christmas cake made its debut with the coffee, decorated with a piece of artificial holly, 'In lieu of icing,' she said. I should have known she wouldn't go the whole hog with marzipan and royal icing like Ma had always done. I also should have known that she'd spoil it for nibbling. When I lifted up my slice, it reeked of brandy; she'd been dribbling the stuff on every week to keep the cake moist, she said, looking pleased with herself. 'It really improves the taste, don't you think?' Finn agreed enthusiastically and neither of them noticed my glum face. I'd counted on being able to white-ant that cake for weeks.

But the surprises waiting for me under the Christmas tree more than made up for the ruined slice I had to leave on the plate.

Stella gave me a long thin flat box with a delicate silver and marcasite necklace inside, saying, 'You need a decent bit of jewellery.'

'But you've already given me your presents! And it looks much too expensive.' Her impulsive generosity was getting embarrassing. She had had to spend her November salary on having the French drain outside the kitchen dug up and relaid, and I knew they were struggling with the repayments on their bank loan because I sometimes heard them arguing about it at night.

'It didn't cost anything. It's one of mine.' She was using her most off-hand tone. 'Pa gave it to me when I turned fifteen so I'm just handing it on, really.'

I moved my hand, making the coloured lights on the little Christmas tree flash from the necklace's many facets. Pa had never given me any jewellery. I wondered how much he'd loved Stella – more than me? If he had, throwing her out of his home must have been agony. Maybe she'd depleted his entire stock of daughterly love, turning him into the grumpy misogynist I remembered. 'Pa used to tell me that jewellery and makeup were unnecessary vanities.'

She let out a disbelieving snort and said, 'He always was an old hypocrite.'

'What do you mean?' He'd just been an elderly father to me.

'He'd say one thing and do another. He had a girlfriend once, did you know?'

Pa? A *girlfriend*? I was stunned.

'Some tittuping secretary in the mine office. Ma found out and left him, taking me with her. We lived with Aunty Mavis for years before the girlfriend dumped him, and Ma and he made it up. I always thought she was a fool to go back; she was much too good for him. You were the end result of the reconciliation.'

Understanding came like a bolt of lightning out of a clear blue sky. This was the reason for the big gap between Stella and me, and probably also the reason for Ma's headaches. I'd often had to tiptoe around the house when I got back from school in the afternoon because Ma was lying on her bed with the curtains drawn and what she called, 'One of my dreadful sick headaches.'

In the darkness Stella's face and spiky hair were defined only by a rim of lamplight from the living room window. I said, 'Did they love each other?'

'Who knows? Who cares?'

'I care. I'd hate to think that I was just a mistake. The unexpected result of saying sorry.' Here was a new anxiety to add to my others.

'I reckon it's a good thing we never know why we were conceived. Or how. When you think about it, most of us probably happened because our parents were just feeling randy that night. Conception is a totally random procedure.' She let out a bark of laughter.

But I wasn't laughing. It's hard to come to terms with the fact that your parents are sexual beings; harder still to look back and realise that whatever they'd had going between them had gradually died in front of your eyes, eroded by

195

betrayal and disappointment. Poor Ma. No wonder she had retreated to where she couldn't be reached. I hoped it wasn't forever.

Stella said, 'You needn't look so stricken, Izz. We were a perfectly normal family, good and bad in parts. Pa just grew difficult in his old age and you were the one who got it in the neck. He and Ma rubbed along quite well together most of the time.'

I stood up and went to kiss her. 'Thanks, Stell.' Maybe I could stop feeling guilty about being relieved Pa wasn't around any more to criticise.

Finn's Christmas presents for me were a Box Brownie and two rolls of film and a tiny bottle of French perfume which he gave to me saying, 'This is to use for the New Year's Eve party and the special boy.'

I gaped at him, speechless. How did he know about James?

He laughed. 'It is obvious for all to see. You forget that Stella and I know what it is like to be in love.'

I went a hot red and gasped, 'I'm, well, he's –'

Finn's arms went round me in a bear hug. 'Don't tell his name. If you tell, some of the magic will go. Yust enjoy.'

Night after night I dreamed in glorious technicolour about the big New Year's Eve party that was held every year in Two Rivers, courtesy of the Herald Company. Everybody went, Titch had told me when we passed the town hall one day. My dreams were all the same. I would float confidently into the town hall in the pink tulle ballerina dress with the exquisite matching satin shoes, my budding bosom uplifted by a self-supporting bra, my hair swept up in a gleaming chignon, my makeup flawless, surrounded by an irresistible aura of French perfume. The crowd would part and fall back and James would be standing there in a white tuxedo, struck dumb by my incredible beauty. We would gravitate towards each other, attracted by the mysterious magnetic force that created the universe. Then he would put his arms around me and we'd glide off across the floor, dancing the night away oblivious to everyone else as we fell deeper and deeper in love.

The reality, alas, was different. I had to wear the red skirt and the white shoes and the angora bunny jacket again, though I had learnt enough from observing the other girls at Titch's party to supplement my ensemble with a homemade corsage made from a frangipani flower backed with a spray of fern; Stella helped me wrap the stems in cellophane and pin it on the bunny jacket's lapel. She also fastened the marcasite necklace round my neck saying, 'I hope it brings you more luck than it brought me.'

How could she talk about more luck? I turned to her in shock. 'But you've got Finn.'

She was wearing pale green that night: not a dance dress puffed out with stiff petticoats like everyone else would be wearing but a pair of clingy satin lounging pyjamas the colour of mint creams that she had found in a second-hand clothing shop in Durban. They were wonderful pre-war quality and very stylish, she said, but I had the usual sinking feeling about having to walk next to her in one of her more outrageous outfits, knowing that everybody would turn and stare. She stood looking down at me and said in an odd voice, 'Yes, I suppose I've got Finn.'

'What do you mean, "I suppose"?' I felt icy fingers reaching up to clutch my heart.

Her mouth went up in a crooked smile. 'Don't look so stricken, Izz. I just mean that it's tempting fate to imagine that the things you value will last forever. Life changes overnight sometimes. Look at Pa dying so suddenly and poor Ma taking it so hard.'

'Going mad.' It came out in a whisper of dread.

'No. Just getting sick for a while. Don't worry about things so much, kiddo.' She put her arms round me then and it felt really good, like proper sisters. I didn't even mind about her slipping in the 'kiddo'.

Though it was only a few blocks away, the three of us drove slowly up the main road to the town hall with me in the dickey seat holding a gauze scarf over my party curls. Stella said we should arrive in style because it was New Year's Eve, but I think the real reason was that she didn't want people to see the Rosholts walking up from Coolietown.

James was at the party (elation!) but sitting on the far side of the hall with his parents; he spent most of the evening duty-dancing with their decrepit old friends' wives (gloom and despondency). The average age of the celebrants that night was at least forty, not counting the over-excited children who tore around yelling and squirting cooldrink everywhere. Fortunately they began to collapse one after the other as the evening wore on, making sticky little heaps under blankets in various corners, guarded by impassive nannies who sat watching their employers get plastered enough to dance with each other. The only other black people in the room were the Indian waiters, sleek and watchful in their festive red jackets with black lapels, carrying trays loaded with drinks. Free company booze was the main attraction of the evening – far more so than the free spread on trestle tables in the foyer outside.

Dicky Gould, looking like a badly-preserved cadaver in a dinner jacket so old that it had turned green, was making sure he would get his full quota by lining neat brandies up by the half-dozen on the table in front of him. His trousers were covered in flakes from the scabs he kept picking at. His sister Dorothy would never have come, of course. Stella had told me after our Christmas charity visit to the sagging old house in Darjeeling Road, where we took a tin of biscuits made by Eslina, that Dorothy Gould was afraid of crowds and preferred talking to her budgies.

Titch and I tried a few dances together, moving with aplomb now, and were sitting on two folding chairs speculating on how long Dicky would manage to stay upright when James materialised right next to me. My heart skipped at least ten beats, then began hammering like a frenzied steam piston.

He said, 'Hi, you two.'

You two. Oh God, was he assuming that I was Titch's girlfriend? If so, what could I do about it? How could I distance myself enough from the boy I'd been sitting laughing with to show James that I was fancy-free, yet not hurt Titch's feelings? I sat frozen, gaping up at the dazzling vision.

Next to me, Titch said, 'Howzit, Singles.'

'So what's new?' James slumped into the chair on the other side of him.

'Nothing. The usual crap.'

198

'I'm thinking of jacking it in.'

'So early?'

'My old folks're giving me the pip.'

Titch grinned. 'So what's new?'

In my catatonic state I was thinking, Do boys always communicate in monosyllables?

'Let's go out, have a beer.'

'Great idea. Coming, Izz?'

I nodded, still speechless. A look of annoyance crossed the god-like face; clearly James hadn't meant me to be included in the invitation.

'Want a beer too?' Titch had got up and was beckoning at a waiter as though he did it every day.

Why not? I thought. I'd need some Dutch courage to brave the odour of James's disapproval. My tongue loosened enough to say, 'Thanks.'

Titch and James walked out carrying three bottles of beer each as inconspicuously as possible under the blazers draped over their arms. I sidled out of the hall in their wake, trying to look as though I was on my way to the Ladies but imagining every adult eye in the room following us. That is the absolute worst thing about growing up: the feeling that you're doing it under close scrutiny, and not managing very well either.

That New Year's Eve wasn't the romantic idyll of my dreams, but I celebrated it in a way the schoolgirl of a few months earlier couldn't have dreamed of: sitting with two boys on the lawn in the square getting dizzy on love and beer. With our backs against Old Man Herald's obelisk and my tongue beginning to work in the normal way at last, we talked about our schools and our friends, about Two Rivers and the deadly dull people who lived there, and finally about our hopes for the future. Standard teenage stuff, but then it all seemed shiny and new and pregnant with exciting possibilities. I'd never talked like that with boys before.

'I'm going to be a biological scientist,' Titch said. 'I'll go to university and study zoology and botany and organic chemistry and all that sort of stuff, and then I'll change the world somehow. Make an amazing discovery or find a new species and write books about it. Become famous. Win the Nobel Prize.'

'Big head.' James lifted his glorious classic profile to look up at the stars. 'I have more modest ambitions, as befits my father's station in life.'

'Oh, bullshit,' Titch said, sounding irritated.

I wondered if James was getting a dig in at him because he was the boss's son, or because scholarship boys often got their noses rubbed in their humble origins at their school. Growing up unaware of one's wealth in relation to others makes people insensitive; nobody knows this better than black South Africans. But the insensitivity to black concerns that apartheid would exacerbate was taken for granted then, and black anger was prudently hidden most of the time.

In a place like Two Rivers where the races historically mingled with each other at the edges like wet watercolours, it would burst through in occasional ugly spurts as I had noticed in the incident looking down from my mango tree, but Two Rivers was unusual. In most places 'white' meant largely pinky-beige with pockets of suspiciously dark tan, and 'black' ranged from pale beige through coffee to nigger brown (a popular fashion colour in the Fifties) to ebony, not counting the unfortunate albinos. The new Nationalist government already had plans in motion to make the white areas impeccably white by evicting and banishing the occupants of any black settlements to distant tracts of otherwise useless land, then bulldozing their shacks flat. People would be happier in their own areas, pure and unsullied, they said. It would also avert unnecessary conflict.

And people like me let them do it. If we made protests, they were not sustained. I can admit it now. *Mea culpa*.

But this is hindsight. Then all I could see was James's head outlined against the stars.

He was saying, 'No, really. I can't just assume I'm going on to university.'

'Balls. You're much cleverer than I am. You'll cream all the bursaries.'

The chiselled god-mouth relaxed into a wistful smile. 'If I do, I'd like to be an engineer. Design hellish complicated roads and dams and bridges. That would be really great, to see things grow out of formulae on paper.'

'And you, Izz?' Titch's eyes reflected in miniature the town

200

hall's colonnades strung with coloured lights. The crowd inside was beginning to sing *Auld Lang Syne*.

Me? What did I want to do with my life? Right then, have James fall head over heels in love with me and maybe even marry me one day. I'd never thought seriously about a career or anything; girls weren't encouraged to then. You finished school and did some training, usually as a secretary or nursing or teaching, then you got married and lived in a nice house and had four children.

What could I say to these two clever boys, both looking at me now? It would be feeble to say that I wanted to get married. What else could I do? The only thing I was really good at in school was English. I could be a poet, I supposed. Or – 'I want to be a writer,' I lied.

All those years ago, right at the beginning, I was already lying my head off about important things. Maybe that's the moment when things really started to go wrong for me: New Year's Eve in Two Rivers, with 1952 a few minutes away. And Srinivassen Pather letting his home town know that he was back by driving his shiny red MG round and round the square where the whites were celebrating, wheels squealing as he hooted his defiant wealth.

Isabel

She opens the door to Janine in a faded blue tracksuit who flings her arms round her in an enthusiastic hug. 'Hullo, Mum. Sorry I'm late. How are you?'

Janine has always been the most demonstrative of her children, and the most forthcoming about what she has been doing since they saw each other last. One of the things Isabel misses about having no children in the house is the daily chatter over meals which kept her in touch with their lives. When she and George are alone they eat in silence over the newspaper or a book.

'I'm fine.' As they pull away from each other, both smiling, Isabel says, 'Thought you usually got away earlier than this?'

Janine shrugs as she dumps her gym bag next to the hall table. 'Got held up at school. Some of the Standard Eights have been bunking sport and I had to administer suitable punishment. God, I hate being a teacher, always having to do the heavy adult number on kids. I'm not that far off being one myself. *And* I've been asked to take an extra aerobics class for two evenings. *And* Steve phoned from Bloemfontein and asked me to drive down for the weekend.'

'You take on far too much. I don't know how you fit it all in.' Isabel is envious of her daughters' ability to dovetail demanding jobs and seemingly inexhaustible social lives.

'Nor do I sometimes. Am I late?'

'No. Chryssa only came a few minutes ago. I have yet to hear what all the drama's about.' She says this in a questioning voice with raised eyebrows, hoping that Janine will give her a hint as to why Chryssa is crying on the veranda.

But Janine shakes her head in warning and says, 'She's all psyched up to tell you the moment I get here. Moral support

202

and all that. I just want to have a pee and wash my hands before I come and join you.'

Pausing by the veranda door, Isabel watches her squeaking down the passage in her scuffed training shoes. She is the one who looks most like herself at that age: hair a darkish blonde and slender arms and legs, but already going heavy round the hips and upper thighs, despite all the exercise she takes. Janine is the peacemaker in the family. When there is a disagreement, she will talk to both sides and try to make them see each other's point of view. She is tenacious, calm and resourceful, and has an army of brisk athletic friends who play gregarious team sports: hockey, water polo, soccer, cricket. If only she would see The Gorgeous One for the vain bastard he is, Isabel thinks. She deserves a good man.

Her minds flits briefly to her lover and the still-silent telephone, then away again. She goes out on to the veranda and sits down in the chair next to Chryssa's, leaning forward. 'Tell me what's wrong, darling.'

Chryssa chokes out, 'Was that Janine? I said I'd wait until she came.'

'She's just gone to the lav. Would you like your tea in the meantime?'

The bent head whips up and she gets a red-eyed glare. 'What good can a cup of tea do?'

'Clear your mind. Give you a nice warm core. I'm a great believer in the soothing qualities of tea.' Isabel reaches out to pull the trolley closer and pours milk into the three cups, then picks up the teapot.

'That's an old fogeys' myth. Give me coffee any day.' But Chryssa has stopped crying and is wiping her eyes with the back of her hand.

Enjoying the sight of the amber arc of tea she is pouring, Isabel says, 'The time I like to have coffee is when I'm working. It really helps me to concentrate.'

'Working at what?'

It is the suspicious question of a child who senses that a parent is up to something mysterious. Isabel has nearly let the cat out of the bag again. She produces a quick laugh and says, 'Oh, some research I'm doing.'

'Research?'

203

Wrong word. Dull middle-aged mothers who've been housewives all their lives never do anything as glamorous as research. She says vaguely, 'It wouldn't interest you. I'm just –' and is saved by Janine, who comes squeaking out on to the veranda smelling of soap and demanding food because she's starving.

They go through the ritual of handing round the cups and the sugar bowl and slices of almond tart, and Isabel watches Chryssa out of the corner of her eye settling back in the basket chair, her face visibly smoothing in the steam rising out of her cup. It is a warm sunny afternoon. The garden sprinkler is waving its crystal fan of water back and forth over the lawn and the flower bed next to the veranda steps, and there is a comforting smell of wet earth. Down at the bottom of the garden, the plum tree she planted just after Ralphie was born has shed most of its fruit, which lies rotting in the long grass because there are no children in this garden now to pick it. She remembers them running back to the veranda with crimson mouths and sticky little hands, homing in.

As though reading her mind, Janine says, 'This veranda always makes me feel that I'm really home. Every time I see basket chairs with fat buttoned cushions like these, I'm reminded of it.'

'It was Stella who taught me to love basket chairs. I had one in my bedroom when –' Isabel stops herself again, thinking, Why can't I keep my big mouth shut? If I start talking about Two Rivers, it'll all come pouring out. Over the years, she has told George and her children only the bare facts about what happened in that year of painful growing up.

Janine says, 'How is Stella? You went down to Durban to see her a few months ago, didn't you?'

Isabel thinks, Actually I went down to meet a clandestine lover in the cottage, but I did manage to spare a few hours for Stella. With only a trace of a blush, she says, 'Poor thing. She's very ill now. The doctors don't expect her to last more than a few months.'

'I've always thought you're the unlikeliest sisters. Stella's so sharp and opinionated, the epitome of a successful older businesswoman, while you're –'

204

She can't help breaking in. 'Round and boring, the epitome of an unsuccessful older housewife?'

'I didn't say that!' Janine is defensive. 'It's just – as though Stella's been painted with layers and layers of lacquer until she's become so implacably shiny that you can't see who she really is underneath, you know? While you're someone people know they can come to for help when they're in trouble.'

Isabel thinks, Brilliant. Janine has a real gift for bringing a conversation round to the point. She turns to Chryssa, who is gazing out at the hypnotic sprinkler, and says, 'Spill the beans, love. I think we're all properly fortified now.'

Chryssa blurts, 'I'm pregnant.'

14

January crawled, smothering-hot and muggy and windless. You couldn't move an eyelash without breaking into a sweat. Stella was bad-tempered and snappy because she had the sensitive pale skin that goes with red hair and suffered from heat rashes. People walked round with glum faces at having to go back to work after the long holiday and the giddy hilarity of New Year. Even the continuous sale running down both sides of the main road in Coolietown, with each shop offering ever more extravagant bargains, seemed half-hearted.

With Titch away in the Cape visiting grandparents and the convent only due to open towards the end of the month, I was in a friendless limbo – one of those terrible hiatuses in the process of growing up when you're afraid you might literally die of boredom. I'd explored the town from end to end, and sitting in the mango tree was beginning to pall. I didn't want to read all day, or practise cooking on the coal stove with Eslina when it was so hot. I was even getting tired of lurking in shop entrances as I lay in wait for James Singleton, who never appeared anyway. Perhaps he was away too?

My refuge was the pharmacy, which was kept cool and airy by a slowly revolving ceiling fan. Finn made me feel important and necessary despite the fact that with the Christmas rush over, there weren't enough customers to justify an extra assistant.

My job was to wrap up customers' purchases in squares of green paper from a huge roll in a cast-iron holder bolted on to the wall; it had a heavy flap to help you tear the paper off in a straight line. I learnt how to make neat parcels with short strips of stickytape and the raw edge folded down, squaring up the boxes of toothpaste and aspirin and boracic powder and cough drops, the bottles of magnesia tablets (blue) and syrup of figs and friars balsam and gentian violet (brown), the Eno's and Mum and Vicks and Dettol and Zambuck ointment, and the pale pink hand lotion that the Zulu women liked.

Finn had a whole range of low-priced toiletries like the hand lotion which he made up in bulk in the dispensary, then put into small jars and bottles with gold labels which I helped him stick on. He explained, 'Most of my black customers can't afford the things in fancy packages, so I try to provide cheaper formulae. It's important for poor people to feel that they can also afford to look and smell good.'

The most frequently muttered request was for Love Drops, a powerful brownish scent which Finn bought by the gallon and decanted into glass-stoppered phials using a miniature funnel. He told me as I was helping him to prepare a new set of phials in the dispensary one day, 'It's wonderful stoff, this scent. My hottest line. It smells like all the spices of Araby, women believe it makes them irresistible to men, it lasts for several months – and all this glory for a shilling.'

He was looking so pleased with himself that I hesitated before saying, 'Don't you think scent is a bit of a swizz, really? I mean, people think it does all these things when it's only a nice smell.'

I got his deep sea look. 'The things of the mind are important, Izzy. If a woman believes that smelling good makes her more attractive to her man, then the scent will give her the confidence to *be* more attractive.'

'But isn't a shilling expensive for someone who doesn't earn very much?' I knew that Eslina got five pounds a month plus bus fares – and that was generous pay then.

Finn gave me his most approving nod. 'In relative terms it is expensive. But we are coming to the matter of personal freedom again. If a woman chooses to buy scent that makes her feel good, that is her choice. And I like to give her the choice. My Love Drops make only a tiny profit, but I see them as an essential customer service. Like the flowers.'

The pharmacy with its chrome and glass counters and pale

green rubber-tiled floor and orderly shelves of patent medicines was an island of hygiene on the uncertain borderline between the white shops and Coolietown's raucous street-long bazaar. It could have been intimidating for the people from the slum houses and mud huts in and around Two Rivers if Finn had been one of those superior pharmacists who behave like medical miracle workers only a degree less important than doctors. But he was a friendly soul, and of course spoke Zulu because of being brought up on a mission station. He would call out a breezy welcome as each customer came tonking in through the door, and spent as much time counselling a woman with bare cracked feet and a few nervously clutched pennies as he would on the company wives who came swanning in for expensive cosmetics. And he always made sure there was a vase of fresh flowers on the counter nearest the door – not the brash marigolds and hibiscus that grew in everybody's gardens but extravagant flowers from the florist in the town square. Apple and peach blossom in spring, roses and carnations and fleshy pink gladioli, and once a graceful arrangement of white azaleas from the mist belt, Japanese in their twiggy simplicity.

The expensive flowers infuriated Stella. I often heard her complaining, 'You know we can't afford them, Finn. They're an unnecessary extravagance.'

'But I like them,' he would say, 'and they're good for business too. Yust you watch my customers, the way they come in to admire and stay to buy.'

He was right. Women with shiny sweating faces, weighted down by bags and parcels, would drag themselves up the steps from the hot dusty pathway to come into the pharmacy and make some small purchase so they could look at the flowers. Sometimes they wouldn't buy anything, just bent over and smelled them and smiled at us and went out into the enervating heat again with their heads held a little higher. Children reached tentative little hands to stroke the petals. Old men, vain as peacocks, would beg a single flower for a buttonhole, making gaps in the arrangements which I would have to fill with sprigs of the maidenhair fern that grew in the dank shade of the water tank by the kitchen door.

Finn sometimes stood near the plate-glass window where the cosmetics were displayed when he wasn't busy, looking down into the road. He liked to watch people. The row of big-bellied apothecary bottles filled with coloured water reflected the summer sunlight in jewel colours on his white side-buttoned jacket: sapphire and emerald and amethyst, and a brilliant translucent ruby. He and Govind wore clean jackets every day, washed and starched by Eslina who pegged them across a wire in the back yard.

Finn's hands when he made up prescriptions were scrubbed pinkly clean, the fur on their backs lying in damp submissive curls. He was attentive and calm with all his customers, explaining to the illiterate over and over again how to use a medicine, until he was sure they understood. I'd hear him saying, 'Give the baby muti from this bottle, one teaspoon now and one tonight. One teaspoon and one teaspoon, you onderstand? And make yolly sure he doesn't get too hot. Use your lips to feel his forehead, like this.' And the mother would mumble her thanks, pay with carefully unknotted coins, hitch the child up and go home satisfied that she had got the best possible advice.

Asha had begun to come in every other day. If Finn was busy with other customers, she would linger by the flowers or pretend to be looking at the imported soaps in a cabinet with sliding glass doors until they went away. Then she would go to Finn and droop over the counter in her shimmering pastel silks to whisper her request, which often resulted in her going back into the dispensary to consult with him. The few times Govind went over to try and serve her, his adam's apple jerking up and down in his throat, she turned her head away and said something sharp in Tamil that made him go red. After several rebuffs, he stopped trying. She couldn't stop him following her with his eyes, though. I'd shiver, watching him. There was something devouring as well as devoted about the way he looked at her.

She talked to me sometimes while she was waiting for Finn, though she was shy about her English, often raising an apologetic hand to cover her mouth when she thought she'd made a mistake. I wondered what was wrong with her and tried to find out from Finn once at the end of the afternoon when the shop emptied, but he was as tight as a duck's arse (Titch's expression) about customers' problems. He answered, 'Nay, you won't get a small peep out of me. One thing people demand absolute of a pharmacist is discretion.'

'But Asha's so damn perfect.'

I must have looked as aggrieved as I felt, because he laughed and said, 'Stop fishing, Izzy. First for compliments; you're not onattractive yourself.'

Jeepers, I thought, he really means it! I'd never considered myself even remotely attractive. The socially adept Evelyn Simpsons of this world were attractive, not self-conscious gawks like me.

'And secondly,' Finn was going on, unaware of my astonished delight, 'stop fishing for confidential information. A pharmacist cannot talk about his customers' problems, OK? And it's high time we closed.' He raised his voice. 'You skedaddle along now, Govind. Izzy will help me lock up.'

He often said that to Govind at the end of the afternoon: 'You skedaddle along now.' He must have got it out of a film or one of the cowboy books he used to read as a boy to keep up his English. I couldn't imagine one of the old missionaries telling people to skedaddle.

But Govind hated it. Hypersensitive as he was, he seemed to think that Finn was using the word to insult him. That afternoon he glared daggers at us before unbuttoning his white jacket to expose a virulent green shirt, then stomping out into the small yard behind the dispensary where he parked his bicycle. And it was the same afternoon that he got knocked off his bicycle by Srinivassen Pather's MG.

We both saw it happen. I was standing on the platform at the top of the pharmacy steps next to Finn, who was pulling the steel grille across the glass front door. (We always went through to the house via the dispensary door.) We were talking about pacifism. Finn had just told me that he would have registered as a conscientious objector if he had been called up during the war, and was saying, 'The troble is, you see, when soldiers and politicians have been in power for too long they become like scabs, hard and separate from the flesh beneath, and –'

He broke off. A shiny red open sports car came barrelling

down the main road just as Govind shot off the path in front of the steps, his bicycle clips making whirling silver blurs as he pedalled. Seething (as he so often did) in his bubble of black resentment, he turned his head only to check the traffic approaching from the side he would be riding on. He did not see the oncoming MG swing out in a broad turn on the wrong side of the empty road so it could pull up directly facing Pather's Jewellers. Nor did the MG's driver see him until the last minute. When the red fender clipped the bicycle's front wheel, Govind's head was still turning. His handlebars gave a violent sideways jerk and he fell in a tangle of thin limbs, landing with a heavy thump on one shoulder at the bottom of the pharmacy steps. The MG slewed sideways on to the path behind him with arcs of sand and gravel spurting from each wheel. The driver was laughing.

Finn said to me in a furious voice, 'It's Srini Pather playing silly boggers again,' and ran down the steps shouting, 'Can't you look where you're going?'

The MG slid to a stop in a cloud of dust and a stocky young man pushed the low door open and climbed out. He had the plump, swarthy good looks of the Hindi film idols on the posters outside the Delhi Palace bioscope, set off by a cream shirt and modish tan trousers. He stood with both hands raised, palms facing Finn, smiling and saying, 'Sorry, sorry. I didn't see the fellow.'

'It's not me you should be saying sorry to.' Finn had reached the crumpled body and knelt down to run his hands over it, moving with swift expertise as he checked the vital signs.

I felt a lurch of horror. Was Govind dead, then? He was lying very still.

The driver strolled towards them saying, 'He's OK, man. Just winded. Not serious. You'll see.'

'I'm not so sure.' It was Finn's grimmest voice.

Leaning over the parapet of the steps above them, I thought, Oh God, another dead person in my life. Maybe I'm bad luck.

Then Govind's body twitched and he started gasping and struggling to suck in some of the wind that had been knocked out of him. When Finn tried to roll him over, he let out a dreadful strangled noise.

211

'Get the doctor, Srini. He's broken something.' Finn looked up. 'Go on. Get moving.'

The driver's lower lip pushed out. 'Listen, this wasn't all my fault, Mr Rosholt. You're my witness. You saw him dash out into the road without looking. He should have been more jolly careful.'

'Get the bloody doctor!'

'But it wasn't –'

'And I certainly hold you responsible. You were driving like a maniac.'

'But –'

'Go! Now!' I had never seen Finn so angry.

Grumbling, the driver went back to his car and got in, saying as he slammed the door, 'I'll try for Dr Singh, but if he's not there I have no time to go searching around. Not for a –' he used a word I didn't know '– like that one. I have better things to do.'

I saw Finn rear up in rage above the gasping man, and thought, There's going to be a fight. Stella will be *mad* if he fights in the street. He'll never hear the end of it.

The driver must have got the same idea, because he lunged for the MG's key shouting, 'OK, I'm going! I'm going!' He twisted it in the keyhole and began tugging at the starter knob. The engine gave a feral growl, then died.

Finn began walking towards him, calling up to me in a tight voice, 'Come down and keep an eye on Govind, Izzy.'

I didn't know what to do. Stella had driven into Durban for the day and wasn't back yet and Eslina had already gone home, so I couldn't run and fetch them. From my perch on the steps I could see people beginning to gather as they always do at a public spectacle, stopping on the pathways on both sides of the road and seeping out of doorways to stand and stare in whispering groups. The sun was low and orange, turning the whole scene a dangerous copper. The driver was yanking the starter knob again and again, each time more desperate, but the engine wouldn't take.

And Finn was closing on him with long angry strides, saying, 'I'm going to –'

What? I thought in panic. Get the doctor? Beat the driver up? Questions whirled in my head. What about his commitment to pacifism? Was this man in a raging temper the real Finn? Was this what Stella had been talking about on that first morning when she'd said, 'I wonder what else they know?'

But I never did learn what Finn would have done when he reached the driver. In the time it took me to sidle down the steps to where Govind lay moaning on the path, a third force intervened. Hurrying across the street from the jewellery shop came a knot of women in saris, clucking like agitated hens. The one in the middle was tall and hatchet-faced with frizzy grey hair escaping in wild tufts from her bun.

Suddenly seeing them, the driver abandoned his starter knob and jumped up in the car shouting, 'Mummy, Mummy, stop him!'

The tall woman called back, 'I'm coming, Srini-baba! Hold on. I won't let anyone hurt you.'

One of the bystanders chuckled, then another, and soon everyone was laughing. It came from both sides of the road, a rising tide of laughter augmented by hooting from passing cars and trucks and buses whose drivers were slowing down and hanging out the windows to see what was going on. Mostly, I think, people were laughing because Srini Pather getting his comeuppance after years of hooligan behaviour was the first decent bit of entertainment since New Year's Eve. He was the only son in a family whose conspicuous wealth was much resented, and had been outrageously spoiled. Except for my tentative arm-patting, Govind's agony was ignored in the general mirth.

To my huge relief, Finn slowed down and began laughing too. Well before Mrs Pather and her cohorts had reached Srini in his MG and surrounded them both in a defensive fluttering circle, Finn had his head back and was roaring until the tears came; I don't think I ever saw him laugh so hard. He was still breaking into little chortles when Dr Singh arrived, called by a nearby shop-owner, and injected Govind with a painkiller before getting several men to carry him up into the pharmacy, where he bandaged his left arm high across his chest to set the broken collar-bone. By the time he was strapped up and sedated, Stella had got back from

213

Durban in the car and Finn drove him home with the buckled bicycle in the dickey seat, vowing to arrange for suitable compensation from the Pathers. But he told me later that Govind never forgave him for laughing after he had been hurt in the accident. The fact that Finn the conscientious objector had nearly beaten someone up defending him didn't count, apparently, against the fact of his laughter.

Finn had incurred Mrs Pather's wrath too. She sent a curt note across the road next morning saying that as he had publicly humiliated Srinivassen and therefore insulted Pather honour, he was no longer welcome to visit the jewellery shop. 'Not under any possible circumstances, please,' the note ended.

When she read it, Stella said, 'Did you have to alienate Mrs Pather? She's one of the few I can talk to.' That was her main criterion with Indians: the ones 'she could talk to' had to be either well educated or rich enough for education not to matter.

Finn was frowning. 'Alienate? That's a strong word when I was not the guilty party. Srini could have killed Govind. His driving was at the very least reckless.'

'You must have done something to put her back up.'

'She didn't like the fact that he was exposed as a mummy's boy in front of everybody.' He gave a reminiscent chuckle. 'You should have seen it, Stella. A grown man crying, "Mummy, Mummy, stop him!"'

'You must have done something more,' she insisted.

I kept quiet about the furious Viking I had seen heading for the red MG. My loyalty to Finn was strong, though it had been shaken by his transformation for a few frightening moments from teddy bear to warrior.

After consulting Mr Reddy, he sent a carefully worded note back to Mrs Pather explaining the circumstances, suggesting that she speak to Srini about his driving and compensation for Govind, and apologising for any distress he may have caused the family. An envelope came back with fifty pounds wrapped in a piece of paper marked 'For the bicycle and medical expenses', but not a word more. If Finn found himself approaching any Pathers after that, they would cross the road before a meeting could happen. There was a total breach between the owners of the two opposing shops, and its repercussions at the Mariamman festival three months later were to be devastating.

Isabel

The announcement of a possible grandchild is the last thing Isabel expects to hear. This eldest daughter has been so intent on her career that there has never been talk of children beyond a vague, 'One day we'll have some, I suppose.'

'It's a disaster. I don't know what I'm going to do.' Chryssa's voice is turgid with misery.

Isabel is too stunned to say anything. She is thinking, I could be a grandmother soon. Is it proper for grandmothers to have lovers?

Janine is saying, 'Go on, Chrys. All of it.'

The words come out like flat stones skipping across a deep reservoir of doubt. 'Tom says I can fly over to England for an abortion if I want to. It's nothing nowadays, just a brief surgical procedure. Have you ever had an abortion, Mum?'

'No. I didn't conceive very easily.' Isabel almost believes the worn excuse now, though she manufactured it herself to conceal the fact that George was an infrequent lover. She adds carefully, 'If you feel that an abortion is the right thing, of course we'll support you.'

'But I don't! That's the whole trouble.' Chryssa starts to cry again. 'I keep thinking that this, this, well, tiny little living being is part of me – Tom and me. So how can I kill it?'

Isabel kneels in front of the basket chair and puts her arms round her anguished daughter, thinking, Thank God I never had to make terrible decisions like this. Women today have a much harder time in some ways than we did. They get inoculated early with the idea that they can have it all, careers and marriage and children, but nobody tells them how damn hard it is to achieve success in even one of these things. Let alone all three.

She says, 'There are two ways of looking at abortion, Chrys. Some see it as killing, yes. Others say that a foetus isn't viable for the first few months, and that it is simply your choice whether you decide to go ahead or not. Are you quite sure you're pregnant, by the way?'

'Oh yes,' she sobs. 'It shows up on the scan already.'

'I thought you were on the pill?'

'I *am*. I'm as careful as anything, never miss one! But the gynae says that there are times when the pill doesn't work: if it passes through your gut too fast, for example. And both Tom and I caught a tummy bug that gave us the screaming runs a couple of months ago – remember? That must be when it happened. If only I'd known, I'd have been more careful.'

With a twinge of sarcasm, Isabel thinks, These girls have such touching faith in the pill. We knew that nothing's infallible. There are always mistakes.

She sits back on the woven grass veranda mat that smelled of fresh hay when it was new, but is now silted with dog fur and biscuit crumbs and general family living. Seeing the dog fur reminds her of their much-loved old Rudy who died a few months ago. She wonders if the fact that they have not replaced him is indicative of the state of their marriage. Does George mind that they have become strangers to each other? Perhaps he wants out as much as she does . . . It is an exhilarating thought.

Janine has been sipping her tea and eating her slice of tart with hungry relish, and now leans forward to cut herself a second, more generous slice. 'If you can handle being a granny, Mum, I rather fancy being an aunt.'

Chryssa wails, 'But I don't *want* to be a full-time mother yet. I've got my life all planned out, and having a kid now would ruin everything.'

'What does Tom think?'

'He says it's up to me, and we try to respect each other's decisions.' Chryssa blinks and fishes in her jacket pocket for a tissue. 'But I'm beginning to suspect that he secretly wants this child.'

'What makes you think that?' Janine is making a show of licking her fingers. 'I thought Tom was also dead against having kids early.'

'He looks wistful when we talk about it.' Chryssa pulls a face. 'If you can imagine him looking wistful.'

Isabel can't help laughing. Tom is one of those urgent young executives in striped shirts and hand-stitched suits who are heading for the top via a degree in accountancy, graduate business school and extra lessons in golf, squash and wine appreciation.

Janine says, 'I can. He's quite a softie under that suave exterior. You should have seen him teaching my Standard Sixes how to make a kite that flies properly during our last creative arts weekend.'

'Really?' Chryssa looks astonished. She remembers being away in Taiwan when Tom, with a cancelled golf date, was roped in by Janine to help at her school.

'It made me like him a lot better,' Janine admits.

'Have you discussed the practicalities of having this child?' Now that Chryssa has stopped crying, Isabel feels she can get up and pour herself another cup of tea. She sits down in her chair again, rubbing the pins and needles in her legs.

'Endlessly. It's just not possible with our current commitments. The bond on the townhouse was only granted because we're both earning good salaries, and there are all our other repayments.' She trails off. 'And I don't want to stop working. I'm just getting to the point where my bosses are starting to take me seriously. If I apply for maternity leave, they'll write me off as a fashion buyer because I won't be able to travel overseas. Women with kids can't travel unless –' She breaks off.

'What?' Janine prompts.

'Unless they have a reliable child-minder on call. That's the only way we could do it,' Chryssa says in a rush, turning to Isabel, 'if you could help out with the baby during the week, Mum. And when I have to go away.'

Isabel's first reaction is, The bloody nerve! And then, So that's what they've been leading up to. They really believe that their mother has such an empty life that she will be willing – even eager – to take on a small child again. They want me to subject myself to more years of worry and responsibility, to endless nappies, my shoulders smelling of baby sick, slaved-over meals that get thrown on the floor,

218

clean clothes that get dirtied in minutes, shrill little voices crying, leaky noses and bottoms that need wiping, and the ever-present dread that I'll leave an essential door or a gate open.

She gives her eldest daughter a big creamy smile and says, 'Oh, no. Don't even think of it. I've brought up three babies, and that's enough. There is no way I am going to take on a small child at this age.'

'But Mum –' Chryssa is wailing again. 'I can't do it otherwise.'

'That's your problem, dear old thing,' Isabel says, getting up and crashing her teacup down on the trolley. She stands with her hands planted on the back of her chair looking down at them, fiercer and more emphatic than they have ever seen her. 'If you want to have children, you must take responsibility for them. That's the deal, and there's no wriggling out of it. As for me, I've done my mother and housewife bit.'

'But you can't have much to do all day.' Chryssa is beginning to sound aggrieved. When things get particularly frantic at work, the image of her mother sitting on this veranda idly drinking tea often slides into her mind, bringing with it a surge of angry envy that she doesn't understand because she has never wanted to be anything like her mother.

Janine uses subtler persuasion. 'I remember you saying just before last Christmas, Mum, that you wanted to find meaningful work. Wouldn't a baby be much more fulfilling than some boring office job?'

'I'm really touched by your concern.' Still smiling, Isabel throttles back the impulse to further sarcasm. 'But I have more than enough to do at the moment and it is extremely fulfilling.'

The surprised expression on both her daughters' faces is gratifying. Chryssa accuses, 'You haven't mentioned getting work.'

'Why should I?'

'You always tell us what you've been doing.' Janine is looking aggrieved too now.

'Not everything. You never seemed very interested anyway. Too busy with your own lives.'

Both have the grace to look guilty. Janine says, 'I'm sorry, we've been neglecting you lately.'

'Actually, I've been too busy to notice.' Isabel is wondering, Shall I tell them? I don't know if the writing is even passable enough to talk about.

'Too busy doing what?' There is growing alarm on both faces; their mother is being unusually secretive.

'It's not what you might call lucrative work but –'

Chryssa bursts out, 'Oh, for God's sake, Mum, you haven't gone and got involved with some wingeing charity, just when I need you most?'

Isabel looks at her with real dislike. 'It's not a charity, Chryssa, and I think you forget that I'm not at your beck and call any more.'

'I didn't ask you to be!'

'You damn well did. You think of me as a doormat.'

'I don't!'

The quiet voice of the family peacemaker cuts in, 'Won't you tell us what it is, Mum?'

Looking at Chryssa's peeved red face, Isabel thinks, Dammit, she wants to use me and I won't be used any more – not by anyone. She says, 'I'm writing.'

'Writing!'

'What?'

'About Two Rivers.'

'Is it a book?' Janine looks awed.

'I'm not sure yet. Maybe.'

'How can you not be sure what you're doing?' Chryssa's tone implies that she would never undertake a project without being crystal clear about her goal.

Isabel thinks, That's rich, under the circumstances. But I mustn't snap back too hard at her; she's under a lot of strain. She says, 'I'm feeling my way as I go. I don't know whether it's good enough to get into print.'

'And if it is?'

'I have plans that I'll announce when I'm good and ready.'

Janine says, 'You're being incredibly mysterious, Mum. Won't you tell us what –'

Chryssa overrides her as she so often did when they were

small. 'So that's the reason for the research you said you were doing. Does Dad know about all this?'

'No. And I'd rather you didn't mention it to him. Or any of this to anyone else.' She leans over the chair-back now on her elbows, trying to change the subject; she does not want to discuss her work any further. 'If you decide not to have the baby, Chrys, just take some leave and fly off and say you're going on holiday. It's nobody else's business but yours and Tom's, and if you keep it to yourselves you'll avoid the malicious whispers. If you need help buying your ticket, I have some money set aside.' She has begun calling it her Escape Fund.

Her eldest daughter nods, for once not knowing what to reply to this newly assertive mother.

'And if you want to know what I'd do in your position – I'm sorry, I can't tell you. My generation usually didn't have the choice between a career and motherhood; we just got married and had kids as a matter of course.'

'Is that why you're trying to write a book, because you never had a career?' Judging by the curiosity on her face, this is the first time Chryssa has ever thought of Isabel as a distinct person with her own needs, rather than simply a mother.

'Yes,' she says, 'yes, I suppose it is.' Admitting this to her daughters, she acknowledges for the first time the growing frustration of recent years. 'You young things today have an amazingly judgemental attitude towards those of us who became "just housewives", without having the least sympathy for the very different conditions we had to face as young women. If we'd had even half the encouragement and the opportunities you've had, don't you think we'd have grabbed them?'

'What would you have done if you'd had the chance?' Chryssa again, really interested now.

'I would have given my eye teeth to have gone to university and studied English. But Granny couldn't afford it.' Isabel feels a familiar lump growing in her throat at the memory.

Chryssa persists, 'Was it your goal to be a writer?'

Isabel finds her continued air of surprise galling and says

with asperity, 'Why not? I won a first prize for essay writing at school.'

Her elder daughter flushes. 'Sorry. I didn't mean it to sound as if you couldn't.'

The look of dawning respect on both faces is a gladsome sight after the years of being taken for granted, and she thinks, I'd love to tell them more – about him, too. My lover. But now is not the time. She says, 'I really can't talk about it yet, least of all to Dad. He wouldn't be sympathetic.'

'No, he wouldn't. He's a real old dork. Lost in the past somewhere. I don't know how you've put up with him all these years, Mum.' Chryssa dismisses the twenty-five-year marriage with a shrug that says, I chose my husband much more carefully.

Janine says, ever more diplomatic, 'I never know what to talk to Dad about. He's always somewhere else in his mind, you know?'

I'm not the only one! Isabel feels a flooding relief. His daughters find him dull too. And Ralphie?

As though his presence has entered her mind before she knows it, the doorbell rings again and Chryssa says, 'That must be Ralph. He said he'd come as soon as he could.'

The basket chair creaks with the sudden loss of weight on its back as Isabel stands up in alarm. 'Have you told him? Isn't he rather young to be involved in this?'

Now the look on both faces is pitying. 'Of course he knows. Ralph's not a kid any more.'

No, he isn't, she thinks as she opens the door to him. She is looking at him objectively for the first time as he is today, not overlaid by the anxious little boy he used to be. And sees that he's a young man, rather pale and thin and scholarly in his glasses, but with George's classic bone structure and fine blond hair that breaks into a suggestion of curls behind his ears. When he fills out, he will turn heads.

As she reaches out to hug him, he blurts, 'Sorry, I forgot my k-keys. Have you agreed? Are you going to look after the baby? I hope so. Chryssa can't just go and k-k-k-'

'No, I haven't.' She is smiling behind his head. 'I'm not the old doormat you all think I am.'

222

He pulls away. 'Of c-course you aren't. But Mum, Chryssa really wants it. So does Tom.'

'I know they do. So do I.' Isabel is filled with a sense of pleasant anticipation at the thought of a new generation – as long as she doesn't have to look after it.

'But she can't do her job *and* have it.'

Isabel nods. 'If she wants to have that baby, she's got some tough decisions coming. But they'll make a plan, you'll see. The urge to reproduce is very strong. Practically impossible to resist.'

'I'll baby-sit. I'm used to it.' His familiar grin flashes. 'My girlfriend's mother married again and has a k-kid who's only nine months old. He's great.'

A girlfriend, she thinks. Then he's definitely not a kid any more. What the hell am I worrying about? Turning to go into the house in front of him, she says, 'That's wonderful, Ralphie. I hope you'll bring your girlfriend home to meet me one day.'

He reaches out an urgent hand to stop her. 'Mum.'

When she turns back, his face is wearing a familiar anxiety. She thinks, He must be worried about the college confrontation tomorrow, and says, 'What is it?'

He blurts, 'Do you think you c-could start calling me Ralph now? Ralphie's embarrassing. Specially in front of girlfriends.'

Now who's lacking in sympathy? she thinks, remembering that his sisters are already calling him Ralph. And says, contrite, 'Of course, darling. I'm sorry. I should have stopped long ago. Mothers can be quite stupid sometimes.'

He says, 'Not you, Mum.'

As they walk down the passage, the phone rings.

15

'Oh, my giddy aunt!'

The first words I heard at my new school came ringing down a high bare brick passage with a vaulted ceiling. Stella and I were sitting with a group of tense mothers and cowed new girls on a wooden bench outside the Mother Superior's office the day before school began, waiting to be interviewed.

A nun came swooping past in a fluster of black gabardine and veils and flapping wimple and disappeared through the office door repeating, 'Oh, my giddy aunt!' She pronounced it 'ant'.

Stella whispered, 'That's Sister Kathleen Killeally. She's Irish, with a temperament to match.'

My heart sank. Sister Kathleen was to be my form teacher.

A voice inside the office said, 'What is it, Sister?'

'Disaster! Frank says that the plumber says that the kitchen geyser's given up the ghost.'

The second voice said with a hint of a chuckle, 'Not holy, I trust?'

'Holy? I don't understand.'

'Ghost, dear. Holy ghost. Just my little joke. I've always suspected that kitchen geyser of being one of the devil's abodes. It has a wicked way of spurting pure steam. How much is this disaster going to cost us?'

'It's a special type of geyser. Frank says that a new one will set us back a good forty pounds and maybe more.' Sister Kathleen added a breathless, 'Holy Mary save us.'

'Forty pounds. Oh, dear. The fees aren't in yet, and the plumber said no more credit.' There was a considering pause. 'I'm afraid there's only one thing we can do. Another prayer cycle.'

'Oh, no.' Sister Kathleen's brogue intensified as she wailed, 'I was after spendin' two whole *days* in the chapel when we needed money for the new domestic science room. Me knees have been giving me – pardon, Mother – merry hell. Matron says it must be the ligaments. Please couldn't it be someone else's turn?'

The second voice said, 'It has to be you, Sister. You're far and away the best supplicator we have. You always get results.'

'But it's not at all fair! I still have the register to draw up and all the new books to apportion before school starts.' It was the closest I ever came to hearing a nun cry.

'This work is more important, so into the chapel with you, Sister –' there was another hint of a chuckle '– and don't spare the horses. Try for a round hundred while you're about it.'

There was a mumble of grudging assent and the sound of a chair being scraped back.

I could feel Stella shaking with silent laughter next to me. She told me later when we were walking home that the nuns, perennially short of money, were famous in Two Rivers for their ingenious thrift. Habits and boarders' sheets and even dishcloths were darned until they fell apart, and 'making do' was practically the school motto. When need became pressing, they held a fête at which long-suffering parents and patrons were skilfully bullied out of far more cash than intended. The tactic was for the jollier nuns to bustle about among the stalls and games and donkey rides, letting their hair down and generating a lot of fun and laughter, which made it seem churlish to refuse to join in. Stella said they knew to the last penny how much could be squeezed out of a situation, and she hadn't known that they applied similar tactics to their Lord.

Sister Kathleen's skirts brushed past my knees on her way out and I looked up at a fanatic's face, gaunt and bone-white. My heart sank to my new school shoes, brown lace-ups worn with beige socks. (The convent uniform was a nightmare for sallow adolescent complexions like mine: a putty-coloured cotton dress and a brown blazer with drab ochre stripes that had to be worn in the street, whatever the weather. There was also a white panama hat that a few months' wear and coastal humidity would reduce to the colour and shape of a wood fungus.)

Mother Beatrice was a pleasant surprise, though: one of those humorous, clever, worldly-wise nuns who make you wonder what could possibly have driven them to bury their considerable talents in a convent. She gave me a brisk welcome and quizzed me in her precise diction about the good marks for English on my previous school report.

'We pay special attention here to reading and writing, Isabel. The Archbishop, bless his heart, offers an essay prize this term and I hope you'll be entering.'

I gave her the demure eye-droop I'd learnt at my last convent. 'I'd like to, Rev' Mother.'

Her shrewd eyes were as black and round and shiny as the rosary beads that hung from her belt, whose energetic clicking was a useful indication of her whereabouts in the school. 'I'm not a Reverend, dear. Call me Mother Beatrice. Or The Old B as I'm more generally known. Not inappropriately, mind.'

I put my hand up to my mouth to suppress a giggle, and got an approving nod. 'You've been taught some manners, I see. They go with the name, of course.'

'The name, Rev' – I mean, Mother Beatrice?'

'Your name, Isabel. Do you know that it is used in France to describe a colour, and that the story from which it derives is associated with two queens?'

I shook my head. I hadn't known that my hated name had royal provenance. It wasn't exactly glamorous, though. Mother Beatrice was saying, 'You probably won't much like the sound of the colour, which is dun yellow, the yellow of soiled calico, but I guarantee that if you're tough-minded, you'll like the story. Are you tough-minded? It's a useful quality, you know. I've no time for namby-pamby women who let their lives be ruled by romantic notions and domineering male relatives.'

The black eyes seemed to be boring into my head to try and see if I was good enough for her school. It was a surprise. Usually I was the one giving the new headmistress across the desk a wary once-over to see if her school was good enough for me. I blurted, 'I've had to be. My Pa's just died and my

Ma's in –' What was the proper word for the loonybin? I tried to think of an alternative to 'lunatic asylum'. Ma wasn't a lunatic, was she? She would get better as the doctor and Aunty Mavis had said, wouldn't she?

'I know about your mother, dear. Stella told me.' The nun's voice was gentle. 'That is why I am talking about toughness of mind. You'll need it to get through the difficulties you face: being without your mother, having to cope with a new situation and a new school. I want you to know that I understand, Isabel, and if you need any sort of help that your sister can't give you, I'm here. Right?'

'But I'm not a Catholic.' It was another blurt.

She clucked her tongue. 'And I'm not talking religion. Empathy, rather. I too lost my parents close together. I coped with it by burying my nose in books, which is where I learnt about the two Queen Isabels. Isabel of Austria, the daughter of Philip II of France, is supposed to have vowed at the siege of Ostend not to change her linen until the place was taken. The siege lasted three years, so you can imagine what her linen looked like.'

As she said this, with distaste and humour equally mingled on her shiny-clean nun's face, there was a little 'ting' from the office next door and she gathered speed as she went on, 'The story about Isabella of Castile is similar, only *she* is supposed to have made a vow to the Holy Mother not to change her linen until Granada fell into her hands. Dirty linen must have been a prevalent colour in those days, of course. And it was a popular colour too; Queen Elizabeth I's inventories mention "one rounde gowne of Isabella-colour satten". All three of these women were admirably tough-minded. You could do worse than emulate them during your first term with us. I hope it's a good one, dear. Welcome to the convent.'

Mother Beatrice had a way of bombarding you with ideas and opinions and general charm, then switching off with a smooth dismissal to make way for her next engagement. She could reduce wrongdoers to jelly one moment, coax school fees out of a reluctant parent the next, then hurry down the passage and give a brilliant lesson to one of her English or history classes, talking for an hour without notes. She was

227

one of the most capable and devious women I've ever met, and would have gone far in politics.

Before we left that day, Stella gave me a guided tour of the brick classroom block with arched cloisters built round a courtyard where gravel paths crisscrossed trim squares of lawn. During morning assembly we would stand in rows along the edges of the paths to gabble our Hail Marys and listen to Mother Beatrice's rousing daily exhortations to work and play hard and learn to be tough-minded women. The convent smelled of red stoep polish and exercise books and the boarders' boiled cabbage that lurked in odd corners like whiffs of bad breath. And the following week I was thrown in the deep end again: a whole schoolful of new faces and the usual tangled web of unwritten rules to learn. I was to acquire a lifelong friend there, however, as well as a formidable enemy in Sister Kathleen.

The afternoon before term started, Titch stood me to a farewell icecream soda in the Paradise Milk Bar, where it turned out that he had been at primary school with spotty Percy Smuts. I had to spend ten minutes fending off leers while they traded desultory schoolboy news across the social divide that now separated them. Percy had passed his Junior Certificate at technical college and had a paying job and a motorbike and a certain skill with his battery of streamlined chrome blenders, and he clearly saw himself as a man of the world compared with a mere schoolboy. Titch, however much he may have mocked the Two Rivers hierarchy, was the general manager's son bound for university. I played the part of piggy in the middle that day: yearning to be the university person, but unwittingly destined to marry the other.

It was a relief to move on to the next part of our farewell, an illicit ride on Ram Pillay's *Sweet-Smelling Jasmine* all the way to the Isipingo Beach terminus, where we would just have time for a quick swim, and back. I had told Stella that I'd been asked to his house for tea, and he had told his mother that he'd been asked to mine; if our lies were discovered, we'd look embarrassed and say we had gone down to the river. Neither of them would have appreciated our need to carry the memory of the rattliest bus on the South Coast through to the Easter holidays – Titch in particular.

He had returned from the Cape moaning that he had been forced to spend two whole weeks of his precious freedom being polite to aged grandparents and assorted relatives, and getting dressed up for meals. One of the things he said was, 'You're damn lucky you don't have your old folks around. Interfering ones like mine have a way of nibbling into the edges of your private life until there's none left.'

I thought, Am I lucky? and realised that indeed I was, to have escaped my quiet dull home for this new life – motherless and fatherless, perhaps, but excitingly different. I could never have dreamed of getting around on an Indian bus in the mining town, let alone with an interesting boy. The afternoon took on a golden tinge.

Titch was saying with cold fury, 'And now it's school again. If you only knew how much I hate it.' We were standing at a bus stop that couldn't be seen from the pharmacy, just before the main road went over the temple bridge. He was giving the bus stop pole savage backward kicks with the trodden-down heel of one sandal; he and Finn were soulmates when it came to old clothes.

'Why? It's supposed to be such a good school.' My parents would never have been able to afford to send me to an ordinary boarding school, let alone a posh one.

His scowl was thunderous. 'I've told you already: you lose every vestige of independence. The masters are either nagging you to get better results because it's so important for the school to maintain its wonderful academic record, or shoving you around making you play team sports because it's so important for the school to maintain its wonderful sporting record. I fucking hate team sports! People who want to do something different from the common herd just don't shape in places where traditions going back to the ark dictate every bloody thing you do.'

It was the second time I'd heard someone say 'fucking' out loud. That Titch should have used it so casually in my presence was a rare sign of friendship at that time; I felt honoured to be the recipient.

He was raging on, 'And the level of humour is totally puerile. Guys have farting competitions half the night in the dormitory, flaming A's and so forth.'

229

'What's a flaming A?'

'You don't know?'

I shook my head.

'Primary school stuff.' He glared down at the muddy brown river sliding beneath us towards the lagoon. 'You save up a fart and then you lie back with your bum in the air and light a match and hold it next to your arsehole while you let fly, and if you get it right there's a whoosh of flame. It's the methane gas catching alight.'

A row of boys shooting flames out of their bums in a darkened dormitory sounded like a real hoot, and I had to make an effort not to grin as I said, 'Don't they get burnt?'

'Not through pyjamas.'

I turned away so he wouldn't see the expression on my face. Titch had been at boarding school for years so he wouldn't have understood the desperate need I'd had, alone in a house with two aging parents, to be giggly and silly sometimes.

As the *Sweet-Smelling Jasmine* came shuddering down the road towards us, he gave the pole one last kick and said, 'I can't stand it much longer, Izz. If I didn't want to go to varsity so I have to get a decent Matric, I'd leave school and bugger off, honest.'

'Really?' I was thrilled by his daring.

'Really. There must be more to life than learning a whole lot of irrelevant crap and being forever at other people's beck and call. I want to do what I want to do. I want to fly, not bloody crawl! I want to get out of Two Rivers and see how the world works.'

But I was happy to be in Two Rivers. It was where the divine James Singleton lived, for one thing, though I only caught a distant glimpse of him before he too went back to boarding school.

My confrontation with Sister Kathleen began during her first religious instruction lesson, which the non-Catholics had while the Catholics went to catechism. (The two Jewish girls in the class were banished to a bench out of earshot to practise their hemming.) She always started the school year, I had been told, with a comparison of different faiths during

230

which Catholicism emerged as the runaway winner. Five minutes into the lesson I had one of those sudden thought-connections: Mary was a mother goddess like Mariamma! Could the ancient Hindu mother have been a spiritual fore-bear of the similarly named Mary? The idea had a satisfying symmetry to it. Mr Reddy had told me about the Lord Krishna's saying: 'Whatever god a man worships, it is I who answer the prayer.'

I made the mistake of putting up my hand and sharing my thought with Sister Kathleen.

From her reaction, you would have guessed that the devil himself had appeared in a roomful of innocents. 'Do you dare, do you *dare* to compare out loud, in my class, a dirty heathen idol with our Holy Mother?' Her face was as white as her narrow wimple, her eyes coals of wrath.

'But Mariamma's not a heathen idol.' I was indignant; I'd actually seen her at home in her wedding cake temple among her worshippers, which I was sure Sister Kathleen hadn't. 'I mean, she may be just a wooden statue to look at, but she's one of the good Hindu goddesses. Mr Reddy called her benign.'

'Heathen!' Sister Kathleen snatched up a ruler and ad-vanced like the wrath of God on the desk where I was sitting. The girls sitting on either side of me started edging away. 'I've never heard anything so entirely disgostin' in me life! Take it back at once.'

'But –'

'Take it back! Confess in front of all to a wicked intention, and I'll not whack yer.' She held the ruler in a hand that trembled high above her starched scapula.

I was still indignant, not yet alarmed. The girls sitting nearby knew better; they were scrambling for cover behind their desk lids. I said, 'But I wasn't intending to be wicked, Sister. I just had this interesting thought. Honest.'

My persistence in heresy inflamed her even more. My hands were lying unwittingly side by side on top of the desk and the ruler swished down, leaving a line of tiny red beads of blood where the steel edge had bitten through the skin. 'Ow!' I snatched them inwards.

'Take it back! Confess!' she shrieked.

231

Dumb with shock, I shook my head. The ruler swished down again, this time on my bare forearm. It wasn't as sore as the first blow, but it left another blood-beaded line. 'Confess!'

Of course I confessed, not wanting to end up cross-hatched in thin red stripes, and was shrieked at some more and sent to stand outside the door in the passage for the duration of the class. The episode earned me Sister Kathleen's passionate loathing for the rest of my time at the convent and a new friend, a girl called Opal Laverty who whispered out the side of her mouth as she passed me leaving the classroom, 'You've got a hell of a lot of guts.'

She filled me in at break about Sister Kathleen. 'I think she's going potty, the way she carries on. Quite a lot of the parents have complained already. But The Old B always talks them out of doing anything. She says that Sister Kathleen's one of her most useful and trustworthy nuns, invaluable to school discipline.'

Keeping quiet about my mother who had already gone potty, I thought of what Stella and I had overheard in the passage the day before. School discipline, hell. Sister Kathleen was the nuns' best money-raiser on the heavenly charity circuit, and she was more than likely suffering from sore knees and a ragged temper after having had to kneel for so long. But it didn't excuse child-beating. I said confidently, 'My sister's the art teacher here. When she sees these ruler marks, she'll be in Mother Beatrice's office like a shot.'

'Don't underestimate The Old B's powers of persuasion,' Opal warned. 'Tough-minded women make impossible head-mistresses. You can never get under their guard.'

She was right. Stella got the full treatment: Sister Kathleen was prone to lose her temper at times, poor thing, it's her nerves, frayed ragged with worry about the kitchen plumbing. She had been spoken to before about using a ruler, we don't believe in physical punishment at all, dear, but *you* know how the children can try your patience sometimes. And so on, until Stella was convinced that I must have provoked Sister Kathleen and was being quite unreasonable about a couple of small weals that had almost disappeared the next day. Round One to Sister Kathleen.

But Stella was right about the school, which wasn't too bad. The teachers (about half of them nuns) were kind and competent and didn't load you with unnecessary prep. Though sport was supposed to be compulsory, nobody checked whether you were playing netball or lining up dutifully on the ant-heap tennis court for lessons where you got to hit one ball every ten minutes or so. I spent most of my sports periods in the school library, galloping through the shelves of novels that Mother Beatrice deemed suitable for convent girls, and there were some surprising choices.

She announced the details of the Archbishop's essay at assembly a week after the beginning of term. 'The St Francis de Sales Prize is in honour of the patron saint of journalists, as most of you already know. It carries a certificate and a sum of money which has been increased this year to twenty guineas.'

There was a collective gasp; it was riches then.

Beaming down at us, she went on, 'His Grace has decided on a topic that will make you think before you sit down and write: "The Fifties: Our New Decade". Now, girls, I expect you to do me specially proud in view of His Grace's generosity. I want as many as possible of you to enter, juniors as well as seniors. We are looking for a quality of thought and expression that has nothing to do with age. We are looking –' she paused for effect with her wimple quivering '– for a Future Writer.'

I felt a covetous thrill run down my spine: could I, a new girl, dare to enter? Why not? Mother Beatrice had been encouraging when she'd seen my English marks, and twenty guineas was a fortune. For starters, I quizzed Stella and Finn about what they thought the Fifties would be like.

Stella said with a sarcastic laugh, 'Probably just as bloody as the Forties, judging by Korea and the Mau Mau. Mankind seems to thrive on confrontation.'

Finn sat for a long time wreathed in pipe smoke, then said, 'I hope for peace because the world is sick of war. But I also worry about this atom bomb, Izzy, that the scientists say is of course only a deterrent. Bigger and better weapons have never stopped men going to war, yust made them want to try

233

out the frickly things to see if they work. And this new government of ours has some fonny notions about black people. If I must be honest, I'm not too sure about the Fifties.'

It wasn't much to go on, but it started me thinking and looking for ideas in the newspaper and making notes. Trying to write an essay was something to do besides homework in the long Titch-less afternoons after school.

The happiest surprise of the convent was Opal, a blithe gangly boarder with a sharp sense of the ridiculous who became my best friend mainly, I think, because of the delicious sandwiches Stella made. The food in the boarding house was an extra form of penance for the nuns, Opal would say as she slowly savoured the other half of whatever I was eating. I bought her friendship shamelessly, and it was one of the best investments I ever made. We have written to each other for years, exchanging our deepest confidences. Of course, with a surname like Laverty she was always being called 'the lavatory' or 'toilet' or 'WC', but she didn't seem to mind, just laughed and said sewage is in the eye of the beholder.

She became my ally in the ongoing war with Sister Kathleen, deflecting her rage with diversions like dropping a pencil box or putting up her hand to ask to be excused. Sister Kathleen had been forced to relinquish the steel-edged ruler but she had other weapons: a mean pinch that left no mark, cutting sarcasm, ways of demeaning me in front of the other girls, and the ability to hand out detentions. I would have to stay behind after school nearly every other day writing essays on subjects like 'Why I Must Not Answer Back In Class' and copying long passages out of the Bible. 'To save yer wicked little soul,' she'd hiss in justification. 'I've made it me special crusade. I'll not let the devil have his way in my classroom.'

'But Sister –'

'Heathen!' She'd spray me with fine spit. 'Idol-worshipper! Unbeliever!'

Her hostility gave me the status of a dubious scapegoat in the class: the other girls were relieved that I was catching all the flak that term, but avoided me in case what Sister Kathleen said was true.

Except for Opal. When I complained about the unfairness of my situation, she said in her practical way, 'There's nothing much you can do about it, Izz, until she goes totally over the top and does something Mother Beatrice can't explain away.'

'But I'm getting Hail Maryed to death.' Praying on your knees was Sister Kathleen's most severe form of punishment, and when I'd said I wasn't Catholic and Hail Marys didn't apply, she'd answered that it didn't matter whether you were Catholic or not, God was always listening.

'The trouble is, you've become a challenge to her,' Opal said. 'She's determined to save your soul.'

'But I think I'm an atheist, and they don't believe in souls.'

'Precisely. Atheists are like red rags to holy fanatics.'

Opal had blunt fingers with the nails bitten away, a figure like an ironing board and frizzy brown hair from a home perm that had gone wrong; her best feature was the dirty chuckle that often goes with a deep contralto voice. Her father was assistant manager on one of the Herald cane farms further down the coast, and she and her two sisters were weekly boarders. 'We're going down in the world because he drinks,' she confided, 'and Ma's given up trying.'

I went home with her one weekend mainly out of curiosity; she tried quite hard to put me off, but I persisted because I wanted to know what it was like to go down in the world.

It was awful. The house was cramped and hot and dirty and neglected, with a kitchen smelling of 'off' meat and shabby furniture and a stinking outside long-drop. Mr Laverty was a wan man with stains down the front of his shirt and red-rimmed watery eyes that wouldn't look at me; Mrs Laverty hid in her bedroom the whole weekend. Opal and her sisters did all the work and cracked endless silly jokes to hide their embarrassment at having an outsider witness their family's humiliation. Being fetched by Finn on Sunday afternoon was like being picked up by a clean arctic wind and whirled away to normality.

I didn't go to Opal's house again. She came to mine on the weekends she was allowed to, and we explored Two Rivers even more thoroughly together on two old bicycles that Finn dug out of a storeroom, saying that he and Stella used to pack picnics and ride them down to the beach when they first came to Two Rivers. After consultations with Opal's parents, we were allowed to ride in a limited radius in the white residential area of Two Rivers, as long as we kept together and stayed off busy roads.

It was fun having a girl of my own age to hang around with and talk to about our futures. Stella wasn't much help in the futures department because she always suggested things like art or design courses, or going in for teaching. With Sister Kathleen breathing fire and brimstone down my neck every day at school, teaching was the last profession in the world I would have considered.

When I asked Opal what she wanted to do, she said, 'I want to be a cook, actually.'

'A *cook?*' All the cooks I knew were black, except for Ma and Finn, who only made occasional forays into the kitchen. 'Wouldn't that be boring?'

She shrugged. 'It's something I know how to do. I've had plenty of practice at home. And it means I can get a job as a trainee in a hotel or a restaurant, if I'm lucky, and leave home as soon as school is finished. I've got to get away or I'll get sucked down too.'

The only fly in the ointment of our friendship was that she thought Stella the most stylish person she'd ever met, and of course Stella basked in it. To be hero-worshipped, even if only by the daughter of an alcoholic assistant farm manager, was an affirmation of worth neither Finn nor I could give her, hard as we tried. Opal would rave on and on about the brilliant way she made sandwiches and transformed old pieces of furniture and how lovely the house looked. I'd often have to trail off and make the tea, feeling like a spare part, while they got into a huddle over the magazines that Stella bought at fêtes and secondhand bookshops for new ideas. I'm only beginning to understand now, writing this story for very similar reasons, how badly Stella needed the impartial approval of her achievements. We are so much more alike than I've ever wanted to admit. Proper sisters.

I'm sure she never meant to lure my new friend away from me, but she did – geographically, anyway. When she became a success after fleeing to London, it was Stella who lent Opal money to do the cordon bleu course in Paris that led to her becoming a restaurateur. Stella who is dying now in Durban. I must go and see her soon before she slips away, and pay the

236

debt of thanks I was too bitter to honour when we both left Two Rivers. Poor foxy, passionate, self-obsessed Stella. Whenever I start to feel sorry for myself, being tied to a man I don't love, I think of Stella who isn't tied to anyone.

Isabel

She snatches up the receiver of the ringing phone as Ralph goes out to his sisters on the veranda thinking, Their greetings are always noisy. They won't hear me if I talk low enough.

But it still isn't him. A voice says, 'Is that the dragon lady? Fire and brimstone for hire, no questions asked?'

'Opal!' She feels a surge of delight; she hasn't seen her for several years, and she's missed her.

'The very one. Many-faceted, mysteriously brilliant and in town next week, on Thursday the sixth. Could I come and stay the night?'

'Of course! Are you flying? Want me to fetch you?'

'Don't worry. I'll be hiring a car to get around to a series of meetings. Should be finished around five, then I'll come straight over. Probably land up on the doorstep simultaneously with the dreaded George. How are things with you two?'

Opal has always called him 'the dreaded George'; she is the only person Isabel has ever felt able to talk to about her dreary marriage and less than satisfactory life. Living as they do at opposite ends of the country, they have written to each other regularly and visited when they could, but it has never been enough. Opal has become the sister that Stella tried to be so long ago.

Isabel laughs and says, 'Things are worse than ever in one respect, and absolutely amazing in another. You won't believe what I have to tell you. So much has happened recently.'

'I can hear it in your voice. Will we be able to chat without running the risk of George eavesdropping on our girlish confidences?'

'Able to chat' is their private shorthand for catching up on

238

each other's lives without interruption. Isabel says, 'I think that's the day George has arranged to go with a friend to join the local bowling club. Retirement planning, you know? So the coast should be clear for a while.'

'It'll be great to see you.'

'Can't wait. Have a good flight.'

Isabel puts the receiver down and lets her hand rest on it, hoping that if she wishes hard enough it will ring again with her lover's voice to still the nagging worry. What's wrong? she wonders for the hundredth time. He had said, 'Before it's too late.' Has he been told that he's seriously ill? Is he facing the prospect of death all alone in the mountain cottage? How can she sit here calmly drinking tea with her children and making plans to see her best friend when the person who has come to matter most to her could be in mortal agony?

Because I'm locked into my life more than he's locked into his, she thinks with despair. Will I ever be able to shake myself free so we can be together openly?

'What's wrong, Mum? You look upset.' Ralph has come inside after saying hullo to his sisters and caught her wishful thinking by the telephone.

She snatches her hand away like a guilty child caught in the act. 'Oh, nothing.'

'Who was that?'

'Opal. She's coming up next week and phoned to ask if she could stay.'

After she has noted the date of Opal's arrival in her diary, they go out on to the veranda and she pours tea for Ralph while he jokes with his sisters. Watching them, she thinks, They have an ease with each other that George and I have never had. What is it that makes some family relationships work and others fail dismally? Is it unrealistic even to think of creating a happy family when the basic union of father and mother is so unsatisfactory?

The answer lies in front of her eyes. Chryssa is leaning back in her chair watching her brother with a slight smile, her frown temporarily smoothed away. Janine is laughing. The affection on both their faces warms Isabel's heart, because it has not always been this way. There have been endless childish fights over the years, many arguments and tedious tugs of war: 'But it's *mine*, not yours! Mummeee, Ralphie's hurting me! Make him go away!' And now they've suddenly grown up into people I really enjoy, she thinks, pleased.

Ralph has always been the entertainer in the family: the capering little shrimp of a kid brother showing off and cracking jokes to hide his anxieties. At school he had taken stock of his assets and drawbacks and decided that the only way for a nerdy kid with a stammer to make an impression was to become the wag of the class. But it had only been partially successful. His imitations and witty cheek towards his teachers had earned him a reputation for daring but not improved his social standing; a nerd remained a nerd when friends were chosen, however amusing. His marks had trailed and his reports were full of 'Could do betters'; in high school he had mostly relied on his computer for companionship.

Yet here he is, grown up and with a girlfriend, entertaining his two older sisters with aplomb. Isabel thinks, You can't predict which way children will go. Their personalities change like chameleons. Just when you think they're going to turn into one sort of person, they sprout new interests and enthusiasms and dash off in another direction. And when they finally grow up (finally!), as if to underline the recurrent teenage refrain, 'I'm not like you were, Ma, I'm different,' they turn into quite unexpected people.

It works the other way too: I'm turning into someone *they* didn't expect, with new priorities in my life. Unnoticed by Janine and Ralph, Isabel gets up and goes to the bedroom to try and telephone the mountain cottage one more time. Only Chryssa's pink-rimmed eyes follow her, speculating.

Extract from the official report of the Sandham Commission of Enquiry into the Easter 1952 Riot:

'. . . Mr Bhiraj Abjee, an attorney practising in Durban, testified that he had acted for the Natal Indian Congress and the Mariamman temple committee in the matter relating to the expropriation of the temple tower in Two Rivers.

He then made a strident statement to the effect that in his opinion the judgement for expropriation was wrong in law, since consecrated ground should by rights remain so in perpetuity. He further stated that the courts, "Would not have dared to ride rough-shod over a Christian church's objections. It's only because we're coolies that they think they can push us around. But this coolie is tired of being pushed around! This coolie has had enough! This coolie is going to take the case of the Mariamman temple to the highest courts in the land!"

Mr Abjee was ruled in contempt of the Commission, placed under arrest and escorted from the room. He was later sentenced to twenty pounds or two weeks and warned by the Bar Council for professional misconduct. It is recommended that the police be instructed to keep a close eye on this potential troublemaker, who openly professes his belief in socialism and the passive resistance methods practised by the late Mahatma Gandhi.

Mr Shunmugam Moodley had to be subpoenaed to appear before the Commission. He would admit only to being the initial convenor of the group of young Indian men known as the temple guardians, and thereafter refused to answer any questions. It is understood that his eldest son Sivalingum Moodley, who was one of the most active guardians, has not been seen since the first night of the riot. The police believe that he has left the country . . .'

16

January turned into February, King George VI died and white Natal went into mourning; half the girls in the school were sobbing their eyes out the day we heard it over the news. When I told Stella, she said, 'Typical. Those are the ones whose parents still talk about Home, though they've probably never even been to England. I can't stand grovelling over royalty.'

The following week, a huge furore blew up over the temporary road camp that had suddenly appeared on the far side of the sugar mill. They had come to widen first the temple bridge over the Umsindo river, the road engineer said, and then the Herald bridge over the Umlilwane river, preparatory to widening the main road. The temple tower would have to be pulled down as soon as the final expropriation documents had gone through. It appeared that the broad pathway and flamboyant trees on one side of the road were doomed too – he wouldn't say on which side. That same week the plinth at the base of Old Man Herald's granite obelisk developed a curious crack and a rumour spread that he was turning in his grave.

A mutinous residents' meeting was held in the town hall and a petition of protest was drawn up and signed by hundreds of people at tables in the square and outside the Coolietown shops. Stella manned the one at the bottom of the pharmacy steps, which she covered with photographs of flamboyant trees cut out of old company brochures featuring the town; in front of it she hung a banner with HANDS OFF OUR TREES! in screaming red capital letters. White and Indian protesters got together in indignant huddles everywhere, for once united by a mutual resolve. There

242

were no Zulu protesters; as one old woman said to Finn with a sarcastic cackle, 'Why should we worry, baas? We not allowed to live here anyway.'

The serious trouble started when Mr Reddy called on Major McFadyen to ask him to sign the petition on behalf of the Herald Company, and was told that this was impossible as it was the company who had asked for the main road to be widened in the first place.

Their conversation was reported by one of the secretaries who worked in the anteroom to the general manager's sanctum.

Major McFadyen said, 'The main road is far too narrow for the increasing traffic load it has to carry, most particularly during the crushing season from May to December when our cane trucks are running. Widening it will be of great benefit to Two Rivers which is getting impossibly congested on working days.'

'I am disputing that it will benefit us in any way, Major.' Mr Reddy spoke in a deadly quiet voice when he was angry. 'The traffic will get heavier, the pathways outside the shops will almost disappear and the shopkeepers will suffer.'

'No reason why they should. Increased traffic surely means more customers?'

'Not if it is passing through our town to get to somewhere else. We do not need a wider road. The cane trucks could easily be sent round via side roads, I think.' I could picture Mr Reddy leaning towards him in the earnest way he had done when talking to Stella.

'The company considered doing that, believe me. We don't want the pleasant ambience of Two Rivers to change any more than you do. We live here too, you know.' The Major gave the hearty laugh he used to jolly along inferiors. 'But it turns out that the bally bridges on the secondary roads weren't built to take extra-heavy vehicles like cane trucks. Widening the main road is the only possible solution, and since the two bridges involved are inadequate for the increased traffic volume they will have to carry, they must be widened as well.'

'But it means our temple tower has to go! That is not acceptable to us.'

243

'I'm sorry, Mr Reddy, truly, but we must look to the future. Besides our cane trucks, people are starting to buy cars again now that the war's well and truly over and wages are going up, and more cars mean wider and better roads.' The Major produced his trump card. 'You have one yourself, I think, a blue Studebaker?'

'Please do not be turning your argument around to attack me personally.' The listening secretary reported that she had had to move closer to the door of the Major's sanctum to hear Mr Reddy's furious reply. 'The land next to the temple bridge is long-time sacred ground to our people. It cannot be bought.'

'This is most unfortunate, most unfortunate, but there's no alternative, I assure you.' Major McFadyen got up and went round his vast mahogany desk so he could shake Mr Reddy's hand before dismissing him. (One had to observe the niceties with a wealthy Indian.) 'Perhaps the company could help with the building materials for a new tower when your committee decides where it should be placed?'

The secretary, peeping through the crack of the half-open door, reported that Mr Reddy ignored the Major's outstretched hand, joining his own two hands under his chin in a deliberately Indian gesture as he said, 'We are not for bribing, Major. This is a matter of extreme principle. We intend to fight the expropriation in the Durban courts.'

'Fight away, then. I'm afraid you'll find that mere religion can't stop the march of progress,' Major McFadyen said, causing Mr Reddy such offence that he would never speak to him again.

The urgent application to the courts barely made a paragraph in the *Natal Mercury*, and was not reported at all in *The Herald*. The temple committee lost against the Natal Roads Department, of course. The following week, notice was served that the tower should be vacated before the first of April, when bulldozers would start tearing it down.

The emotional temperature in Two Rivers went up another notch when the committee formed a band of young Hindu men called the temple guardians. They took it in turns to patrol the temple two at a time, dressed in Indian clothes:

loose white tops, dhotis and black scarves knotted round their heads with the long ends dangling down on one side. Each carried a long wooden stick and as they roamed the temple grounds they would lightly thwack the trees and the jasmine-covered walls and the stone steps as if asserting claim to them: These are our things. This is our land. Watch out!

After their presence had been reported to him, Sergeant Koekemoer got on his 500cc Triumph and chugged over to the temple in full uniform: navy serge jacket and trousers, Sam Browne belt buckled on top with his police revolver in a shiny brown leather holster at his waist, police cap with brass badge, motorcycle boots. He must have sweltered unbearably in that uniform – February was the muggiest month of the sauna summer in Two Rivers – but he always wore the full regalia on official business. Finn said it was crazy in that climate to wear anything but cotton, though he understood why the Sergeant felt obliged to sweat it out in serge. It had to do with the carrying out of the law: if people want a decent, well-ordered society, they must learn to respect the police. 'And in yust the same way the police, of course, must respect and uphold the rights of the people,' he added.

Opal and I happened to be walking down the main road towards the bridge after school when we saw Sergeant Koekemoer stop the Triumph near the steps that led down to the temple, kick the stand into place and go over to the parapet to look down into the temple grounds. We sauntered as close as we dared and leaned over to see what he was looking at. Two of the guards were walking up and down in front of the entrance porch, thumping the worn stone paving with their sticks at each step; the templegoers and beggars who would usually be clustered on the flight of steps leading down from the porch had drifted elsewhere, leaving them bare and showing their age. Ferns and moss grew in deep cracks in the cement, and so did cigarette butts and peanut shells and orange peel and the blood-caked feathers that flew when chickens were slaughtered.

After watching for a while, the Sergeant spotted several members of the temple committee leaving the main door and called down to them, crooking a thick forefinger to indicate that they should come up on to the bridge.

Opal nudged me and whispered, 'This should be interesting.' We shrank into the shade of one of the concrete columns that supported the parapet and the iron railings beneath it.

Two men detached themselves from the group and came toiling up the worn concrete steps. Both were sweaty and panting when they got to the top: Mr Reddy from age, Mr Moodley from fat. Mr Reddy said, 'Yes, sir?'

The Sergeant's heavy jaw shot out. 'I don't like the military look of those boys you've got guarding the temple. It's got to stop, you hear?'

'They are doing nothing illegal, sir.'

'If I don't like something, it stops. I am the law in this town.' A fist banged down on the parapet.

'Pardon me, Sergeant, but I think the law allows private guards on private property.' Mr Reddy, about half the policeman's size and at least twice his age, stood his ground with utmost politeness.

The jaw shot out at least another inch. 'Who are you to say, hey?'

'I have spoken to my attorney, Mr Bhiraj Abjee, about the matter, and he says –'

'I too have spoken to my attorney,' Mr Moodley wheezed, looking anxious.

'You two ch –' the Sergeant apparently bit back the 'charras' he was about to say and substituted, 'You people want to argue with me?'

'No.' Mr Reddy shook his head. 'We are just wanting to avoid any trouble at our holy place, so we have volunteers patrolling there.'

'If it's a holy place, why do they need fighting sticks?'

'Those are not fighting sticks such as the Zulus carry. They are lathis, Sergeant. A weapon much used by the Indian police.' Mr Reddy managed a thin smile. 'We are thinking them appropriate for the occasion.'

Without admitting defeat, the Sergeant agreed reluctantly that perhaps the guardians could continue to patrol the temple, but banned them from leaving the grounds. 'If I see even one of your boys on the roads or hanging around with those sticks, I'll lock him up, you hear? Just seeing a weapon in another man's hand makes some people pick fights.'

246

'Yet you don't stop the Zulus carrying their fighting sticks?'

The Sergeant gave them a grim smile. 'Never. It would be like trying to cut off their cocks. You've got to be realistic so far as the Zulus is concerned.'

'How enlightening,' Mr Reddy murmured. 'I had no idea we blacks were being treated with such kid gloves.'

The Sergeant took a while to digest that, then he glared at each man in turn and said, 'My problem with your boys is, they might get into fights with the Zulus. I won't have any fighting in this town, finish and klaar. You tell your boys: they put one foot wrong and I'll have them locked up so fast they won't know if they coming or going. OK?'

As the two men nodded, they must have been glumly aware that they were being asked to do the impossible: restrain the sons and grandsons who were vowing in anger not to be pushed around by the whites as their parents and grandparents had. The gift of education is a two-edged sword, Mr Reddy said once, and at last I understand what he meant.

Govind came back to work after a week with his arm still strapped across his chest, complaining of constant pain. Every time he moved there would be an ostentatious wince and a sharp intake of breath to show us how much he was suffering. Finn had offered to put him on half pay for as long as it took the collar-bone to mend, but he had insisted on coming back to work because his mother needed the money, he said. The Pathers' fifty pounds had been used up paying the doctor and the repair shop that mended his bicycle and outfitting the younger brothers and sisters in much-needed school clothes. 'And we have to eat too, you know, sir?' I heard him say, lowering his eyelids so it wouldn't sound too offensive.

But Finn was snuffling in distress and didn't notice. 'I hope the family isn't going hungry, Govind. Is there no other source of income?'

'My mother sells rotis down by the school on weekdays but I am the only wage earner, sir.' His adam's apple did a double jerk. 'It's a heavy burden on top of the night school.'

'It must be. I'll try to help you all I can.' Finn patted him on the wrong shoulder, causing a genuine wince and himself more distress. He hated hurting people even when it was for

247

a good reason like drawing out a splinter or a thorn, as he was often asked to do. He trimmed corns and dressed boils and bound sprained ankles too, and kept pumice stones which he would lend out for weeks at a time to people with badly cracked heels. 'A pharmacist in a small town with not enough doctors has to be a yack of all trades,' he told me. 'Yust as well I did two years of medical training.'

'You were going to be a doctor?' Stella had never told me this.

He got his deep sea look. 'I wanted to very badly, but the war came along the year after I started at university and that was that. Norway had no money to send its missionaries and I had to get a yob, so I went into pharmaceuticals. It was as close as I could get to medicine, and being a protected occupation I knew I probably wouldn't get called up.'

I remembered how he'd said that he would have registered as a conscientious objector. 'Didn't people mock you for not wanting to go to war?'

He shrugged. 'Ya, of course. There was a madness in the young men then that you can see today in the temple guardians. They are so furious to put the world to rights that they don't think straight. I yust couldn't see myself using a gun to kill people, Izzy. Not for any reason.'

I had been seven when the war ended and had seen my share of war films: glorious sagas of derring-do in which brave airmen like Guy Gibson and gritty old generals like Monty and Ike and McArthur took on and vanquished the Huns and the Eyeties and the Japs, saving Western civilisation from evil incarnate. It would be another fifteen years before Vietnam would change the general attitude to war. I said, 'But what about murderers? What if someone strangled Stella or bashed a baby's head against a wall? Wouldn't you want to kill them for doing something so bad?'

There was a moment when his face grew sadder than I had ever seen it and his eyes a shade of blue that was close to ink. Then he gave a dry laugh and said, 'Sometimes I want to strangle Stella myself. Don't you?' And the moment was stored away in my mind until today.

Finn was a pacifist to his core, yet his actions caused terrible hurt. It was the one paradox that Stella, who loved paradoxes, could never forgive.

Isabel

This time the phone is answered: his voice chopping the words off. 'Yes? What is it? Did you see her?'

She thinks, 'Her'. That means he's got someone else. It's over. He's had enough of me phoning and pestering him and shilly-shallying about my family. I've blown it. My chance of a lifetime. She stands numbly listening to the crackling line, unable to make her mouth do anything but gasp with the pain she feels.

'Vince, is that you? Talk louder, man. This line's terrible. Can you hear me now?'

She remembers that Vince is his publisher and says, 'No, sorry, it's me.'

'Isabel!' It is an explosion in her ear, a sharper stab of pain ramming into her head. 'What the hell has happened? Why the telegram? Is anything wrong?'

'I thought –' She stops, uncertain whether his anger is at her or for her.

'*You* thought! Hell, I've been worried crazy up here. Would have got into the car and driven down straight away if it wasn't for my fucking deadline at the end of the week. Izzy, what's wrong, my dear love?'

She feels a spreading warmth soothing the nerve endings that have made her skin feel like velvet rubbed the wrong way all day. 'Nothing. Everything.'

'Why didn't you phone back? I kept trying from this end, but no luck. When the telegram arrived half an hour ago, I phoned Vince and told him to make sure that you're all right. I thought maybe that bastard had found out and had a go at you.'

'No. It's nothing like that.' She thinks, How can I explain

250

my terror at the thought of losing him without sounding clingy or pathetic?

'What, then? One of the kids in trouble?'

'Yes, but that's not why I sent the telegram.' She tries to marshal her feelings so that she can express them properly, and fails. The words pour out. 'When I spoke about coming for the weekend, you sounded so angry. You said that I must stop creating obstacles and make up my mind about leaving George because life is moving on for both us. You said that you want all of me before it's too late. Why too late? Are you ill? Oh God, are you dying? And then the phone went dead and I couldn't get through to you and I've been almost out of my mind with worry all day –'

There is silence at the other end of the crackling phone. She turns her head to make sure that Chryssa and Janine and Ralph are still down at the bottom of the garden picking the last of the plums to take home, then shouts into the receiver, 'Are you there? Answer me! Talk, damn you!'

Her answer is a rumble of laughter that gets louder and louder until he is bellowing. He laughs and laughs and laughs while she sits on the edge of her bed holding the phone away from her ear, wondering if he is quite sane. Perhaps visiting Ethiopia again, seeing the dreadful suffering, has tipped him over the edge.

Still chuckling, he manages to say, 'Izzy, dear lovely Izzy, I was in a foul temper this morning because I hit the wrong series of buttons on my computer and wiped the whole of yesterday's work. I just meant before it is too late for us to enjoy each other. And here we are both getting ourselves into knots because the telephone department is mending the lines down the road and keep cutting me off. It's the bloody government's fault again.' He breaks off and clamps his hand over the mouthpiece; she can hear continued muffled laughing in the background.

'So you're not mad with me? I can still come?'

She hears him take his hand away and the deep beloved voice, still amused, saying, 'What a question. I can't wait. Two whole days of you.'

'There's a lot to talk about. Things have changed a lot in the past few hours.'

251

'What things?'

Again there is the leap of hope in his voice and she thinks, amazed, He really loves me. Here I am well over halfway through an indifferent life and suddenly it feels as though the moon and stars – the entire Milky Way! – have fallen into my lap.

'Izzy? What things?'

'Can't talk now. Tell you at the weekend.' She makes a quick calculation, based on the time when George said he would be leaving for Sun City. 'I should be there around eleven. What would you like me to bring?'

'Ambrosia,' he says. 'Nectar. The elixir of youth. I want to enjoy you forever.'

'Be serious, love. We can't live on fresh air, and I'm sure there are things you need.'

His answer is a growling, 'Don't fuss about details. All I need is a jug of wine, a loaf of bread and thou beside me, etcetera. Come quickly.'

'I can hardly bear to wait,' she says, and puts the phone down thinking, He must be the last romantic man left in the world. And I the luckiest woman.

When she turns round, Chryssa is standing in the doorway with a basket of plums. 'We're just leaving. Who was that, Mum?'

Caught in the act. But Isabel, moving in a bubble of joy now, doesn't flounder for an explanation as she would have only yesterday. She says firmly, 'Just a friend I'll be spending the weekend with while Dad goes to Sun City.'

'Who?'

'None of your business, dear old thing,' Isabel says, sailing out of the room to say goodbye to her children and answer Vince's phone call with a cheery, 'I'm fine. Never been finer.'

17

I slaved over the Archbishop's essay for a full month before handing it in on the due date at the end of February. Stella had asked the convent secretary to type it out for me in return for a bottle of imported hand lotion that Finn couldn't sell in the pharmacy because its box had got damaged. (She was a genius at bartering unwanted goods for services she needed; it matched her skill at buying things on sales and bidding at auctions.)

Aware of the paramount importance of neatness in convent schools, I had borrowed one of Stella's lettering stencils to print the essay's title on the front of a cream cardboard folder – THE FIFTIES: OUR NEW DECADE – and underneath, BY ISABEL JANE POYNTON, STD 8. Then I'd punched double holes in the typescript and bound it into the folder with a length of narrow satin ribbon in the school colour, ochre (a subtle touch, I thought) threaded through and tied in front with a flat bow. I thought it looked wonderful: a truly professional piece of work.

But standing outside Mother Beatrice's office with the other hopeful essayists, I thought of her saying, 'We are looking for a Future Writer,' and was struck dumb at my cheek in even thinking I could enter. The girls chattering round me were mostly older and seemed dauntingly clever. Their essays were thick wodges of lined paper covered in scholarly writing, unlike my elegant cardboard folder which in the cold light of day seemed to be trying to masquerade as a chocolate box. Trust me to get it wrong, to be seduced by Stella's passion for making things look good.

I was sidling towards the bare brick passage wall so I could sneak away and hide my shame in the cloakroom when the

253

office door jerked open and a hand clamped down on my arm. 'Is this your offering, Isabel?'

I stood gaping up at Mother Beatrice with my mouth opening and closing like one of Finn's goldfish. Finally I managed to croak, 'Yes, but I – I–I've had second thoughts about it.'

'Why?'

Major squirm. 'It's, well, just not any good.'

'I'll be the judge of that. Come in, child.' She hustled me into her office and expertly wrested the beribboned folder from my clutch. 'This looks very attractive. Ten out of ten for presentation. I hope the contents are as good as the cover.'

I hung my head. 'That's the trouble, it's probably useless. Though I worked jolly hard.'

'In between detentions? I haven't had very good reports of you from your form teacher.' The shiny-clean face surrounded by starched cotton gave off chilly moon rays when Mother Beatrice was displeased.

I blurted, 'She doesn't like me, I don't know why.' Sister Kathleen had been diligent about broadcasting my alleged sins; I was getting wary looks from the other teachers when I walked into their classes.

'She says your behaviour is rude and argumentative and unbefitting a convent girl.'

'It's not! I just seem to rub her up the wrong way. And I don't always agree with the things she says.'

'What things?' Mother Beatrice's shrewd black eyes were as effective as twin thumbscrews.

'About religion. It's not wicked to go into other people's holy places and find out about their gods, is it?'

'Ah. So you've been out and about exploring our little town.' To my surprise, she looked approving. 'We're a tangled skein here, child. Christians and Moslems and Hindus and people who believe in a host of tribal religions rubbing along together as best we can, and that means not very well. But – how can I put this to you most simply? – what's important is not the different gods people worship, but to have faith in the One God to whom they all lead. We must tolerate each other's differences in the knowledge that we ultimately believe in the same thing.'

254

But the trouble was, I didn't think I believed there was a God at all. You just couldn't be *sure*. And if there wasn't a God, what else was there to believe in? But I couldn't ask Mother Beatrice these questions, however sympathetic she was being. Since nuns' whole lives were based on the fact of there being a God, to question his existence was to suggest that they were wasting them.

I said, 'Sister Kathleen doesn't seem to tolerate me very well.' There was a lump in my throat at the unfairness of being singled out for having unusual ideas. It was hard enough being a semi-orphan and a new girl without having to cope with an ongoing vendetta being waged by my class teacher as well.

Mother Beatrice bent forward and put her hand on my arm; disembodied by the voluminous sleeve of her black habit, it was very white and smooth and cool. 'Perhaps you could practise a little diplomacy, Isabel? Sister Kathleen is one of the most fervent and single-minded believers I have ever met and such faith leaves little room for tolerance, I'm afraid.'

I could feel my lower lip pushing out. 'Why should I be diplomatic and tolerant when she isn't? She goes out of her way to be horrible to me. She called me a pox the other day. It's not fair.'

Mother Beatrice sighed and took her hand away. 'Life is seldom fair. That's why it's important to be tough-minded, so we can cope with unfairness and intolerance. If I tell you that Sister Kathleen led a life of hell as a child, would you try to understand the way she is now? Her father and mother both drank, and her uncle –' She broke off with an abruptness that I only understood years later. 'Don't discuss this with the other girls, will you? I've told you in confidence because I think it may help the situation between you. It's difficult for her to change now, but you're at the beginning of your life. You can roll with the blows and come up smiling still. And I'll speak to Sister Kathleen again, right?'

The smile she gave me was one of mingled complicity and encouragement. Crossing my fingers so she couldn't see, I said, 'I won't tell anyone.' Of course Opal would have to know. We were allies in the classroom war.

Mother Beatrice nodded. 'That's settled then. I shall look forward to reading this beautifully bound essay, Isabel. Get along to your class now, dear.'

There was a week to go before the result of the essay competition was announced. I was on tenterhooks, half the time hoping that I had an outside chance of at least coming third or fourth, and the other half plunged into misery because I was sure I'd written absolute rubbish which the adjudicators would toss aside with the contempt it deserved.

My fifteenth birthday fell during that week and instead of a present, Stella drove Opal and me into Durban and treated us to a mixed grill in the Greenacres tea room and a bioscope at the Playhouse called *Thunder on the Hill*, starring Claudette Colbert, Ann Blyth and Gladys Cooper. It was about a nun who solves a murder mystery in a convent, and on the way home in the dickey seat with the wind blowing our hair into brush-defying tangles, we made up a murder story to fit our own set of nuns. Sister Kathleen would be the victim (naturally), Frank the dour school handyman would be the psychotic killer, and Opal and I would be the intrepid girl detectives who solved the mystery.

'We could corner him in the basement amid hissing steam pipes,' Opal was improvising as we pulled up behind one of Naidoo's buses which had stopped on the temple bridge. There was something blocking it in front.

'And I'd knock him out with a plumber's wrench.'

'Wouldn't it be better to have him slip on a patch of oil and fall into the open furnace and suffer an agonising fiery death? Then we wouldn't actually have to do anything violent ourselves.'

'But the convent doesn't have a basement or a furnace. We'll have to think of something else. How about Frank creeps up behind her while she's praying in the chapel and strangles her with her rosary? The camera could zoom in on her face going all purple and her eyes bulging and her mouth drooling spit and –'

'– and her stinky old black shoes drumming helplessly on the floor until they give one last twitch and flop sideways. That could be an amazing scene.'

256

'Heavens, you two are bloodthirsty,' Stella called back from the driver's seat.

'It's just our unusually vivid imaginations,' I said. 'I'm going to be a writer, Stell, did I tell you?'

She turned round with a snort of laughter. 'You don't say. A writer of what?'

'Novels, of course. Passion. Romance. Adventure. Murder. I'm going to be rich and famous one day.'

'I dreamed of being rich and famous too, kiddo, and look where I ended up: Coolietown.' She looked around, her foxy eyes narrowing as she took in the littered bridge and the temple tower sticking up through the trees and the line of shacks that ran alongside the muddy river below us. 'Not exactly a launching pad to success. I wonder what's holding up the bus in front?'

Stella had this way of blowing out a fine sour mist that could dampen your fun in a moment. It wasn't that she meant to be a spoilsport. It was just that her discontent kept showing like a dirty petticoat under the hem of a dress, giving you little shocks of realisation at what really lay beneath.

When we had finally crawled across the bridge and the bus pulled off the road at the bus stop, we saw why the traffic had been held up. There was a procession of Indian men walking along the middle of the main road behind a banner saying: !!! HANDS OFF OUR TEMPLE !!!

Stella said indignantly, 'They've pinched my slogan. And why wasn't I told about this protest march? I would have joined in – hell, I'm going to join in! I'll just park the car outside the pharmacy and you two can scoot inside and tell Finn.'

The photograph that appeared in the *Natal Mercury* next day said it all. I have it here before me in the scrap book, opposite the stubs of our bioscope tickets and the birthday card with 'Love from Ma' in shaky writing inside. She was getting better slowly but steadily, Aunty Mavis had said when she last telephoned. The doctors were pleased with her progress. She was beginning to feed herself again.

The newspaper photograph shows Mr Reddy and fat Mr Moodley walking past Old Man Herald's obelisk holding the banner between them. Behind stretches a line of men with angry shouting faces, some with their fists in the air. Marching next to Mr Reddy is Stella in the outfit she had dressed up in to take us into Durban: a men's linen jacket in a size too big for her so it was loose instead of fitted like everyone else's, flappy black trousers and huge gold gypsy earrings. She is facing the camera with an insolent glare and her hair is sticking out in spikes, ruffled by the wind that blew their shouting away that afternoon in clouds of dust off the pathways, so people in the white parts of Two Rivers didn't even know that a demonstration had taken place until they saw it in the paper the next day. The caption underneath reads: 'Defiance campaign erupts in Two Rivers over road-widening dispute. Police are investigating.'

Stella came banging through the glass door into the pharmacy afterwards, hoarse and elated, crowing, 'Sergeant Koekemoer nearly fell off his motorbike when he saw me. Siding with Indians, what next!'

'You're yust lucky he didn't arrest you.'

Opal had gone home, and Finn and I had been standing in his favourite spot by the apothecary bottle window, watching out for Stella. Now he had both his furry bear's paws on her shoulders, trying to calm her down. Stella could fly right off the handle when she got really excited about something.

'I'd like to have seen him try.' She threw back her head with a hooting laugh. 'I'd have given him stick in front of everybody. You can't arrest people for making a peaceful protest. Gandhi knew that when he started the passive resistance movement. Did you know that Gandhi actually lived in Two Rivers for a while as a young man? Mr Reddy was telling me while we marched.' The excitement of defying authority had given her a brilliance I had never seen before.

Finn, looking down at her, stroked her hair saying, 'You get involved so deep, my Stellen. I hope it doesn't bring troble.'

'What trouble? Let them try! Let them just try and stop us now! We're not going to allow the roads department to move in and wreck our lovely little town, tear down the trees and the temple tower and take away our wide pathways just so that more trucks can come grinding through, choking us

258

with exhaust fumes. We're going to fight them every inch of the way! We're going to lie down in front of the bulldozers! Just watch us, Finn. Just watch!'

She had a bilious attack at supper that night which turned into a migraine like the ones Ma used to have. I was hovering outside their bedroom when Finn came out after making her swallow some tablets and sitting by the bedside until she fell asleep.

'Is she OK?'

'Nay, Izzy, she's feeling very bad. It has happened several times now, this terrible headache. If she's not better by the morning, I'll call the doctor.'

'Ma has headaches like that. Maybe it runs in the family.'

'Maybe.' As he turned away to take the empty glass he was holding to the kitchen, I saw the same thought as I was thinking reflected on his face: maybe Stella too would have a nervous breakdown. We both knew she wasn't happy. We had both seen the brilliance.

The announcement of the winner of the Archbishop's prize took place at the last morning assembly in February in an atmosphere of highly charged seriousness. Mother Beatrice always gave the essay competition a major build-up because she reckoned that a good standard of English impressed parents and got better fees out of them, Stella said.

We were lined up as usual along the edges of the paths that crisscrossed the classroom block courtyard. (The nuns had a mania for making us line up; we always had to walk in a crocodile on class expeditions outside the school grounds.) Mother Beatrice stood at her lectern on the raised brick platform outside the chapel. Next to her sat the Archbishop, a surprisingly young man with a long pale face and long pale fingers that looked as though they had been recently laundered. He wore a purple satin skullcap and a matching wide sash over a long black cassock with a row of buttons like purple Smarties running down the front. Round his neck was a silver chain with a huge cross hanging from it.

Ranged on either side of the dais sitting on classroom chairs were the teachers, lay on one side and nuns on the other; Stella wasn't there that morning because she'd woken up with another migraine. Sister Helga sat at the foot-pumped organ just inside the chapel door where she played the accompaniment for our hymns and brisk jolly marches to get us back to our classrooms in a good mood afterwards. It was Sister Kathleen's day for turning the music pages, so she was standing next to the organ with her face in the chapel shadows.

Mother Beatrice began, 'Girls, it is my great pleasure this morning to introduce His Grace the Archbishop again. He has come to award his most generous annual essay prize: twenty guineas and a certificate.'

There was a flurry of clapping. His Grace the Archbishop inclined his head with a keen smile.

'But before I hand over to him, I would like to comment on the standard of entries received this year. With the exception of the top three essays, it was poor. We were hoping for thoughtful speculation about our new decade, the Fifties, but we received an assortment of wild prophesies ranging from robot servants to men on the moon.'

Everybody laughed.

'I am also,' Mother Beatrice went on, looking grim, 'quite appalled at the bad grammar, atrocious spelling and even worse handwriting that we adjudicators have had to wade through. This is not good enough for a school that sets great store by reading and does its best to encourage Future Writers.' She always made it clear, by slightly hushing her voice as she said them, that the words had capitals. 'Starting tomorrow, there will be daily spelling tests and extra grammar lessons, and slovenly writing will be severely penalised.'

Everybody groaned.

'Spider scrawls, inkblots, excessive crossings out and erasures are banned henceforth from any piece of work that is handed in. Grammatical mistakes will be corrected and written out ten times. Persistent offenders will receive regular detentions until they mend their ways.'

Everybody sighed. The Old B was serious.

She unleashed the most ferocious smile I had ever seen. 'Girls, in this convent we will strive for neatness and order and a strict adherence to the King's English. We don't want the poor man, bless his soul, turning in his newly dug grave.'

She moved sideways, holding out a commanding arm. Mother Beatrice knew how to dramatise occasions. 'And now, Your Grace, over to you.'

I was standing near the front of our Standard 8 row with Opal behind me. The sun had not yet risen high enough to reach into the courtyard, so it was still cool; through the cloister arches to the right of the chapel, the gardens sloping down to the river were flashing with a million sparkles of sunlight after rain during the night. It seemed a good portent: a diamond morning, rare in that muggy climate. And for once the town had stopped smelling of boiling sugar. The cane-cutting season had ended on the last day of January and the mill stood silent while its machinery was being overhauled.

The Archbishop got up and swished towards the lectern, watched by a hundred and fifty silent girls in putty-coloured uniforms and the entire teaching staff poised on their chairs, the nuns with their faces following their spiritual father like a row of imperturbable penguins. Hairs were prickling on the back of my neck. Any minute now one of us would be twenty whole guineas richer . . . not that I had a chance, of course. I wondered who it would be: some clever Matric girl from a well-off family, most likely, who wouldn't need it. Life was like that, Stella used to say, quoting what she claimed was the only thing she remembered from Bible readings at Sunday school when she was a kid: '"To them that hath shall be given." It always seemed so bloody unfair until I found out that it was true.'

The young Archbishop turned out to be lively, erudite and funny. He cracked three jokes to start with, allowing the pent-up anticipation in his audience to escape in laughter, then went on to extol the virtues of good writing, and in particular, essays.

'The essay prize is named, as you know, for the patron saint of journalists, St Francis de Sales. If we are to have good journalism, we need writers who can put their points succinctly, with insight and authority and a modicum of wit. Newspapers provide daily commerce with the world outside our small parochial lives, and one should be able to rely on them for objective, well-written reporting.

261

'I offer a monetary reward as well as a certificate for this prize because, being a more worldly man than I may appear –' the nuns twittered '– I know that cash is a splendid incentive when you don't have very much. And I am very keen that as many girls as possible should enter every year. Nothing venture, nothing gain, as the actress said to the archbishop.'

The nuns looked a bit shocked but everyone else laughed again. I was thinking, He's a good advertisement for Catholics. Much more fun than boring old Reverend Mundy at St Agatha's was.

'And now for the winners.' The Archbishop's smile sharpened as his eyes trawled the assembly for every last ounce of attention. 'As Mother Beatrice has already told you, there are three essays which we adjudicators felt were worthy of note. For this reason I am awarding special certificates to the two runners-up, and these are –'

My heart began to thud in thick heavy beats.

'– Linda Todd and Denise Johnson. Both submitted interesting entries of a good standard. Will they come forward to receive their awards, please?'

There was polite clapping as they went up to the platform for the Archbishop's handshake and their certificates. Opal bent forward and whispered in my ear, 'You've still got a chance, Izz.'

I shrugged as casually as I could. How had she known I'd entered an essay? I'd kept it a deadly secret and she hadn't been at school on the day I handed it in. But the encouragement was typical of her generous spirit.

'As for the winner.' The Archbishop paused. 'Her use of language is exact, her construction logical and her ideas interesting – particularly her conclusion. We cannot enjoy the sunshine of peace, she says, without being aware of the still-present shadows of war. I found this essay outstanding.'

Was I hearing right? My heart began to thump so hard against my ribs that I thought people would start turning round to see what was making all the noise.

'This person is a reader as well as a writer, girls, and I cannot recommend the virtues of reading too highly. Books have been constant and faithful companions in my own life –'

the nuns looked moist-eyed '– and they have given me endless pleasure and instruction. It is on this note that I would like to ask for a fanfare on the organ – Sister?'

Sister Helga's black laceups began to pump the organ pedals and a burble of music swelled out of the chapel then subsided again.

'And now –' The Archbishop raised one finger as silence fell. I stood in a stunned trance, wondering if my heart would burst under the strain of all the pounding it was doing.

'– and now it is my great pleasure to ask Isabel Poynton from Standard 8 to come up and receive the St Francis de Sales Prize for 1952: twenty well-deserved guineas and a certificate.'

The clapping started again and Opal cheered and thumped my back. 'Go on. Go up. You've won!' Dizzy with astounded joy, I stumbled up the path towards the platform. Other hands were patting my back, other voices saying, 'Well done' and 'Shot, hey?' and 'Lucky you'.

I was within touching distance of the lectern when Sister Kathleen Killeally exploded out of the chapel door, her usually white face burning, both hands raised palm forwards like the martyred saints in holy pictures, her habit billowing in a black storm cloud behind her, shrieking, 'It cannot be! This child is a heathen!'

I faltered to a stop. Behind me, it seemed that the whole school drew its breath and gasped.

She came charging towards the platform, spraying spit. 'This child should be cast out of the school and damned for her wickedness!'

The frieze of lay teachers on one side and nuns on the other sat with their heads turned towards the commotion and their mouths gaping, for once speechless.

Mother Beatrice, standing next to the Archbishop, was the first to act. She swooped to intercept Sister Kathleen saying, 'Sister, calm yourself.'

They met in a clash of rosaries and starched cambric, Sister Kathleen howling, 'We should be excommunicating this sinner, not giving her prizes! She has maligned our Holy Mother, comparing her with graven idols.'

It was the worst imaginable nightmare. I stood rooted to

the gravel in front of the lectern, feeling a violent blush climbing up my neck. This public calumny was my punishment for not believing properly in God. Maybe he did exist after all, and Sister Kathleen was his instrument of revenge.

'She is anathema!'

Mother Beatrice was hanging on to Sister Kathleen with one hand and making frantic gestures at the other nuns for help, but they sat paralysed. Several had swivelled towards me in horror, as if looking for horns sprouting out of my head instead of a ponytail. I turned away and found that every girl in the school was staring at me, frozen between the applause of a few seconds before and fear of some unspeakable abomination lurking inside me.

'Antichrist! Devil worshipper!' Sister Kathleen yelled, struggling to free herself from Mother Beatrice's arms, her mouth bubbling spit and ancient curses.

You'd better pray, kiddo! I told myself in Stella's bossiest voice. But how could I if I wasn't sure anyone was listening? Is trying to make yourself believe in God good enough? My head writhed with serpent questions that coiled round and round each other, their beginnings and endings indistinguishable.

'Demon! Beelzebub!'

It was the second most horrible moment of my life. I yearned for the ground to yawn open and swallow me, even if it meant plunging into the eternal damnation that probably awaited me, a soul irrevocably lost.

'Lucifer! Fiend! Satan!'

All of a sudden foam gushed out of Sister Kathleen's mouth and she fell down on to the brick platform and lay there jerking and jerking about a yard in front of me, her back arching and her eyes rolling up with only the whites showing. Her wimple and veil fell off, exposing an old woman's pink scalp and wispy grey hair – so much for the school wisdom that the nuns shaved their heads.

The shocked silence was broken by one of the younger girls sobbing which started off a whole lot more, and it galvanised Mother Beatrice. She waved her arm over the assembly and commanded the teachers, 'Get the girls out at once. Use the fire drill to hurry them back to their classrooms, then explain what has happened. Sister Helga, call the Matron and then the ambulance. I'll stay here.'

She saw me standing stricken and said something to the Archbishop, who descended from the lectern and gathered me under his arm and swept me away from it all: the chaos of crying girls, flustered nuns, barking teachers and Sister Kathleen's spectacular frothing fit.

I remember his cassock swishing and then the electric light gleaming on his purple skullcap as he stood looking down at me in Mother Beatrice's office. And the skin-warmth of his silver archbishop's ring as he held my hand and told me what a marvellous essay I'd written and not to worry about the wild accusations of a sadly deranged sister in Christ. 'It's clear she needs psychiatric help. You're not to let this incident upset you, my child.'

My heart was still pounding. My face felt like a boiled beetroot. I was so upset that I didn't register the 'my child' until long afterwards. I said, 'She called me a devil, but I'm not, really. Am I?'

For a few terrible seconds until he answered I stood there wondering if Sister Kathleen was right and I was not merely an unbeliever but an actual devil from hell. A dreadful thought came with a jolt like an electric shock: Jeepers, didn't devils have red faces?

You don't see an archbishop as a flesh-and-blood man until you get really close. He had a nick on his pale cheek from shaving and peppermint on his breath, and I'll always be grateful for the fact that not even the trace of a smile showed on his face. If he had smiled, I'd have gone on believing in some deep recess that I really did have devilry in me.

He said, 'You write like an angel, Isabel. So how could you be?'

There must have been less than five minutes between the second most horrible moment of my life and one of the best. While the horrible moment taught me that it was expedient to keep my opinions strictly to myself – I would lie myself silly rather than let anyone else know what I believed in – the Archbishop's graceful and confidence-building compliment sustained me for the rest of my school years. Later too, when my marriage went sour and I needed something of my own to work on and think about, this was the memory that sent me out to the stationery shop to buy the first notebook that was to become a series of private writing journals.

I'm not sure to this day whether there is a God or not, but bless you for saving me from the devil within, Your Grace.

And for the unbelievable riches in those days, the twenty guineas. They were earmarked for the dreamy pale pink ballerina with the strapless satin top and layers of tulle skirts and matching pink shoes and pearl-beaded clutch bag in the shop window labelled 'For That Special Evening'. James bait.

Isabel

On the long drive to the mountains, Isabel has plenty of time to think about the interview with Ralph's student counsellor and its aftermath.

They had met their son in the reception office of the college where he was studying computer science, and sat for a fraught fifteen minutes while George badgered him to explain why they had been called in and Isabel kept smiling nicely at the woman behind the counter so she wouldn't think that Ralph's problems stemmed from an unhappy family background.

It wasn't unhappy when the children were small, she thinks, and after things began to deteriorate between us, we tried to keep our disagreements private. Though I'm sure they must have been aware of the squabbling; you can't keep angry voices down low enough to prevent them from leaking through doors. The main thing is, they've never lacked for love – from me, anyway. And George? He used to be so good with them, happy to organise games and cart them round the zoo and museums, explaining things; I'd forgotten what a benign daddy he was in the beginning. But when they grew up and started to argue and he found himself no longer the ultimate authority, he got offended and started grumbling about how ungrateful they were, and the inevitable rot set in. It's sad that they see him now as stuffy and pompous and boring. Saddest of all for him. Poor limited George. How could I ever have fallen for him?

Thinking back over the family life that started so well and has now shrivelled to a level where she and George hardly communicate, she can't shake off the niggling worry that they are responsible for Ralph's stammer and Chryssa's selfish consumer lifestyle. Are parents ever able to absolve themselves from guilt? she wonders.

For the college interview she had worn what she always thinks of as her mother hen outfit: a suit in beige tweed with small brown and red flecks, her pearl earrings and matching brown leather handbag and court shoes. That morning as she put on her makeup (a discreet touch of eyeshadow and not too much lipstick; it wouldn't do for a mother to look like a tart), she had thought, This person in the mirror isn't me. I'm not a mother hen any more; I feel like a bird of paradise. I'm going to dump these dreary middle-aged clothes when I leave.

'Make like a tree and leave,' she murmurs now, remembering Ralph's mirth at the schoolboy joke. It's not going to be easy to pull up my roots. Or to abandon finally the image of the mother tree – the mother hen – whose main purpose in life is to shelter and nurture her young.

'For God's sake, Izzy,' she hears her lover say, 'they're not your young any more. They're grown up. They have their own lives. You can help them best now by being a reliable friend.'

Can I? she wonders. Was I a reliable friend the other day for Chryssa, struggling with her terrible decision? She came to me expecting to be bailed out and I refused – but dammit, she's got to take responsibility for her own actions. I did her a favour, cutting another apron string. As I did with Ralph yesterday.

The student counsellor had been blunt. 'Your son is a bright young man with considerable ability, as he demonstrates in his practical work. Yet he attends less than half his lectures and seminars. When asked why, he told me he was bored. We have no room for bored students in this college. If he doesn't pull up his socks he will not get the duly performed certificate he needs to write his exams at the end of the year.'

George had blustered. Ralph had sat silent and sulking. The student counsellor had been by turns avuncular, superior and threatening. It had been left to Isabel to ask Ralph why he was slacking off.

'Because I *am* bored, Mum. They haven't taught m-me anything I don't know already. I'd rather be working with

268

c-computers than sitting around having theory rammed down my throat.'

'Why didn't you speak to us about this?'

'Because you wouldn't have listened.'

'I've always tried to be –'

'You've been too wrapped up lately and Dad never listens. He pushed me into c-college to do c-computer science, and he'd never admit he was wrong.'

George's face had registered aggrieved shock. 'I was doing what was best for you.'

'I'm the only one who knows what's best for me.'

George had, as if to prove Ralph's point, not listened. 'Everybody knows that you need a diploma or a certificate to get a decent job today. I spend all this money sending you to college to get one, and all you do is throw it back in my face.'

'M-money,' Ralph sneered. 'It's all you ever talk about. M-money.'

'I'll bloody cut your allowance if that's how you feel!'

'C-cut my allowance, then! I can get a job without a stupid diploma. It's what I want to do anyway. Working in c-computers will pay me double what you earn.'

With her new feeling of detachment from her family, Isabel had felt sorry for them both: the father who thought he was doing his best and the son blundering his way to manhood with hurtful insults. She had thought, I must keep the peace between them. They'll need each other when I've gone away.

Over coffee in the clattering student cafeteria afterwards, she had persuaded George to let Ralph leave college and get a job, and Ralph to apologise to his father. 'You know it's not going to be as easy as you think?' she had warned her son. 'You'll have to support yourself now.'

'Piece of c-cake.' He had flashed her his little boy's grin, all confidence. 'There are plenty of jobs going in c-computers, and Janine said I could m-move in with her for a while until I find some digs to share.'

'Suits me,' George had huffed. 'Our income's going to halve when I go on pension. We may have to sell the beach cottage.'

Oh, no, Isabel had vowed. That's mine. He can have the house and I'll have the cottage for a love nest. She had laughed out loud at the thought, making them both turn and look at her in surprise. It had not been a wife and mother's laugh.

Now she lifts her driving glasses to rub the bridge of her nose, then settles them again. The sign she has been watching out for is a few kilometres further on and she turns off on to a gravel road, slowing down as the car skitters over the corrugated surface. The road winds through foothills and then through a gorge of fissured sandstone with dark green knots of bush where ledges and crevices offer a toehold. She is just wondering if the pebbled river rushing next to the road is the one he swims in, with the gin and tonic pool, when she sees the second sign.

'It's a track from there on,' he had warned over the phone. 'Go slowly, and watch out that you don't catch your sump on the middel-mannetjie.'

'I've driven on mountain roads before.'

'Not this bastard. It chews sumps for breakfast.'

'How far is the cottage from the turn-off?'

'Couple of k's. I'll be waiting outside when you get there. It's one of the advantages of living up here; you can hear your guests coming at least fifteen minutes before they arrive.'

And he is waiting in front of a thatched stone cottage: a shock of grizzled beard over a tan sweat shirt, faded jeans, thick socks folded over climbing boots, and a beaming smile.

She is wrapped in his arms, welcomed with nuzzled endearments. 'Izzy, you've come. It's been so long.'

'A month and five days.' Said into the hairy warmth of his neck.

'Ethiopia took longer than I thought. Dear love, I missed you.' His hands move over her body, caressing.

She begins to pull back. 'Me too. So much has happened.'

'Tell me later.' His breath scorches her cheek.

'We should unpack the car.'

'Later. Later. God, it's been so long.'

There is a log fire in the bedroom and woven carpets and a down quilt which they throw off after a while. His urgency arouses her to a passion she has never known before, until she is shouting: 'Come! Come now!' It is glorious, to make

270

love with abandon; to give of herself with absolute trust after a lifetime of holding back and wondering if there is something wrong with her that she doesn't enjoy sex. Every cell in her body feels as though it is singing hallelujahs. The world contracts to the touch of his fingers on her face and the liquid crackle of a log fire.

'My dear love,' he murmurs.

She smiles into the pillow and reaches down to pull up the quilt.

'Have you finished the update on the Ethiopia book?'

They are sitting cross-legged and facing each other on the sofa in the living room, devouring the picnic lunch she has brought with her: crusty Italian olive bread, cheese, salads and a bottle of late harvest wine. The room has a soaring roof of thatch over tarry log beams, a wall of books, a stone fireplace where more logs are burning and a broad window filled with mountains.

He nods; there are crumbs caught in his beard and his mouth is oily with salad dressing. 'Posted the manuscript off yesterday afternoon in the village. We've got the whole weekend to ourselves. What would you like to do?'

'Talk first. Then have a swim in the rock pool you keep going on about. I presume there's nobody around to see if we take our clothes off? I've always wanted to swim naked in a mountain pool. I must have a naiad fixation.'

'Only the odd baboon, and there are hikers sometimes. But the water's freezing cold,' he warns. 'Maybe we should just get under the quilt again and talk there.'

She laughs. 'Forget it. I'm all tuckered out. The old bod isn't used to such strenuous gymnastics.'

'Give it time.' He puts his plate down on a side table and reaches for her hand. 'How much time now, Izzy? You said that so much has happened since I've been away.'

She leans towards him with her greying hair swinging forward, scented with the citrussy shampoo he loves. 'I had a long talk with the children, for starters – ' She tells him of the afternoon they came for tea, about Chryssa's dilemma and Ralph's leaving college and her own admission that she is trying to write. 'It was quite galling, the way they reacted,'

271

she admits. 'Made me realise what an idiot they've always thought I was.'

'Nobody who knew you could possibly think that.'

'George does.'

'You know what I feel about George. Have you spoken to him yet?'

She feels herself blushing. 'No. But I'm going to soon.'

'I've heard that one before.'

As his hand drops and his eyebrows contract into a frown, she says, 'Really! I'm just waiting for the right moment. The big relief for me is that the kids think he's –' what was the word Chryssa had used? – 'a boring old dork too. I am not alone.' She says it with an accent, like Garbo.

'I am alone.' He is serious, unseduced by her joke. 'Please, Izzy, don't draw it out much longer. I feel – sometimes I feel that you're still hovering between me and your family. That you haven't yet made your final decision.'

'You're wrong. That's what's been happening to me this week: I've made the decision.' She snatches his hand up again with both of hers. 'Darling, with Ralph cutting loose I have no one to keep me at home any more.'

Still unsmiling, he says, 'Have you brought more writing with you?'

She nods.

'How is it going?'

'Hard to say. I haven't any experience to go by. Some days it just sort of comes out, but on others I can sit for hours and nothing happens.'

She is looking down at the hands that won't always do her bidding and doesn't see his frown relaxing. 'Common problem. But it gets easier with practice.'

'I still have no idea if it's any good.'

'You'll get an honest opinion from me.'

'I know. That's one of the reasons I've come up this weekend.'

'Not for my fair body?' Laughing again, he leans forward to give her a kiss that tastes of salad dressing.

'That too, of course. But mainly I wanted to tell you that I don't feel responsible for Ralphie – Ralph – any more.'

'Then bingo, right?' But there is still doubt on his face.

'Bingo,' she says confidently, trying to dispel it.

'I'll be counting the days.'

'Me too. And I haven't yet told you the best thing that happened this week. Guess who phoned?'

'I'm no good at guessing games. You know that.'

Ignoring his growl, she says, 'You must remember her from Two Rivers. It was Opal – Laverty, she used to be. She's coming to stay for a night next week.'

'The many-faceted and mysteriously brilliant one?'

'You remember!'

'I remember everything about Two Rivers. Every single bloody detail.' His face is as dark as the angry cumulus clouds boiling up above the mountains for the afternoon thunderstorm. 'God forgive me.'

18

The Archbishop was understanding as well as kind. He and
Mother Beatrice were a powerful combination. He poured me
a cup of tea and stirred in two heaped spoons of sugar ('For
shock,' he said) and talked about his favourite boyhood books
while I drank it. Then he announced that I was being
granted a day off school as an extra reward for winning the
essay prize.

'And I hope you'll keep on writing, Isabel,' he said as he
swished me down the stairs and along the vaulted brick
passage towards the front door. 'You have an unusual ability
to express yourself well in good clear English.'

I blushed and mumbled something that ended with '. . .
Your Grace,' but I was listening to the noise coming out of
the classroom windows: the mad mutinous buzz of swarming
bees. Teachers were having to pitch their voices higher to
make themselves heard. Whenever I heard bees for years
afterwards, I thought of the hysteria that hummed just below
the convent's surface that day. Sister Kathleen had upset the
whole beehive with her outburst.

As we reached the chauffeur-driven episcopal Austin in
which I was to ride home, the Archbishop took my hand into
both of his, patting it and saying, 'I'm sure you'll find it in
your heart to forgive Sister Kathleen. You know that it was
her illness speaking, not herself?'

I looked down at the sharp blue stones of the gravel drive
which had been freshly raked for his visit and nodded, but it
was a lie. I knew she was sick but I'd never forgive her for
turning me into someone whom my peers couldn't quite
trust. Never.

The long pale fingers increased their pressure on my all too

274

stubby ones. 'Forgiveness is hard but for your own sake you must try. I pray that your wounds heal without a scar, and I promise you that Sister Kathleen will have no further contact with young people.'

I followed the row of purple Smartie buttons up his cassock and past the hanging cross and saw that the concerned face under the purple skullcap understood very well how hard it would be. So what could I do but nod again and say, 'I'll try,' and climb into the big black car trying to look suitably forgiving?

'Bless you then, my child. Go in peace.' The Archbishop laid his hand lightly on my head through the window as the car began to move. 'And I hope that you put the twenty guineas to good use.'

Would he have approved if I had told him that the money was earmarked for an evening dress to snare a boyfriend, rather than improving books? I told myself that an archbishop who cracked jokes would surely understand, and gave him a wobbly smile.

The tears I had managed to hold back so far started leaking out on the way home and burst into a flood as soon as I was inside the garden gate. I ran into the house to tell Stella what had happened, but her bedroom door was closed and Eslina came tiptoeing down the passage hushing me not to disturb her. So it was Finn I told first and who slammed out of the pharmacy in a rage, leaving Govind in charge, and stormed over to the convent to confront Mother Beatrice.

When he got back, he came to my bedroom where I had taken refuge with Edgar Bear in the wicker chair, looking unusually stern and pharmaceutical in his white jacket. Above it, his eyes were the deepest sea blue I had yet seen, almost navy. He must have been communing with his pipe on the walk back because the smell of tobacco smoke overlaid the piney soap he always used when washing his hands in the dispensary.

He pulled up the stool from the end of my bed and sat down beside me saying, 'You are not to let this thing with Sister Kathleen worry you. She's a mad woman, and mad people are not responsible for their actions.'

'Is she mad like Ma is mad?' It came out in a whisper.

275

'Nay, you know she is not. Your mother –' he was upset enough to pronounce it 'modder' – 'has yust had a temporary nervous breakdown, that's all. The doctors expect her to get completely better. Completely, ya? But Sister Kathleen has a mental illness that goes back to a very hard childhood, I have been told. What makes me furious is that the order let her go on teaching, knowing this.'

'She's their best pray-er,' I said, trying to make it sound funny. But I couldn't seem to control my lips.

He leaned forward and gathered me into a bear hug. It always made you feel so safe, being hugged by Finn. He said with his lips close to my ear, 'She should not have been put in charge of a class. Mother Beatrice admits it now. I am so sorry this happened while you are in our care, Izzy. Try to forget the whole frickly business.'

I said against his shoulder, 'I'll try,' but it wasn't easy. Despite the fact that Eslina made my favourite chocolate cake for tea and Finn took me to the bioscope that night in the Town Hall and drove me to school in style for the next few days, the spectre of Sister Kathleen haunted both my dreams and my days at the convent. Though Mother Beatrice had done her best to repair the damage by explaining to each class in turn the fanatic nature of Sister Kathleen's illness, it was not enough for the girls to be told that I was innocent of sinful practices. Many were jealous that a newcomer should have won the best prize of the school year, and rumours about me flew about like flocks of raucous mynahs.

When my gloom had not lifted by Friday, and with Stella still shaky after the migraine, Finn suggested that Opal should come to stay for the weekend to cheer me up. 'We could all three of us go for a nice picnic,' he suggested.

I was languishing on the sofa in the living room, which always irritated Stella. 'It's infuriating, seeing you lolling about like that!' she'd fume, plumping cushions all round me.

'You used to.' I remembered only too well how she would spend recumbent hours talking to her friends on the phone when I was a kid, shooing me away when I tried to get her attention or started whining that I had no one to play with. My revenge was sweet. 'I'm not getting in your way by just sitting here, am I? Everybody's entitled to sit, surely?'

Finn said, 'A bicycle picnic, that's what we'll have. I'll ask Govind if I can borrow his, and you and Opal can use mine and Stella's. A ride in the fresh air will be yust the ticket, you'll see.'

Riding a bicycle certainly helped me to forget my woes that Saturday – it was as good as having wings – but it generated other woes.

Finn suggested that we use the occasion to go on an all-day expedition, exploring parts of Two Rivers that Opal and I hadn't seen before. When we sat down on Friday evening to plan the route, he was like a schoolboy poring over the map and writing out a list of things to take in our saddle bags. Even Stella's grouchy, 'For God's sake, who'd want to explore this one-horse dorp?' didn't dampen his enthusiasm.

'First we'll make a long ride out into the contry to the west of town. Then we'll follow the Umlilwane river path all the way down past the station to the confluence of the two rivers where they run into the lagoon – here.' His finger stabbed at an expanse of pale blue. 'A friend of mine has a cottage with a rowing boat which we could paddle across to the sand spit where the lagoon runs into the sea.'

'What friend?' Stella looked up from her magazine.

'Yust one of my so-called disreputable fishing cronies.' Finn's voice had the sarcastic edge I noticed it took on sometimes when he talked to her.

'Oh.' She went back to reading.

He bent his head next to Opal and mine again. 'South of the sand spit there's a high dune with a secret hollow where we could have our picnic looking down on the sea, then go for a swim afterwards. We can ride back the other way, up the Umsindo river to the bridge at the temple, here. That way we can do a round trip and come home like conquering heroes. Or heroines, as the case may be,' he added, stretching out his arms and giving us both a furry hug.

Next morning he and Eslina put together a picnic that was to be a surprise, packed in a series of cake tins that went into our saddle bags and his canvas fishing bag, which had been specially washed out for the occasion. I felt like an explorer as we set off on foot along the main road pushing our bikes.

Stella had put on a lot of makeup to disguise her paleness and gone off to Abjee's where yet another protest meeting was being held in one of the empty auction sale rooms. Bulldozers had arrived at the road camp and feelings were running high among objectors to the road-widening.

As we turned into Darjeeling Road and mounted our bikes and pedalled off, Finn in front, then Opal, then me, I felt Sister Kathleen's malevolent presence falling behind like a shed snakeskin and found myself muttering, 'Get thee to a nunnery, go!' We were studying *Hamlet* that term.

Our route took us past the Goulds' house with its rampant jungle of weeds, then winding through the two-acre smallholdings where mostly poor whites lived, still dreaming that they were farmers in their squat tin-roofed houses with rusty cars and fowls and sad little patches of mealies in the back yards. Stella would never have taken us out that way; she was scornful of poor whites. When we passed drab mothers trailing dirty barefoot kids along the pavement, their heads shorn for lice and the veld sores on their legs splodged with gentian violet, she'd make disparaging comments like, 'Those women are fools, allowing themselves to be treated like rabbits.' Taking somebody else's home-made jam and biscuits to Dorothy Gould was about as far as her compassion for the weak and feeble went, though she would march and shout and work like a demon for a public cause like the road-widening. Maybe Stella should have gone into politics rather than interior decorating; she had the intelligence and the drive – and the detachment.

It was blissful to be whizzing along the dusty gravel road with the wind in our ears, flicking in and out of the circles of shade thrown by the flamboyant trees, standing up on our pedals to peer over fences and revelling in our superiority over mere pedestrians. After half an hour Finn led us down a dirt track to the Umlilwane river bank where a broad path took us past the lower end of the convent grounds; on the opposite bank, the company estate's orderly battalions of cannas in their red and yellow plumes marched from the lily ponds and palm-lined terraces down immaculate lawns to the water. Through the trees I could just see the green tin roof of Titch's house, and wondered when he would be home again.

Talk of the devil. (Sister Kathleen wriggled into my mind as I thought it, then mercifully slipped away again.) Round the next bend we came upon Titch and Kesaval squatting on the bank next to a white enamel slop bucket with a vented lid, fishing in the water with nets. They turned round as we slid to a crunching stop.

'Hey, I didn't know you were back. Did you manage to get yourself expelled, or what?' I felt comfortable enough with Titch now to chaff him.

He stood up, tipping his pith helmet back with a muddy hand. 'Hullo, Mr Rosholt. Howzit, Izz. This is half-term weekend, when we get time off at home for good behaviour. Sorry to disappoint you.'

We did all the usual hullos while I added, 'Do you know Opal, my friend from the convent?'

She put in quickly, making it sound like a joke, 'Opal Laverty, many-faceted and mysteriously brilliant.' She always introduced herself like that; it was her way of skipping over the embarrassing surname.

'Hi.' Titch gave her an assessing glance that surprised me; he hadn't seemed to be interested in girls. Opal noticed it too and looked pleased. She was shy with boys because she didn't know many and thought she was ugly; being around them made her gangle worse than usual, I'd noticed.

'I am pleased to meet you.' Kesaval flashed his sudden smile at her. Unlike Titch in his grubby shorts and shirt and clay-caked sandals, he wore his blue jeans with a checked shirt and polished leather moccasins. Did he feel he had to dress better than his white friend? I wondered. Or did his family insist that he wore clothes which indicated their standing in the Indian community? I remembered him saying, 'I trust girls.' What did he think about white girls? Could he trust us to see him as a person and not just another coolie-boy?

Opal nodded at him, blushing a bit. 'Likewise.'

There was an awkward silence while the four of us stood there not quite knowing how to handle the unexpected boy-meets-girl situation. Finn broke it by getting off Govind's bike and lowering it into the grass next to the path, saying, 'What are you two doing?'

Titch brandished his fishing net as we parked our bikes

279

too. 'Trying to catch platties and collect some frog spawn and tadpoles for a school experiment.'

'Platties?'

Kesaval said, 'Platannas. The clawed toad, a species of frog, you know? Titch's biology master wants them.'

'Oh.' Losing interest, Finn wandered away along the bank peering into the water to see if any mullet had got this far upstream. In his old shorts and bush shirt and sockless velskoens and what he called his farm hat, a shapeless felt mushroom he wore to prevent the thinning top of his head from getting sunburnt, he looked from the back like the tramp Stella was always accusing him of wanting to be. Finn scorned appearances as much as she valued them; they were incompatible in almost every respect, those two. When I grieved for them in the months and years after the terrible night of the Mariamman festival, I told myself that they would never have stayed married anyway. Yet I was never convinced. The oddest marriages last, for the most illogical reasons. Look at mine.

That day on the river bank, I said to Titch, 'What does your biology master want frogs for?'

'To cut up so we can compare the different stages of growth. Don't you cut things up in biology?' He bent down and lifted the lid on the bucket so we could see inside. It was half full of river water polka-dotted with wriggling tadpoles; three long skinny frogs were kicking around the surface in frantic circles.

Opal let out her dirty chuckle and said, 'At the convent? Anathema. Girls cutting up God's creatures for questionable scientific purposes, what next?'

I shuddered. 'Don't say that word.'

'Which word? Why not?'

She slid her eyes sideways at me. 'Shall we tell them about The Episode With The Nutty Nun?'

'No.'

We had tried to transform the appalling scene with Sister Kathleen into comedy by giving it a funny name, with little success. The trouble with being called a heathen and a sinner and a devil-worshipper in front of the entire school was that however deranged my accuser clearly was, doubts lingered.

280

Except for Opal and a few stalwarts in my class, I was being shunned. Girls made elaborate detours to keep out of my way in the playground and the brick corridors; the teachers gave me peculiar looks when I walked into their classrooms and stopped asking me to answer questions; even the nuns, who must have known only too well how disturbed Sister Kathleen was, kept a prudent distance from me. When I'd tried to tell Stella how hurtful it felt, she'd just said, 'It'll soon blow over. You won the prize, didn't you?'

Titch was saying, 'Nutty Nun has got to mean Sister Kathleen.'

I felt as though all my blood was draining away. 'How do you know? Has somebody told you?'

He shook his head. 'You forget, I'm a convent old boy. I've had personal experience. What has she done now?'

'Gone clean round the bend and attacked Isabel in public,' Opal said. 'It was gruesome.'

Titch whistled. Kesaval looked impressed.

Emboldened by the reaction, Opal said, 'Go on, Izz, tell them what happened. The more you talk about it, the less horrible it'll seem in retrospect. And they should know about the prize.'

'No.' I didn't want to talk about any of it.

Titch said, 'We'll find out for ourselves if you don't tell us. I have my sources.'

'Me too.' Another flash from Kesaval.

They moved closer to us to emphasise the threat. Looking back now, I realise that those two boys had learnt about the uses of power from experts. Whether consciously or not, Titch's father and Kesaval's grandfather had taught them who really ran Two Rivers: the people with money. Perhaps that was the basis of their friendship. Each knew that the other would be somebody in the community when they grew to manhood – Kesaval wealthy, and Titch a product of one of the elite schools whose old boy networks supplied most of the top positions in South African business, and took care to recruit new talent from within their ranks. Things changed when bright cocky boys from the wrong side of the tracks started graduating from business schools in the Seventies and Eighties, convinced that their theories and formulae would transform the world, but in the Fifties it mattered very much which school you had gone to, and how much money you had.

In a last-ditch stand against revealing all, I muttered, 'It was nothing. She just shouted stuff at me.'

Titch leaned so close that I could see right down into his green glass eyes, past the brown scribbles. 'We want to know every single beautiful gory detail, Isabel-Necessary.'

He knew it would make me mad, but I didn't stoop so low as to call him Timothy Montague etcetera in front of the others. I'd get him back some other time. The fact was, I suddenly realised that I had an interested audience – something which an almost-only child like me finds irresistible. So I told what had happened, embroidering shamelessly with Opal's help, and enjoyed the sensation of being at the centre of the drama so much that it became the first of many tellings. I dined out for years on my encounter with Sister Kathleen, and used the aura of wickedness it gave me to throw my weight around at the convent for the rest of the term. If people thought that the devil lurked behind my schoolgirl facade and avoided me just in case, why should I disabuse them? It only gave me more space. I became an outlaw and a rebel.

But Sister Kathleen's attack wasn't the only reason. The other was an incident that happened at the fag end of the day of the bicycle picnic which started off so well, with Finn persuading Titch and Kesaval to join us further down-river under the station bridge and Titch saying, 'I'll give James a bell and see if he wants to come too,' as they hurried off with the bucket between them, making my heart do a flipflop.

That day is a pillar of fire in my memory because James did come, and the five of us and Finn cycled through what felt like endless summer down the river path. Where it ducked into the wild fig and milkwood bush, there'd be monkey vines and drifts of snake lilies sticking up like red-tipped paint-brushes; where it burst out into the sun again, there'd be stubby palms and wild bananas and amatungulus and tshwala-ka-inyoni shrubs with sunbirds hovering over their small sweet orange flowers. The tide must have been out because the muddy brown river was sliding seawards. Sudden rustles in the reeds were striped legevaans and once a vuzimanzi, swift squiggle of water snake arrowing away. We had to get off and push the bikes through bamboos and clumps of escaped sugar cane taller than elephants and small hidden patches of sweet potatoes with their nodding heart-shaped leaves interplanted with dagga – probably hoed and planted by homesick contract workers, Finn said, in their spare time. He showed us how the dagga plant's narrow serrated leaves grew like fingers from a central point, and we crushed some between our fingers feeling wicked and worldly (this was the fabled hashish!) but they smelt like blackjacks.

When we reached the fishing shack owned by Finn's friend and parked our bikes and turned over the upside-down rowing boat outside, all three of the boys wanted to row. Finn had to settle the argument with a flipped penny from his pocket before we could wobble across the lagoon and brave the squelching mud and reeds on the other side to pull the boat up on the sand spit.

And for a while the magic continued as we picnicked in the hollow of the high dune looking down over the sea, first dividing up Eslina's delicious cold meats and salads before moving on to the doorstep sandwiches and packets of chips and slabs of chocolate that the boys had brought with them. Stella had secretly packed a bottle of Grand Mousseux in Finn's fishing bag – the flamboyant surprise was typical of her – and we popped the cork and passed the bottle from hand to hand, getting light-headed as much on the thought as on the teacupful of sweet bubbly wine. Afterwards Finn pulled his hat over his eyes and lay back among the dune creepers and slept, and we sat talking about ourselves in a rainbow bubble of self-absorption: sharing our dreams and aspirations, problems at school and with parents, communing with each other in that high sunny place, after that wine, in a way that would never have happened otherwise.

I remember Titch saying, 'I wish I'd had brothers and sisters. The pressure of being the only one gets harder every year. All the expectations heap up on you.'

And Kesaval saying, with feeling, 'You should maybe try

being an Indian grandson with your father dead and your grandfather pushing, pushing you every day to do things that will bring honour to the family. I don't want to go to Oxford. It's too far away.'

And Opal turning on him. 'You've got nothing to moan about! My father drinks. He's disgusting. I have to wipe up his sick sometimes.'

And James turning his beautiful face to her, vivid with relief that someone else shared his shame. 'My father too.'

For the rest of the afternoon they were side by side, talking. I don't think he even saw me after he discovered that Opal was battling many of the same demons as he was. I pretended I didn't care, laughing and joking with Finn and Titch and Kesaval as we swam and body-surfed in the sea and paddled back across the lagoon and rode home up the Umsindo river bank, past the Coolietown shacks. I pretended I was a dragon lady spurting fire and brimstone instead of silliness and sea water; they weren't to know that it was actually heartache and bile. I didn't need to squander the twenty guineas on the pale pink tulle ballerina dress with its matching satin shoes and beaded evening bag, because James was Opal's after that day.

I kept a wrapper from the chocolate bars we ate and pressed the flowers we collected from the dune creepers and the sturdy dune aloes to stick in my scrapbook. They are there still, faded reminders of cruelly dashed hopes. My one consolation was that Opal's and my friendship survived the weeks of agonising disappointment that followed. I didn't tell her for years how I'd coveted James – just as she didn't tell me in the letters we wrote to each other after I'd left Two Rivers that he'd dumped her a few months later for a prettier girl. It's a good thing that the parameters of friendship are more flexible than those of a love affair, otherwise we'd all be friendless.

The sunset that evening was spectacular. February had been unusually dry and there was a lot of dust in the air which turned the sky into a blaze of curry colours: red chillie fading to turmeric and fenugreek and the greeny yellow of ground coriander and cumin where the sky darkened. We walked

284

through eddies of spicy cooking smells hanging on the hot still evening air. Being a Saturday, there was a bazaar gaiety about the family meals being eaten under the trees in the corrugated iron enclosures of each back yard: strings of coloured lights hanging in the trees, laughter and children's voices, the clash of dice and slapping cards, gossiping women, clinking tea cups. After we said goodbye to Kesaval and he turned down the road where he lived, we were a cluster of silent white faces pushing our bikes through occupied territory, our eyes uneasily searching the shadows. Mine did, at any rate, after Finn looked at his watch and peeled off too, saying he was going to Govind's house to return his bike, and for Titch and James to deliver us home safely. They were only boys, and the boisterous darkness was not the Coolietown I knew by day.

When we'd said goodbye at the garden gate, where James leaned forward to brush Opal's cheek – oh, Judas! – with his lips and Titch gave me a comradely punch on the shoulder, we found Stella waiting among the ferns on the veranda.

'Where the hell have you been? Where's Finn?' Her face glimmered pale as the frangipani flowers.

'It was a long picnic.' A few hours earlier I would have raved about it, but the day had gone sour. 'He's returning Govind's bike.'

'I wanted him to get some bread from the café so we can have it with cheese for supper. I didn't have time to make anything because the meeting went on for ages.'

And you slept all afternoon, I thought. She still had the bruised migraine rings under her eyes, and was always grumpy when she woke up.

'We'll go,' Opal said, ever-willing to be helpful.

'But it's already dark.'

I could see Stella thinking, White slave trade. Rape and battery. They'll be attacked. Run over by a bus . . . God, she could be infuriating. I said, 'So what? We made it as far as the beach and back. I reckon we can make it down the road without tempting fate too much. Come on, Ope,' and let my bike clatter down on to the paving stones and marched out through the gate.

Which is how I came to be walking just ahead of her past

285

Ismail's General Dealers which stayed open until late on Saturdays. Through the moth-spotted window I saw a couple standing at the haberdashery counter, the young woman fingering a sari length with rapt fingers; when she turned her head, I saw that it was Asha. I stopped to watch her lift the apricot silk and stroke her cheek with it, saying something to the man behind the counter who nodded his head and looked pleased. In the lamplight and framed by the window, it looked like a painting in warm gold and ochre and russet oils, shading to sable where the shadows encroached at the corners. Not far enough, however, to obscure the face of the man standing next to her: Finn.

Into the picture, in front of the window, stepped Govind in one of his violently patterned shirts. As he stood staring at them, his face began to twist like a brown wax crayon melting in the sun.

Coming up behind me, Opal said, 'What are you looking at?'

I turned and fled. 'Nothing. Nothing!'

'Wait for me,' she called, running after me.

So she didn't see what I'd seen, and I didn't tell anyone. I just grew a harder shell so I wouldn't care too much when my new family fell apart too. Or when people avoided me at school, the girl who had been accused of being a devil-worshipper and worse.

If that's what they thought, if that was the way things were going, I didn't give a damn. I'd kick and scream and argue and lie and be as bad as everyone expected. If I played my cards right, I might even be able to tell Evelyn Simpson a thing or two when I got home.

Isabel

It is late afternoon and she sits at her desk thinking, My legacy from Sister Kathleen was a ferocious determination to prove to everybody that I was utterly trustworthy. I had to be the most loyal wife, the most dependable mother, the dogs-body friend who would always produce a cake for a charity sale, pick up a child, lend an appliance, do emergency shopping and provide tea and sympathy at all hours. Hell, I've been knocking myself out for other people for years without paying enough attention to my own needs. How stupid of me.

She gathers up the day's work and carries it to the hiding place among the sheets in the linen cupboard, realigning them carefully before she closes the door.

As she goes on down the passage she is thinking, I must find some way of warning my daughters against excessive do-gooding. Though Chryssa is probably too selfish, Janine is in danger. She's much too vulnerable to lame ducks.

Opal arrives on the doorstep twenty minutes later with a bottle of chilled chardonnay and an armful of flowers from a trendy florist who specialises in 'country garden' bouquets: cornflowers and poppies and grasses and intricate dried seed-heads.

Hugging her, Isabel murmurs, 'Lovely expensive gifts. Thank you, dragon friend. What's the occasion?'

'Tell you in a mo.' Opal pulls back to look at her. 'But first I'm dying to hear your news. Is George still out? I didn't see his car in the drive.'

'He'll be standing rounds at the bowling club, so we're safe for an hour at least.' Isabel slips her hand through her friend's arm and hurries her inside. 'Let's put the flowers in a jug and get some glasses and sit on the veranda. We've got so much catching up to do.'

As they go down the passage and into the kitchen, they are eyeing each other for signs of change since their last meeting. Isabel sees that Opal's modishly square-cut hair has gone auburn – much more successful than last year's ash blonde. Having her hair well cared for is one of the ways in which she tries to banish her miserable childhood. Years of cooking and tasting have thickened her once thin gangly body, and the lines on her face have deepened and multiplied, but they are the laughter lines of a good marriage and fulfilling work. Opal and her husband Colin own a famous restaurant in the Cape, where they have managed to bring up four children while seducing a generation of guests with haute cuisine, fresh herbs and unusual wines. Isabel has visited them several times, though only once with George who distrusts what he calls 'fancy cooking'; he always makes a show of drinking a violently fizzing glass of Eno's in the bathroom afterwards. Her relationship with Opal has always been tinged with envy – Until now! she exults, running water into a pottery jug to hold the flowers.

Opal sees more grey in her friend's hair, but there is a lightness to her movements and a radiance that has erased the aura of growing disappointment she has given off in recent years. Praise be, she's in love, Opal thinks. And it's reciprocated. About time. Now she'll be able to shed the dreaded George. I just hope the kids won't hold her back.

They go out on to the veranda, Opal carrying an ice bucket holding the wine and Isabel carrying a tray with wine glasses and biscuits and cheese and olives. The sun is setting through the trees, slanting dusky gold across the lawn and the flower beds and through the hanging ferns. Late afternoon is Isabel's favourite hour; she loves to spend it on this sheltered veranda where the garden blends into the house and the creaking wicker chairs wrap their padded arms round her. Comfortable and homely, it is a place for confidences and quiet times, for afternoon tea and sundowners and still summer evenings.

Opal picks up the bottle in a rattle of ice cubes, operates the corkscrew with practised ease and pours out the wine. She holds her glass under her nose to savour the bouquet, then raises it to Isabel saying, 'Congratulations. Who is he?'

Reaching for her own glass, Isabel laughs and says, 'You've guessed?'

'It's coming out of your pores, old dear.'

'George hasn't noticed.'

'George is so self-centred that he wouldn't notice if the sky fell down. Can't think why you ever married the pompous twit.'

Isabel shrugs, raising her own glass. 'Didn't know any better. And he was OK in the beginning, really. He just hasn't aged well.'

'You can say that again. I think you're a saint for having hung on for so long.'

'It was the children mainly. I used them as an excuse, told myself they had to have a stable home, etcetera. But I've been doing a lot of soul-searching recently and I've come to the conclusion that I've made a mess of my life because I'm basically feeble. It's not only George who's been the problem, it's me.' Opal is the only person to whom she can admit this. 'I should have planned things better, been much more assertive about what I wanted instead of allowing circumstances to dictate the course of my life. If I'd just hung on with Ma in that awful flat and not married the first presentable man who came along, maybe I'd have got off on the right foot to start with.'

'Oh, bull. I've never known anyone less feeble. You were unlucky, that's all. The person who said that life's a lottery was dead right. The older I get and the more horror stories I hear, the more I'm convinced that chance is the major factor governing our lives. I mean, just think how different your life would have been if your Pa hadn't died when he did. We'd never have met, for one thing.' Opal takes another considered sip. 'How do you like the wine?'

'Lovely, thanks.' Isabel is not sure what else one should say about the taste. Though she enjoys wine, she has never had a chance to explore its variety. George, wedded to his brandy, can't see the point in spending money on expensive bottles and says boxed wine is quite good enough if she must drink the stuff. She adds, 'It's a real treat in this parsimonious household. Tell me what we're celebrating?'

With her familiar dirty chuckle, Opal says, 'Colin and I are about to embark on a new venture. You're looking at the future co-author of a cookbook about Cape food. That's why I'm up here, to talk to our publisher.'

'Great! That's wonderful. I'm also –' Isabel stops, not wanting to detract from her friend's moment of glory by announcing that she too is writing something.

But Opal pounces, quick as always to pick up nuances. 'You're also what? Come on, Izz, tell me all! You're bursting with secrets. Who is he? Someone I know?'

Isabel nods, unable to restrain her beam of joy.

'Who? Is he from the Cape too?'

'No. From way back.'

'How far back?'

'Two Rivers.' The words drop between them, stones that sink in muddy water sending out ripple after concentric ripple of memories.

Opal is flabbergasted. 'From back *then*? But who?'

'Let me tell you what happened first . . .'

For the next half hour while they nibble cheese and olives and the level in the wine bottle sinks lower and lower, Isabel regales her friend with an account of how she met her lover again, their trysts down at the beach cottage, her need for meaningful work, her decision to start writing about what happened in Two Rivers, and the growing manuscript hidden away from George in the linen cupboard. Draining the last drop from her glass, light-headed as much from the relief of telling someone as from the wine, she ends with, 'The story has just come pouring out as though it's been waiting all these years to be written.'

'Maybe it has. Have you shown it to him?'

'Had to pluck up the courage first. You know how spare you feel when you're showing something to an expert? But he actually seemed to like it, says it's good and I must keep going. I still feel quite amazed by the whole thing.'

'I don't. Remember how you snatched the Archbishop's essay prize from under all our noses?'

Isabel leans forward and clatters her empty glass down on the table. 'Don't remind me of that day.'

'It was nothing compared with –' Opal breaks off, hesitates, then changes the subject. 'Do you feel confident enough to show what you've done to a publisher? I'm sure ours would be interested if it's been praised by someone so well known.' She chuckles again. 'I can't believe that you two have got together.'

'We're not together yet.' Said quickly.

'Surely you're going to leave George now?' Opal lunges forward to grab her friend's hand. 'Just dump the bloody man! You don't have anyone to hold you back now that the kids are grown and gone.'

'Ralphie – Ralph hasn't quite gone. He ran into problems at college and we agreed to let him leave. He's staying at home until he finds a job, then he'll move in with Janine for a while. I'm pleased about that. She's in love with a beautiful but brainless cricketer who goes away all the time and never stops looking at himself in the mirror. He's not nearly good enough for her, but she can't see it and I can't say it, because that would only make her stick to him even harder. You know how loyal Janine is. I'd hate her to make the same mistake as I did with George.'

'Maybe the scales will fall from her eyes when she has Ralphie around for comparison. He's a lovely kid, that one. So bright and questioning under the shyness.'

'He's not a kid any more. That's been part of his problem at college, apparently; he was way ahead of the others in Computer Science. And he wants to be called Ralph now that he has a girlfriend. Can you believe it? I've been worrying myself sick for years about what seemed like an unhealthy involvement with computers and the fact that he never seemed to make friends, and he turns round and says he has a girlfriend.'

'They seem to be children for so long, and then one day you find that they've grown up without your noticing.' Opal thinks of her four, all flown the nest now. She and Colin are somewhat guiltily enjoying the peace that has descended on their home. 'Have you spilt the beans to them yet?'

'Some of the beans. I told them about the writing but didn't think they were ready to hear that their mother has taken a lover. They were all at the house yesterday afternoon, as a matter of fact. We're in the throes of a family crisis: Chryssa is pregnant and wants me to look after the child so she can go on working.'

'No! You can't consider it, Izz. Not now, with –'

Isabel's laugh rings out into the darkening garden. 'Exactly what I said. It's her and Tom's problem, not mine. These past months have shown me that there's a whole big exciting world outside this family I've cocooned myself in for too long, and I want to explore it.' She remembers her lover saying, 'Having found you so late, I am overwhelmed by greed. I want you with me all the time so we can make up for the lost years.' She says, 'I'm going to make up for the lost years. I'm going to be greedy and please myself now. I'm going to ask George for a divorce.'

It is the first time she has said it out loud and, as if in confirmation, they hear the sound of his car coming up the drive.

'Bravo,' Opal murmurs.

'He'll want his supper now.' Isabel pulls a face. 'We'll have to continue the gossip tomorrow morning. What time is your plane?'

'Ten-thirty. I'm flying home via Durban so I can see Stella. How is she?'

'Haven't seen her in the last month, though I've been thinking about her constantly since I've been writing about Two Rivers. It's made me understand her a lot better.' Isabel tries to shrug off her guilt at being too self-involved to go and see her dying sister, and fails. 'She finds it hard to talk on the telephone, though I keep in touch with her doctor, of course.'

'Is she on her own? I'd have thought –'

Isabel cuts in, knowing exactly what her friend is going to say. 'I wanted her to be near me but she can't take the thin air at this altitude, so she chose to go to a place in Durban where she can have full-time nursing care. You know Stella. Always does the exact opposite to what's expected.'

Opal gives a sympathetic nod. She understands how it has always been between the two sisters: they have an irritable affection for each other that has never had a chance to become love. They are too different, and the ghost of Finn inevitably comes between them.

292

'Fly with me,' she urges. 'Even if it's just for the day.'

Wallowing in her new sense of release, Isabel says, 'Maybe I should. There are things I want to ask her about Two Rivers – though I don't think I'll tell her that I'm writing about it. She would hate to know that it was all being dragged up again. She never mentions Finn.'

From the hallway comes the sound of George tossing his keys on the table and putting his briefcase down.

'Do come. It would be less traumatic if there were three instead of two of us. I've been dreading saying goodbye to her, both of us knowing it's probably for the last time.' Opal speaks in a low voice so he won't hear. 'I'll stand you to the return ticket and we can catch up with the rest of our news on the plane down.'

'Killing two birds with one –' Isabel stops herself. 'I don't mean that. Poor Stella. Of course I'll come, but I wouldn't dream of letting you pay. I've got money tucked away for emergencies and things George kicks up a fuss about buying.'

He comes out on to the veranda smoothing his hand back over thinning hair and says without enthusiasm, 'Hullo, Opal. Long time no see. What do I kick up a fuss about?'

'So-called unnecessary expenditure.' Isabel sits looking at her husband outlined against the passage light; at the last tailor-made suit he could afford, bagging at the knees and elbows now, the tie knot pulled loose and the red brandy stains high on his cheeks. George who was once so dapper is now shabby. With a mixture of pity and exasperation, she thinks, I don't want to live with this man any more. It's enough now. She says, 'I'm going to fly down to Durban with Opal to see Stella tomorrow. I'll pay for the ticket.'

'Bit sudden isn't it?'

'George, you know how ill she is and I –' Hearing the defensive tone in her voice, Isabel stops herself and says crossly, 'I don't have to explain. I'm just going.'

'Suit yourself, but don't pretend to Opal that you're paying when we all know that it'll come out of the housekeeping. And you'd better enjoy it because there won't be money for air tickets when I retire.' He swings round and goes back inside.

As his footsteps recede, Isabel raises her eyebrows at her friend and says, 'QED. Time to go.'

'ASAP,' Opal replies, and they find themselves giggling as they used to in Two Rivers during the long hot afternoons, when they would lie on Isabel's brass double bed under the knotted-up mosquito net talking endlessly about boys.

Extract from the official report of the Sandham Commission of Enquiry into the Easter 1952 Riot:

'... Mr Perumal Pather, current chairman of the Mariamman temple committee, testified that acting on his instructions, Mr Bhiraj Abjee applied first to the Durban courts, then to the Supreme Court in Pietermaritzburg, and finally to the Appeal Court in Bloemfontein for an urgent interdict to stop the bridge-widening. All three applications were turned down, the judges being satisfied by the argument presented by counsel for the Natal Roads Department to the effect that, though they regretted having to demolish the tower of the Hindu temple, the ground on which it stood was essential to the widening of the already dangerously congested Umsindo bridge.

Mr Pather then read from a prepared statement, making loud and unseemly accusations against the Natal Provincial Administration and its attitude towards what he called "taxpayers who are having no say at all over the way their own money is spent, just their sacred buildings pulled down willy nilly."

It was pointed out to him that the Hindu temple was not the only structure affected by the road-widening. The gates to the Herald Company offices and housing estate are also due to be pulled down to make way for the widening of the Umlilwane bridge.

This elicited a second outburst. Mr Pather shouted, "You are comparing a gate with a place of worship? I protest! You people deliberately set the Zulus on us, trying to get rid of your coolie problem in the same way as Hitler got rid of the Jews."

He was ruled in contempt of the Commission and placed under arrest. After consultation with Sergeant Koekemoer, who affirmed that the police suspected Mr Pather, a jeweller, of illicit diamond buying, it was decided not to grant bail but to hold him pending further investigation . . .'

19

The road camp had been pitched just off the main road
running north to Durban, on the stubble of a cane field that
was due for replanting. Every week it sprouted more prefabs,
water tanks, trucks, bulldozers, earth compacters, cement
mixers, tar barrels and heaps of river sand and crushed blue
gravel. Construction men began digging holes to relocate the
poles that carried the telephone lines. Starting on the far side
of the mill complex, a survey team moved along the main
road sighting and measuring and leaving rows of steel pegs
and angled wooden markers hammered together out of rough
pine.

When they began slapping whitewash crosses on the syringa and mango trees between the temple tower and the
bridge, there were renewed howls of protest in Coolietown
and the temple guardians were called out to form a living
cordon round the marked trees. Ram Pillay, who sometimes
assisted the temple priest, spent hours up a ladder that night
rigging up a defensive floodlight on one corner of the tower,
and caught a chill that turned into pneumonia. Dr Singh
ordered him to bed and for the first time since anyone could
remember, *The Sweet-Smelling Jasmine* was rattling around
being driven by someone else. The new driver was too much
in awe of Mr Naidoo, the Durban tycoon who owned the bus
company, to allow any free lifts.

Sergeant Koekemoer was a policeman who did things by
the book and was dedicated to what he called 'the maintain-
ance of law and order at all times'. As soon as it became
apparent that the road-widening would be controversial, he
had made preparations. The morning after the living cordon
appeared, he chugged across the bridge again in full uniform

with a court injunction banning gatherings of more than three persons anywhere along the main road until the widening operation was complete. The injunction was backed up by a police detachment brought in from Durban to patrol the roadworks in day and night shifts. The temple guardians withdrew, muttering. The whitewashed crosses continued their relentless march across town, appearing on all the flamboyant trees on the west side of the main road.

Stella was furious because it was our side. I heard her raging at Finn, 'We're going to lose our pathway as well as the trees! The road will come right up to the pharmacy steps and the traffic will be twice as heavy. You've got to stop this desecration – this brutal rape of our town!'

'How?' He was exhausted, trapped between the all-day anger being voiced by his customers and Stella's eruptions at night. She was more tense than ever, caught up in a passion of protest that whirled her off to meetings and marches and then slammed her back on to her bed with migraines. She had asked Mother Beatrice to release her temporarily from teaching, saying that effective protest was vital before it was too late. Mother Beatrice, short-staffed by two now, doubled up the art classes and taught them herself.

Eddies of unease at the protest activity and the presence of extra policemen in Coolietown spread through the white parts of Two Rivers, made worse by the horrifying stories that were beginning to appear in the newspapers about Mau Mau attacks on white farmers in Kenya. People started locking their doors during the day, and uniformed guards were posted at the gates to the company estate and the golf course opposite. As the end of March approached, even the elements were restless: a cold front sweeping up the coast brought wind and driving rain.

There was talk of the annual Hindu charity fête being cancelled. Finn told me that it was held each year on the last Saturday of March in the adjacent gardens of the Reddy and Pather mansions, with part of the fence between them being taken down. Everybody in Coolietown went, he said, as much to ogle the domains of the wealthy as to spend money in a good cause. Even a few whites had been known to brave the rigours of Indian crowds in search of bargains.

Sarcastic remarks like these were new coming from Finn. I wondered if it was because he was tired, or a result of what I had seen through Ismail's window on the night of the bicycle picnic. I had hardly been able to look him in the face since then because my feelings were in such turmoil. Clearly he was having an affair with Asha; she came into the pharmacy every day now for private consultations in the dispensary. I couldn't help remembering our conversations about beauty and grace; he'd said, 'Grace is a rare attribute in people.' And Asha was demure as well as beautiful and graceful – the epitome of the comely, pliable, willing Eastern woman men are supposed to admire – whereas Stella was opinionated and selfish and prickly, volatile as methylated spirits. Her foxy eyes looked more and more like those of a wild animal caught in a trap; her already scant patience snapped under the least strain. Even though she was my sister, could I blame Finn for falling out of love with a wife who kept brushing him aside for things she considered more important, who criticised and argued and wasn't even sure if she loved him?

No, I couldn't, because I did love him. But I was also furious with him for allowing himself to be snared by the whispered confidences and shimmering silks of a girl only a few years older than I was, who belonged to a different, forbidden race (the Prohibition of Mixed Marriages Act had been speedily passed in 1949, the year after the Nationalists came into power). He had no right to Asha, and from the look of angry resentment on Govind's face every time they disappeared into the back room together, I knew that he thought so too. Which made me even more furious because I didn't want to ally myself with skinny Govind and his horrible jerking adam's apple against Finn.

The air in the house behind the pharmacy was thick with unspoken recriminations. Even Eslina felt it, because she said to me one day, 'Izzy-weh, I think my grandmother she is calling to me, and she is very cross. I must go to the sangoma straight on Saturday to find out what things I must do.' Her grandmother had been dead for over ten years, but she still took regular offerings to her grave and spoke of her as a bossy old woman who kept a sharp eye on family affairs.

'Aren't you going to the Hindu fête, then?' Since both Finn and Stella were preoccupied and Opal was going home for the weekend, I had planned to ask Eslina if I could go with her and her friends, who always went for the good quality second-hand children's clothes. 'Those coolies, ai! They spend too much money on their kids,' she'd said, pearl earrings jiggling as she shook her head.

The fête committee had finally been given permission to hold it as usual by Sergeant Koekemoer, on condition that they agreed to let him station a police patrol at the gates. When they'd protested, he'd first said, 'Doesn't you people know that the police force is here for your protection? I'll put in a request for a Indian patrol, if you want.' Then when they'd managed to convince him that navy blue serge uniforms and holstered revolvers could also be seen as a threat, whatever the race of the wearers, he'd said grudgingly, 'So OK then, I'll keep my men out of sight around the corner. But they must stay until the fête is completely over and finished. I'm not standing for any trouble, you hear?'

Eslina said, 'I'm go to the fête early-early nine o'clock, Izzy, if you want for to come. Then I must go to the sangoma.'

The women who ran the fête had worked for months making sweets and knitting baby clothes and embroidering household linen and collecting old clothes and books and donated items for the white elephant and the tombola stalls. If it hadn't been for the Indian music and the food being sold – samoosas and rotis and chilliebites and cartons of blistering curry and rice – it could have been any South African fête. Fat aunties sold packets of sticky pink coconut sweets, sweating fathers stood in makeshift booths with sacking walls trying to get people to throw balls at targets to win various useless objects, kids giggled and screamed and wailed, boys chased each other, and on trestle tables covered in crêpe paper, cracked vases stood next to ugly lampshades and tattered copies of Kahlil Gibran and the *Victoria League Cookbook*.

Lured by the prospect of books for the taking, Dorothy Gould had made one of her rare public appearances and was hovering nearby with a large shopping bag, eyeing them;

Mrs Chetty was keeping a kindly watch on her from behind the stall. Nobody would mind if Miss Dorothy was taking any books that remained at the end of the day, she whispered to me, smiling, but they wanted to sell what they could before they let her loose. Dicky was there too, shuffling around the food stalls picking at his scabs and looking hangdog. I even saw Percy Smuts, and melted rapidly into the crowd in the opposite direction; if he latched on to me in public, I'd die. He'd phoned Stella several times to ask if he could take me to the flicks, a fate worse than death which I'd managed to avoid by making desperate signals that I wasn't at home. I could just imagine what Evelyn Simpson would say if she heard I was being regularly propositioned by a boy with yabs and a quiff who worked in a milk bar.

Eslina left after an hour with two bulging string bags of clothes for her children and I wandered around keeping a watchful eye out for Percy and feeling disappointed. I had expected something more exotic: mysterious oriental tents with silken drapes and stalls laden with antique ivory bangles and tinkling silver necklaces and painted wooden elephants. Why did everything have to be so ordinary? Now that I had become the convent pariah and things were going wrong between Stella and Finn, and (worst of all) James was writing letters from boarding school to Opal instead of me, the gilt was wearing off Two Rivers.

It was getting near lunchtime and the sky was disappearing again behind fast-spreading storm clouds with a gusting March wind behind them. I'd get caught in the rain if I didn't go home soon. On my way out I drifted up the lawn towards the Pathers' Spanish-arched veranda, hoping to sneak a look through the windows and see if the inside was as luxurious as the Reddys' house. As I got to the steps, however, people came out of the main doorway – the Reddy and Pather families descending to grace the fête with their presence. Or so I thought at first. They were dressed to kill: the women in glittering saris, the men and boys in immaculate long white cotton jackets and trousers. They walked in procession, with the parents in front followed by Kesaval and Asha and Violet Reddy on one side and Srini Pather and his brothers on the other.

301

I hadn't seen Kesaval in anything other than jeans and school clothes, and he looked different and foreign: not a boy who caught fish and frogs on the river bank any more, but an Indian. A worshipper of many-armed gods. Dicky Gould's contemptuous 'chilliecracker' surfaced in my mind too, I'm ashamed to say. The trouble with racial slurs is that they slip so easily through the cracks of correct thought; they're like eels wriggling in under the mud.

I shrank back behind a yesterday-today-and-tomorrow bush so he wouldn't see me and guess what I was thinking. To this day the horrid purple and mauve and white flowers with their heavy scent remind me of ugly thoughts I would rather forget – and of the look on Asha's face when Mr Pather stood on the top step and announced to the hushed crowd below her betrothal to 'our dearly beloved eldest son, Srinivassen.'

That was the first time I saw Mr Pather, standing next to his forbidding wife who was resplendent in an emerald green shot silk sari edged with a broad band of intricate gold embroidery, her hand on Srini's shoulder, her expression challenging anyone to deny that he was the most handsome, most accomplished son in the world. Mr Pather had a hawk's nose and hooded eyes sunk into grottos overhung with brambles; unsmiling even on this happiest of occasions, he seemed to hover above the crowd like a bird of prey. Stella said afterwards that he mesmerised people, and it was true. Once I met him on the pathway outside his jeweller's shop and when he stepped aside with his hands clasped behind his back, chillingly polite, I faltered to a stop and stood gaping up at him, unable to move for agonising seconds. When I could, I scurried off like a mouse.

Asha looked as though she felt much the same that day. Her face was almost hidden under the head-folds of her sari. Standing next to her, his hair combed into sleek careful waves, his fat-lipped smile gleaming with gold fillings, Srini was basking in the cheers and shouted congratulations of the crowd. He was taking them as his due, rather than hers. He hardly looked at her during the whole ten minutes that the families stood there announcing the dates of the betrothal and the wedding. I lurked behind the bush, watching. Now

302

that I was closer to him I saw that his skin had a buttery sheen, as though he ate too much ghee and it was coming out of his pores.

Though I felt sorry for Asha – having to submit to marriage with someone you didn't like must really be a fate worse than death – I was sending up silent cheers too. It meant that she would be out of Finn's reach. The whole thing was suspiciously sudden, though. Neither she nor Kesaval had mentioned a word about a betrothal. Had her mother and grandfather heard about the clandestine meetings with Finn and hurried it forward?

People had crowded up to the veranda to listen to the announcement, leaving the fête stalls deserted with their sacking sides flapping in the wind and the unsold goods – the ugly and the shopsoiled and the badly made – lying forlorn on trestle tables with their concealing crêpe paper in tatters. The leftovers would be given away to the poor, no doubt, who would have to accept them with grateful expressions and renewed feelings of helpless umbrage. For an odd moment I thought, looking down over the scene, It looks as though a refugee camp has sprung up in the two gardens, the poor invading the rich. Was this what revolution looked like? Sackcloth shanties crowding mansions, street people gathering like ants round the honeypots of the wealthy hoping for a share, trampled lawns, rubbish everywhere . . .

Big drops of rain began to fall. As Mr Pather speeded up his closing oration, there was a commotion round the side of the house. Jantu Soobramony came running along the path that led to the veranda with two Indian policemen in hot pursuit, shouting, 'Bulldozers! Come!'

Heads swivelled towards him. Mr Pather stopped talking and glowered at the running boy.

'Bulldozers!' Jantu flung out a whiplash arm in the direction of the temple.

The crowd swirled away from the veranda steps making a growling noise. The two policemen skidded to a halt and held up their arms. 'Stop! You are not permitted to leave these premises!' one shouted, while the other fumbled in his holster for his service revolver. 'Stop, please!' But they were both overrun long before the revolver had been wrestled free and then dropped and lost in the chaos of running, jostling bodies. And I cowered behind the yesterday-today-and-tomorrow bush until they were all gone, watching Dorothy and Dicky Gould systematically loot the remaining books and abandoned plates of food in the rain. Then I scuttled home.

According to Finn, who heard from breathless customers what happened, the fête crowd surged out of the dual Spanish gates and along the main road and across the Umsindo bridge unhindered by the small police detachment round the corner. Sergeant Koekemoer was away in Durban that Saturday refereeing a police rugby match, and there were no reinforcements on call. Down at the temple, two yellow bulldozers had crashed their way down through the bamboos and small trees along the road verge and stood on either side of the base of the tower. The white operators, seeing the angry crowd boiling over the bridge, had switched off and made a dash for the road camp. Within seconds people were climbing all over the machines, shouting their defiance. By late afternoon, both had been trussed in chains wrenched off railway trucks used for carrying sugar cane that were standing empty in the mill siding.

Next day was a Sunday and Finn went fishing. After he had gone off in a cloud of tobacco smoke Stella said, 'There's a protest delegation going down to the police station about the bulldozers. Shall we go too?'

Her face was lit up like the windows of Pather's Jewellers at night. She thrived on arguments with authority. I said, 'But are we allowed?'

'Don't be so wet, Izz. We're co-protesters on the road-widening issue. The least we owe our Indian neighbours is moral support.' She stormed happily into her bedroom to choose a suitable protest outfit.

On the way to the police station charge office, I remember thinking, She's forgotten how much she hates living behind a shop on the edge of Coolietown. Now the coolies have become her neighbours. Maybe with Asha out of the way, it's going to be all right between her and Finn.

Standing across the charge desk from the Sergeant, Mr Pather and Mr Reddy and Mr Moodley were bolstered by a solid phalanx of angry templegoers. Stella and I sidled in behind them and stood against the wall.

Mr Pather was fuming, 'The Roads Department has no right to demolish until the first of the month! The expropriation order is only for Tuesday. We are planning the final ceremonies for tomorrow.'

'Those bulldozers was being moved early into position. That's all.' Sergeant Koekemoer's face was swollen with fury at not having been forewarned of the move by the Roads Department. Finn had said that he prided himself on knowing exactly what was going on in every corner of Two Rivers.

'For Tuesday? Aikona, Sergeant. That is a very useful Zulu word, nè? Aikona! It looks to us like there were orders to demolish the tower at a time when nobody was there to protest against it. A cynical – I might say typical – fait accompli.'

The Sergeant insisted, 'I'm telling you, man, it had nothing to do with the fête! They was just getting things ready.'

'And I'm telling you, Sergeant, that if any single person is touching our tower before Tuesday, there will be serious trouble. That is a holy place. Our mother goddess, Mariamma, is already very angry.'

'Goddess, jislaaik,' I heard the Sergeant mutter under his breath. Finn had also said that he was a good Calvinist and despised the fancy trappings of other religions, particularly the heathens.

'We are not joking, sir.' That morning, Mr Moodley looked more like Genghis Khan than a fat spice merchant.

The Sergeant raised his voice then so everybody in the charge office could hear. 'Listen, you people better not make any more trouble, you hear? Else I'll be forced to call in reinforcements.'

'So will we,' Mr Reddy said, deadly quiet. 'So will we, Sergeant.'

Rumours raged through Coolietown the following day like cane fires in a strong wind. People whispered that Mariamma was displeased at the imminent destruction of part of her temple – so displeased that she was likely to call up one of her darker aspects, Kali, the destroyer of evil. The name was spoken in fear with soft explosive k's. You heard it everywhere you went. Kali. Kali is coming. Kali has put a curse on

305

anyone who tries to pull the tower down. Kali. I heard Govind muttering it. From the mango tree I heard the Soobramony children passing it round with the stolen fruit in the shadows of their father's storeroom.

Pictures appeared in some of the shop windows showing a fierce four-armed blue goddess with bared teeth and her tongue sticking out, standing on the prostrate body of a man. I asked Finn to explain about her, and he said that the man was her husband, the god Shiva. She represented the vital energy of the mother goddess, and destroyed evil so as to lay the basis of the good to follow. In three of her hands she held a shield, a sword and the grinning severed head of a demon; the fourth was in the assurance pose, which Finn said assured her devotees of her protection. She wore no clothes, only a garland of skulls and the severed hands of the demons she had killed strung together and used as a skirt. Blood from the stumps dripped down her legs.

Thrilling with horror, I wrote a letter to Evelyn Simpson wallowing in the gory details. With things so chancy between Stella and Finn, and Ma getting better by the day according to Aunty Mavis, I could be sent home sooner than expected. It would be foolish not to prepare the way for a triumphal return to my old school as an authority on Indian exotica and boys from posh private schools. I'd probably have to write James off as a bad job, I realised, but I was sure I could persuade Titch to write me letters on Michaelhouse notepaper.

By the morning of Tuesday the first, April Fool's day, the rumours were saying that Kali had come. I heard the muttered word everywhere on my way to school. Kali. Kali. Kali. And I see now through the prism of my wiser years the dangerous paradox of that morning: the schoolgirl walking through the convent gates with her bouncing ponytail into a smug white world of ordered lessons and superior godliness, while behind me the angry spirit of Kali trailed her bloody skirt of severed hands through the tin shanties of Coolietown, swearing to destroy anyone who dared to desecrate the temple tower.

306

Isabel

Speaking on the phone to her publisher next morning, Opal tells him about Isabel's manuscript, adding that it has been commended by the well-known writer of political biographies and travel books. Isabel has not told Opal that her lover is also the anonymous writer of the novel about middle-aged sex whose sales are still rocketing. It is a secret they are determined to keep to themselves, he because authorship of a sizzling bestseller would undermine the public perception of him as a serious writer, and she because she doesn't want her new-found joy invaded.

'I don't mind what you write about our astonishing orgasms – the book obviously gives a lot of people new hope, or they wouldn't be buying it like they are – but I would mind them knowing that I'm the role model.'

'You don't hanker to be a sex queen?'

'Only to you,' she had said, reaching for him.

Remembering the occasion, she is smiling when Opal turns away from the phone and says, 'Gerald says that he'll certainly take a look at your manuscript, as long as it's typed.'

'He will?' Isabel breaks into a nervous laugh, floored by the suddenness. 'But I've never learnt how to type. Never had any reason to.'

'Don't you know someone who types?'

Isabel shakes her head. 'But – but it's quite easy to read. I've written it all out in neat.'

'In neat! Oh, Izz, you sound just like the nuns. What an imprint convents leave on their pupils.' Opal turns back to the telephone and says, 'I'll take it home and get it typed up by our secretary. Thanks, Gerald. You're a star. 'Bye.'

Aghast, Isabel bleats, 'It's not ready yet.'

'Doesn't have to be. A good editor can tell at once if a piece of writing is worth anything. Go on, Izz,' she urges. 'Let me take it home now, or you'll spend weeks agonising over every little word.'

'No. It's too soon. And you're being damn bossy.'

'Somebody's got to give you a shove.'

'I'm afraid. So much depends on what he says.' Isabel is whispering. 'You can't believe how much.'

'All the more reason to get an informed opinion before you go any further, and Gerald can give you that. Colin and I are very impressed by his ideas. He has some innovative publishing projects on the go and actively seeks out new authors, which is how he got on to us.'

'I don't even know if what I've written is history or biography or just rubbish.' Now that it has come to showing someone her work, Isabel feels her confidence haemorrhaging. 'And I haven't got to the most important part yet, the Mariamman festival and the riot and –'

'Write a synopsis explaining what happens.'

'But we're leaving for the airport in less than an hour, and I haven't packed.'

'I'll help you. Come on, dragon lady. Get a pen and paper and write down what happens in the rest of the story while I pack your case.'

Remembering how Isabel would sit dreaming up her mango tree while she procrastinated over things she didn't want to do, Opal is relentless. She bullies her into unearthing the manuscript from the linen cupboard and sketching out a two-page synopsis, then wraps it in brown paper and stows it in her attaché case saying, 'I won't let this out of my sight till I get home. Your offspring will be safe with me, I promise.'

As they get into the hired car to drive to the airport, both dreading the visit to Stella in the Durban nursing home that lies ahead, she says, 'I'll ask our secretary to do two copies of the manuscript so you can keep a copy to work from when you take it in to Gerald.'

Isabel looks doubtful. 'If I can pluck up the courage.'

20

Nothing happened at the temple until the afternoon of Tuesday the first. All available members of the committee and the temple guardians had gathered there just after dawn ready to shout their protests when the tower was pulled down, but no one had come.

Mother Beatrice let us out of school one period early that day, telling us to go and play our April Fool jokes elsewhere because our teachers were too busy trying to think of sensible comments to make on our end-of-term reports to bother with such silliness. Agog to see how far the demolition had progressed, I persuaded Finn to leave Govind in charge of the pharmacy to walk with me down to the bridge.

But the temple stood unchanged in its quiet grove of trees by the sliding brown river, leaf shadows and monkeys flickering among its wedding-cake decorations. The crowd that had gathered earlier along the railing had thinned out as people drifted home or back to their jobs, though temple guardians were prowling everywhere thwacking steps and pillars and jasmine-hung walls with their sticks, faces clenched under the black scarves knotted round their heads, dying for a fight. The yellow bulldozers squatted at the foot of the bridge embankment amid the wreckage of trees and bamboos they had crashed through, still entangled in the chains they had been trussed in on the day of the fête.

We leaned together over the parapet where we had leaned with Mr Reddy, looking down at the doomed tower. Among the shells and peacocks and crescent moons, gods and goddesses sat and stood and danced in stately frozen whiteness as before, with those faint, all-knowing, celestial smiles that seem to be above petty human concerns, yet curiously sympathetic. Above them the golden urn rose out of its lotus-petal base with the still flame licking skywards for the last time.

Beside me, Finn was drawing on his pipe as though it had hellfire in its bowl instead of the rank Magaliesberg tobacco he had taken to smoking, mainly to annoy Stella, I think. It came in calico bags, one of which he had stuffed into the pocket of his trousers under the starched white pharmacy jacket, with the drawstring hanging out.

'The sculptors who made all these marvellous decorations must have worked with their hands.' His lips kept plopping as he smoked. 'They must have moulded those statues day after day with fingers that were sore and shrivelled from the wet cement, standing barefoot on the rickety bamboo scaffolding, sometimes falling down with tiredness. Yust imagine it, Izzy. They were simple men building for the same reason as the medieval masons who built the great cathedrals of Europe, to the glory of their gods. Yet here we are destroying their devoted handiwork in the name of progress.'

He was teasing out his ideas with an exasperation stoked in equal measure by the distress of his Hindu customers, his respect for other people's cherished objects, and Stella.

'And it's not yust a holy place that's being desecrated. We're violating a trust too. People who create temples and churches have a right to expect a reasonable continuity – to know that a lovely building like this will stand for a century, at least.'

More savvy now about my expected role when out walking with Finn, I put the opposing argument. 'But what about all the cars and trucks that have to come through Two Rivers? We can't just wish them away.'

'Nay, it's true, we can't.' He lifted his head and looked upriver. 'Maybe the answer is to take roads past cities and towns instead of through them. There's plenty of space for a main road through the canefields op there. Then we could live in peace and quiet without having to bulldoze everything that gets in our way.'

It was a prophetic thing to say in the early Fifties. The irony is that though a six-lane highway runs exactly where Finn envisioned a main road that day, the small town of Two

Rivers was invaded and almost obliterated by the blight of factories that spread south from Durban during the boom years. With prudent foresight, the Herald Company had already relocated its corporate headquarters and golf club and management housing to a landscaped estate even further removed from Coolietown and the grimy mill that smelled of boiling sugar for nine months of the year, and where there were no little black particles of burnt cane trash fluttering in the air.

Remembering the whispers I'd heard on the way to school that morning, I said, 'Why is Kali always so – so frickly?' 'Frickly' was a wonderful word, one of Finn's best gifts to me; it could mean anything from medium horrible to gruesome to ghastly.

He nodded. 'Thought you'd ask. The skulls and the severed hands make her specially eye-catching, I think. Like the statues of the saints in those old cathedrals used to be – not plain wood and stone as we see them now, but painted in bright colours. See, the theory is that when your congregation can't read, you can entice them to God with spectacles like miracle plays and holy pictures and stained-glass windows. But these are yust the trappings, Izzy. Even this lovely tower is a diversion. Try to see past the blood and the incense and the gold filigree to the pure belief that lies beneath.'

He was gazing down at the river sliding beneath us, gurgling on a pipe that had gone out. We were getting into deep water for a weekday afternoon. I said, 'But, I mean, I don't understand how the Hindu gods work. Is there one main one like we've got who keeps appearing in different disguises, or is there supposed to be a whole team of gods and goddesses?'

'Does it matter?' He looked up at me, his eyes fathoms deep. 'In my opinion, the Hindus beat Christians hands down with their goddesses; it means that they aren't dominated by Popes and celibate priests who see women as lesser beings. The concept of the mother goddess goes back to the earliest times when women were worshipped as the creators of life. Mother Nature, you know? For the Hindus, this supreme mother is Sakthi, and Kali is the most warlike of her many aspects. Mariamma is a more yentle aspect, the goddess who is responsible for people's ailments. At the Mariamman festival

311

on Good Friday, you'll see people bringing her thank-you gifts for making them better.'

'But what do people mean when they say that she is calling up Kali? Why is everyone so afraid?'

He began knocking his pipe on the parapet to clear out the burnt ash. 'Kali is like the big gun when people are in troble. She has the power to destroy evil, so she is the natural one for Mariamma to call op onder the present circumstances.'

'But just widening a road isn't evil, is it?'

'It's not yust the road, Izzy. Here in Coolietown people feel powerless on two counts: because most of them are poor, and because they belong to a small minority group dominated in nombers by black people and in every other way by tight-fisted whites. Kali may be frickly, but Hindus feel they can rely on her to be on their side if it comes to a fight.'

I shivered in spite of the afternoon heat. The cold unsettled weather had moved on up the coast and we were back to muggy days and stifling nights when you would lie awake sweating inside a grey cloud of net, listening to the thin high irritating whine of mosquitoes. Did Kali come visiting at night like Lakshmi was supposed to at Deepavali? Would the severed hands bang softly against her thighs as she dripped her bloody way across the floorboards, moving closer and closer in the moonlight?

A shout snapped me out of the frightening vision. It came from a group of the temple guardians who had been sitting on the steps at the base of the tower eating curry out of cartons. Now they were standing up clutching their long sticks, drawn together in a taut defensive line and looking towards a Roads Department truck that had pulled up on the embankment near the bulldozers and was disgorging labourers who carried sledge hammers and picks and shovels. Behind them, Sergeant Koekemoer sat revving the Triumph at the head of a squad of white policemen with rifles.

Finn said, 'And so it begins.' He pulled out his bag of tobacco and began tamping a large pinch into his pipe, letting half the shreds drop as he always did when he was upset. 'I hope there's no troble now.'

We watched as five men came out through the archways of the temple's portico and walked towards the Sergeant, who switched off the motorbike, kicked down the prop, climbed off and scrambled down to them, pulling out of the inner pocket of his uniform jacket a sheet of folded paper which he handed to the first man. After reading it, he gave the Sergeant a curt nod and passed it to the other committee members.

The Sergeant turned and shouted up to the road gang foreman, 'You can carry on then! Start on the wall and the chains whilst me and my men clear the area. Let's get this show on the bleddy road.'

Finn and I stood looking down as the road gang foreman directed some of the labourers to knock away a section of the wall that joined the tower to the main building. A man with an oxy-acetylene torch released the chains that bound the bulldozers and they were dragged off. The police squad spread out and began urging people to move away from the tower and its vicinity. The temple guardians made a show of resistance but were chivvied towards the steps on the far side of the sacred pool with the help of a dozen rifle butts; they sat there seething and tapping their sticks. Portable barricades were set up round the tower and at both ends of the bridge, ready to be pulled across at the critical moment to stop the traffic. The crowd along the railing began to swell as the news flashed around Coolietown and people came running. Soon they were lining both river banks too. This would be a spectacle of spectacles: not only a tower falling, but a whole panoply of gods and goddesses and sacred lotuses and elephants dropping out of the sky and crumbling to dust.

The muttering began again, exploding all around us like small muffled firecrackers. 'Kali. Kali. Kali.'

I pressed closer to Finn. 'I'm scared.'

He put his free arm round me in one of his bear hugs. 'Shall we go off home, then?'

'No. I want to watch.' How many other girls from my old school would be able to boast of seeing a temple tower destroyed? If I played my cards right, Evelyn Simpson's exploits with boys on the back seats of motor cars would be forever eclipsed.

I was getting squashed against Finn in the press of people. Down below, the road gang foreman was directing the placing of long steel cables that looped from one bulldozer to the other through the demolished part of the wall and round the tower. When I asked if the bulldozers could pull it over just like that, Finn said, 'The tower's not so high – only two storeys, I would say. And he's obviously hoping the old brickwork is deficient in lime, and crombly.'

The foreman was a peevish, shambling old man with a sagging felt hat that had a line of dark sweat where the band had once been. His khaki trousers were held up by braces; when he stood directly under us, you could see a line inside his frayed collar where the weatherbeaten skin gave way to pasty white. He kept shouting at the workmen, 'Get a fokken move on, julle! We haven't got all day. Shesha, man, shesha!'

One of a group of off-shift millworkers who had gathered near us on the bridge began to laugh and jeer, 'Shesha coolies, isonto lizowa!'

'What does that mean?' I whispered.

'He's taunting. It means, "Hurry, the church will fall down".' Finn had begun to look grim. 'I don't like this, Izzy. We should go.'

'No. I want to watch.'

'Stella will be mad if anything –'

I grabbed his pipe-holding hand. 'You want to watch too, don't you?'

He gave a reluctant nod. 'The death of a building has a terrible fascination, I must admit. Tell you what, we'll move along to the other end of the bridge where the crowd is thinner.'

'Please can't we stay here? It's right opposite the tower. We'll get a grandstand view.'

'I thought you said you were scared a moment ago?'

The lie burst from my lips in full flower. 'I'm not any more. Honest. There are cops all around us, anyway. They'll guard us.'

The policemen had spread out and were standing at regular intervals along the bridge and the barricades with their rifles by their sides, trying unsuccessfully to look nonchalant. There is a special watchfulness to a policeman in a crowd: he keeps his face impassive, but his arms are held slightly away from his body and in the shadow of the blue peaked cap worn low

314

in front, his eyes weasel everywhere. In Two Rivers then, we trusted policemen.

The millworkers were hanging over the bridge railing now, laughing and chanting in unison: 'Shesha, coolies, isonto lizowa! Shesha, coolies, isonto lizowa!'

The policemen standing near us began drifting towards them.

Finn said in a sudden harsh voice, 'Come, Izzy. We can't stay.' He stuffed his pipe in his pocket and began pulling my arm. 'This way. We must get home.'

'Please –' I tried to hold him back.

It was the first and only time he got really angry with me. He bent down and barked, 'Listen to me now! We must go. This is a bad situation. Anything can happen. To be in such a crowd at such a time –'

There was a coughing roar as one of the bulldozers started up, and then the second. Terrified screeching monkeys fled in every direction. People began shouting and booing, trying to lean further over the railings to see. The millworkers chanted louder: 'Shesha, coolies, isonto lizowa! Shesha, coolies, isonto lizowa!' The policemen who weren't busy moving the barricades into place at each end of the bridge were shouldering through the crowd with their rifles held high, trying to reach the jeering men and hustle them away before an angered Indian raised his fist and started a fight.

Finn shouted, 'Come, this way!' and began dragging me through the crush of struggling bodies.

The pitch of the bulldozers' engines rose higher as they clanked backwards. People were yelling, women sobbing into their saris, children crying with fright. Through a gap in the scuffling legs, I saw drooping steel cables tighten to parallel lines. One of them slipped upwards and dislodged a statue, which toppled and fell into the jasmine thicket at the base of the tower, somehow staying intact.

A deafening roar went up. People were packing tighter and tighter round us, jostling for a better view. Finn kept tugging me in the opposite direction, nearly pulling my arm off. Desperate to stop him, sobbing with terror that I was going to be torn apart, I tried spreading out my elbows and digging my heels into the gutter at the edge of the bridge pavement, and felt myself falling against the railing.

'Izzy!' His face swam down to me through a nightmare of trampling legs and shoes and feet. 'Hang on,' he bellowed, 'yust hang on, I'm right here!' I felt his body arching over me, making a cage of furry arms and starched white jacket. Even so, my head was being squeezed against the railing and I was struggling to breathe. I remember thinking, I'm going to die here.

And then the tumult and the shouting eased and the bodies stopped struggling. I could turn my head again. Through the railing I saw the bulldozers bucking and straining, their metal treads churning up an ugly porridge of muddy soil and smashed trees, their taut steel cables vibrating like fishing lines trying to reel in something huge and struggling – and the tower still there. The cables had worn grooves in the plaster and there were some deep vertical cracks, but otherwise it stood as solid as ever.

As I struggled to my feet, people were beginning to cheer. Relieved smiles flashed in dark faces all round us. The firecracker words began to go off in little explosions. 'Kali. Kali. Kali.'

Finn had his arm round me and was urging me away. 'We must go while we can.'

My heart was still hammering in shock, but I managed to choke out, 'Can't we just –?'

His face swooped down at mine, his mouth in a furious parabola. 'Stupid girl! Stupid, stupid girl! You could have got killed there. Now we go, ya?'

I couldn't see for tears of self-pity as he frogmarched me home through the jubilant crowd. Finn had called me stupid. Now I had nobody to love me.

People kept tugging at Finn's sleeves and saying things like, 'You see? Our tower is too strong, Mr Rosholt,' and, 'They made good cement in those days, nè?'

'Ya, ya,' he said, propelling me ahead with a firm hand on my shoulder. 'It's good. I'm pleased for you.'

When we reached the barricades at the Coolietown end of the bridge and Finn had to slow down, I turned round and looked back. Policemen were prodding the sullen group of millworkers past a double line of halted traffic towards the compound gates. Down the embankment, the bulldozers were slackening off, defeated. The temple tower soared above them, its gods and goddesses serenely smiling, its crowning golden urn vivid in the late afternoon sunlight. People hung over the railings cheering and shouting, 'Kali! Kali! Kali!' Behind loomed the corrugated iron mill buildings with their skyward-stabbing chimneys, the grim industrial sows that fed off the living green of the canefields to suckle endless truckloads of sticky brown sugar.

Next day, the temple committee sent Abjee's son the lawyer back to court. A different judge issued an injunction preventing the Natal Roads Department from making another attempt to pull the tower down until after the Mariamman festival on Good Friday, on the grounds that weakening the structure could endanger festival visitors.

Coolietown hummed with rumours. People whispered that both Mariamma and Kali were enraged by the attempt to pull down the tower. Both goddesses would have to be suitably propitiated to keep the death curse from spreading to all who had watched the attempted demolition of the tower.

The toppled statue of Ganesha, the wise elephant god to whom Hindus always pray first, son of Shiva and Parvathi, was lifted out of the cushioning jasmine creeper where it had fallen and carried reverently inside to a place of honour in the inner sanctum. There was a noticeable rise in the numbers of people visiting the temple with offerings of fruit and incense. Camphor fires burned all week in the grove of trees that surrounded it, drifting in pungent wisps across the river. Finn and I saw them from the temple bridge, where we had gone on a peacemaking walk so I could apologise for being stubborn and childish and he could apologise for losing his temper.

'I don't know what came over me,' he said. 'I feel that our lives are all at sevens and sixes these days.'

The fourth of April was the last day of school before the Easter holidays. As Opal and I went gossiping out through the gates, I couldn't know that it was for the last time. The seeds of the terrible Easter riot had already been sown. After their deadly harvest was reaped, I would be sent back home.

317

Isabel

Stella lies propped up on pillows in a hospital bed angled so that she can look out over the nursing home's gracious Berea garden. Just below her window is a lily pond with a stone parapet like the one in the courtyard at Two Rivers. She has lain for weeks watching the yellow waterlilies bud and bloom and die, bud and bloom and die, remembering Finn and their time together. It is the first time in many years that she has allowed herself to think of him; it seems pointless now that her life is ebbing to keep trying to banish his tall stooped fond shade. Isabel and Opal are flying down to see her this morning, and they will no doubt conjure up more memories.

They've obviously been told I won't last much longer, she thinks. And I hope I don't. This farce has gone on long enough. Life has no meaning when it is reduced to a desperate struggle for each breath. Would I have started smoking in the first place if I'd known what decades of nicotine would do to my lungs? Probably. I always was pigheaded. I didn't stop or even cut down when the warnings about lung cancer and emphysema and heart disease began to crop up everywhere like poisonous mushrooms. Finn hated my smoking. Hated those affected Black Russians I'd save up to buy because I thought their black cigarette paper and gold tips were the height of sophistication. And of course to scandalise the tea-swilling lady wives of Two Rivers. Bloody boring hypocrites. They were so easy to shock. I had to try much harder in London.

She makes an effort to divert her thinking towards her long and successful career as an interior decorator of top British restaurants, but the London years seem curiously remote. Her friends and colleagues there are melting into the

318

shadows of her mind; it is Finn she sees now, quite clearly. The hurt in his blue eyes when she said something nasty in one of her rages, and the way the curly blond fur on the backs of his hands went limp when he washed them. His courteous mission-bred manner, so otherworldly and unambitious, and so infuriating when she was crackling with a hundred ideas to set the world on fire. If it hadn't been for the baby – the baby that never was – they would never have gone as far as marriage; they were too different. And he wouldn't have died. Was it her fault, that he was driven to his quixotic end? Is this agonisingly slow, dreary death her punishment?

She remembers Isabel, teenage-gawky in baggy blue jeans and that ridiculous stub of a ponytail she was so proud of, mooning around the house and garden feeling hard done by. Stella thinks, She was sure she loved Finn more than I did. It shouldn't have irritated me – psychologists would say it was quite natural for her to transfer her father-feelings from a crabby old man who died to a much kinder, younger man who treated her like the intelligent growing adult she was – but it did. I hated the way she would make adoring sheep's eyes at him and put on little commiserating smiles when I said or did something bitchy. Afterwards, I was happy to dump her on Aunty Mavis and flee to England.

Stella feels a new thought seeping into her consciousness, slowly as all her thoughts do these days. I dumped Ma on Isabel too. Was it my fault that she chose to escape by marrying that preening idiot George? Surely not. It can't all be my fault. I've done good things too. I've been a success. I've worked hard all my life and done a lot for young people who needed help.

But not enough for my family, she thinks. Such as it is: Isabel who never became a proper sister, and her children. Nice kids, what I've seen of them. I can make amends now. I've left my money to all four of them, in equal shares. I hope it does them more good than it did me. Maybe they'll think kindly of me sometimes.

Hearing footsteps approaching the door, she reaches for the bright red lipstick on her bedside table thinking, I hope this visit won't be too painful. I couldn't stand another dose of sheep's eyes, not today when I feel I'm at last beginning to make my peace with Finn. He was a lovely man, just not right for me.

As they go towards the bed, Isabel and Opal try not to let their shock at Stella's appearance show. Her face is ravaged, a death mask made all the more terrible by the gash of badly applied lipstick. Her arms are two arrangements of inert bones on either side of a skeleton covered by a sheet. Only her foxy brown eyes seem alive, kindled by the morning's memories.

She gasps, 'Hullo – you – two.'

'Stella.' Isabel leans down to kiss the bony forehead that is damp with the effort of her breathing. The hair closest to her scalp is grey, shading to the faded henna of her last treatment. It has been cut short in a parody of her wispy Fifties crop. She will not ask for it to be dyed again; her vanity is as exhausted as her body now.

'Izzy. Can – I – call – you – that – now?' Stella turns one hand up to clasp Isabel's in a surprisingly strong grip.

'Of course, love. It doesn't bother me any more. How are you?'

'Nearly – at – my – last – gasp.' The gash of lipstick parts in a ghastly smile. 'About – time – too.'

'It's not like you to give up so easily.' Isabel blinks away the threatening tears, remembering how Stella hates them.

'Not – easy.' She stops for long seconds to draw in a shuddering breath. 'Bloody – hard.'

'I know.'

'You – can't – know!'

There is no answer to a dying person's anger at being robbed of life. Isabel squeezes her hand and moves sideways so Opal can bend over and kiss her too, stroking the two-tone hair. 'Hullo, old thing. It's awful to see you laid so low.'

'Lower – than – a – snake's – belly.' The foxy eyes are blazing up at them. 'Don't – let – your – children – smoke. Not – worth – it.'

Isabel shrugs. 'I've tried, but you can't tell kids what to do after a certain age. Chryssa started at school and smokes far too much.'

Opal says, 'So does my Leon.'

'Bribe – them – to – stop! Tell – them – my – horror – story.' Stella has to summon all her failing strength to convey her urgency to these two rather solid middle-aged women bending over her with such concern. What became of the teenagers I remember? she wonders. Opal so gangly and enthusiastic, and Isabel dreaming of boys and glory up in her mango tree.

Isabel is saying, 'You can hardly call your life a horror story. I've always admired you so, Stella. You did the things most of us only dream about. You've had an amazing career.'

'And you've done so much for others, starting with me.' Opal wishes she could find the right words adequately to thank this woman who helped her escape her hopeless family and achieve the initial training that has led to her lifelong involvement in fine cooking.

'But – I – was – always – lonely.' Stella turns away to look out at the sunny garden. 'I – missed – Finn. You – never – appreciate – people – till – they're – gone.'

Sensing the approach of a touchy area, Opal says, 'Will you both excuse me a minute? I'm going to drum up some tea,' and leaves, closing the door behind her.

Isabel remembers Finn's funeral, when Stella picked up one of the gaudy marigold wreaths sent by the Indian families and tore it to pieces. She remembers Stella screaming, 'I'll never forgive him, never! He's ruined my life.' And looking down at the pathetic remnant of her once-vibrant, passionate sister, she thinks, I've spent a lifetime condemning her for the mistakes she made, and never gave a thought to the magnitude of what she lost in making them. I may have led a dull life in comparison, but I have my children and now I have my new love. I have been blessed with so much more than she ever had. How could I have pushed her away for so long?

She sits down in the chair next to the bed and leans close to her, saying, 'I haven't appreciated you enough, Stella, and I'm so sorry. I could have been a much better sister.'

The death mask moves slowly away from the garden to look at her. 'We – can – be – proper – sisters – now?'

'Proper sisters.' Isabel hugs her. Despite the sadness of the wasted body in her arms, it feels good to be healing the long rift between them.

'Better – late – than – never.' It is gasped into her ear. 'Remember – me – to – your – enviable – children.'

She pulls back. 'They send their best love. You've always been their ritzy London aunt, you know?'

'Too – distant – to – be – of – any – use.'

'Not at all. You sent them the most exciting, unusual, exotic presents for their birthdays and Christmas, which gave them endless pleasure. Plus the privileged status of receiving parcels from overseas.'

'They – wrote – such – lovely – thank-you – letters. Nice – kids. Well – done – Izzy.'

'George helped. In the beginning, at least.'

'Never – liked – that – man.'

Isabel admits, 'I've gone off him too. I'm thinking of leaving him now that the children are off our hands.'

'Good – show!' There is another ghastly smile, then a searching look. 'Is – there – someone – else?'

Isabel laughs and says, 'Believe it or not, someone even more controversial than you were. You may remember him from Two Rivers.' She tells his name, and about the years as a journalist and the travel books and the novel that has scandalised the nation. She can tell Stella the secret because there is no danger of it going further.

There is a glint of amused approval. 'Quite – a – catch. Won't – be – easy – though.'

All of a sudden, Isabel feels the need to confide in this rediscovered sister. Until Opal dropped in out of the blue, she had not been able to talk to anyone about her new love and the decision she is about to make, and now she has a second sounding board. It is such a relief to talk openly about her options. She describes how she met him again, and how well they get on together. 'We've been lovers for nearly a year now. He's made me realise how badly my relationship with George has deteriorated.'

'What – the – hell – are – you – waiting – for?' Though Stella's strength is waning now, her hoarse whisper is fierce. 'Dump – bloody – George.'

'Things aren't as clear-cut as that.' Isabel looks down at their still-clenched hands. 'I need to know that I can stand on my own as a person, not just rush from one relationship

322

into another. The problem with George and me is that we painted ourselves into our respective corners. He has always seen himself as The Noble Provider carrying the entire burden of the family, with the rest of us hanging off him like succubuses.'

Stella gasps, 'Succubi. Children – can't – be – succubi. They're – female – demons – who – were – supposed – to – sneak – sex – with – sleeping – men.'

'Exactly!' The image is so precisely how George sees her that Isabel throws back her head and laughs. When she stops and looks at Stella again, she is laughing too, soundlessly. 'And I have seen myself as the indispensable mother, which was really stupid. When the kids leave, who needs a full-time mother?'

'You – and – I – made – opposite – mistakes.'

'What a pair.' Isabel sighs. 'The point is, I have to feel that I am going into this new relationship with something. As a person of value in my own right, not just a failed wife.'

Stella gives a nod of understanding. 'What – will – you – do?'

'I'm doing.' Isabel tightens her grip on her sister's hands as she confesses. 'I'm writing about what happened in Two Rivers. I hope you don't mind.'

Stella's first reaction is to close her eyes to shut out the flooding pain. Two Rivers. Isabel wants to drag it all up again and chew it over like rotten cud and spit it out for everybody to see: her life, her stupid mistakes, her arrogant certainty that she was right and everyone else was wrong. 'Can't – we – just – give – that – terrible – year – a – decent – burial?'

'I will if you ask me to.' When she opens her eyes, Isabel's are searching her face. 'But I want you to know that he thinks it's good. He says my writing is mature and confident. Isn't that amazing?'

Seeing her sister's pride of achievement, Stella feels her objections dwindling. What does it matter when I'll be gone soon? she thinks, bone-weary of the constant struggle to breathe. There'll be no one to feel the pain. To make her a gift of approval is an even better way of making amends for being such a lousy sister.

'You – always – said – you – wanted – to – be – a – writer.

323

So – go – ahead. Tell – about – Two – Rivers.' Her whisper is very faint. 'Just – be – fair – about – Finn – and – me. He – wasn't – a – saint – you – know.'

Isabel leans forward until her cheek is touching her sister's deathly pale bony one. 'Thank you, love. And I promise that I'm trying very hard to be fair. One thing I've learnt is that nobody's totally saint or sinner. Even poor George has his good points.'

'Could – have – fooled – me.' They are holding hands and beaming at each other when Opal comes into the room with the tea tray.

21

In the build-up to Good Friday, I was still child enough to wonder whether Stella would buy me Easter eggs as Ma still did. I loved the bitter dark chocolate and would hoard my eggs for weeks, making them last by breaking off one thick little chunk at a time to nibble. Today's flimsy, anaemic milk chocolate Easter eggs aren't a patch on the ones we used to get.

Titch phoned up on the morning of Friday the fourth. Stella had to call me down from the mango tree where I had retreated with a book and some crunchies and a ready-mixed bottle of Oros, for want of anything else to do. The house was hot and silent except for the buzzing of a late-summer plague of flies that zoomed in through the flyscreen doors every time you opened them, then sat around on the ceiling rubbing their horrible spindly little front feet together; Eslina was going through the house twice a day with the hand-pumped Pyagra spray. Everyone else had something to do except me. Stella was at her desk, preoccupied with sorting out the paperwork for the next protest meeting. Opal had gone home for the first weekend of the holidays, and Finn had driven off in the Ford to an appointment in Durban, leaving Govind in charge of the pharmacy. I never offered to help behind the counter any more when Govind was there alone; he stood around looking aggrieved all the time, which made me feel more uncomfortable than ever. Thin people seem to get so much more consumed by their emotions than we more solid citizens. Maybe it's because their feelings radiate out in their original intensity, unfiltered by the mitigating cushion of flesh.

'Got home last night.' Titch sounded grouchy. 'This was

the most futile, time-wasting term I can ever remember. How about another bike expedition to get the taste of boarding school out of my mouth?'

For pride's sake I paused before answering as though I had various options to consider, then said, 'I can think of worse things to do.'

'Split bomb!' It was that year's trendy expression for 'Great!' Only now, as it tumbles out of yet another dusty recess in my memory, have I realised that it was an expression of nuclear-age chutzpah: a boast to mask our suppressed fear, so symptomatic of the Fifties. Titch was going on, 'We could ask James and Opal to come too, as long as they promise to keep their hands off each other.'

All I'd dreamed of the whole term was having his hands on me. I gave an ironic laugh and said, 'Why should they? Doesn't bother me.'

Sister Kathleen would have felt triumphantly vindicated if she'd heard me utter such a gross untruth, but she was gone: packed off to what Mother Beatrice called at final assembly, 'A nun's rest home, bless her poor tormented soul,' further down the South Coast. Linda Todd swore that she'd seen Sister Kathleen being carried out to an ambulance at dead of night in a straitjacket but nobody believed her because, unlike me, she was a known liar. To this day I wonder what happened to Sister Kathleen. Did she go stark raving mad or was she just an eccentric zealot who overstepped the mark because I triggered off some dark uncontrollable force in her?

Titch made the noise Zulus make with their tongues when they're exasperated. 'It's boring being with people who imagine they're in love. James is the worst when he falls for a new girl: he hangs around holding her hands and gazing into her eyes like a pained camel.'

I cheered up at the thought that Opal might be just a passing fancy. 'She couldn't come anyway because she's gone home already. And I bet you've never seen a camel.'

'I bloody have. Dad took Mum and me to Egypt last year to show us some of the places where he spent the war, and we saw herds of camels. Every single one of them looked pained.'

It wasn't fair. I'd always wanted to go to Egypt and see the Pharaohs' tombs and the pyramids and meander up the Nile in a felucca with a white sail like a swan's wing, but exotic travel wasn't an option for working families like ours. I wondered if Titch was aware just how privileged he was.

He said, 'Are you still there, Izz?'

'More or less.' I was in Egypt, actually, wearing a gold circlet with a cobra rearing above my forehead and doing a sideways dance.

'I'll be there at ten. Wait by the pharmacy steps, OK? We'll take the Umsindo river path that goes upstream from the bridge past the temple. I want to try and catch some freshwater crabs and look for cane-rat colonies.'

'Sis!' I said. 'You can count me out if you're going on a rat hunt.'

'They're not ordinary rats, dumbo – more like giant brown guinea pigs that live in the reeds. You needn't worry about them running up your legs because we're not likely to see any; they're nocturnal.'

'Don't be wet.' He made me mad when he put on his superior act. 'Wild guinea pigs sound weird. Why do you want to find them?'

'To breed, of course.' From the sound of his voice, I knew he was grinning. 'Zulus love cane-rat meat and train their dogs to catch them; they reckon that they're more succulent and tender than buck or rabbits. Our biology master expects us to do a project this year, and I thought I'd build a riverine environment in the back yard and see if I can get a pair to mate. If they'll breed in captivity, they could be commercially viable.'

'Sis. I can't imagine anyone wanting to buy rats to eat.' Stella hated the word 'sis', so I was schooling myself to use it as often as I could. She was so easy to annoy when you wanted to get back at her for something.

'Now who's being wet? You've got to keep an open mind if you want to be a scientist.'

'I do not want to be a scientist, heaven forbid,' I said with a shudder. 'I want to be a writer.'

'Even more reason to keep an open mind.'

One up to him. He was better at repartee than I was: nimble-minded and quick to flash back an answer where I took time to find the right word. I said, 'I *have* got one, believe it or not.'

He clucked his tongue again, impatient as always to get going, 'We're wasting time. I'll be there ten sharp. See you later, alligator.'

He rang off before I had time to say the requisite, 'In a while, crocodile.'

Waiting with Stella's bike by the pharmacy steps, I watched some scruffy white boys playing marbles on the sandy pathway, squatting in a shouting circle vying for the moment when one could swagger away victorious with his pants half down from the weight of conquered glassies and ironies and alies and queens. Several of the shorn bullet heads were dabbed with gentian violet for ringworm.

Also watching them from the doorway of the vegetable shop next door with his face in the shadows was Jantu Soobramony. It was unthinkable for him to expect to join in. Where the wealthier Indian families like the Reddys and the Pathers commanded a grudging respect for their feat in rising so far above their indentured labourer origins, poor Indians were non-people to even the scruffiest white kid. Coolies. And they didn't get much more sympathy from black people like Eslina either, who saw even the poorest as members of the money-grabbing shopowner class. No wonder the residents of Coolietown revered Finn; he never made distinctions based on the group to which people belonged. When those deep sea eyes looked at you, he seemed to see beneath the surface into your real self, the one you kept mostly hidden. I wonder now if it was a talent he was born with, some sort of mystic Norwegian troll wizardry, or just the way his nature shaped him as he grew up on the remote mission station in Zululand, giving him the ability to accept people the way they are without loading his expectations on them.

When Titch came, a familiar scowl bobbing along under the grubby pith helmet, we pushed our bikes through the crowds of jostling shoppers down to the bridge. Coolietown was always extra busy on Friday mornings, partly because it was the day before the weekend and partly because the Moslem-owned shops closed between twelve and two so their owners and assistants could go to the mosque. Under the bridge, the muddy water was backing slowly upstream. Although you couldn't see the sea from Two Rivers, you always knew it was nearby. Seagulls sat on the rooftops sometimes and the rivers slid both ways according to the tides, and the air was so damp and muggy that things you kept in cupboards and didn't use grew mould on them: leather shoes and old suitcases and sheets that had been folded damp.

We clattered the bikes down the steps on the far side of the bridge and stopped next to the doomed tower, looking up. Apart from the torn-away jasmine creeper and the grooves left by the bulldozer cables and the hole where the statue of Ganesha had been and the vertical cracks, it looked exactly as it had always looked: solid and four-square with its ornate tiers diminishing upwards to the golden urn on top of the dome, the fine detail of its decorations blurred by half a century of whitewash. Close up, the gods and goddesses had the smooth featureless faces of ghosts.

Having vanished for a week, the grey monkeys were back too, slipping between the statues and scampering over the temple roof and peering down from their vantage points in the trees, scrutinising passers-by for snatchable offerings of food. I've never liked monkeys; their small sly black faces and grasping hands are too human for comfort. Eslina was terrified of them because she said that they sometimes bit babies out of spite. The Zulu word for monkey sounds just like the noise they make: 'Inkawu! Inkawu!'

'Where are the bulldozers?' Titch demanded. 'Dad said they've been stopped from having another go at the tower until after Easter, but I thought they'd still be here.'

'Gone. Clanked off in high dudgeon when they couldn't pull the tower down.' I'd been dying to use 'high dudgeon' out loud ever since I'd read it. The retreat of the bulldozers had been ignominious. Jeered at by the crowd that seemed to gather instantly whenever something threatened to happen at the temple, their operators had manoeuvred them in clumsy jerking circles to climb the embankment and trundle back to the road camp, leaving behind a trail of smashed trees and bamboos.

'Did you see them trying to pull the tower down? Hell, I always miss the best stuff when I'm away at school.' He took off his pith helmet to wipe his cross sweaty face on his sleeve.

The temple glade could have been in the Amazon that day: its hot jungly shade dappled with sulphur-yellow sunlight and the smell from the midden of rotting fruit even stronger than usual.

'Saw the whole catastrophe.' I tried not to sound gloating, but it was hard. 'The bulldozers heaving, the statue falling, people screaming and panicking and muttering, "Kali. Kali. Kali." It was creepy.' I looked around to see if there was anyone near enough to hear me, but the glade was empty except for the monkeys and two of the temple guardians sitting on the far side of the scummy green sacred pool, tapping their sticks and staring at us. I dropped my voice anyway. 'Finn says that Hindus believe Kali has the power to destroy evil. Do you know she's supposed to wear a necklace of skulls and a skirt made of the cut-off hands of her enemies?'

Titch shrugged. 'Mr Reddy told us, remember?'

I wasn't getting much credit for my original eyewitness account. To elevate the drama level, I said, 'You hear her name everywhere in Coolietown now. She's supposed to be coming to take revenge, and maybe she's already started. I nearly got squashed against the railing when the crowd were shouting at the bulldozers, but Finn saved me.'

'He's strong for a tall thin guy.'

Being terse was Titch's way of holding down his annoyance at missing it all, but the remark about Finn got my goat. He was a lot more than a tall thin guy. I shot back, 'At least he's not a short-arse like you.'

'You're no oil painting yourself, Isabel Necessary.'

'Hey, listen, you can't –' I hadn't expected such a swift and deadly riposte. I had a lot to learn about the war between the sexes.

'Even stevens, so let's change the subject, OK? It's my first day of freedom, and I don't want to fight.' He jabbed at the ground with the toe of his sandal. 'Dad says he's never known so much unrest in Two Rivers. People seem to be really mad about the road-widening and it spills over into other things. There's trouble in the millworkers' canteen too.'

'Do you think it's because Mariamma is angry about her tower being pulled down?' The moment the words were out

330

of my mouth, I felt a dreadful hot red blush rising up my neck. It sounded so childish and superstitious.

But he didn't laugh. He just gave me a level look and said, 'It's possible.'

Searching his face, I thought: I wonder if he really believes that? Could he possibly have the same fear I have sometimes, that God will reach down a huge gnarled holy hand and punish me for doubting him? I felt the very roots of my hair burning.

Titch was fiddling with his bicycle bell and saying, 'You can't discount a fact because it hasn't been proven. That's a basic tenet of scientific research. There could just as easily be a Goddess instead of a God, or a whole lot of them like the Hindus believe. Or nothing at all.'

I thought, If there's nothing out there (up there?), we humans have gone to a hell of a lot of unnecessary trouble. Finn had talked about the faith that went into building holy places; what if it was misplaced? Was an act of faith worthwhile in its own right to the person who made it, even if it was misplaced? I mumbled, still hot-cheeked, 'I just don't seem to be sure about anything like that.'

'Nor do I.' There was an answering pinkness under his freckles. We stood facing each other over our bicycles, locked in our agony of mutual doubt.

'But how can anyone ever be sure?'

He said, 'If you're anything like me, you're still trying to sort out what you really believe from what you've been told to believe all your life by people who call themselves your elders and betters. It's a bugger, being fifteen.'

I felt a surge of recognition: we were struggling with the same problems, however different our family circumstances. I'd never had such a deeply personal discussion with a boy, and it was a revelation to know that he too seethed with uncertainty under the confident surface. I mumbled, 'It's hard deciding what you really believe. The elders and betters keep shovelling their ideas and experiences all over you, and they always think they're right.'

Titch nodded. 'Typical. Old folks are a drag.'

He's lucky to have some, I thought, dredging up a soothing dollop of self-pity. (There are advantages to being a semi-orphaned child.)

Silence descended. I shuffled my tackies on the path's gravel. Titch tinged his bicycle bell and cleared his throat, then looked up at the temple. Following his eyes I saw Kesaval standing in one of the portico arches looking down at us, dressed in his unfamiliar Indian clothes.

'It must be a lot harder for someone like him, having to stick to the rules of an old culture like this in today's world.' Titch raised his voice to call out, 'Howzit, Kes.' When he raised an answering hand and started down the steps towards us, Titch looked relieved. We had been drifting into deeper waters than a bicycle ride warranted.

I nodded my hullo, still a bit shy of Kesaval. He seemed even more foreign in the long white tunic and loose pants than he had on the day of the fête: darker, more Indian, almost forbidding. I had a strong feeling – never felt on previous visits – that we were trespassing that day. Maybe it was because Kali had moved in and didn't want us there; we represented the forces that wanted to destroy Mariamma's tower, after all. We came with the brick dust of progress on our clean white hands.

'What are you two doing this morning?' Kesaval sounded wistful.

'We're on our way up the river path but stopped to look at the tower. We've also been moaning about our so-called elders and betters.' Titch gave an embarrassed laugh. Clearly, indulging in confidences with a girl was a new departure for him.

'You're lucky you can moan.' Up close, Kesaval's mouth looked sour and red as though he'd eaten too many amatungulus. He had the beginnings of a fine black moustache on his upper lip and a cluster of pimples on his chin. I wondered who he saw when he looked into the mirror: the adolescent he was or the man he would be?

Titch punched him on the shoulder (I noticed that boys did that a lot). 'What's wrong, man?'

'Everything.' The dark eyes were angry-hot. 'I'm going through a terrible time with Asha's betrothal. That's why our two families are here today, for the formal ceremony.'

'Why terrible? Engagements are supposed to be happy.' I'd been so pleased when I heard, because it would keep Asha

332

away from Finn. She had only come into the pharmacy once to consult him since the fête.

'Not when you hate the man who's been chosen for you. I don't know what to do, I'm telling you. She just sits and cries all the time. I'm her brother, I should be her protector. I keep asking myself what my father would have done – married her off in this way, or let her be a modern girl and find her own husband? – and I don't know.'

When Finn told me that the Reddys would probably arrange a marriage for Asha, I'd never imagined that they'd make her marry someone she didn't like. I thought of Srini Pather: the swarthy good looks and fat-lipped smile and sleek black hair. He was rich and had a red MG and his father owned a jewellery shop, so he should have been a good catch for Asha. But she had kept her face hidden in her sari on the day the betrothal had been announced. 'Why doesn't she like him?'

'Because he's a bully. We always played together, living next door. Srini was the biggest kid and used to getting his own way. I don't think his mother has ever told him "No". He bossed us around and hit us when we didn't do what he said, and sometimes he pinched us in secret places, specially the girls. So Asha hates him. She's very shy and gentle in her ways, you know?' He glared at us.

'She's lovely,' Titch said after a while.

'For months she's been begging my mother and the aunties and my grandfather not to choose him, but they wouldn't listen. It's a highly suitable marriage between two good-class families, they say, and all the god signs and the birth dates are right. Older people know who will make the best husband for a girl, they say. It's so old-fashioned. It makes me sick, this forcing.'

'Is there nothing Asha can do?' Jeepers, it was like the worst kind of fairy tale: the princess and the frog without the happy ending. Srini looked like a frog, come to think of it, with his plump suave smile. For a moment I felt as though we had been whisked from our prosaic little sugar town into a mythical time-warp where gods spoke and people trembled and virgin daughters were interchanged to unite the families of robber barons.

Kesaval said, 'Nothing! And nothing I can do either. I'm not a full man yet, see?' He made a furious gesture that mocked his boy's slenderness. 'They want it both ways. I must fill the gap left by my dead father, but I can't take any of the decisions he would have made.'

'But surely Mr Reddy wouldn't –'

'You don't know my grandfather. Not at all! He doesn't care that we are already living in the second half of the twentieth century. He wants to hide in being a Hindu and in the past and keep us all there with him in the traditional kutum, the extended family group. Indian people must look inwards and rely on their own strength in a country where we are so greatly outnumbered, he says. What happens will happen because it is the will of the gods. But that's old man's talk! I won't spend my life hiding. I'm going to get out of this place.'

'Me too,' Titch said, with feeling.

'Me too.' I wasn't to know that my casual echo of their need to escape Two Rivers would come true for me much sooner than for them.

We stood talking in that hot green place with the muddy river sliding past the wrong way, our voices hushed but intense: Titch and I the interlopers with our bikes, Kesaval the iconoclast, united in teenage rebellion. Then someone called from inside the temple and Kesaval flashed an uncertain smile at us and went up the steps, and the moment was gone.

That expedition was the last. If I'd known, I'd have tried to fix every detail in my mind so I could call up the memory later when I really needed to, back in the mining town with my sad, subdued mother and bossy Aunty Mavis. But I only remember odd things ... The colour of sunlight angling through river water, beer bottle brown. The squelch and suck of our wheels on the muddy path. The scrabbling sounds of the captured crabs in Titch's canvas fishing bag. The vari-egated squadrons of vegetables marching through the market gardens we passed and the turbaned old men who toiled there, lifting their heads from their hoeing and weeding to give us snaggle-toothed greetings.

Beyond, where the canefields began, the path was over-grown with sedge grasses that we had to push our bikes through like explorers in some primaeval savannah. Titch showed me the hollow tunnels made by cane-rats and flattened places in the reed beds with little piles of oval droppings, though we didn't see any. He tried to scare me by saying, 'They do so much damage to sugar cane that the cane farmers encourage pythons to keep their numbers down. If you hear a rustling in the grass, run,' but I pooh-poohed it, laughing. Only later when I told Finn did I learn that it was true, and felt a retroactive terror. Pythons squirmed through my dreams for years afterwards, scaly coils thick as a man's arm wrapping themselves first round my legs and then higher up to trap my arms against my body and squeeze the living breath out of me. Freud would have made a banquet out of my python dreams.

I remember getting home afterwards with scratched legs and a sweaty red face and a bad headache that made Stella say crossly what a silly little fool I was to go out in that heat and get exhausted. Didn't I know there was a polio epidemic on? She made me have a tepid bath and lie down on my bed under a sheet and brought me freshly squeezed orange juice in a glass with blue rings on it. She could be so nice sometimes.

As Easter got closer, rumours burgeoned like fungi in Coolietown and the general unease grew. People whispered that the road gang foreman had said that if the bulldozers couldn't pull the tower down at the next attempt, he would have to use dynamite, which could damage the main temple building. Mariamma's fire-blackened wooden statue on the altar inside the inner shrine was said to be weeping resin tears of sorrow. Even piling marigold garlands round it and burning camphor and incense all day didn't help: she kept on weeping. It was muttered that Kali was rampaging round the town at dead of night in a fury, leaving trails of spattered blood. I was shown some actual evidence arcing across the gravel on the pathway outside Abjee's sale rooms but when I told Finn, big-eyed, he just laughed and said it must have been made by a carcass being delivered to the butchery next door.

There was continuing trouble at the mill compound: the

Zulus were talking of going on strike because the food was too little, they said, and they were trying to persuade the Pondos to join them. Knots of off-shift labourers roamed the town carrying sticks and making threatening gestures at each other. My exploring privileges were withdrawn at once. Stella and Finn forbade me to set foot outside the garden gate on my own.

When Stella went to visit Dorothy Gould with a box of Eslina's crunchies, rather guiltily because she hadn't done so for months, she found her in bed under a filthy sheet splattered with budgie droppings, too ill even to put the hissing dentures in. 'That miserable drunk Dicky isn't feeding her properly,' she fumed when she got back, and rushed off to tell Lilah McFadyen. By phoning round town, they bullied a roster of company wives to supply the poor old thing with at least one meal every day. It wouldn't take much effort on the part of the women who had volunteered; all better-off families had a cook and a maid then, and usually a garden boy as well who could be sent round to Darjeeling Road with a covered basket.

Afterwards, Lilah came to a victory tea – she never seemed to mind slumming in Coolietown – and Titch came with her, as we needed to talk about the Mariamman festival. Stella and Finn and the McFadyens had withdrawn permission for us to go because of the general unrest, but Titch had a plan: if we went in a group with James and Opal and two of his friends from school who were coming to stay for the Easter weekend, he was sure we could persuade the old folks to let us go.

'Even if it's just for a while,' he said. 'As well as the fire-walking, you've got to see the torchlight procession and the devotees with hooks in their backs pulling the decorated chariots and the people with needles stuck through their tongues. They're amazing sights. And there's a fun fair that comes down from Durban too, so it turns into a huge party.'

We were sitting on the edge of the lily pond while Stella and Lilah murmured together on the veranda over their tea and granadilla cake. The heat wave had got worse and the cloying scent of frangipani was everywhere. I picked one of the perfect creamy flowers from the tree above us and twirled it in my fingers to send it helicoptering down to float on the water. 'Stella will never let me go. She thinks every man who lives in Coolietown has designs on my fair white body.'

Titch gave an uncomfortable laugh, as if for once he didn't have a scientific explanation for the phenomenon.

I was sunk in gloom at the prospect of missing the sight of Mr Padayachee fire-walking. He had gone into religious seclusion for nine days, Finn had told me, praying all the time and seeing no one and refraining from all pleasures of the body, which included going on a spiritually cleansing fast of bananas and milk. It was necessary to concentrate the spirit on the forthcoming ordeal, Finn said.

'Stella will change her mind if I can convince my father that it's OK. What he says, goes in this dorp.'

Titch's confidence in his father's omniscience was touching, but I knew Stella only too well: once she'd said no to something, she didn't like changing her mind – specially if someone put pressure on her. 'It'll never work.'

'Give me a few days. Kesaval might have some ideas too.' He shot out his hand to try and catch one of the iridescent blue dragonflies hovering over the pond, but it was too quick for him and darted away.

'He's got his own problems.' Neither of us had seen him since the day at the temple. Both families involved in the betrothal had begun the complicated round of ceremonies, preparations and exchanges of gifts that would lead up to the wedding. As a prospective bride, Asha had been confined to the big Spanish house. I kept thinking of her looking out the window of her bedroom like the Lady of Shalott into the Pathers' garden and seeing Srini her frog prince strolling there, and her blood freezing slowly and her eyes darkening wholly as she cried, 'The curse is come upon me.' I thought that since Finn was out of the picture, she had no loyal knight and true. But I was wrong.

Titch was saying, 'Never to worry, Izz, we'll make it. By hook or by crook.'

He was determined, and though he would never have admitted it, as used as Srini was to getting his own way. Trailing his fingers in the water to feel the goldfish feathering past them, he sat hatching plan after ingenious plan to get us to the Mariamman festival.

But he needn't have bothered because Finn suddenly changed his mind. Over breakfast on Wednesday when I was moaning at Stella how bored I was at being cooped up in the house and how furious I was to be missing the festival, it wasn't fair, etcetera, he said casually, 'I think we should let them go, as long as they agree to stay together. I'll be there on Friday, so I can keep an eye on them too.'

'What?' She swung on him. 'You can't! It's dangerous. We've already forbidden them to go.'

'It's a holy festival, Stella.' He was scraping butter across his toast with slow deliberate knife strokes; it was one of the things he did that infuriated her, the buttering and scraping, buttering and scraping, and I suspect he used it sometimes as a weapon in their unacknowledged but growing conflict. 'Yust last night I spoke with Mr Abjee and Mr Chetty of the temple committee, and they say that they've arranged for extra-tight security on Friday because they don't want any troble. Sergeant Koekemoer will have plainclothes detectives in the crowd and a uniformed squad on call, and the guardians will patrol the perimeter of the temple grounds. I can't see why the yong people shouldn't go.'

'It's not safe!' She got up, letting her chair crash on the floor, and blundered towards him. 'This town's not safe any more. We can't let those kids run around on their own, specially when they could get caught up in a crowd of religious fanatics.'

I'll never forget that moment in the cavernous kitchen with its frieze of forget-me-nots and the rows of blue and white plates on the big wooden dresser and the morning sun slanting thick and hot under the jasmine creeper on the veranda outside. The dark blue hydrangeas in the willow-pattern jug on the table were already beginning to wilt.

Finn said, 'They are our neighbours and this town is our home. We will make it safe.'

'Our neighbours are one thing. Fanatics and mutinous millworkers are quite another.' She reached him and put her hands on his shoulders and started to shake him. 'Wake up, Finn! You can't make things safe just by wishing.'

'It's not yust wishing.' He was looking up at her with his most intent expression. 'It's a matter of mutual trust. We'll never get anywhere in this contry ontil we trust each other. Suspicion and fear only breeds more suspicion and fear, can't you see that?'

'We're not talking about the same thing at all.' She stopped shaking him and stood up, her copper hair sticking out, her foxy eyes the shiny brown of sucked humbugs in her pale morning face. 'You're talking about an ideal world which doesn't exist. I'm talking about the trouble that is obviously brewing in this town, the real world.'

'I think it is a thonderstorm in a tea cup.'

'You're deluding yourself, then. You always do.' Her voice was despondent. 'If you can't see the facts in front of your face, I give up.'

He took her hands in his, smiling up at her. 'Truly there's nothing to worry about. The road-widening and the pulling down of the tower are yust making people more opset than usual.'

'What about the trouble at the mill?' She shivered. 'And there are terrible rumours going around.'

He got up then and put his arms round her and rocked her against him murmuring, 'You worry too much, my Stellen. This is a good little town.'

'I hate it.' Her voice was very low.

'I think you have never given it a proper chance. Or me. We are not so prosaic as we seem.'

They had forgotten I was there, because he kissed her and it lasted so long that I turned away and pretended to be studying the lettering on the coal stove. But when they pulled back from each other, I saw that the bruised rings under her eyes were deeper than ever.

I am still not sure what happened between them that morning, but she was very quiet for the next few days.

Isabel

'Opal was sneaky and sent the typescript straight to her publisher, Gerald, and he actually likes it! He likes it!' Isabel is shouting down the phone.

At the other end of the line in the mountain cottage, her lover holds it away from his deafened ear and lets out one of the comfortable rolling laughs that have become more frequent as his life has steadied.

'What do you think of that?' She is giddy with delighted astonishment. 'He phoned me this morning and told me what she'd done and asked me to come and see him. Of course I went in fear and trembling, thinking that he'd give me a polite brush-off and a pat on the head for trying. But he said he liked what he'd read and would I please finish the manuscript so he could assess it as a whole, with a view to possible publication. Here I am at fifty plus with more water under the bridge than I care to remember, and someone is talking about publishing what I've written. I can't believe it.'

'My dear love, I can. I am so proud of you.'

It is the best thing he could have said. Pride is exactly what she feels, and what she most wants him to feel. This is something she has done all on her own, without help from anyone.

She has told herself all along that writing is like giving birth, but this exhilarating sense of personal achievement is quite different. She had never doubted that she would give birth to healthy children and be a good mother afterwards. If she had had time to ponder Motherhood when she was busy having babies, she would have reasoned that it was probably programmed into the genes like the ability to build

340

nests is into birds. In those days, childbirth wasn't the scientifically controlled process it is now, with scans and foetal monitors and prenatal classes and elaborate tests for detecting problems almost before they happen, and nobody expected it to be painless. She had gone through the long hard physical process three times in the certain knowledge that there was a team of skilled people helping her, and a unique reward at the end of it.

The labour of writing has not been painful so much as undertaken in trepidation and uncertainty, with the ever-present fear that the end result could be a stillbirth: all those months of intense soul-searching work come to nothing. She has not dared to tally the hundreds of hours of thinking and planning and jotted notes, of committing her narrative to paper, agonising over each word, of alterations and additions in tiny writing in the margins, of revising and crossings out and rewriting, for fear that they have been wasted. There had been a greater fear too: that her sense of quiet satisfaction when the work had gone well was based on false pride. Because her happiness pivots on the success of this endeavour, there has been strain and heart's anguish in the writing, and until her last conversation with Stella, worry that she would hurt someone she cared about by telling tattletales.

But her doubts have been banished by the publisher's enthusiasm. 'This is good,' was the first thing he had said as he looked up from her manuscript to her tense face on the other side of his desk. 'I'm not sure how we would classify it – biography, or perhaps with a little reworking, fiction – but it's good. I'm pleased that Opal went behind your back. You're a promising new talent, Isabel Poynton.'

She had scribbled her maiden name on the manuscript when she gave it to Opal, partly in memory of the long-ago schoolgirl who had dreamed of being a writer, and partly because she did not want to use the surname that had come with George.

'Do you really think so? Really?'

He had given her the pleased, smug smile of one who senses he is on to a good thing. 'The only thing that puzzles me is what you've been doing all these years?'

'Building the nation. Bringing up children.' She had given a self-deprecating laugh.

'You've never written anything before? Things for women's magazines, perhaps?'

His assumption that 'things for women's magazines' are all housewives are good for had riled her. She had summoned all her dignity and said, 'I've been writing most of my adult life, actually.'

'Who for?' His face had registered dismay that she wasn't going to be his own discovery after all.

'Myself. Journals and odd poems.' A brief sharp smile. 'All consigned to an old tin trunk because I didn't think they were up to much.'

'You didn't show them to anyone?' When she had shaken her head, he'd said, 'I'd like to see more of your writing, when you feel ready.'

Now her voice sings down the telephone. 'He wants to see more of my work, and says I must finish the manuscript as soon as I can. I'm going to have to work my arse off to get through it, but at least I know it's leading somewhere.'

'No trysts for a while, do you mean?'

'Wot, no sex?' Her laughter is uninhibited, light years different from that of last year's Isabel. 'Oh darling, you know I'd die if I didn't see you. I'm going to need lots of reassurance and bolstering and egging on, not to mention –' Her voice drops to a murmur as she goes into detail. She still finds it unnerving to talk intimacies over the phone, even though she knows the likelihood of a crossed line is small.

'And George?' he cuts in. 'Has he been told yet?'

'I've been trying to pluck up the courage since I got back from Durban,' she admits, and for the first time her voice falters. 'It's a good thing Opal and I went to see Stella. They phoned last night to say that she's in a coma and they don't think she'll last more than a day or two.'

'Will you go down again?'

'No point. She wouldn't recognise me.'

'I'm so sorry.' Out of delicacy for her loss, he does not point out that she has changed the subject away from George. Yet again.

'She wants to go. Poor Stella, she's exhausted. It was terrible to see her so close to death. She was always so vital, so impatient. Like you, in many ways.'

342

'How can you say that?' he growls. 'I think I've been the soul of forbearance over your reluctance to break off with that bloody man. If it had been me –'

'That's the other thing I wanted to tell you,' she puts in quickly. 'Stella wanted me to know that she's leaving her estate to me and the children in equal shares. It's quite a lot.' Her laugh is a gentle echo now. 'When I leave George, I'll be able to come to you as a woman of independent means as well as a writer in my own right.'

'When?' He is not to be mollified.

'Soon.'

'When, dammit? How long do I have to wait? How many more times will you say in that jolly hockeysticks voice, "Soon"?'

With a sinking heart she thinks, This is it. You've finally run out of excuses. He can't be charmed with 'soons' and 'maybes' any more. It's time to tell George. She gulps and says, 'The children are coming round to supper this evening. I'll tell them first, and then I'll break it to George.'

'Promise? Cross your heart?'

'Cross my heart and all the way up to heaven.' It is the formula she used as a little girl. 'I'm sorry it's taken so long. It's just so hard to break out of a life you've been jogging along in for so many years. Do you understand?' she begs. 'It's not for lack of love for you, my darling.'

He is about to snap a sarcastic, 'You could have fooled me,' but the urgency in her voice stops him. I've mellowed since I met her, he thinks. Learning how strong her ties are with her children, I've begun to understand that families can be binding in a positive way, not just stifling as mine was. 'I understand,' he says. 'And I am waiting with all the patience I can scrape together. Come to me soon. You'll finish your manuscript all the quicker up here in the mountains with no family distractions.'

She closes her eyes and nods, picturing the bliss of being able to be with him all the time and work whenever she pleases without hiding whatever she writes under the folded sheets in the linen cupboard, away from George's prying eyes. 'Or by the sea. I long for us to be together in the cottage again. The waves are like a constant heartbeat that tells you

343

the world is still alive. I'm going to tell George I want the
cottage when we split up.'

'You'll speak to him this evening, for sure?' he demands.

'For sure,' she says, and puts the phone down dreaming of
white cotton sheets and sunlight streaming through sliding
glass doors with the blue sea just visible through the bush
outside.

22

On Thursday, Finn walked me down to the temple bridge so we could hang over the parapet and watch the fire pit being prepared. A long rectangle about twenty-five feet by four and thigh-deep had been dug near the tower, and an old man was supervising the laying of dry twigs and logs for the fire that would be lit early next morning. Women were scrubbing the portico and steps and working at a trestle table set up in the grove, preparing the trays of camphor to be cut into squares and wrapped in newspaper for sale to templegoers the next day, Finn explained.

In the open ground between the temple and the Indian mill staff cottages, a fun fair was being assembled. Men in overalls were bolting girders together for a giant wheel and a wall of death and a rickety-looking figure of eight; others were hanging seats on a swing roundabout and an octopus and fitting gaudy panels over the oily machinery that made everything go round; huddled dodgem cars stood waiting to be hooked into the power supply. A network of pipe scaffolding circled the main attractions, draped with tarpaulins and lengths of canvas crudely painted to look like stalls. An electrician on a ladder was winding strings of light bulbs round their edges. It looked a very poor relation of the dazzling giant fun fair at the Rand Easter Show that my mining town friends and I flocked to every year.

When I confided this to Finn, he just laughed and said, 'It'll look better at night. You didn't expect Yohannesburg sophistication in Two Rivers, Izzy?'

'I don't know what I expected. There wasn't time after Pa – after –' I still couldn't say out loud, 'After Ma went into the loonybin.'

He put his arm round my shoulders. 'Courage, Izzy. Yust concentrate on enjoying our little town. Myself, I think it's very special.'

'Me too. I love being here with you and Stella.'

'Really?' I got a searching blue look. 'It hasn't been so easy for you, coming to a new home and a new school and having that frickly Sister Kathleen attacking you.'

'Really and truly.' How could I convey my enormous gratitude to this beloved brother-in-law who had taken two problematic sisters into his home and his heart? 'I don't know how to thank you properly.'

'You don't have to. It's been good for Stella and me, having you here with us. Like being a family.'

But I didn't want to hear the sadness in his voice, not that day. So I went barrelling on, 'You've both been great. Jeepers, I'd've gone mad if I'd had to go and live with Aunty Mavis. She's so fat and *boring*. Her stockings swish together at the top when she walks.'

It worked, because he laughed and said, 'We should call her Thonderthighs.'

I laughed too then. Thunderthighs was a perfect name for Aunty Mavis, conveying her bossiness as well as her size. Finn was good at nicknames. And I'm so glad that at least I tried to say thank you to him that day. I didn't know it was my last chance.

And then it was Good Friday – one of those days that you know are going to be stinkers because the air already feels stale when you get up, as though it has been breathed by too many people during the night. It started quietly like all public holidays in Coolietown: first the muezzin calling in the still grey hours, but after that no early morning traffic, no trains being shunted, no banging and scraping of shop shutters being pushed open. The sound of single footsteps could be heard crunching past on the sandy pathway outside the garden wall instead of the usual weekday shuffle. The early sunlight shone in a dull gold bar across my drooping mosquito net; when I cleaned my teeth, the water running out of the cold tap was tepid and tasted of iron.

Even the mynahs seemed listless as they pecked at the

crumbs I scraped off my plate into the back yard. With the pharmacy due to open for an hour only in the late morning, Finn and I had decided to prepare a special breakfast for Stella: floppy heart-shaped Norwegian waffles made with his mother's hand-held waffle iron heated on the coal stove, served warm with melting butter and honey and proper percolated coffee. But the phone had rung at the wrong moment and she had spent ten minutes talking to Lilah McFadyen, and her waffles had gone cold by the time she sat down.

'Sorry I spoilt your treat,' I heard her saying as I crossed the veranda from the back yard.

Finn shrugged. 'I'm sorry too. They're better warm.' He raised his newspaper to go on reading.

She put her hand out to hold the newspaper down. 'Don't be offended. I wasn't just having a gossip. Lilah and I were making contingency plans for tonight.'

'What plans? I've told you already that I'll be there. I can watch over the yong people. For God's sake, Stella, don't start with your meddling now.' He gave the newspaper an irritable shake to dislodge her hand.

I lingered outside the doorway, sensing another confrontation. I hated being in the same room when they were arguing.

'She's worried about their safety and so am I.' Stella dropped her voice to a murmur. 'There's going to be a big crowd there tonight and we've decided to go along too. We won't let the kids know that we're there; we'll just hover in the background somewhere.'

'That's yust a ridiculous idea.' He crashed the paper down on the table. 'I tell you that nothing bad is going to happen. And if by any chance there should be troble, what can two women do in a crowd?'

'You admit there could be trouble! I knew it. It's not safe for those kids to go. I'm going to phone Lilah back and tell her –'

'No, you won't.' I saw Finn reach out and hold her arm in a tight grip. 'For once I am going to put my foot down on the ground. The yong people will be allowed to go because they are curious to see this festival of another religion, and they have good open minds for learning new things. Don't you see

347

what a big opportunity this is for them, in a contry where people are afraid to step over the borders of race and colour, and the government is making it harder and harder for those who dare? I feel very strong about this. They must go. I guarantee their safety.'

'How?' Her voice swooped upwards. 'How can you guarantee that? You're not God, you know.'

'I have spoken to the temple committee and the guardians about them, and I have also asked Ram Pillay to keep a special look out. These will be the most watched over yong people in the whole world tonight.'

But Stella was not listening. Her thoughts were running along an all-too-familiar track. 'You're not the ministering angel you like to think you are, Finn, graciously bestowing hygiene and medicinal largesse on the unwashed masses. You're just an ordinary man.'

'So you have told me many times. And I have never claimed to be anything else.'

'You always take the moral high ground.'

His face had gone as pale as hers. 'And you always accuse. Always. I think it is nearly finished between us, Stellen. You have no trust in me any more. You want to pull me down all the time.'

'I don't! At least, I didn't mean it to sound like that. I'm just worried about Isabel being in that crowd and all the awful rumours going around and –' she looked down at her hands '– and you and me. We never seem to agree any more. We just wrangle.'

He nodded. 'We are growing away from each other.'

'But I don't want to.' Her mouth curved down like a sad clown's.

He reached out his other hand and touched her cheek. 'Sometimes we can't control these things. Sometimes two people yust don't make good chemistry together.'

I shrank away from the doorway and the sight of their stricken faces and tiptoed across the veranda to lose myself behind the jasmine creeper. It would be devastating if they separated, specially now that Asha was out of the picture. I'd have to go with Stella – where? – and I'd lose Finn and Two Rivers and all my new friends.

It was turning into a Bad Friday.

But they managed to paper over the cracks as they must have done many times before. When I ventured back into the kitchen, Stella was clearing the table and Finn was washing up because Eslina's husband was expected for the long weekend and she would not be coming into work.

'Ai, when that man is coming home,' she had said to me the day before, 'we must clean and cook and have everything too nice.'

'Isn't it hard for you, only seeing your husband twice a year?'

'Not so hard.' She had given her head an emphatic shake that set the pearls jiggling in her ears. 'This way, I am the boss of my house for most of the year.'

'What about his other wife?'

'She is the boss of her house.' I got a small tight conspiratorial smile. 'We work it OK between us.'

'Just OK?'

'Very OK.' The smile broadened. 'Maybe I see you Friday night there by the fun fair. I make a promise to the kids to take them if he brings money home.'

'Doesn't he always? Bring money home, I mean.'

'When he has been too much with the town girls, aikona.' She clucked her tongue. 'But this is not for you to hear, Izzy-weh. This is big woman troubles.'

Looking at Finn clattering the soapy dishes in the sink and Stella wiping down the table with one hand as she ate her last cold buttered waffle with the other, I thought, They're having big troubles too. And I wished with all my heart that they would somehow learn how to work it OK before it got too late.

Excitement began flickering around Coolietown as the morning grew steadily hotter and more humid. Whole families left their homes dressed in new clothes for the festival and took to the pathways, which soon spilled over into the roads. Cars and buses were having to inch through crowds of meandering pedestrians that had been further swelled by workers from the mill compound and surrounding cane farms and reserves, since Good Friday is one of the four statutory holidays of the South African working year. The Palm Café and all the eating houses and Ismail's General Dealers were open (the Ismail family being Moslem, it would close only during the usual mosque prayer hour at lunchtime) and doing a roaring trade in food and cooldrinks and icecreams. Down at the station, trains were disgorging more festival-goers from Durban and the stations in between.

I don't remember a hotter day in Two Rivers; it had turned into a stinker of stinkers. The only cool people in town must have been the kids running and laughing and getting wet behind the water cart as it trundled up and down the side roads spraying the gravel to keep the dust down over the holiday weekend. Mr Padayachee's two eldest sons were leading the mule that day because he was still in seclusion, preparing for the fire-walk.

I climbed the mango tree to my observation post and was rewarded by seeing the tail end of a procession of tinselled, flower-decked chariots jogging down the middle of the main road, pulled by sweating men in dhotis and cheered on by the crowds. Perhaps because it was a holiday, but more likely because the tormentors were white, people did their best to ignore the gang of barefoot kids running along behind it jeering, 'Coolie Christmas! Coolie Christmas!'

From across the courtyard, Finn called, 'I'm yust opening the pharmacy for a while, Izz. Want to come and help? Govind's busy at the temple today. They've made him a special assistant to the priest.'

'Sure.' But few people came in. It seemed that aches and ailments were forgotten on festival days. We closed up early.

As I helped him lock the door grilles, Finn said, 'Tell Stella I'll be late for lunch. I'm going along to church to pay my respects.' He had changed his pharmacist's jacket for a linen one and put on a tie.

'But I thought –' From what he'd said on that first silver morning, and from his sympathetic interest in Hindus and their temple, I'd assumed that he'd stopped believing in our Christian God as I had (well, mostly).

He said, 'You shouldn't confuse arguments with beliefs, Izzy. I may disapprove of the trappings but I am still a

350

believer. Still my parents' son who needs to talk to God sometimes. Specially on days when He and I are both down in the dumps.'

Watching him walk away, his tall stooped figure moving so courteously along the crowded pathway towards the sedate, church-going, golf-playing white Good Friday, I wondered what God would have to say about his decision to join in the Hindu goddess's festival that night. Would He be miffed or tolerant? Did it *matter* how many gods there were, as long as you believed in the mystery?

Opal's father brought her in the early afternoon, as wan and apologetic as ever; he was sobering up from a bad week, she said in a cool voice that forbade any questions. Titch phoned to say that he and James and their friends from school would be dropped off by his mother around five o'clock, so we could walk together down to the bridge where we could watch the Kavady ceremonies taking place on the riverbank before going on to the temple.

'What's Kavady?' I asked Finn as we sat in the ferny coolth of the front veranda, eating mangoes. Tackling a mango was much more of a business then than it is now, because they had fibrous strings that got stuck in your teeth and you had to wash the juice off your mouth straight away so as not to get mango sores. Or perhaps that was an old wives' tale? You never hear of mango sores now, or veld sores, for that matter.

Finn put his mango pip down on the pile of peelings – sucked mango pips always remind me of tonsured monks with fringes of ginger hair – and leant forward to dabble his fingers in the bowl of water in the middle of the table. 'Before I explain Kavady, you should onderstand the ancient belief that time hangs in a delicate balance when the seasons change and the forces of nature are in a state of crisis. At such moments evil threatens the forces of good, and people must intensify their devotions to keep the world safe and going along its proper path. So we have Kavady, which is a yeneral ceremony of thanksgiving for favours granted by the gods. Here in Two Rivers, where most people are Tamil, the penances are done and the sacrifices and thanks given to Mariamma.'

351

'What penances? Do you mean, like, those men pulling the coolie Christmases around town?'

I got a warning deep-sea flash. 'Those aren't the words I'd use for a religious procession, Izzy.'

'Sorry.' I felt a rising blush. It was humiliating to have Opal watching his reproof.

He smiled to take the sting out of it. 'See, it works this way. People go to the poosalie, the temple attendant, if they have a problem and need help – say, in a matter of health. And the poosalie whisks a peacock feather around them and says, "Make a vow to the goddess that if she solves the problem or makes you better, you will thank her with sacrifices." These can be live goats and chickens or fruit or sweetmeats, or sums of money, or candles and incense and camphor to burn. Sometimes you will see a small silver model of the part of the body that has been healed. Or the devotee might promise to take the needle or walk the fire or carry Kavady, which is an offering of milk and rice in two pots hung from a wooden frame carried on the shoulders and ornamented with flowers and tinkling bells. This is what Titch is talking about.'

'Is it sore, carrying Kavady?'

He shook his head. 'No more than carrying a heavy weight. And I don't think the devotees feel soreness from the more serious penances either – the piercing of the skin on their backs with hooks and the needles through the tongues and even the fire-walking – because they are in a state of ecstasy. It is like a trance, self-hypnosis perhaps, helped by the fact that they have been fasting for days before. You'll see.'

It sounded thrilling. I could hardly wait for five o'clock to come, when Opal and I would be on our way to a pagan ceremony where people stuck needles and hooks into themselves and walked on fire – with no less than four Michaelhouse boys. Eat your heart out, Evelyn Simpson! was ringing through my brain. If things dissolved between Stella and Finn, at least I'd be able to go back home to the mining town with a substantial advantage over a smalltime sexpot who had never seen an actual, genuine sacrifice. I made a mental note to find out whether the live goats and chickens had their throats cut straight away or were saved until later.

'What are agni chettis?' Opal was asking. 'I heard one of our farm foremen saying that he was going to carry them.'

'Agni chettis are clay pots full of hot coals that devotees carry in their hands. Like the fire-walkers, they yenerally come out the other end with not even a redness on their skins. It's remarkable,' Finn said. 'Some day I would like to study this phenomenon. I wish –'

But he didn't tell us the wish, and I've always wondered what it was. Did he wish that he had done more with his life? If there had been no Stella and no threatening baby, would he have become an artist or gone into pharmaceutical research and made extraordinary discoveries? He certainly had the enquiring curiosity of a researcher, as Titch had; I think that was why they liked each other so much. And I think that Finn was a lot more ambitious than Stella imagined, only he hid his disappointments and frustrations better than she did. Looking back now, I realise that shotgun marriages hurt the men involved as badly as the women.

When the boys came clumping across the courtyard in their school shoes, white shirts and grey flannels, there was a period of awkwardness while Opal and I were introduced to Robin and Wally and we all shook hands self-consciously. But Finn got us over it in his easy way by starting to talk about the festival and explaining what would happen, with interjections from Titch and James who had seen it before. Lilah disappeared into the house to find Stella; I heard them talking in the passage.

'I'm glad to see that you yong people are dressed proper for the occasion,' Finn concluded. (Opal and I wore blouses and skirts and our Indian sandals – I had perfected my clenching technique – and I'd tied a red bow round my ponytail.) 'Yust remember the important things about what you're going to see. The Mariamman is a two-sided festival, both of penance done in fulfilment of vows made to the goddess, and of thanksgiving. I don't need to remind you to keep to the background and not get in anyone's way. Try to watch and learn, and not to comment out loud. It is not right to be critical of other people's religious rituals.'

We all nodded solemnly. I felt my heart thumping with excitement.

'There's been some silly talk in town about the pulling down of the tower and the goddess being angry and so forth. It's nonsense, of course. But if there should be any troble, any at all, I trust you boys to look after the girls and get them home as fast as you can.' He turned to Titch. 'You and James especially.'

Titch gave an emphatic nod.

Finn turned to James who had managed to sidle round so he could hold Opal's hand. I pretended not to notice, but it was hard. 'You hear me too, James?'

'Yes, Mr Rosholt. Don't worry, you can trust guys from over the bog stream.'

The boys all laughed; I assumed it was a boarding-school joke.

'Right.' Finn smiled round at us. 'I'll be there, and Ram Pillay and the temple committee members have promised to keep a close eye on you. Make sure you get back home by eight at the latest.'

I said, 'It doesn't give us very long. Can't we go to the fun fair afterwards?'

'I think not, Izzy. That would be pushing things.'

'But —' Looking sideways at Robin, I was thinking, He doesn't seem too bad at all. Maybe if I went on the giant wheel with him, it would make James jealous.

Finn said in a stern voice, 'Eight o'clock, no later. That's the deal. You all promise?' He extracted a nod from each of us in turn. 'So. Have fon.'

We all stood there for a moment, looking at him. It's one thing to plan an expedition into unknown territory, and quite another to have someone saying, 'Off you go, then.'

Then Titch said, 'OK, let's hit the trail,' and we all trooped across the courtyard and through the gate into what became the biggest adventure of our lives.

The path outside the garden wall had turned into a noisy, shoving, pushing, cheerful river of people moving slowly towards the temple bridge. Many of them were carrying baskets of fruit and sticky sweets nestled in banana or syringa

354

leaves, coconuts and bowls of decorated cooked food and rice; others carried marigold garlands head-high to keep them from being crushed. I saw people leading goats with flowers and ferns wound round their horns, and others with live chickens under their arms.

At first we drifted along between the edge of the crowd and the shops, through eddies of incense and hair oil and camphor, chilliebites and curry, bubbling fat and dust and smoke and sweat. The sun was setting in a hot red ball behind shanty roofs, glinting off glass bangles and running in gleams along the bands of gold embroidery edging brilliant silk saris. There were shuffling grannies in white cotton, bawling babies, kids weaving through everybody's legs, shouting vendors, trapped cars and taxis honking, people hanging out of bus windows, happy chaos everywhere.

'We've got to keep together! Grab on to each other!' Titch called out as the road began to narrow towards the bridge and the crowd grew denser, and we clasped slippery hands and allowed ourselves to be carried along by the current. Apart from the strangeness of being so far outnumbered, I didn't feel afraid or out of place; it was a holiday crowd keen to celebrate, and peopled smiled and nodded at us and one man even said, 'Welcome to Coolietown, nè?' and bared a mouthful of bad teeth. The talk about Kali taking revenge seemed to have been forgotten; we didn't hear her name mentioned once.

But she was there, already starting to work her inscrutable mischief. Hardly noticed at the edges of the river of festival goers were the strong counter currents of contract millworkers and men from the farms and reserves heading for town with their fighting sticks and cane knives, hungry for food and tobacco and their own holiday entertainments. Including the white man's booze that they were forbidden to buy by law, but was freely available at inflated prices in the backyard shebeens that flourish in any shanty town.

At the bridge, some of the crowd peeled off down the steps to the near river bank where they would be able to watch the Kavady rituals across the water. Titch gestured that we should make for the far side where we would be able to look down on what was happening, and we ended up jammed together against the railing. It was the closest I ever got to James, having my face pressed up against his shirt pocket.

Down below, smoke was drifting through the trees from the camphor offerings being thrown into small fires whose flames licked up in places against the temple walls, blackening the new whitewash. The pillars of the portico arches had been bound in banana leaves threaded with marigolds; more were hanging from strings stretched between the trees, now beginning to curl and dry in the smoke and heat from the fires.

The grove was seething with people. Some had gathered round the fire pit which had already died down to a bed of ashy coals with red glowing through underneath; you could feel the heat even up on the bridge. The usual complement of beggars lined the main flight of steps up to the temple: pathetic mothers with thin children and gnarled old women and cross-legged holy men in dhotis with ash-smeared bodies and long straggling grey hair. Dicky Gould in his khaki shorts had insinuated himself among them, a vermilion dot prominent among the other blotches on his forehead. He was trying to appear nonchalant by looking around with a vague expression as he picked at his scabs, but his eyes kept flicking back to the leather-rimmed black beret upside down on the steps in front of him, into which people were dropping coins as often as they dropped into the cupped hands of the Indian beggars.

'Maybe we should try that sometime,' I heard Wally say to Robin. 'We could make a stack. Spend it all on the chicks.' There was an answering snigger, and bang went any ideas of going on the giant wheel with him. I wouldn't be seen dead with anyone who called me a chick.

People who had come with offerings were dipping them in the olive-green water of the sacred pool then sprinkling them with turmeric before walking barefoot round and round the temple with them – they'd do it seven times, Finn had told us. Some of the child walkers had sprays of syringa leaves tied over their new clothes with string. Then the offerings would be handed to the priest, who waved each one several times over the fire on the altar platform at the top of the steps, lighting the candles from the fire with a taper. He had a droopy untrimmed moustache and a shock of greying hair that looked like Finn's badger shaving brush; he leant against the temple pillars between offerings, watching the walkers.

'He has to be pure in heart,' Titch said in my ear.

'What happens to the sacrifices?'

'Mostly they go to the beggars. And the poor.'

Govind was standing next to the priest, soberly dressed for once in a long white shirt that emphasised his thinness. His job was to smash the coconuts down on the round stone lingam so that the coconut milk ran all over the altar in little rivulets; he did it with the same slow, deliberate precision as he did things in the pharmacy, hitting the coconuts on the same point each time so they split into neat sections. Other assistants poured offerings of milk down a hole and walked the goats away and carried live chickens up a ladder to a wire cage that had been built on the roof of the portico, tossing them in with flailing wings. After a lot of startled squawking, they would join the group huddle that sat very still looking down into the grove, mesmerised by the smoke and noise.

'Doesn't look like they're going to be sacrificed straight away,' Titch hissed.

'Damn. I was dying to see how they did it.'

Opal gave an ostentatious shudder. 'Don't be so blood-thirsty, dragon lady.'

'I'm not!' Was she showing off for James? What could he be thinking of me?

But Titch leapt to my defence. 'It's pure scientific curiosity, can't you see? The question is: which is less cruel, breaking the neck or a swift slice with a knife or beheading with a chopper?'

'Sis! How can you?'

She was definitely showing off; I'd never known Opal to be the least bit squeamish. Even best friends can disappoint you sometimes. I turned back to the railings and hung over.

The thickest crowd had gathered down by the river where the Kavady devotees were milling around chanting and singing and getting ready for the procession which would start half an hour after sundown. Most of them had already lifted

357

frames like little wooden benches crowned with a semicircular arch on to their shoulders; they were hung with bells and tinkled each time the carrier moved. The arches were wreathed with tightly packed marigolds threaded in places with purple bougainvillea; some had long curving peacock feathers sticking up like antennae. You could see the two brass pots holding milk and rice hanging down in cloth slings on each side. The whole contraption looked gaily festive rather than burdensome, as though carrying Kavady was a contribution of singing colour rather than solemnity to the goddess's day.

'Look! Look!' Opal was nudging me. 'That man's putting a needle through his tongue.'

It was one of the marvels of that singular evening, seeing gold and silver needles shaped like tridents at one end being pushed through people's tongues and cheeks, and savage fish hooks with limes and other weights hanging from them being threaded through the skin on their backs and arms, and never a wince of pain or a drop of blood spilt. The procession and the fire-walking that followed would be even greater marvels, Titch promised, but they'd only happen when it was completely dark.

'Meanwhile, let's try to get to the steps so we can work our way down. I reckon the light will be gone in half an hour, by which time we should have found a position near the tower where we can watch everything. Stick close to me.'

We began to squirm through the dense crowd, holding hands again to keep together. Once when I was near the railings I thought I saw Finn in the crowd below, but when I looked again the tall figure was gone. Beyond the tower in the parking place between the fun fair and the main road, dozens of pale blue Naidoo buses had lined up after disgorging their festival goers. Titch and I spotted *The Sweet-Smelling Jasmine* at once because Ram Pillay was standing on the dented bonnet rewinding strings of marigolds that had worked loose from the roof rack. We called out and waved to him but he couldn't hear us. Even a person who wasn't deaf would have battled to hear individual voices over the buzzing crowd and the Indian music blaring from loudspeakers and the tinny carousel that had started up in the fun fair. And the drums.

Three men had begun a regular stuttering on hand drums, breaking every now and again into a frantic tum-t-t-tum-t-t-tum-t-t-tum before slowing down again. It was a heartbeat spiked with adrenalin that went on throughout the evening, a compulsive tempo that made your pulse race faster as the drums speeded up to announce a special moment.

The first happened when we were struggling down the stairs in a mass of bodies and trampling feet and all the coloured lights went on at once, outlining the temple and the tower and the fun fair rides and looping between the trees. Everybody stopped to gasp and ooh. The grove was transformed into a wonderland of light and fire and smoke, the glittering stalls of the fun fair beckoning like treasure caves, the wedding-cake temple rearing above us in majesty, its white-washed domes and serenely posed gods and goddesses glowing against the dark in all the colours of the light bulbs. To the east of the bridge the moon had just risen and hung over the river like a spanspek melon, making a path of orange sparkles on the water.

It is the moment I try to keep in the forefront of my memory of that night: when the lights went on. Before the horror blotted out the magic.

Isabel

She is still preparing supper when the doorbell rings, and has to wipe grated cheese off her hands before she goes to open the door. George is out at a pre-retirement course and won't be home until after ten. She has been psyching herself up all afternoon to tell the family, and then him, that she plans to leave as soon as she can tie up all the loose ends in her life. She has made their favourite supper: fresh tomato soup, lasagna and home-made icecream with hot chocolate sauce. Guilt food, she thinks as she turns on the front door light.

Janine bursts in with a red face and puffy eyes from crying. 'I've given Steve the push! The bloody bastard was two-timing me. Oh, Mum.' She buries herself in her mother's arms. 'What am I going to do? We took the flat together.'

Suppressing an urge to cheer, Isabel comforts her and says, 'Ralph's supposed to be moving in, isn't he? I'm sure he can pay his share of the rent.'

'It's not the *rent*. It's splitting up after two years. Stopping being a couple. I thought I was going to marry him, and he –'

She starts sobbing, and it is twenty minutes before Isabel has soothed her enough to resume putting the lasagna together so she can get it into the oven. Janine sits at the kitchen table shredding lettuce into smaller and smaller pieces until Isabel has to say, 'That's enough now, darling. Just put them in the salad bowl. And could you make some dressing?'

Janine uses a fork to beat oil and vinegar to a white froth, pulverises some herbs from the kitchen windowbox, hurls in mustard, salt and a pinch of sugar, gives the pepper-mill a few vicious grinds, thrashes the whole lot together, and feels better. By the time the doorbell rings again, she is

360

ready to answer it with a rueful smile for Chryssa and Tom and a brief, 'Don't ask where Steve is. I've chucked him out.'

'Good riddance,' is Chryssa's response. She is not as diplomatic as her mother.

'Good riddance to who?' Ralph materialises behind her.

'Boring old Steve, the body beautiful. Janine has finally seen the light and told him to get lost.'

'About time.' Ralph is pleased; this means that he'll have his sister and her flat to himself.

'I thought you both liked him!' Janine is stung. It is always hurtful when you realise that your family and friends have been hiding their antipathy towards the man of your choice, specially when you are still in shock from discovering that he has feet of clay. Even worse is the knowledge that your judgement has been at fault and everyone else knew it before you did.

'He messed you around, J. Cricketers are notorious for it, of course.' Chryssa goes into the house looking smugly married. Janine has to resist the urge to hit her.

'Find someone better. Like me.' Tom hugs her. 'I could check around the guys at the office and find out if any of them have –'

'I'm quite capable of organising my own love life, thank you very much.' Janine wants to hit him too, though she knows it is kindly meant.

'Remember what Dad always says. "Boyfriends are like buses; one comes past every fifteen minutes."' Ralph slips past her laughing before she can unleash her anger on him.

Janine is left to close the door and blink away renewed tears before she joins the others on the veranda with its candlelit supper table. Isabel has pulled out all the stops tonight: roses from the garden, the embroidered linen tablecloth and the porcelain plates, each one in a different pattern like Stella's cherished tea cups all those years ago. As a young mother with very little money and a yearning for nice things, she had blessed Stella's teaching for the expertise she had developed at spotting good value in sale rooms and junk shops. She hopes that George will be generous when they part and let her take her treasures: the plates and the silver cream jug, the Victorian candlesticks, the glass bowl that looks as though it could be Lalique but isn't, and others.

They have been good friends, cheering her through bad times by the very fact that she possesses their small contribution to the world's sum of beauty.

'What's all this in aid of?' Chryssa says as Isabel comes out on to the veranda bearing wine glasses and the ice bucket with a bottle of the same kind of chardonnay as Opal the wine expert brought. Everything must be of the best tonight.

'Some special announcements and a celebration.' Isabel hands the dripping bottle to Tom to open.

'Celebrating what? Oh Mum, is it to do with the writing you told us about?' As so often happens, Janine picks up the unspoken straight away. Isabel has often wondered if her second daughter has second sight.

She can't restrain her beam of pride. 'Yes. Opal bullied me into giving her the part I'd completed to be typed by her secretary, then sent it to her publisher without telling me, and he likes it. Wants to see more.'

She spends the next few minutes basking in surprised congratulations and being bombarded with questions, most of which she can't answer. 'But I can tell you that it's about the time I spent with Stella and her husband down in Two Rivers when I was just turning fifteen.'

'You've never told us much about him.' Chryssa is blazing with a suppressed excitement that she can't hide. She has also not taken more than a sip of the wine.

Isabel thinks, She and Tom have made their decision, and it's yes. I'm so glad. A grandchild will be lovely. But I'll wait for them to tell me. She says, 'Stella's husband, Finn, was the nicest, kindest man I have ever known. I've been writing about their tragedy, and about my growing up too. It's amazing what you remember when you try. These have been wonderful months for me, rediscovering my past and unearthing a talent I didn't even realise I had.' She looks down at the writer's bump on the middle finger of her right hand. 'Which brings me to the first announcement. It's sad news, I'm afraid. Stella died early this morning.'

Their shock and sorrow are touching; for all her generosity in sending presents over the years, Stella has been a remote aunt. How much she missed, not having children, Isabel thinks, and remembers again the baby that never was.

'The good news is that she's left her estate to the four of us in equal shares. She told me to tell you that you're splendid young people, and she hopes that the money will enrich your lives and make you independent enough not to make the mistakes she did. It's quite a lot, when you convert pounds to rands.' Isabel smiles round at them and names the sum each will inherit.

The supper that follows is euphoric, with everyone making delighted plans for the unexpected windfall. The chardonnay is followed by glasses of honeyed noble late harvest to go with the icecream. By the time Isabel is ready to make her second announcement, they are all a bit tiddly.

She tings her spoon on her glass and says, 'I want to tell you something else before Dad gets home. I've decided to leave him.'

This time their shock is absolute. Isabel finds herself looking round a table of disbelieving, suddenly sober candlelit faces. The questions come like arrows.

'Leave Dad?'

'You mean, move out?'

'When?'

'Why?'

'It should be obvious why.' She challenges each of them in turn. 'We've grown apart. I have my life to lead, and he has his. Specifically, I have met someone else and I intend to go and live with him.'

'You're going to *live* with someone? Mum, you can't!' With herculean effort, Chryssa manages to hold back, 'At your age.'

'Why not? I love him. And happily he seems to love me.' Isabel gives them a Cheshire Cat smile.

Her children and son-in-law sit looking at her in stunned amazement. She is surprised how galling she finds their expressions. Do they think I'm completely unattractive to men? she wonders. Why aren't mothers allowed to be sexual beings in their own right? We're not numb from the neck down, for God's sake. My body's not in bad shape. I have the benefit of experience and I've learnt some interesting new ways of making love in the past year. In fact I'm quite a good lay, even though I say it myself.

363

She lets out a hoot of laughter and says, 'You needn't look so startled. I'm sure you'll grow to like him when you get over the initial shock.'

'Who is he?' Chryssa demands.

'Anyone we know?' Janine has forgotten her own foundered love affair in the light of her mother's revelation.

Isabel shakes her head. 'You don't know him. He's someone I knew way back in Two Rivers, and he became a writer. It's because of him that I started writing.'

'Tell us who he is.' Chryssa again.

'Not yet. I'd prefer to introduce him to you when things are cut and dried between Dad and me. I'd feel disloyal if I did it any other way.' She turns to Ralph, who has not spoken since her bombshell. 'What do you think about all this?'

'You're breaking up the family!' Ralph bursts out. 'How can you? What will Dad do?'

She puts her hand on his clenched one and does not speak until she has engaged his eyes. Then she says, 'The family has dwindled down to me and Dad, and we're not happy together any more, Ralphie.'

'Ralph,' he says. 'Call me Ralph.'

'Ralph. All of you.' She looks round the table. 'Understand that I'm living in limbo here in this big house. You've all gone and Dad has other interests. I want to get out and do something with my life.'

'But you've done so much! Had kids, made a lovely home, kept our family going –'

'Something for me now,' she says in the quiet steady voice that they remember from the times in the night when they woke in terror or sickness and she came. She always came. 'And I am asking you all to try and understand. I'm not begging for favours. I'm not suggesting that you take sides with me against your father. That would be even more disloyal. I'm just telling you that I've paid my dues as a wife and mother and now I want to be an individual again. It's my right.'

'But if you're going to someone else –'

She cuts in, 'I am going to him as an individual. And he accepts me as such.'

They look at their mother and she looks back at them over

364

the guttering candles, summoning up all her dignity. This is the moment she has been dreading, the injury of a broken family inflicted on her children. She knows that her confrontation with George will be sharp and painful, but also conclusive: once he has accepted the fact that she actually wants to leave him, the Provider, he will probably be relieved to be rid of her and her obsession with scribbling. He'll be able to spend whole days and nights with the boys, playing bowls and drinking brandies and exchanging long-winded anecdotes. He might even find a biddable woman to put up with him; there are widows who would exchange crushing loneliness for a nice house and occasional company.

It is Tom who speaks first. 'You deserve it, Isabel.'

Smiling over the table at him, she thinks, It's easier for Tom, of course, but thank God for nice sons-in-law.

And he has broken the spell, because they all start talking at once and the worst is over. When she gets up to fetch another half bottle of the noble late harvest, they watch her sail into the house like a confident schooner in full rig.

'She's changed.' Janine is twirling her empty glass. 'When you think about it, she's been preoccupied for months. And I don't remember her ever being so outspoken about what she wants.'

'Positively assertive,' Chryssa agrees. It is a quality she admires, and has never thought to find in her usually accommodating mother.

Ralph mumbles, 'I'm sorry about Dad, though. It would have been better if they could have made it up.'

Janine shakes her head. 'I don't think there's much left between them. You know how Dad is.'

They fall silent. They know how Dad is, what he has become, but have closed their eyes to the effect that his increasing self-absorption must have had on their mother. It will take each one of them months to come to terms with the fact that even longstanding marriages sometimes fail. It is tempting to think that investing your emotional capital year after year in someone else will pay good dividends in the end, but relationships don't work that way. Like stock markets, they are unpredictable and often subject to conditions beyond one's control.

'It's going to make our lives more problematic, having to visit them at different times. And places, probably. I hope she's not going to move away.' Chryssa picks up Tom's hand. 'We're counting on her to baby-sit occasionally in the evenings.'

'You've decided! That's wonderful!' Janine jumps up to hug her sister and prances round the table singing, 'I'm going to be an aunty, I'm going to be an aunty.'

'I can baby-sit.' Ralph gives Chryssa the shy grin she remembers from when he was a little boy struggling to tell something important. 'My girlfriend and I, that is. She's used to it because she's got a kid brother.'

'A girlfriend now? Well well. You're certainly not a kid brother any more.' But Chryssa's answering grin takes the sting out of her words.

They have all gone and Isabel is clearing up in the kitchen when George comes home with the telltale red brandy stains on his face, demanding food. She heats some lasagna up in the microwave and puts it down on the kitchen table in front of him, then makes herself a cup of tea and sits down and listens to his grumbling about the retirement course. It is past eleven when she begins to speak, and nearly two in the morning before his initial disbelief has turned to rage then to shouted blame then to wounded pride, and finally to a grudging admission that maybe it would be best if they called it a day. 'But you won't get a bloody cent of my pension if you go off with another man.'

'What about my pension?' she demands. 'I've put in my time too, George.'

'Time! You've sat around on your arse at home all these years while I've been slaving my guts out in the office.'

She closes her eyes to try and shut out the ugliness of this bitter end to what had been an unsatisfactory rather than a bad marriage, and says, 'I only want what is my due for being your housekeeper and bringing up your children. Pension schemes usually have a formula for divorced wives.

'Not if they remarry! Who is the bugger, anyway?'

'I don't know if I'm going to marry him.'

George is incredulous. 'You're just going to run off with

some fucking gigolo to spite me and live in sin with him so you can keep your sticky hands on my pension, is that it?'

'No, that's not it,' she says. 'And will you stop harping on about your pension as though I want to rob you of it? I don't. I just want my fair share.' She doesn't mention Stella's legacy, which is a windfall that she intends to invest. It doesn't belong in the equation between her and George.

'You want to break me!'

'I want what's right.'

'You can't talk about what's right,' he jeers. 'You're the one who's walking out. Deserting.'

'But you've just agreed that it's the best thing for both of us. Can't we be civilised about this? Part amicably? It would be easier for the children.'

'The kids won't give a damn. They'll be too busy gathering like vultures for the spoils.'

She would like to pound her fist into his aggrieved, self-righteous face, but instead snatches the opportunity to say, 'While we're on the subject, if I can have the beach cottage, you can keep the house and its contents. Except for my personal stuff and the things I've bought over the years that have meaning for me. That's fair.'

'What things? I'm not going to have my own home denuded.'

It is another hour before she finally gets to bed exhausted, leaving him prowling round the house with a notebook and one of the dozens of ballpoint pens he has stolen over the years from the office, drawing up a precise inventory of their belongings. He has agreed to her having the beach cottage and her car and a few selected items that she must specify, but she can whistle for anything else, he says. He has not mentioned the children again.

She lies in bed trying to send a telepathic message to her lover: It's done. I've broken free. I'm coming!

And imagines his deep voice saying, Oh my dear love. At last.

Extract from the official report of the Sandham Commission of Enquiry into the Easter 1952 Riot:

'. . . The flashpoint of the riot appears to have been an incident which occurred in the Palm Café at approximately 6.30 p.m. on the evening of Good Friday, 11 April. The circumstances were as follows:

Almost all able-bodied members of the Hindu community were at their temple celebrating the Mariamman festival. Many of the establishments that remained open in the area known as "Coolietown" (notably the Palm Café, a number of low-grade eating houses and certain illegal shebeens) were staffed by inexperienced temporary assistants, and they were busier than usual because it was a public holiday.

The overcrowded facilities were further strained by bus-loads of male Bantu traditional dancers who had come in from the reserves to take part in a dance competition in the Herald compound, usually followed by a beerdrink, and large numbers of off-duty millworkers who had refused to consume any canteen meals that day on the grounds that they were inedible, and had come into town to buy food. These men were both hungry and belligerent. Most, if not all, carried weapons because of the ongoing faction fighting in the compound.

Another factor was clearly insufficient policing. Sergeant Koekemoer testified that because of the unrest in the Hindu community over the imminent demolition of their temple tower, he had decided to station the strongest force of uniformed men (including the detachment from Durban) near the temple grounds, with plainclothes detectives patrolling inside the grounds. Only a skeleton force remained to man the police station and there were no town patrols operating that night. It is the opinion of this Commission that these placings constituted a gross error of judgement on Sergeant Koekemoer's part, as he was fully aware of the possibility of further faction fighting breaking out among angry armed men with a grievance and access to alcohol.

At the Palm Café, it appears that a Bantu male (it is not clear whether he was Zulu or Pondo) purchasing tobacco was given sixpence too little change by one of the temporary Indian assistants; when challenged, he became nervous and denied that he had made a mistake. The Bantu threatened him with the cane knife he was carrying, the assistant called for help, and a fracas ensued during which the Bantu was hit over the head with a tubular metal chair and fell to the floor shouting that he was being killed.

The men who came to his aid first assaulted the Indian staff (one of whom subsequently died of his injuries), then wrecked and set fire to the café. The mob was further swelled by men who poured out of the eating houses and shebeens, their already belligerent mood heightened by holiday drinking, the general unrest in the town due to the expropriations, and a persistent rumour that Indian shopkeepers intended to raise their prices to pay for a new temple tower.

As the fire spread to adjacent shops, looting began that led to fighting between Pondo and Zulu factions. Within minutes the fighting had erupted into a frenzy of arson, rape, assault and murder that soon spread from the main road shops to the residential and shanty areas beyond. All the Indians in the vicinity were forced to run for their lives. Eyewitnesses report shouts of "Kill the coolies!" as gangs of berserk men began to move down the main road and over the Umsindo bridge towards the temple . . .'

23

When the lights went on in the temple grove, people's faces sprang out of the noisy dusk: milling about under the trees, gathered several deep round the fire pit and the chanting devotees down by the river, lining up for the fun fair rides. Lovers twined in the shadows, stall vendors called out their wares, kids tumbled and chased each other, mothers scolded, old women shuffled round and round the temple barefoot, praying with mumbling mouths. Knots of youths with slick hair and linked little fingers and white shirt collars spread open over the lapels of new sports coats drifted about, eyeing every girl they passed. Almost naked old men sat with crossed legs and rapt faces and ash rubbed all over their dreadlocks and beards and bodies, so still among the hubbub that they could have been statues of holy men.

It was a spectacle as far removed from my previous experience as the medieval world of the Breughel painting it so resembled, updated to depict a Hindu festival in modern Natal with the faces and arms bronzed instead of dull flesh pink. We six teenagers goggling from the stair rail appeared to be the only whites there, if one didn't count Dicky Gould and Sergeant Koekemoer's plainclothes policemen patrolling the crowd in burly pairs, and Finn whom I thought I had seen earlier.

Titch nudged me and pointed. The Pather and Reddy families were standing together in one of the arches of the portico, a fresco of privileged worshippers backlit by the smoky light of the candles burning in the temple. At the near end were Asha, wearing silver jewellery and silk that shimmered like the moon on midnight water, and Kesaval in the slender white jacket buttoned from neck to knee; both had their heads turned to one side as if waiting for someone. Next to them, Mrs Reddy looked more like a seal than ever with her sleek hair and questing, sharp-nosed face and dark purple sari; bobbing at her side like a small disagreeable blimp was Violet in a frilly white dress. Mr Reddy and Mr Pather were conferring with two other members of the temple committee in the middle of the group, and the formidable Mrs Pather was haranguing her sons on the far side. Srini appeared to be paying her no attention; he was watching a group of passing girls who were making eyes at him, giggling under their hands.

Titch said, 'Come on, we've got to get near the pit if we want to see the fire-walking. This way.'

We struggled after him, edging our way down through the jostling mass on the bridge steps towards one of the walls next to the temple which he thought we could reach if we climbed along the branch of a nearby syringa tree. Being Titch, he was right. After a nervous scramble in the dark with our sandals in our hands, Opal and I found ourselves sitting in the middle of a row of four boys high above the crowds, with a grandstand view of what was happening only partly blurred by smoke. The jasmine creeper covering the wall prickled up through our thin skirts. I wished I had worn my unrespectable jeans.

The bell clanged several times and the drummers started to beat louder: tum-t-t-tum-t-t-tum-t-t-tum. Round the corner of the temple pulled by a group of women came Mariamma's chariot, a decorated platform mounted on four rubber wheels. The little wooden goddess had been freshly painted and was sitting on a stylised horse with spots on his haunches, her face shadowed by a fringed umbrella with green and red tassels surmounted by a tinsel arch lit by tiny winking Christmas tree lights. The red and gold everyday sari had been exchanged for a gorgeous pink silk one edged with gold embroidery; gold necklaces and marigold garlands had been heaped round her neck and a bunch of red carnations threaded through a hole in one of her four hands. The trident was still there, held in the highest hand, proclaiming her to be the wife of Shiva – as Kali was too, of course, but there

371

was no sign of her presence. (Yet, I have to add in hindsight. Yet.)

The bell clanged again and the drums quickened: tum-t-t-tum-t-t-tum-t-t-tum. Below us, the crowd became still and tense. My heart began to thump. I grabbed Titch's hand and held on. The chariot's platform rocked as a man climbed up to light the candles in the upturned glass lampshades below the goddess. As each candle was lit her gold face grew out of the darkness and became more vivid, appearing to move as the flames flickered, aglow with radiant life. Bundles of incense sticks were lit and put into holders next to the lamp-shades, their pinpricks of light ringing the goddess like a bevy of smoky fireflies. The grove was filled with incense and mystery, and awed murmurings and children being shushed.

Then the drums burst into a rattling tattoo and the chariot lurched forward, pulled by the women and followed mostly by women and boys. The Christmas tree lights in the tinsel archway winked on and off as the goddess began to move in a jerking curve down to the river bank where the devotees had gathered, pierced and hooked and holding burning pots and ready to walk over red-hot coals to honour their vows to her. The sensation of life in the small golden face being carried along above the crowd in the darkness and the smoke was startling. I wondered if Mariamma was really there looking out of the painted eyes, and shivered.

Titch whispered, 'Are you all right?'

I nodded. 'It's just – it feels creepy, as though the gods are really here tonight.'

'Maybe they are. Who can say for sure?' His eyes were as dark as the sacred pool.

'What are you two muttering about?' Opal leant forward, James's arm round her shoulder.

'The gods. Do you feel them here too?'

'Are you serious?' She looked at me, her frizzy hair an unlikely halo in the glimmering shadows, then let out one of her dirty chuckles. 'For pete's sake, Izz, it's just an ordinary old festival. Nothing to write home about. Hindus have them all the time.'

'Can't you feel anything?' I wanted to say, A sense of brooding holiness. A presence that couldn't be explained, though it was strong. But she was in a different world that night, in thrall to the moon and James's hand that I saw creeping under her arm and the cap sleeve of her blouse. So I just gave a hard laugh and said, 'Never mind, it's probably all rubbish,' and turned away so she wouldn't see how jealous I was. Evelyn Simpson had maintained that boys were always trying to get their hands into her bra, and I had been dying for someone to try it with me. It was a gross unfairness that Opal should be favoured first.

To quell the lump of self-pity in my throat, I looked around pretending not to care. The grove was getting hotter and smokier with all the fires, and the different kinds of music wailing from stallholders' gramophones and blaring from loudspeakers and the fun-fair carousel were beginning to set my teeth on edge. The wall of death had started up too, so the sound of a motorbike racing round and round added to the cacophony. I was just thinking that maybe quieter, more sedate churches like ours were preferable when I saw Ram Pillay standing at the top of the temple steps looking towards us, and nudged Titch and we both waved. He at least wasn't being bothered by the noise. He answered us with a bringing together of palms and an almost toothless grin under the walrus moustache.

The Pather and Reddy families began to move down the steps between the beggars towards a special roped-off area with chairs on the far side of the fire pit where the other committee families were sitting. Beyond it at the base of the tower, I thought I saw Finn in the hazy darkness, but couldn't be sure. Is he following us to make sure we're safe? I wondered. And had Stella and Lilah McFadyen come as they threatened to? I tried to see if they were lurking under the bridge with a flying wedge of company guards ready to force their way through the crowd to save us if we seemed to be in danger, but there was no sign of them. Only Sergeant Koekemoer's plainclothes policemen seemed to be taking any interest in us; they kept walking past the wall giving us meaningful upward looks as if to say, What the hell are you white kids doing here among all these Indians?

After a short ceremony at the river that Titch explained were purification rites, the chariot began to move again with its procession of women and boys swelled by chanting devotees: first along the river path as far as the bridge so the people on the other side of the river could see her, then back in a wide arc to circle the temple three times before coming to rest near the fire pit. The crowd standing round it drew back as Mariamma was lifted reverently off the painted horse by temple guardians and placed on the throne that had been prepared for her: a carpeted platform under a canopy decorated with marigolds and carnations and syringa leaves and more Christmas tree lights. In front of it was a shallow trough of pink-coloured milk for the fire-walkers to cool their feet in. From where we sat she looked shorter and squatter now, a little dressed-up wooden statue with a painted gold face that undulated in the heat waves radiating off the coals. Women were bowing down before her with offerings of flowers and fruit and sweetmeats; one of them stroked scented oil over her feet.

The thought came to me again that Sister Kathleen had so violently objected to: was there a spiritual link between the ancient mother goddess Mariamma and the similarly named Christian holy mother Mary? Hadn't Mary Magdalene anointed Jesus's feet with oil too? Why did the various religions fight and despise each other over details of worship when they all professed to believe in God? It was a mystery to me then in the noisy smoky temple grove on that sauna-hot April night, and remains one now when I am almost sure that there is no God anyway. Almost.

The chanting devotees gathered at the river end of the fire pit, leaving a clear space for each walker to stand and pray or meditate before he or she stepped on to the coals. The men beating the drums stood to one side, and had muted them now to a quiet tap-tap tap-tap tap-tap. Members of the temple committee left the roped-off area to bow low with their palms together at each corner before throwing camphor on the coals, followed by some leaves that shrivelled immediately to black specks. ('Betel leaves,' Titch said in my ear.) Then the priest scattered a handful of powder in a special pattern, and followed it with the flicked-out contents of a small brass bowl. ('Ghee,' Titch said.)

The coals flamed up in a blazing, crackling burst that

turned all the watching faces copper. It must have been some sort of signal, because the loudspeakers and the fun fair carousel went dead and the gramophones were turned off and the chattering voices of the crowd died down. And the drums began to rattle again in their disturbing, pulse-quickening tempo: tum-t-t-tum-t-t-tum-t-t-tum.

The first devotee stepped forward, his tongue and cheeks bristling with needles, ash daubed on his head, his legs bare from the thighs down, and stood teetering with closed eyes and joined palms at the edge of the glowing pit. He's really going to walk, I thought with a shiver. It hadn't been real until that moment, but now it was a frightening equation: ten or twelve steps across a red-hot bed of coals must equal burnt human flesh. Maybe his feet would be seared off and he'd come hobbling out the other end on charred black stumps. Maybe he would trip and fall forward and shrivel to a human ember in front of our eyes. How could anyone be so brave – or so foolish? I sat kneading Titch's hand in an ecstasy of horror.

Then the man stepped forward and strolled quite calmly over the coals. And others followed: men and women, some walking, some running, some carrying brass urns with more coals in them, some with needles through their cheeks and tongues, some with rows of hooks stuck through the skin of their backs, some with both hands raised in exaltation. Most of them were smiling when they reached the other end, though there were others who gritted their teeth or sobbed, and one elderly woman who was howling. It was, and still is, the most extraordinary sight I have ever seen: a demonstration of faith and trust that any god or goddess should be proud to receive.

One of the last to walk was Mr Padayachee, who ambled across the coals with a forest of needles through his tongue and hands up in the air, his flowing beard lifting like grey smoke in the updraft. He had a peaceful, faraway look on his face as if he were in a realm no one else could see, a private paradise. Maybe that's where heaven is, in the deep places of our minds where we go when we have done something good and are feeling peaceful and satisfied and happy?

It was when he stepped into the pink milk with a beatific

smile that I noticed the noise coming from the shanty town across the river: banging and thumping and the shouting of angry voices. And screaming.

Titch's head snapped up.

I said, 'What's that?'

'Don't know. Doesn't sound too good.' He leant behind me and tugged James's sleeve. 'Hey, can you guys see through the trees? What's happening over there in Coolietown?'

James stood up, holding on to Opal's shoulder to steady himself. 'People making a hell of a racket.'

'Who?'

'Can't see. Plenty of them.'

Down below us, the crowd watching the fire-walkers had heard it too. Heads were turning, among them Dicky Gould's; he had shuffled down from the temple steps to try and wheedle money off elated devotees. I saw plainclothes policemen shouldering through the crowd towards the bridge steps.

'We'd better get down from here.' Titch sounded worried.

'I'm sure it's nothing. Just drunks. A lot of the millworkers from the compound went into town tonight.' James sat down and began to put his arm round Opal again.

'Come on, man. I promised Finn we'd be home by eight, and it's well after seven now. We'd better get back. We've seen the fire-walking, anyway.'

'Can't we stay just a few minutes longer?' Opal had a dreamy look on her face.

And it made me mad. I got up and said in a bossy voice, 'I promised Finn too. We've got to go.'

The noise over the river was getting louder and closer to the bridge. I looked towards the crowded steps that led up to it, and now I definitely saw Finn. He was standing in the darkness at the base of the tower with Asha shimmering next to him, looking down at her with his bear's paw on her arm. There was a suitcase lying by her feet on the dying jasmine creeper that had been torn off by the road gang.

The sight was like an immense agonising punch in my stomach. Finn hadn't come to watch over us. He had come to run away with Asha, who had been promised to another man. He was stealing as well as cheating.

376

Another figure joined them: Kesaval, gesticulating towards the source of the noise over the river.

I whipped my head round to see what the rest of the Reddy family was doing, but they appeared not to have heard or noticed anything unusual yet. Mrs Reddy had her head close to Mrs Pather's, talking intently – about the wedding, no doubt. Violet, looking sulky and bored, sat with both sausage legs sticking out in front so she could admire her patent leather shoes while she nuzzled a stick of pink candyfloss. The two older men stood with the other committee members, also talking, and the Pather brothers were clustered round some girls in western clothes and exaggerated makeup, teasing them.

Then all the coloured lights blinked out. But we weren't left completely in the dark. Hundreds of candles were glowing inside the temple, fires still smouldered and smoked under the trees, lights powered by a generator burned at the fun fair and in the car park, and there was enough wan moonlight to see by. Titch scrambled up next to me shouting, 'Come *on*, all of you! We've got to go!' He climbed on to the branch of the tree that we had come up by and held his hand out to me. 'You first, Izz, then Opal. Come on. Quickly.'

James had caught his urgency now, and held my arm steady as I reached out for Titch's hand and felt my way along the branch, which drooped under our combined weight. As I grabbed for the main trunk, my sandals slipped out of my hand and fell into the darkness below.

'I've dropped my sandals.'

'Forget them. Just climb down and wait for us at the bottom.' I had never heard Titch so keyed up. 'Come on, Opal. You next.'

I slid down the trunk and started feeling round the sticky trampled ground with my bare feet, but they kept getting stood on by people pushing past towards the road. One of them stopped next to me and said, 'Missy? You must come thees way.'

It was Ram Pillay, his turban like a swirl of white icecream in the hot smoky darkness.

I shook my head and pointed upwards. Opal was climbing down now, followed by James and Robin and Wally. Titch dropped down behind them.

'All of you. I am promising to Mr Rosholt.' I felt a bony hand on my arm. 'Come now, please, to the bus.'

'Finn's here. By the tower.' I didn't add, Betraying us both, Stella and me.

Deaf to the news of Finn's presence as he was to everything else but the evidence of his eyes that something was badly wrong, Ram Pillay tugged at my arm and beckoned at the others and began pushing through the milling, uneasy crowd round the tower towards the floodlit parking area where the Naidoo buses were lined up. The loudspeaker music had started up again: Nat King Cole crooning in his wonderful brown velvet voice, 'Unforgettable, that's what you are –'

Titch shouted, 'Keep together!'

'But my sandals –'

'Forget your bloody sandals! There's something going on over the river. Sounds like it's coming closer. We've got to get home. Ram will take us.'

My feet were getting battered by trampling shoes and the horny soles of those who went habitually barefoot. I tried to keep my toes curled in, but that meant I had to hobble and Titch kept raging, 'Come on! Keep up.'

The crowd gathered round the fire pit was melting away, though Dicky Gould hovered with his black beret in his hands looking old and forlorn and disappointed. I could feel the intense heat coming off the coals as Titch hustled us past and thought, How could anyone have walked there? It's impossible. Through the dervish dance of the heat waves I saw the wooden goddess's gold face looking straight at me, and got another sickening jolt. Someone had hung a necklace of small skulls round her neck on top of the garlands. Kali had come, as promised. And Govind was standing behind her, his face and throat with its prominent adam's apple lit from below by the dull orange light of the dying coals.

I stopped and looked up at the base of the tower in terrible fear. Finn had his arm round Asha now. She had pulled her sari round her face and was cowering against him. Kesaval was moving away towards the bridge steps. The tower loomed above them, huge and pale in the darkness with the moon hanging like one of Eslina's pearl drop earrings from the bulge of the dome.

378

I remember that moment as one of complete silence, but it couldn't have been. Harrowing noises were drifting across the river: people screaming, thuds, explosions, breaking glass, the hideous liquid crackle of fire. From the car park behind the tower came the sound of a bus being started up.

'That's Ram. Hurry.' Titch.

'My feet hurt. I can't go any faster.' Me.

'You've got to.' Titch again. 'Grab my hand.'

We edged our way through the now panicky crowd at the base of the tower, Titch shoving in front, James and Robin and Wally behind us in a protective semicircle. The policemen had all disappeared. Something horrible was happening over the river. People were battling their way up the packed steps on to the bridge; others were battling downwards. Desperate parents shouted at their children to keep together. Dark people-shapes were running both ways along the river bank.

There was the sound of a bus revving. 'Make for the *Jasmine*. Hurry.'

Titch was nearly dragging my arm out of its socket. We reached the bridge embankment and scrambled up and along, ignoring scratches and splinters from the bamboo debris left by the bulldozers. It was easier to move up there, above the struggling mass of bodies. When we stopped for breath, we could look down on both sides of the tower base.

So we saw it all happen.

And this is the loop of film that ran in slow motion through my head for years, over and over, until I managed to shove it into a remote cranny of my mind and seal it shut. Until I began to think and write about Two Rivers again. This is the loop:

Govind catching sight of Asha and Finn with the suitcase at the base of the tower, and shouting at the Pather brothers.

Ram Pillay backing a reluctant, shuddering *Sweet-Smelling Jasmine* towards the tower, anxious to fulfil his vow to Finn to look after us. So anxious that he starts wheezing and coughing, having not quite recovered from his pneumonia, and his unreliable foot slips off the clutch. So deaf that he does not hear the frantic shouts of warning, or the hands banging on his window.

The rattliest bus on the whole South Coast bucking

backwards and ramming into an old mud-brick structure already weakened by two bulldozers.

A ghastly sound like a lot of airguns going off as the small cracks in the white plaster suddenly craze into a network of gaping crevices, arrowing everywhere.

People crying out, 'Look! Look! The tower!'

Ram Pillay, heedless of the fatal damage he has caused, crashing his gears and the bus jerking forward again.

Finn urging Asha towards the bridge steps with his free arm round her shoulders, looking up at the tower with eye sockets that are fathomless black holes.

Govind running to intercept them, all slowness gone, reaching out to grab Asha's hand.

Srini Pather running behind him, his face contorted with fury, followed by temple guardians brandishing their long sticks.

The first bits of plaster tumbling very slowly in the moonlight to smash on the ground.

Shouting. 'Run! Run! It's coming down!'

The panic to scramble away. People stumbling and cursing. Collisions in the darkness. Screams of fear. The temple guardians dropping their sticks and linking hands to try and clear a space round the tower, yelling, 'Get away! Quick!'

Finn and Govind in an ugly tug of war with a weeping Asha being torn between them, a rag doll in a glimmering midnight sari.

The deep cannon boom as the beautiful white wedding cake tower cracked from top to bottom.

The crowd's huge, horrified gasp and fear-distended mouths exploding: Kali! Kali! Kali!

Govind letting go and falling back against Srini and his brothers.

Asha collapsing in a terrified sobbing heap.

Finn curving over her – echo of her drooping lily over the pharmacy counter.

And the tower disintegrating like a sandcastle washed over by a wave. Just slumping down in a tired rumble – gods, goddesses, cows, peacocks, shells, flowers, crescent moons and dome crumbling to dust as if to say: That's it, I've stood long enough. Old mud and straw, bricks and plaster mixed by hand, underlimed because the community was poor, falling apart.

Burying Finn and Asha.

Bursting plaster and brick debris over Govind and Srini and the temple guardians.

A single chunk of masonry bounding towards that small white blimp Violet Reddy, still sitting in her patent leather shoes with her sticky blob of pink candyfloss by the fire pit, screaming, 'Grandpaaaa!'

Dicky Gould, with a surviving flicker of the instinct that had sent him Up North to fight and lose to the victorious Germans at Tobruk, galvanised into jerking her out of her chair seconds before it splintered to matchwood. And his poor skinny, scabby, scaly old rooster's leg splintering with it.

For a single dreadful moment after the last piece of plaster slips and lies still, a death hush arrests the fleeing crowd and binds it to awed silence. The smoke-hung grove reeking of sweat and camphor and incense is as still as the grave it has become.

And then the panic starts again and is doubled and redoubled by the terrifying sounds of riot and killing and runaway fire coming across the river.

This is the loop of film that runs in my head now, over and over. Unforgettable.

Though many were bruised and grazed and showered with rubble, Mariamma must have stayed Kali's avenging hands – or more likely, she found the sport of rioting more to her taste – because no one else was killed by the temple tower. Only a rooster that had been brought to sacrifice, its dying muscles jerking in spasms as settling dust gradually filmed its bright black eye.

People began running again and trying to struggle up the bridge steps. We saw Kesaval kneel beside the broken bodies under the fallen masonry, trying to push aside huge lumps of it. Titch and I slid down the embankment and tried to help him. I was there when Finn's drained blue eyes finally closed. I hope he saw me. Hope he felt my hands under his bloody head and heard the love I whispered in his ear, struggling through my tears to forgive his betrayal. What a frickly, *frickly* way to die.

Asha had died at once, her slender body crushed by a falling statue, her beautiful Persian face untouched. Kesaval knelt above her, crying in a terrible deep voice that kept splintering.

And then James and Robin and Wally were dragging us away towards the bus where Opal was already sitting under police guard. Two of Sergeant Koekemoer's plainclothes men had been commandeered by Stella and Lilah McFadyen who had been sitting in the Ford in the car park, hidden behind the buses. It was important to protect whites first in a riot situation, of course.

Stella didn't know about Finn then, because he and Asha had not been visible from the car park. And I, speechless with shock, couldn't tell her.

Ram Pillay, oblivious of what he and the *Sweet-Smelling Jasmine* had done when they leapt backwards – he thought he'd hit a tree, he said at the inquest – was revving the engine so it wouldn't dwindle and expire before he got us away to safety. As he did hundreds of other people beleaguered in Coolietown that terrible night, ferrying them through the howling, unreasoning mobs to the temporary sanctuary of the company estate in the sturdy old NAIDOO'S FAVOURITE TRANSPORT bus that defied the sticks and stones and axes and cane knives rattling against its pale blue sides.

I remember that night in nightmare flashes. Faces I recognised from my walks around town, now engorged with hatred and rage. Strong brown muscular arms rising and falling, smashing glass, splintering inadequate shutters. Bone-crushing blows thudding down on cowering bodies. Frantic, desperate, hideous screaming. And the looting lust: the grabbing, furtive greed mixed with gleeful revenge. The tumult and the shouting.

The Easter Riot raged for two days and three nights, spreading up and down the South Coast. Long-simmering grievances against the Indians, exacerbated by three centuries of black repression and encouraged by white antagonism, burst out in an orgy of destruction and murder. It was Indians who died mostly, though a number of rioters were shot dead by the police and the soldiers.

Major McFadyen was instrumental in having a state of

382

emergency declared so the army could be called out to assist the exhausted police. Though the Herald Company was prepared to take in shocked and destitute refugees and set up dormitories and soup kitchens with the nuns' help until further arrangements could be made (a humanitarian gesture not lost on the sugar-buying public), their assets had to be protected.

Stella and I were sitting huddled under blankets on one of Lilah McFadyen's sofas when the Major came and knelt down in front of her and told her very gently about Finn. He did not mention Asha then, nor the fact that the pharmacy and the house behind it had been ransacked. Stella lost everything in one night: husband, home, precious possessions and place in the community. They broke the rest of it to her the next day and she took the news like a stoic, devastated but dry-eyed. It was the whispers about Asha that turned her to granite. Nobody could get through to her after she heard them: neither Mother Beatrice nor Lilah McFadyen, both of whom she had liked and admired, and certainly not me, for whom she had only an exasperated affection.

Nor did a visit from an ashen Kesaval dressed in a grey suit and tie and polished black shoes make any difference. He came to explain that Finn had been helping Asha to run away that night from the arranged marriage she dreaded. She was to have slipped away from the family in the festival crowd and caught a train to more modern-thinking relatives in Durban who had offered to take her in.

'So it's my fault too,' Kesaval confessed with tears running down his face. 'We both killed her. She would have been better married to Srini.'

Stella said in a dull voice, 'Nothing you say makes any difference. Finn betrayed me as he betrayed you. In his mind if not with his body.'

'Mrs Rosholt, please –'

'Go away. Go away!'

It made a huge difference to me, and I managed to catch Kesaval on the McFadyens' front steps and tell him so with the stone lions prowling on either side of us. 'Is it true? I thought Finn was –'

'Everybody thought! People here have mean little minds,

383

always looking for faults and failings.' He gave the step a vicious kick. 'I thought he was different, but I was wrong. He just interfered.'

'But you said – you know he was trying to help her.'

'Is it help, to let someone get killed?' His eyes were sunk deep in their smudged sockets. 'Is it help, to save your sister from one man and let her die in the arms of another? She didn't need our kind of help.'

'It was an accident. It just happened.'

'Nothing just happens! And nothing you say will change my mind. I'm leaving this place the moment I finish school.'

'But what about your grandfather and Oxford and –'

'The steam laundry? It's not for me. Not at all. Forcing a grandson to toe the family line and take over a business is as bad as arranging marriages. I can't live in the past. I want to be part of the modern world.'

I thought of Titch saying, 'I want to get out of Two Rivers and see how the world works.'

I thought of Finn saying, 'It is for you alone to choose how your life goes along, and nobody else. It is a shame, I think, that women have to fight still for the right to make their own decisions.'

And I understood why he had tried to help Asha, and began to get my first inkling of the restless spirit that lives in some men and women. Men like Titch and Kesaval. Women like Stella. Not the rooted ones like me who live in a world of dreams and maybes, and are slow to change their allegiances.

Though I do know what the smells of fear are because I've been there: mud and blood, the foul smoke that belches out of burning houses, stinking sweat and vomit and voided bowels. And afterwards, ash.

Isabel

She and George are going through the house dividing up their possessions. He has a detailed room-by-room inventory on a clipboard, and carefully ticks off each item she says she doesn't want with a black ballpoint. The few things she asks for are marked with a heavy asterisk in red. They look like drops of blood on the paper.

She thinks, I didn't realise this would be so hard, or so hurtful.

His clamped lips could be a badly healed scar across the lower half of his face. There are fine drops of sweat on his forehead which he wipes off every now and then with a handkerchief, stuffing it back into his pocket so that half is left hanging out. He has not looked directly at her since the dreadful night when she told him she was leaving.

Now he says, looking out the window pretending indifference, 'If you're not taking the sofa and easy chairs, what about the TV and the video?'

She thinks, He'll need those most of all when I'm gone. Sitting alone at night when he gets back from the club. 'No, I don't want them. I've never been much of a TV fan, remember?'

There is a brief flare of gratitude on his face, then he says in the grating voice he uses all the time now, 'I remember. You always thought yourself too good for such a mundane activity. Sticking your nose in a book was more obviously intellectual.' The emphasis he puts on the last word makes it plain that he despises people who fancy themselves intellectuals.

'George –'

'Yes?'

'Does it all have to be so unpleasant? I'd hoped we could be sensible.'

'Sensible?' Now he swings on her, the broken veins on his cheeks standing proud of the red stain spreading underneath. 'You leave me to run away with an artsy-fartsy scribbler, and you ask me to be sensible? Christ, you've got a bloody nerve. Another man would have thrown you out on the street with nothing.'

She closes her eyes hoping to make the ugly words pouring out of the mouth scar disappear and says, 'Please don't start up again.'

'Stop whining! You always do it when you're in the wrong. I can't stand that tone of voice. It never ceases to amaze me how –'

He is playing his old game of claiming moral superiority, and goes into a long diatribe about what a useless wife she has been compared to the other wives he knows. And he's right in some respects, she has to admit. In recent years she has been lazy about cooking for just the two of them and has only made a special effort when visitors come or the children drop in. The garden and her charity work and her book club became far more important to her than keeping house; during the past months, her writing has consumed her to the exclusion of everything else.

'– other wives of working men have a bloody sight more consideration for their breadwinners, I can tell you. I'm amazed at the level of gross neglect I've put up with all these years.'

She opens her eyes so she can counterattack in their usual battle mode: feint, pincer movement, flights of barbed arrows, concealed snipers, charge of the mounted lancers, final tank engagement with all guns blazing. But the poison gas of her anger is blown away by what she sees. The hands holding the clipboard are trembling, and he clamps his mouth shut to keep it from trembling too. The ugly words he is uttering are at odds with his body language. She thinks, Why didn't I see this before? We've become two people who wilfully inflict unhappiness on each other. Two adults behaving like children who don't get their way, stamping our feet and each trying to shout louder than the other.

She says, 'George, please let's stop pretending.'

'What do you mean?'

His eyes bulge – Like sourballs, she thinks, and at another time would have laughed at the thought. Now she realises with a pang of guilt that this has been part of their problem all along. He is very much a man of his generation who believes that a woman's place is in the home and that women are wayward creatures who need 'handling'. Instead of confronting him with her increasingly independent point of view during their arguments, however, she has taken the line of least resistance by letting him rail on at her while she mocks and laughs at him inwardly. Anything for peace. But of course he has sensed it and been affronted, which has made things worse. As she has learnt with painful and unwelcome insight over these past few months, the breakdown of this marriage is as much her fault as his. She has misled him by her lack of overt resistance as much as he has disappointed her by his inadequacies.

She goes towards him and puts her hand on his trembling one. 'Let's stop pretending that this marriage has any mileage left. We were fine in the beginning but we've grown away from each other now. We're two very different people and it's better if we go our own ways before it's too late. I'm sorry it hasn't worked out.'

'You are?' He is taken aback at her sudden change in tactics, and suspicious. She can almost see him thinking, What is the woman trying to pull on me now?

She thinks, It would be so much better for everyone if we could end it amicably.

They stand facing each other at the moment which will define their future contacts – inevitable meetings at family weddings and births and holidays like Christmas. However tedious she has begun to find him, he is her children's father. And a good father in the beginning, she reminds herself. Maybe a good father still if I had been more diplomatic and less mummy-knows-best over the years. If I hadn't subtly encouraged the children by laughing when they said he was a boring old dork. Maybe I've helped to create the George I've found it so easy to despise.

She says, 'I'm sorry about other things too. About misleading you as to the kind of person I really am. About letting our relationship slide downhill instead of trying to tackle the problems.'

'You're sorry?' he breaks in. 'I thought you couldn't wait to get out of this house. This prison, I think you called it. Isn't it a bit late to say you're sorry?' The aggression is still there, but less certain.

'It's never too late.' Having said it, she smiles at him and says, 'I sound like that song from *The Boyfriend*, remember? "It's never too late to fall in love, Boop-a-doo, boop-a-doo, boop-a-doo." But I mean it, George. I am sorry it didn't work out. And I'm also sorry that I've let you lose touch with the children. You were such a good father when they were little. You had endless patience with them.' The trite saying pops up in her mind: Love means never having to say you're sorry. She has spent half a lifetime saying sorry to George.

'I was?' But he covers his surprise by adding a sarcastic, 'I thought the kids didn't have time for me any more, now that they don't need me to reach into my pockets when they need something.'

His irritation at being taken for granted as a parent is an echo of her own, which reached its highest level when there were three demanding teenagers in the house. But I didn't want to know about his feelings, she thinks. I was too busy wallowing in mine.

She blurts, 'I'd like to try and help you mend your relationship with the children. They'll need you to be here for them when I go away.'

'Haven't shown any signs of it,' he grumbles, but his mouth scar falls into a downward curve. Until this moment, she has not realised how much he minds the alienation from his children.

With a rush of compassion she says, 'Chryssa and Tom don't know it yet, but they're going to need a good grandfather.' She remembers how George used to enjoy taking the children to places where he could explain things to them, impress them with his superior adult knowledge. 'Someone who can be relied on for walks in the park and visits to the zoo.'

He says sharply, 'Just because I'm retiring doesn't mean

that I'll be at everybody's beck and call. I've got my own life to lead, plenty to do.'

Thank God for that, she thinks. Or should it be Mariamma, or Shiva? There are so many gods in my life now that it's quite a problem working out who to direct pleas and thanks to . . . Smiling at the pun, she thinks on, At least I don't have to worry about him keeping busy. If he doesn't find a woman to move in with him soon, there'll be the housework and the garden to keep up too. Staying on here is going to be expensive for him.

She is opening her mouth to suggest that perhaps he should think of moving to a townhouse or a retirement village when he grates, 'By the smirk on your face I can see that you think I won't be able to manage without you.'

'That's not what I was thinking at all.'

'Don't deny it. I know that look. I've put up with it for years, and you know what? I'll be glad to see the last of it.'

He's accepted the break, she thinks with relief. Maybe we can manage this difficult parting and dividing up without coming to blows.

In his usual way, he is harping on, 'I can manage perfectly well. I'm quite self-sufficient. Don't need other people.'

With only the barest hesitation she says, 'Of course you don't.'

'And you needn't worry about the kids. I'll keep an eye on them – Ralph especially. He gets carried away by his enthusiasms sometimes.' It is said in a gruff voice calculated to reject any pity she may feel for him.

'That'll be a relief to me. Thanks.'

She smiles at him, trying not to make it look like a smirk. This is the moment to tackle him on the matter of her share of the pension and she does so, naming a modest monthly sum. It is not so much need as the principle of fair reward for services rendered that motivates her; she will, after all, be getting the interest from Stella's money and her long-hoarded escape fund. She is only asking for her due, and he is clearly relieved that it is less than he expected.

So the division proceeds without further rancour, and by the end of the day she has packed her precious possessions and photograph albums and books and journals and the few necessities the beach cottage still lacks: bed and table linen, crockery, kitchen equipment and several dhurrie rugs in sea colours, greens and turquoises and blues. The hall is half full of cardboard boxes and tea chests by the time she has finished.

She goes to find George, who is ostentatiously shaving the lawn to within millimetres of its roots. She hopes it will survive the onslaught, then reminds herself that this garden is no longer her problem. No longer hers, though she has created and nurtured it for years. This is what it must be like giving up a child for adoption, she thinks, looking around to drink in for the last time the deep borders and rambling roses and shady terrace under the trees where arum lilies flower in spring, if well watered. I hope he looks after it and doesn't let it all die. I won't have a garden at the beach, only bush.

She has to swallow the lump in her throat to say, 'I'm all packed and ready now. The movers will fetch the stuff in the morning.'

'What?' He throttles the mower down to a low mutter.

'I'm all done, so I'll be going. The movers will come in the morning. I hope I haven't taken too much.'

He waves the idea away with an impatient gesture. 'Nothing I particularly wanted.' In fact, he is relieved that she has taken so little. Sweating over the mower, he has begun to think that perhaps he will sell up and move into something smaller and more convenient now that she's going. Gardens are a hell of a lot of work, and he intends to be out most of the time anyway.

'I – we're staying at the Hampton Court for a few days, if you want to talk to me about anything.' She is shy about saying 'we'.

'Not going down to the beach straight away?' He has not mentioned her lover since the night she broke the news, not even asked his name, and she accepts that this will be one of the rules between them: no mentions, no comparisons.

And, she hopes, no regrets. 'Not straight away. I have to do some things for Opal's publisher before I – we leave.'

'Big stuff, hey?' His vestigial smile is an indication of the jokes he will make in the months to come about his ex-wife, the budding author, to garner what he feels is his fair share

390

of acclaim for supporting her. The concept of fairness seems to be a basic human requirement, yet it is so seldom achieved. It is to Isabel and George's credit that they part feeling that each has been fairly treated.

Her answering smile is understanding. 'Goodbye then, George. I hope you'll be OK.'

'Why shouldn't I be?' He lets go the mower handle and tugs the handkerchief out of his pocket to wipe his sweaty face and neck and repeat his boast. 'I'm quite self-sufficient.'

'Of course you are. Probably planning to move a whole harem into the house tonight.'

He lets out a bark of sarcastic laughter. 'No damn fear. I'm taking a holiday from women. Too many other things to do.'

'So this separation is a relief for you too?'

He shrugs.

She thinks, I'll never get him to admit it out loud, but what the hell. We both know it. That's all that matters. She goes up to him and puts her hand on the vibrating mower handle next to his. 'Shall we kiss goodbye?'

'Don't see any point now.' He moves his hand further along the mower handle, away from hers. Another rule is going to be no touching. 'I hope you know what you're doing, Isabel.'

'Oh, yes.' She turns to look him full in the face. 'It's the first time in years that I've been really sure I'm doing the right thing.'

The moment stretches between them like the shadows lengthening across the lawn. She wonders if he will be able to say, 'Be happy,' or something similar. She would like to part on a high note.

But he only says, 'Go well, then. Keep in touch,' and bends down to turn the mower up again.

She wanders round the house alone as the mower goes back and forth, back and forth outside. It is not difficult to say goodbye because it has an impersonal air now that she has packed away the things that made it her home. She half-closes her eyes and tries to see it as an estate agent would: a shabby family home that shows the depredations of three children — scuffmarks, chipped paintwork, worn carpets, heights measured on a doorpost, thumbtack holes in cupboard doors that once sported pop star and racing car posters. It wasn't a bad life, she thinks. We had a lot of happy times.

The place she finds hardest to leave is the veranda with its comfortable basket chairs and ferns and woven grass mat full of crumbs and dog hair. How many cups of tea have I sat and drunk here, looking out over the garden? she wonders. How many confidences exchanged? Tears shed? Arguments raged over? Dogs patted? Parties held? She remembers the children's birthday parties – making jelly oranges and racing cars out of sponge biscuits with Smarties for wheels and jelly-baby drivers, and George playing Mr Whale behind a blanket pinned across a doorway as each child fished for a present with a rod and a bent pin hook at the end of a piece of string. All the sticky little hands and faces. All the years . . .

And now I'm going away. Goodbye, veranda. Goodbye, life with George. Hullo – oh, God, I hope it's true – hullo, happiness.

She walks down the front path to her car without a backward glance.

24

Nineteen people died in Two Rivers during that Easter weekend, and a hundred and twenty-seven were injured.

Though the white areas were scarcely touched, one of the dead was Dorothy Gould. A police detective pieced together what must have happened to her. Terrified by the sight of the large group of Zulus (thieving, devious, no-good skellums in her shaky old mind) who ran along Darjeeling Road singing war songs and brandishing their fighting sticks, she had fled into her book treasury and tried to burrow into her hoard for refuge. Like dominoes the tottering cobwebbed piles of books had toppled over one by one, burying her in an avalanche of words. They found her when they went to tell her that Dicky was in Durban's Addington Hospital, basking in a hero's glory and the prospect of a generous reward from Mr Reddy for saving Violet's life. Forgotten in the horror of the rioting, Miss Dorothy had been dead for three days and the soft parts of her fingers and one earlobe had been nibbled away by rats. The free-flying budgies lay in little blue and yellow heaps all over the stinking house, having battered their wings in vain against windowpanes furred with decades of grime.

The shanty areas of Coolietown were razed and most of the shops along the main road were burnt-out shells. Pather's Jewellers and the Reddy Steam Laundry escaped the worst of the fury because they were solid structures and well barricaded. The pharmacy and the house behind it were not set on fire, but stripped to the bare walls by human army ants. The garden was a trampled desert, the maidenhair ferns round the water tank dried to brown fuzz. The goldfish were gone from the pond in the courtyard and even the waterlilies had been ripped out and flung down on the stones. Only the jasmine had survived the holocaust, greenly foaming now over an empty, echoing shell. All my lovely teenage clothes were gone, but they had left Edgar Bear with one glass eye torn loose, and my scrapbook.

Nothing of Stella's was retrieved.

'Just as well,' she said in the dull voice she had begun to use all the time. 'I can make a clean start when I leave.'

The Indian community was stunned by the violent hatred that had suddenly boiled up in people who had been their customers and neighbours for almost a century. As they set about rebuilding their damaged homes and businesses and trying to heal the psychological scars, the Natal Indian Congress vowed to make sure that it would never happen again and pressed for an official Commission of Enquiry which took place six months later, chaired by Mr Justice Anthony Sandham. Relations between black and brown in Natal were badly – some say irreparably – damaged by the Easter Riot. It took years for a tentative trust to grow again between the people of Two Rivers, and by then the town was dying under the onslaught of factories that spread south from Durban.

Stella and I stayed with the McFadyens while we waited for the rioting to subside, and for the funeral.

Finn and Dorothy Gould were buried in the new cemetery on the crest of a low hill at the edge of town where Old Man Herald's flamboyant trees petered out. It had trim gravel paths and lawns and young trees, but was too new and exposed and too close to the main road running south to Umkomaas and Port Shepstone to feel like a proper resting place. Only the view was a partial compensation: over the green fairways and palms of the company golf course, across the ambling brown Umlilwane river and the town lying like a navel among the canefields, and beyond to the lagoon and the sandspit and the long blue line of the sea.

The Lutheran pastor conducting Finn's service was a friend of his elderly parents, who were too shocked to make the long journey down from Zululand to their only son's funeral. A lot of people came to pay their last respects to a man who had been greatly liked and respected, but there was a look common to their faces that said: This is the sort of thing that happens when you get too mixed up with charras.

None of them mourned him like Titch and I did. The moment when the first spadeful of red earth thudded down on to his coffin was one of the worst in my life. It was when I realised that he was really gone and would never give me a bear hug or look at me with those deep sea eyes ever again. I started crying and when Titch put his arm round me I knew that he was crying too from the way it shook, even though boys weren't supposed to. Specially not in a Michaelhouse uniform so everybody could see what sissies little gentlemen were. Major McFadyen went stomping off to his chauffeur-driven car afterwards with a face like maas – sour milk curds – leaving Titch and his mother to beg a lift home with us.

No Indians came to the funeral. Many had fled to families in other towns when the rioting started but among those who stayed to clean up and start rebuilding, it was felt that Finn had betrayed their trust by encouraging Asha to run away from the arranged marriage. Whatever his passion for individual freedom of choice and the unease felt by many in the Indian community about outdated customs like arranged marriages, it was not his place to interfere. Mr Reddy was said to be deeply wounded by the actions of a man whom he had considered to be a sympathetic ally among mostly unfeeling whites. Locked in his big Spanish house which had been bypassed by the rioters as too well protected to bother laying siege to, he must have mourned his lovely granddaughter as bitterly as he struggled to control his anger against the gods who had decided her fate. The Pathers next door were said to be enraged that their Srinivassen should be so insulted by the girl chosen for him, and considering suing the Reddys.

Finn's friends Mr Moodley and Mr Padayachee and Mr Chetty from the Palm Café sent their tribute in one of the few rickshaws that had survived the riot: a pile of marigold garlands whose bright assertive orange kept drawing people's eyes away from the genteel pastel wreaths and lilies lying on the mound of raw red earth. When Stella snatched up one of the garlands after the pastor had finished and tore it to pieces, there were murmurs of approval. Then the wind began and everyone went home leaving the mangled flowers to blow away petal by petal into the canefields.

The simple fact was that Asha had died because of Finn's

well-intentioned meddling. That is how most people saw it, anyway. I am still not sure in my own mind what happened in the temple grove that night: a terrible chain of coincidences, blind bad luck for those who were caught in it, or a conspiracy of angry goddesses? Because Kali was definitely present; I saw the necklace of skulls round Mariamma's neck with my own eyes. Even if it was put there by a mischievous boy who caught a lot of rats so he could string their skulls together, who is to say that Kali didn't put him up to it? That's the trouble with matters pertaining to the gods – or to God himself (herself?): you can never be one hundred per cent sure.

And Stella had been right about Two Rivers. As we drove away from the cemetery in the Ford with Lilah McFadyen on the passenger side and Titch and me cramped into the dickey seat holding damp hands, I heard her saying, 'I always said it wasn't safe in this town, but Finn knew better. Sanctimonious bastard.'

Stella was always attracted to paradoxes.

The next day we left the McFadyens' house with the Ford's hood up for the long drive to the Transvaal. Stella was taking me back to Aunty Mavis and Ma, who had been let out of the loonybin and was convalescing at her home.

I had said goodbye to Opal over the phone, as the main road into Two Rivers was still sealed off by the army and her father couldn't drive her in. 'Promise to write?' I begged in a voice that seemed to be permanently sodden with tears. 'I hate having to leave, but it wouldn't be the same without Finn and Stella. She says that as soon as Finn's affairs are wound up, she's going away overseas to forget about Two Rivers. But how could she? I won't, ever.'

'Yes, you will.' Opal sounded miserable, rare for her. 'None of my friends last.'

'I'll be the exception if you promise to keep on writing to me. We can be penfriends. I want to know everything that happens at the convent and in Two Rivers and in your life.' I didn't mention James. Even saying his name would have hurt, knowing that I would never see him again.

'Such as it is. I'm going to die of boredom at school without you there. At least we could laugh together.'

'At least. I'll miss you, oh many-faceted and brilliant one.'

'Me too, dragon lady.' She rang off with a sob.

I wondered where Sister Kathleen Killeally was, and whether she would have gone around saying that the rioting and killing and burning of houses was a judgement on heathens who worshipped graven idols. Mother Beatrice had come to the McFadyens' house the previous evening to say goodbye to Stella and me, her hands as smooth and cool as ever despite the fact that she and the nuns had been running non-stop soup kitchens for the homeless.

'I'm sorry to lose you both,' she had said. 'Stella because of your very real talent as an artist and teacher –' Stella had managed a faint smile for the first time '– and you, Isabel, because the convent could do with more star pupils. Helps no end when it comes to gathering in the fees.' She had bent down to give me a final directive. 'Remember what I have said about the necessity for women to be tough-minded. This terrible time we have been through in Two Rivers is only the first of many such in our country, I think. Your generation will need to be exceptionally tough to survive.'

I could not believe her then, didn't want to believe that such an appalling outburst of unreasoning hatred and violence could ever be repeated, though of course she was right. Sharpeville happened eight years later and Soweto sixteen years after that, followed by violence piled on violence as South Africans shot and killed and raped and burned and necklaced their way to democracy. Our generation failed miserably to find solutions that work, but perhaps the next will begin to make some headway. I want my grandchild to inherit peace and tolerance; if it is a granddaughter, I will start talking about the necessity for women to be tough-minded as soon as she is old enough to understand.

Titch promised to write as well, and gave me my first meaningful kiss from a boy in full view of his mother. As he stepped back, he pulled his pith helmet down over his eyes so I could hardly see them. The last thing he said to me was, 'You're OK, you know, Izz?'

'You too, Timothy Montague Wotherspoon –' But he had disappeared round the corner of the house before I could finish.

Behind me, his mother murmured, 'Altogether less barbaric, wouldn't you say? Thanks to you.'

All I could say before my throat closed up and the tears started again was, 'You've all been great.' She hugged me then, and so did Eslina who had walked all the way to the company estate from her home in the reserve, talking her way through four army roadblocks, to say, 'Hamba gahle, Izzy-weh. Go nicely to that Joburg place. You remember Eslina, nè?'

They stood waving side by side as Stella and I drove out through the company gates to take the detour round Two Rivers that would get us on to the main road going north. Mr Padayachee and his water cart had been engaged to keep the hastily scraped temporary road watered so the heavy traffic crawling along it wouldn't kick up too much dust, and he raised a thin bandaged arm to wave to us. Stella turned her head away but I waved back, remembering how his beard had lifted like smoke as he ambled over the red-hot coals. He was the last person we saw.

I read in the newspaper recently that there is a scientific explanation for the phenomenon of fire-walking. It is a matter of physics. A substance may be hot but will transfer that heat slowly. You can put your hand into a hot oven and touch a baking cake without getting burnt, but you will get burnt if you touch the metal cake tin or oven racks.

During fire-walking, burning embers or hot coals and their ash behave like the cake – they are also poor conductors of heat. And because feet have a high heat capacity, the hot coals actually cool down when walkers step on them. The trick is not to spend too long on the coals as the effects are cumulative. It takes an average eight or nine steps to cross a twenty-five foot bed of coals. At a reasonably brisk pace, each foot is in contact with the coals for no more than a second or two, not long enough to cause burns.

The trouble with rational explanations like this is that they spoil the mystery.

So I prefer to remember the mystery of the temple grove that night and the exalted expressions on the faces of the fire-walkers. And I try to forget that death was there too, lurking in the temple tower and in the sharpened cane knives of men whose erupting anger had robbed them of their reason. The smell of a flowering jasmine creeper on warm stone helps, mantling the jagged memories with its soft living green.

Opal and I wrote to each other every month or so for the rest of our time at school, though less frequently as we got caught up in our adult lives.

She told me that the house on Darjeeling Street was condemned and pulled down and that Dicky Gould, on his discharge from hospital, was tidied away into an expensive old age home paid for by Mr Reddy. He didn't have to pay for long, Opal wrote in a subsequent letter, because Dicky Gould died of terminal sobriety a year later. Unlike her father, who had started getting the DTs.

She told me that Sergeant Koekemoer had been demoted and transferred to Underberg, where he was like a fish out of water in the pukka English atmosphere until someone in police headquarters took pity on him and transferred him to Pretoria several years later.

She told me that Kesaval had left Two Rivers the day after his Matric results came through, vowing that he would never come back, and that Mr Reddy had cast off all the trappings of his wealth and become one of the holy men who sat every day on the temple steps anointing their bodies with ash and meditating. Mrs Reddy was helping the brother-in-law to run the steam laundry and the whole staff was terrified of her twin lasers, which missed nothing.

Opal told me that a newly-qualified Indian chemist had bought and restocked the pharmacy, but that Govind had gone to work for the Pathers where he did very well and became their ace jewellery salesman. Srini eventually married a girl from a rich Durban family, which his mother told everyone was *much* more satisfactory than marrying into stuck-up rubbish like the Reddys. Opal said that she had got very bitter after Mr Pather was jailed for five years for illicit diamond buying.

I used Opal's letters to bolster my reputation at school, embroidering a colourful tapestry of half truths about the now notorious Two Rivers and its Hindu practices and wildly exciting social life and the rioting and killing I had personally witnessed. Evelyn Simpson's nose was out of joint for at least three months until she acquired a boyfriend who worked as a crooner in a nightclub and picked her up after school every day on his motorbike, and my reign as a minor celebrity ended.

I have to admit that she didn't come to a bad end. She became a model and sashayed up and down ramps and through the fashion pages of magazines for several years before marrying a wealthy Free State farmer. You see her on television sometimes talking about the early days of modelling, a maturely beautiful pillar of her Dutch Reformed Church community: Evelyn Viljoen now.

Though I've been tempted to write to her and ask what happened to her father's favourite book, *The Demon Headmistress*, I have refrained because she strikes me now as an admirably tough-minded woman.

Isabel

She would not have felt comfortable introducing her lover to her children in the home that she has shared with George for nearly twenty-five years. So a neutral venue has been chosen: Chryssa and Tom's glossy townhouse, which they have just sold and will soon be vacating. With the baby well on the way now, and with the help of Stella's legacy, they have bought a cluster home in a new suburban development specially designed for young families, with properly staffed day-care facilities for the working mothers. It is the ideal solution because the baby will be with his or her neighbouring friends in safe professional hands, and Chryssa is highly chuffed with herself for finding it.

She and Tom radiate the self-satisfaction of being young and well off and in control of their lives as they welcome Janine and Ralph at the front door. They have not yet had to face the worries and uncertainties that come with parenthood, and are unaware that life is a commodity which defies control.

'What do you think Mum's intended will be like?' Janine struggles into the hallway with a bulging briefcase in one hand and a bulging gym bag bristling with racquets and a hockey stick in the other. She has come straight from school and is dying for a cold beer, though she knows she probably won't get one. Chryssa and Tom drink wine and mineral water.

'Hardly intended. She's just going to live with him.' Chryssa leads the way through the door into the living area, which has two uncomfortable black leather and chrome benches – they are not yielding enough to be called sofas – a black

401

marble coffee table holding three architectural magazines and a round glass bowl of languid red tulips, and an Eames chair. The imported hi-fi is burbling Mozart played by the Modern Jazz Quartet.

'Fancy our mother living in sin. What next?' Janine throws her stuff down in a heap in the corner, ruining the spare ambience of the room. In a few minutes when she is not looking, Tom will whisk it into the cupboard in the hallway. He will never quite get used to the deep litter his two children live in. As he moves up the corporate ladder, his increasingly sumptuous offices will become havens of peace and order to which he flees gratefully in the mornings for cossetting by his minions. As Chryssa will flee to her office, though with a heavier load of guilt.

'I think it's bloody selfish of her, personally.' Ralph is grumpy about losing his mother to a stranger.

'Why? We can't expect her to run her life to suit us any more.'

'What about Dad? He provides her with a home and k-kids and looks after us all for years, and when she's tired of him, she just dumps him for someone else.'

'Ralphee!'

'You don't really believe that?'

His sisters are looking at him as if he has just walked in with dog mess under his shoe. He starts saying, 'If you look at it from Dad's point of view –'

But they cut him off with a familiar double act. 'Don't you see that *he* dumped *her* emotionally years ago?'

'And what was she supposed to do? Stick around forever in that mausoleum of a house while he went out playing stupid bowls?'

'Dad's such an old dork.'

'I can't talk to him at all.'

'They don't talk to each other any more.'

'They probably haven't slept together for years.'

'Do you think she's already slept with the new boyfriend?'

'Must have. Otherwise how would they know?'

'Know what?' Ralph manages to get in.

'Whether they're compatible or not, dumbo.'

There is an awkward silence as they contemplate the idea

of their mother doing things in bed with another man. It is broken by Tom, who comes in with a black lacquer tray carrying wine glasses, chilled bottles of white wine and Schoonspruit, and to Janine's relief, cold beers. She picks one up and snaps it open and takes a long satisfying pull, then balances it on her tracksuited knee. 'I love that first cold prickling swallow. Thanks for getting me some beer.'

'It wasn't for you. We thought he might drink it.' Chryssa will always be short on diplomacy.

Janine shrugs and says, 'Who do you think he is? Mum said a well-known writer.'

They are still speculating on the possibilities when the door chimes sound. Tom puts down the bottle of wine which he has just started to pour. 'There they are.'

But Isabel's children don't move. This is a moment they have been dreading and it sucks them deeper into their seats. Seeing the look on their faces, Tom says, 'I'll get it,' and goes into the hallway again.

'Brace yourself, Sheila,' Janine mutters. Chryssa wraps her hands round her growing bulge for comfort. Ralph shifts uneasily.

Isabel comes through the door first with a tentative smile; she has been dreading this moment too. What if they don't accept him? Will she be forced to make a choice between her lover and her children? She fervently hopes not, because there will be no choice. She is committed to him now. Body and soul, she thinks, hyping up the drama of the moment. I've given them what I had to give, and now I'm asking them to give me something back: loving acceptance.

She says, 'Hullo, darlings. You needn't look so apprehensive. He's quite presentable.'

'Of course we're apprehensive,' Janine blurts.

Ralph is listening to the voices in the hallway: Tom's precise tenor and a deeper baritone. He feels cold sweat breaking out on his hands and rubs them on his jeans. There are footsteps coming towards the doorway, and two figures coming through it.

Isabel says, 'This is Kesaval Reddy. Kesaval, my children.'

Their shock is profound. The man in the doorway is a burly Indian with a grizzled beard, wearing a brown leather jacket whose age echoes the lines that a hard life have incised on his face. It is so unexpected, so extraordinary even in the New South Africa, that they are speechless.

Isabel scans their faces as anxiety begins to cramp her stomach. What if they reject him? What sort of reflection will it be on her, if her white children recoil from the fact of his race?

The cool jazz burbles on in the stark room with its silent audience. Janine sits gripping her can of beer. Ralph sits rubbing his hands on his jeans. Chryssa sits and stares.

Kesaval says, 'You find me quite beyond the pale?' and laughs, though there is an edge to it.

He too has been apprehensive about this meeting, though not for the same reason as Isabel. He is not afraid of personal hostility or even outright rejection. As a journalist, he learnt to relegate racism to the dungheap where it belongs, though he has never underestimated its ugly power over people whose egos are bound up with their sense of group identity. His success now as a respected author enables him simply to dismiss those who have a problem with his being Indian. The only thing he fears is that Isabel's children will make it difficult for her to keep in touch with them, knowing how much they mean to her. He envies her the twenty years she has had with them, now that he has accepted he will never have any. She will be his family.

Isabel moves closer to him and links her arm through his. She says, smiling too brightly, 'Say something, someone.'

It is Ralph who breaks the silence. 'Are you the guy who wrote those travel books?'

Kesaval nods. Isabel's arm tightens against his.

'I've read them – all of them. They're amazing! Make you want to sling on a backpack and c-catch the first plane out. Were you really in Biafra during the war there? And in Lebanon? And in Tibet? And the Galapagos?' He gets up and goes to pump Kesaval's hand forgetting to worry about his own damp one. 'I've always wanted to go to India too. Mum used to read K-Kipling to us. *Kim* was my favourite book for years after I grew out of Rikki-Tikki-Tavi.'

Kesaval looks down at Isabel and lifts a wiry eyebrow. 'Kipling? My dear love, you haven't shown any obvious colonialist leanings.'

'Never thought about him that way. I just used to enjoy reading him out loud.' She is beaming with relief. Galvanised by Ralph's enthusiasm and the look on their mother's face when she is called 'my dear love', Chryssa and Janine have snapped out of their temporary paralysis and are getting up and coming towards them. It's going to be all right. She is not going to lose them.

She hears Chryssa say, 'You've made Mum very happy. I'm glad,' and Janine blurt as she reaches for his hand, 'Welcome to the family.'

There is still some reserve on their faces; they are not going to allow this new man of their mother's to win them over as easily as he has won Ralph. But she knows they'll like him when they get to know him better. They are her daughters after all: bright and capable and argumentative, passionate in their likes and dislikes, sometimes warm and funny and loving, sometimes as stubborn and pigheaded as Stella used to be, and as irritatingly superior in the arrogance of their youth – but always rewarding. Two tough-minded women of whom even the exacting Mother Beatrice would have approved. Isabel is so proud of them. As she is of Ralph, this surprising young man who has evolved from her anxious little son.

She throws back her head to laugh, and the whole town-house rings with her happiness.

25

Of course it had to be Kesaval, the angry boy who fled his claustrophobic family and community after his sister was killed. He wanted to be himself, unique, without any stifling obligations – most particularly the burdens borne by a racial minority and only grandsons. He joined the *Rand Daily Mail*, a liberal Johannesburg newspaper, and after doing their cadet course and struggling through several years of investigative journalism complicated by security police surveillance, fled apartheid altogether. An English newspaper appointed him roving foreign correspondent and sent him all over the world on their most difficult assignments because he was resourceful and unattached and poured scorn on sentiment and family ties.

It couldn't have been James, who became a civil engineer and built bridges as he dreamed of doing, but who had to swear off other girls when he married the boss's eagle-eyed daughter on his way up in the world from that small grim gatehouse to the Herald sugar mill compound. You will find his photograph these days in company reports: sleek, distinguished and beautifully tailored, yet with a look about his eyes of one who has found his dreams wanting.

And it couldn't have been spotty Percy, who sold his motorbike one day, packed his white tuxedo, stole a week's takings out of the Paradise Milk Bar till and disappeared without a trace into the merchant navy.

And it couldn't have been Titch, who lost a leg at the age of twenty after a climbing accident in the Drakensberg and later joined the brain drain to America, where he is now an eminent genetic scientist.

We had kept writing to each other through our last years

of school and his years studying zoology and botany and microbiology at university. He was rapidly becoming an expert on the ecology of Natal rivers, and was leading a difficult climb up the escarpment to the headwaters of the Tugela when part of his equipment snapped and sent him plummeting down into a ravine.

I have often thought that it must have been his unquenchable curiosity that cost him his leg. I can still hear him saying, 'I want to fly, not bloody crawl! I want to get out of Two Rivers and see how the world works.' And I see him reaching out too far for a startling new species of plant that nobody had ever seen before. In those days before helicopters were used, it took the Mountain Club's rescue team two days to reach him, by which time gangrene had set in and the leg had to be amputated. Its loss meant the end of scrambling up and down river banks so he turned in his positive way to genetics, which only needed a powerful microscope to complement his restless, questing mind. Hereditary diseases are his particular field of interest, and quite recently I saw in the newspaper that he is the leader of a team making significant headway in the prevention of muscular dystrophy. Maybe he will win a Nobel Prize one day, after all.

I wrote to his mother after the accident, and kept on through the years. Lilah McFadyen has been a great comfort to me, a wise and dependable second mother. She is very old and frail now and lives in a widow's cottage on the new company estate where she has created an exquisite small garden. Kesaval and I went to visit her there on our way down to the beach. Characteristically, she cut our praise short by telling us with a wicked cackle that her plants only thrived because she fed them a wonderful organic compost made from duck shit. 'Highly efficacious, my dears. Absolute magic. Makes the little buggers grow like weeds.' She shuffles about in old dungarees and a straw hat with wisps of white hair straggling out underneath, but her eyes that are like the greeny-blue glass marbles called ghoens, Titch's eyes, are as young and lively as a girl's.

She told us that he is coming home with his American wife to visit her soon. 'Wants to see the old bag before she finally drops off the perch,' is how she put it. 'They're bringing my

407

grandchildren too – four of them, all brilliant of course. Never still for a minute and besotted with wildlife, like Titch used to be.'

Kesaval and I offered to meet them at the airport, where we plan to present Titch with a new pith helmet to protect his probably balding head from the rigours of the African sun, and in honour of old friendship. It will be strange to be together again forty years on. I hope he hasn't changed too much.

We stopped in Two Rivers as well, for me to be introduced to the grown-up Violet – too plumply complacent to be disagreeable now – and her family of little sausages. To my surprise, I liked her; she received me with a warm chuckling hug and a matter-of-fact acceptance that not one of my friends (except for Opal, of course) has felt able to bestow on Kesaval. Surface appraisals die hard in our country, though this is changing. Opal sent a telegram after I phoned and told her that we were moving down to the cottage together. It said: 'YOU ARE BOTH HENCEFORTH ADMITTED TO THE SELECT COMPANY OF THE MANY-FACETED AND BRILLIANT. BE HAPPY.'

Before we left Two Rivers we went to say a last goodbye to Finn, who lies in what is now an old graveyard above the new motorway, looking down on factories whose noxious effluents and smoke make it impossible to see the coastline only a mile beyond.

His gravestone reads:

FINN OLAV ROSHOLT
1920–1952
'When he shall die,
Take him and cut him out in little stars,
And he will make the face of heaven so fine
That all the world will be in love with night.'

Stella had it erected when she started making good in England and could begin to grieve for the man she had lost. Juliet's words are fitting for the special, loving, big-hearted bear of a man I knew. Like Kipling's Kim, he was a Friend of all the World.

This book is my memorial to him. As I have brought him

to life in these many pages, so I lay him to rest in my heart.

From where I sit at my desk writing these last words, I can see down through the bush to where the green waves rise and curve and topple forward in a glory of tossing white foam, one after the other, reminding us all that life goes on.

Acknowledgements

My warmest thanks to John Meyer for the very generous loan of his painting, *South Coast Morning*; to Narotam Govind Patel and Brenda Kali for their kindness and patience in checking the manuscript and help with names; to Father Roger Hickley and Bergliot Bowles for their advice; to Ray and Sheila Hasson and Marie Weeks for their superior courier services; to my brother David Walters for the electrifying evening at the Isipingo temple; and to my ever-supportive family.

For long-ago information and help which they have probably forgotten, I thank Mrs Bruce who lived over the Casbah Café in Pietermaritzburg, Moonsammy Pillay and the Padayachee family of Tongaat.

For assistance and encouragement above and beyond the call of duty, I thank my indefatigable agent Dinah Wiener, and my sterling editors Jenny Dereham and Alexander Stilwell, for both of whom fine tooth-combs must have been invented.

Publications that have been helpful include the *Weekly Mail*, Fatima Meer's *Portrait of Indian South Africans* and Jay Naidoo's *Coolie Location*.